SOMEDAY

KAREN KINGSBURY

THORNDIKE PRESS
A part of Gale, Cengage Learning

GALE
CENGAGE Learning

Detroit • New York • San Francisco • New Haven, Conn • Waterville, Maine • London

GALE
CENGAGE Learning

Copyright © 2008 by Karen Kingsbury.
Baxter Family Drama — Sunrise Series #3.
Scripture taken from the HOLY BIBLE, NEW INTERNATIONAL VERSION®, NIV®. Copyright © 1973, 1978, 1984 by International Bible Society. Used by permission of Zondervan Publishing House. All rights reserved.
Scripture quotations are taken from the Holy Bible, New Living Translation, copyright © 1996, 2004. Used by permission of Tyndale House Publishers, Inc. Carol Stream, Illinois 60188. All rights reserved.
Thorndike Press, a part of Gale, Cengage Learning.

Thorndike Press® Large Print Christian Fiction.
The text of this Large Print edition is unabridged.
Other aspects of the book may vary from the original edition.
Set in 16 pt. Plantin.
Printed on permanent paper.

LIBRARY OF CONGRESS CATALOGING-IN-PUBLICATION DATA

Kingsbury, Karen.
   Someday / by Karen Kingsbury.
     p. cm. — (Baxter family drama — Sunrise series ; #3)
   (Thorndike Press large print Christian fiction)
   ISBN-13: 978-0-7862-9746-7 (hardcover : alk. paper)
   ISBN-10: 0-7862-9746-8 (hardcover : alk. paper)
   ISBN-13: 978-1-59415-206-1 (softcover : alk. paper)
   ISBN-10: 1-59415-206-3 (softcover : alk. paper)
   1. Family—Fiction. 2. Large type books. I. Title.
PS3561.I4873S57 2008b
813'.54—dc22   2007050919

Published in 2008 in arrangement with Tyndale House Publisher, Inc.

Printed in the United States of America
1 2 3 4 5 6 7 12 11 10 09 08

To Donald, my prince charming
In this sad season of losing my dad, you have been a rock for me, precious love. Working quietly behind the scenes to fill in when I'm on deadline or when the kids need a little extra help with schoolwork and checking in on me more often than before. You understand the great loss we're all experiencing, the void among us now that my dad's smile is forever gone from the here and now. But the thing that showed me again why I love you so much is something you did just this morning. My mom's birthday is tomorrow, and you knew it. With my dad gone less than a month now, and with me on deadline to finish this book, you stopped by the florist, picked up a bouquet of flowers, and wrote my mom a two-page letter, telling her all the reasons why you loved my dad and all the ways that you

would be there for my mom now that Dad is gone. The amazing thing about being married to you is that your love has a way of multiplying. It's no longer about the many ways you find to love and cherish me, but how you love our family . . . and our extended family. Here's the thing . . . you really are my prince charming, Donald. I mean it. I love you more with every passing day, understanding as we settle into these middle years that time is not a guarantee. Today is a gift, and tomorrow is uncertain. And so I treasure these beautiful, loving days, looking forward to our intimate moments in a quiet walk or laughing over something only we would understand. The ride is breathtakingly beautiful, my love. I pray it lasts far into our twilight years. Until then, I'll enjoy not always knowing where I end and you begin. I love you always and forever.

To Kelsey, my precious daughter

You are eighteen now, a young woman, and my heart soars with joy when I see all that you are, all you've become. We prayed that through the teenage years you would stay true to who you are, to that promise of purity you made when

you were thirteen, once upon a yesterday
on a bench overlooking a sunlit river. But
I never dreamed you'd so fully hold true
to that promise. You look forward to that
far-off day when you can share with your
future husband the gift you've saved for
him alone. But in the meantime, you trust
God that with Him, laughter and
friendship and dancing and singing and
spending time with your family are
enough. More than enough. Honey, you
grow more beautiful — inside and out —
every day. And always I treasure the way
you talk to me, telling me your hopes and
dreams and everything in between. I can
almost sense the plans God has for you,
the very good plans. I pray you keep
holding His hand as He walks you toward
them. And when you sing out across that
stage a few months from now, Papa will
have a front row seat in heaven — proud
as ever. Just remember that.
I love you, sweetheart.

To Tyler, my lasting song
I know this has been a tough season for
you, dear son. You and Papa were
kindred spirits in so many ways. Just
tonight, you came in and sat beside me.
"I miss him," you told me. "I miss listening

to classical music with him and talking about old movies and dreaming aloud about the next big play." You leaned your head on my shoulder. "I miss him a lot."

My precious Tyler, I miss him too. But among the ways God has comforted me, there is this — you are so much like him. In you I see his zest for life and love of family, his appreciation of a strong singer, and his passion for theater. You even look like him, the way he looked as a high school boy. Hold on to all you remember about your sweet papa, Ty. Love like him and laugh like him and cherish life the way he cherished it. I'm proud of you, Ty, of the young man you're becoming. I'm proud of your talent and your compassion for people and your place in our family. But two things will stand out when I look back on this time. The way my heart melts when you sing "Proud of Your Boy" and the earnest look in your eyes when you told me last week that maybe — just maybe — you'd want to be a teacher like your dad. A drama teacher, of course. Giving kids the skills to be successful onstage. You're fourteen and six foot two, Ty, no longer my little boy. But even as I see the future in your eyes, I'll treasure my memories of all the stages of your life.

Especially the season where we were all so blessed to have Papa. However your dreams unfold, I'll be in the front row to watch it happen. Hold on to Jesus, Ty.
I love you.

To Sean, my happy sunshine

Today you came home from school, eyes sparkling, and you told me you'd tied the school record for the high jump at track practice. The fact that your mark didn't count because it wasn't in a meet didn't dim your enthusiasm even a little. As you recounted your jump, I was struck by how much the story symbolized everything about you, Sean. You're so happy, so optimistic. You won't have Papa cheering for you from the sidelines anymore, dear son. But you'll have me and Dad and Grandma and a family who couldn't be more proud of you. Sean, you have a way of bringing smiles into our family, even in the most mundane moment. I pray that God will use your positive spirit to always make a difference in the lives around you. You're a precious gift, Son. Keep smiling and keep seeking God's best for your life. Make sure the bar's set high — not only at track practice.
I love you, honey.

To Josh, my tenderhearted perfectionist

Watching you work on your book report the other day, I saw again what always amazes me about you. Your work is so careful, so detailed, I wonder sometimes if I should remind you to be a little easier on yourself. But I've discovered something this semester about you, Josh. You're a wonderful writer! How it thrills my heart to see the creativity you work into every story — even a silly old book report. Whether in football or soccer, track or room inspections, you take the time to seek perfection. Along with that, there are bound to be struggles. Times when you need to understand again that the gifts and talents you bear are God's, not yours. And times when you must learn that perfection isn't possible for us, only for God. Even so, my heart almost bursts with pride over the young man you're becoming. You bear your papa's name as your middle name, and I believe with all my heart you will do it proud in the years to come. You have an unlimited future ahead of you, Josh. I'll be cheering on the sidelines always. Keep God first in your life, and who knows . . . one day maybe you and

Alex Smith will be teammates.
I love you always.

To EJ, my chosen one

We had a family meeting the other night,
one of those talk sessions you kids
sometimes tease us about. The subject
was a reminder that sitting around the
dinner table each night are the very best
friends you'll ever have — your sister and
brothers. And also that everyone needs to
pitch in more. We talked about giving 100
percent, because someday far too soon,
when all you kids are grown and in
families of your own, you'll need to give
100 percent always. That's what love
looks like. In the days that followed our
family talk, Dad and I were thrilled to see
that you truly stepped up your efforts at
helping out. We'd see you standing at the
sink, washing dishes and singing a happy
song, and you'd grin at us. "A hundred
percent!" you'd say. EJ, I pray that you
hold on to that very small lesson always.
It's a lesson Papa believed in too. You're
a wonderful boy, Son, a child with such
potential. Every day, every season, just
give 100 percent, okay? Because God
has great plans for you, and we want to
be the first to congratulate you as you

work to discover them. Thanks for your giving heart, EJ. I love you so.

To Austin, my miracle boy

It's been a month since Papa went home to heaven, and still every night when I tuck you in, you cling to me and whisper the same thing. "I feel empty without Papa. He should be here, Mom." And always I tell you the same thing. "You're right, honey. He should be here. We have to remember everything special about him so we don't ever forget." Papa loved you, the way he loved all of us — with his whole being. He loved sitting in his van next to Grandma, watching you play baseball for the Reds, and no one grinned bigger when you ripped off another huge hit. But he loved more than your performances. He loved the quiet times when you sat next to him and talked about your day. I know that's what you're missing most right now, and I understand. I'm not sure the missing part ever goes away. I can only tell you that our quiet times together are what I love most too. You're my youngest, my last, Austin. I'm holding on to every moment, for sure. Thanks for giving me so many wonderful reasons to treasure today. I

thank God for you, Austin, for the miracle
of your life. I love you, Aus.

**And to God Almighty,
the Author of Life,**
who has — for now — blessed me with
these.

ACKNOWLEDGMENTS

During the writing of this book, my father, Theodore C. Kingsbury, suffered a massive heart attack. He lived eight more weeks before going home to heaven on September 14. I was at a Tyndale dinner the night I learned about my dad's heart attack. Far away from home, in Atlanta with my two oldest children, I stepped out of the banquet room and into a kitchen hallway. There, I dropped to the floor and began to weep.

After a few minutes, I had no choice but to return to my table. Despite the beautiful entertainment happening that night compliments of Mandisa, those around me knew I was suffering. By the time the evening ended, I was surrounded by many, many great Tyndale friends. Ron Beers and Karen Watson were there, as were so many members of the Beers Group. Also Randy Alcorn and Vonette Bright and others.

That night, my friends at Tyndale became

a family. They prayed with me and hugged me, and as I returned to my hotel room to prepare for an early flight home, I had the overwhelming sense that God had heard our collective cry for help. In the days that followed, we held a bedside vigil over my dad, and his initial prognosis — that he would never come out of his coma — fell to the wayside after the first two weeks.

My dad woke up and was alert and cognizant. Though he had a tracheostomy so he could breathe, we were able to communicate and share hours of precious, unforgettable moments. I told him how grateful I was that he was my dad, and I thanked him for believing in me as a writer from as far back as I could remember. I told him if it hadn't been for him, I never would've stayed with writing.

I also had hours when we talked about the Lord and about heaven. My dad loved Jesus very much — he still does. He was sad about saying good-bye, but he wasn't afraid to die. He told me that. I even asked that if he reached heaven before me, could he give my only brother, Dave, a hug for me? In those amazing eight weeks, absolutely nothing was left unsaid.

For that, I have my friends at Tyndale to thank.

This book was due in their offices at the end of July, two weeks after my dad's heart attack. But with my father in the ICU through the end of August, I couldn't focus on my book long enough to write a single chapter. I needed my dad, needed to be with him and talk to him and play hymns for him. I needed to be there with my mom and sisters, filling his room with the sweet presence of God so he wouldn't have a single moment of fear or loneliness.

My dad used to tell me he had just one fear. The fear of dying alone. That didn't happen, and here I want to thank my friends at Tyndale for giving me a chance to be there with my dad until the end.

Dad . . . in my mind, John Baxter will always have your face. You can't imagine how much you are missed.

Also thanks to my amazing agent, Rick Christian, president of Alive Communications. Rick, you've always believed only the best for me. When we talk about the highest possible goals, you see them as doable, reachable. You are a brilliant manager of my career, and I thank God for you. But even with all you do for my ministry of writing, I cherish most your prayers. The fact that you and your wonderful wife, Debbie, are praying for me and my family keeps me confident every morning that God will continue to breathe into life the stories in my heart. I could never find the words to truly thank you.

A special thank-you to my husband, who puts up with me on deadline and doesn't mind driving through Taco Bell after a baseball game if I've been editing all day. This wild ride wouldn't be possible without you, Donald. Your love keeps me writing, and your prayers keep me believing that God has a plan in this ministry of fiction. And thanks for your help with the guest-book entries on my Web site. I look forward to that time every night when you read through them, sharing them with me and releasing them to the public, praying for the prayer requests. Thank you, honey, and thanks to all my kids, who pull together, bringing me iced green tea and understanding about my sometimes crazy schedule. I love that you know you're still first, before any deadline.

Thank you also to my mom, Anne Kingsbury, and to my sisters, Tricia, Sue, and Lynne. Mom, you are amazing as my assistant — working day and night sorting through the mail from my reader friends. I appreciate you more than you'll ever know.

Tricia, you are the best executive assistant

I could ever hope to have. I treasure your loyalty and honesty, the way you include me on every decision and exciting Web site change. My site has been a different place since you stepped in, and along the way the readers have so much more in this ministry of Life-Changing Fiction. Please know that I pray for God's blessings on you always, for your dedication to helping me in this season of writing. And aren't we having such a good time too? God works all things to the good!

Sue, I believe you should've been a counselor! From your home far from mine, you get batches of reader letters every day, and you diligently answer them using God's wisdom and His Word. When readers get a response from "Karen's sister Susan," I hope they know how carefully you've prayed for them and for the response you give. Thank you for truly loving what you do, Sue. You're gifted with people, and I'm blessed to have you aboard.

Thanks also to my forever friends and family, the ones who rushed to our side as my dad's health declined and as he eventually went home to heaven. Your love has been a tangible source of comfort, pulling us through and making us know how very blessed we are to have you in our lives.

And the greatest thanks to God. The gift is Yours. I pray I might use it for years to come in a way that will bring You honor and glory.

FOREVER IN FICTION

A special thanks to Jane Drummer, who won Forever in Fiction at the C.L.U.B. ETHAN auction. Jane chose to honor her friend Ethan Blaine Teeple, age four, by naming him Forever in Fiction. Ethan was diagnosed with cancer just after his first birthday. Since then he has waged a constant fight for his life with the smiling optimism that can only come from a very special child.

Ethan has blue eyes and blond hair. He is friendly, forgiving, patient, and quick-witted. Make-A-Wish Foundation provided Ethan and his family with a magical trip to Walt Disney World, his very favorite place. When Ethan's in the hospital, he likes painting pictures and creating with Play-Doh. He doesn't like staying in bed, and often he and his IV pole have to be chased down the hall by his nurse Lindsay, a special friend. Ethan believes he's engaged to Lindsay and that he'll marry her when he's all grown up. He knows which tubes belong where on his little body, and sometimes he'll inform the doctors if something isn't connected right.

When Ethan's out of the hospital, he loves playing outside — especially T-ball — and spending time with his family — older brother, Trevor, and his parents, Gary and Autumn Teeple. Ethan treasures every moment and continues to battle his disease as this is going to print. Please pray for Ethan and his family.

Ethan's character in *Someday* is that of a sick boy struggling for life. His bright sunshiny presence in Brooke's life prompts her decision to volunteer her time to help reopen the crisis pregnancy center in Bloomington.

Jane, I pray that Ethan is honored by your gift and by his placement in *Someday* and that you will always see a bit of Ethan when you read his name in the pages of this novel, where he will be Forever in Fiction.

Also, thanks to Molly McCabe, who won Forever in Fiction at the Doernbecher auction. Molly chose to honor her niece, Paige Tagliaferri, age six months, by naming her Forever in Fiction.

Paige is a bright ray of light in the lives of her family. She has blue eyes and dark blonde hair and the cutest button nose. She has a bright smile and is the daughter of Megan Tagliaferri, an interior designer, and Jeff Tagliaferri, a produce salesman. Paige loves classical music, particularly Mozart and Beethoven. She was born on Cinco de Mayo and is an excellent traveler.

I chose to make Paige's character that of a young baby under the care of Dr. Brooke Baxter. As a fictional character, Paige's birth was very much planned and replete with difficulties. She is — in *Someday* — a healthy, happy baby and the greatest picture of a life much wanted, much prayed for. Her presence in Brooke's life causes her again to consider the importance of reopening the crisis pregnancy center so all babies would have the chance little Paige has in *Someday.*

Molly, I pray that Paige is honored by your gift and by her placement in *Someday* and that you will always see a bit of Paige when you read her name in the pages of this novel, where she will be Forever in Fiction.

Finally, a special thanks to Diane Geer, who won Forever in Fiction at the Upper Valley Christian School auction. Diane chose to honor her late husband, Louie James Geer, age fifty-seven, by naming him Forever in Fiction. Louie was diagnosed with cancer in 2003 and eventually lost his battle with the illness. His family chose Forever in Fiction as a way of honoring the love and wonder of his life and the way his memory lives on in the hearts of his family and friends.

Louie was six feet tall with a strong build, dark brown hair, and blue eyes. He had a great sense of humor and was very social, kind, generous, and hardworking. He was married to Diane Geer for twenty-five years, and together they had two children — Jamie Anne and Kelly Marie. Louie loved British Columbia, especially Vancouver. He was good at business, an active man who owned his own tour company. In that line of work, he was an excellent host, fun to be with and always bringing a smile and a laugh to his customers. Louie was a strong Christian family man who loved God and put Him first in all things. He is dearly missed.

I chose to make him the fictional deceased father of actress Randi Wells in *Someday*. Randi is struggling in a lot of areas of her life, and it sometimes brings her perspective to remember the kind, gentle Christian man her father was and the role he played in her life when she was younger.

Diane, I pray that Louie is honored by your gift and by his placement in *Someday* and that you will always see a bit of Louie when you read his name in the pages of this novel, where he will be Forever in Fiction.

For those of you who are not familiar with Forever in Fiction, it is my way of involving you, the readers, in my stories, while raising money for charities. To date this item has raised more than $100,000 at charity auctions across the country. If you are interested in having a Forever in Fiction package donated to your auction, contact my assistant, Tricia Kingsbury, at Kingsburydesk@aol.com. Please write *Forever in Fiction* in the subject line. Please note that I am able to donate only a limited number of these each year. For that reason I have set a fairly high minimum bid on this package. That way the maximum funds are raised for charities.

CHAPTER ONE

John Baxter made his decision as his family was leaving the hospital.

Elaine had shared with him and his family a moment of deep tragedy and deep love, a time that had bonded them beyond any other shared experience. He held her hand as they walked silently to the car. In a few hours, everyone would meet back at the Baxter house for dinner. They needed to be together, needed to share about how the brief life of little Sarah, his granddaughter, had touched them, changed them.

But in the meantime he couldn't shake the feeling inside, the certainty that he wanted Elaine in his life not only in moments like this but always.

Elaine's car was parked near his, but before she went to it, she stopped. "You're quiet."

He smiled and a calm worked through his soul. He was worn-out and weary, but he was no longer discouraged, not after what he'd witnessed this afternoon in his daughter's hospital room. "Just thinking."

Elaine would be joining them for dinner after she spent a few hours at home. They all needed some downtime. But the look in her eyes told him that she would stand in the parking lot all day if he needed her. "Wanna talk about it?" She angled her head, her eyes soft.

John could feel the warmth in his heart shining through his eyes. "God's bringing some of the details into focus. About how much I need you."

She looked surprised and touched and maybe a little shy. "That's a good thing."

"We'll talk more about it later." He hugged her, and they said their good-byes.

When John was alone in his car, the decision in his heart took root, writing itself across his soul and changing his picture of the future. The drive home seemed longer than usual and marked by a new sort of thrill and loneliness. He entered the old house, but instead of tossing his keys on the counter, he stopped and leaned against the doorframe. Every inch of the place still held memories of Elizabeth, the way it always would. He walked up to their room and hesitated at the photo of her on his dresser.

"You were there with us today, dear. I felt you."

He gripped the dresser, and his thoughts drifted back to earlier today. Before he left the hospital, Ashley had shown him Cole's picture. The artwork by his eight-year-old grandson had brought him the same much-needed comfort as it brought Ashley and her husband, Landon. Nothing could be more fitting than the image of Elizabeth holding little Sarah in heaven, taking care of her until they could all be together again.

He moved to the card table he'd set up at the end of his bed. Elizabeth's handwritten letters were spread across it, more organized than before, and on one end was a stack already copied. The project had outgrown this space, so later tonight he'd move it to the dining room. When he was finished copying, he would have six sets of her letters — one for each of their children. Each yellowed letter carefully opened and reread had filled his heart with Elizabeth's presence and made him miss her more than ever. But now the emotional, painstaking process was nearly behind him, and he was almost ready to put the letters into scrapbooks and pass them out. He had a feeling there was something in Elizabeth's words that would make a dramatic difference in each of their adult children.

Even with baby Sarah's funeral planned for later in the week, he would focus his energy on the letters. It was time, and it was the right thing to do. When he was finished, he would finally have closure, finally have walked through everything left of the woman he still so dearly loved. He would need that closure because of the decision he'd made an hour ago. The decision that one day very soon he would take the step he had been certain he would never take.

He would ask Elaine Denning to be his wife.

Dayne Matthews gripped the wooden railing of his back porch and stared out at the distant water. Even with the sorrow from earlier today, the sun sprayed a blanket of light across the surface of Lake Monroe. From inside the lake house he could hear the soft voice of his wife, Katy, talking to her agent again, trying to keep the conversation short.

This wasn't a day for business deals.

He squinted against the shine of sparkling lake water and lifted his eyes to the deep blue sky. No matter how many Hollywood roles he'd played, regardless of all the emotion he'd conveyed and seen acted out across the big screen over the years, he'd never seen anything like the strength and faith of his sister Ashley.

The events from a few hours ago came to life again — the call from his father, John Baxter, asking them to come quickly, and the way he felt walking into Ashley's hospital room. His family — Brooke, Kari, Erin, Luke, and their spouses and children, the people he'd missed out on all his life until recently — filled every possible space, circling Ashley's bed.

Of course, Ashley and Landon had known for months that their unborn baby girl wouldn't survive more than a few days. Anencephaly was merciless that way. The miracle everyone prayed for wasn't an unexplained healing but rather what happened today in the few short hours of Sarah's life.

The screen door sounded behind him, and he looked over his shoulder. Even on a day marked with so much sadness, his heart still found room for the familiar awe. Katy Hart had actually married him, agreed to put aside her private life in Bloomington, Indiana, and join him on his public journey of fame.

Now if only they could survive the ride.

He turned and held out his arms.

31

"C'mere."

Her steps were slow, measured, her expression lost and distant, as if the brief life and tender death of their niece Sarah had drained her. When she reached him, she eased her hands around his waist and laid her head on his shoulder. For a long time the only sound was the cry of a lone hawk in a distant tree.

Finally Katy drew a shaky breath and stepped back so she could see his eyes. "We can do it . . . right, Dayne?"

He let himself get lost in her touch, in the sweet caress of her voice. "Do what?"

She sighed. Her expression held fear and determination in equal amounts. "Use the next four weeks to remember what matters. Before the world tries to tear us apart again."

Four weeks. That's all the time they had to savor a semblance of normalcy in Bloomington, to enjoy their lake house and remember the reasons they'd fallen in love. Just four weeks. Frustration built in a hurry and took the edge off his good feelings. He set his jaw, and for a moment he looked past her to the hills beyond their home. What had he been thinking, encouraging her to star in a movie opposite him? As if that weren't enough fodder for the tabloids, in less than a month they would face the debut episode of the reality show based on their shared movie experience. Both the show and their upcoming movie had been moved from a January release to the upcoming fall debut. His agent had explained the schedule change best. "Right now, no one's hotter than you two. The studios realize that." Everyone with a dime to make was counting on the conflicts between Dayne and Katy, racy headlines that during the filming had brought them to the breaking point.

But that was before they returned home to Bloomington. Here, finding love was as natural as breathing. Amid the sprawling country fields and rolling hills and endless sky, love had returned like a summer breeze, washing over them and assuring them that everything would be okay. And how could it not, in the company of the Baxters, surrounded by more love than Dayne had known in all his life?

"You're not answering me." Katy's expression softened, and sadness added to the mix.

He brushed his cheek against hers. "I wish it were four *years.*"

"Or more." Katy rested her head on his shoulder again. "There's no way back, is there?"

She was talking about their upcoming

movies, the fact that in a couple of months she would fly to London and he to Cabo San Lucas, Mexico. For ten weeks they would be separated, fulfilling their obligations while the rags took shots at them. A heaviness settled over his heart.

"Ah, Katy." He held her close. The faint smell of her perfume, her skin, filled his senses and heightened the subtle urgency in their hushed tones. "Someday, maybe. When all this is behind us." He didn't say it, and she didn't either, but what if they never made it to that far-off day? What if his world grabbed hold of him, and her world grabbed hold of her? And what if they found themselves pulled so hard toward distant shores that they lost sight of the promises they made on a beach in the Mayan Riviera what felt like a lifetime ago?

They talked about someday often, especially since they'd been home from Los Angeles. Someday, when they'd say goodbye to Hollywood and acting and every aspect of the celebrity life. When they'd settle down in Bloomington and maybe bring to life again the Christian Kids Theater group Katy missed so much. A time when they'd have walks on the shore of Lake Monroe, Sunday supper with the Baxters, and babies of their own. The picture grew and swelled and filled Dayne's heart and soul because nothing could be better.

But they had a war to win between now and someday, the war they'd welcomed by agreeing to do the reality show. *For Real* was supposed to be a white flag, a way of giving in to the paparazzi without being swallowed whole. But the camera crews didn't land on the set of their recently wrapped movie looking for happily-ever-after scenes. They stirred conflict from the beginning, creating headlines that screamed of doubt and unfaithfulness.

And the show hadn't even aired yet.

Dayne kissed her forehead. "What did your agent say?"

"He wanted to make sure I had a passport." She sounded tired. "I told him I did, of course. Because of our wedding."

For a heartbeat the world fell away, and Dayne could see all the way to the center of her soul, the way he had once seen her before the tension of the past few months. "It was beautiful, wasn't it?"

She smiled. "Sometimes in my dreams I see it again, playing out so real I can smell the ocean air."

He nuzzled his face against hers. "Too bad you couldn't get your movie switched to Cabo."

The sun was setting, casting shadows across the deck and underlining the difficulty of what lay ahead. "It'd be hard to shoot Big Ben from Cabo."

"True." He placed his hands on either side of her face and touched his lips to hers. Their kiss was slow, with a hesitancy born of the tension that had marked the recent weeks. But it kindled a passion that knew no bounds, and after a while, their breathing changed and a knowing filled her eyes.

"I love you, Dayne." Her whispered words betrayed the intensity of her feelings, the way her body responded to his.

Even in the worst of times, their marriage had been marked by a physical love that seemed almost divine — a gift from the God they both believed in, the God who Dayne prayed would keep them together in the coming months when it might look easier to walk away.

"I love you too." He held her closer. "Don't ever stop saying it, okay? And I won't either."

Katy hesitated. "I won't. . . . I won't ever stop." She kissed him again and spoke close to his ear. "Let's go inside."

He swallowed and eased his fingers between hers. As they went in, as they walked past the kitchen and down the hallway toward their bedroom, Dayne still wasn't sure about the someday they dreamed of. But for now they had something else, something that here and now maybe mattered more.

They had four weeks.

CHAPTER TWO

Ashley Baxter Blake held tight to Landon's hand as they stepped into the sunlight and felt the automated hospital doors slide together behind them. It seemed like a week since Landon had rushed her here, since she was hurried into labor and delivery. But the wonderful, terrible moments that surrounded their daughter's life and death had happened only the day before.

The August sun was hot on her face, but Ashley began to shiver. "It hurts, Landon . . . too much."

Landon tightened the hold he had around her waist, but he didn't ask her to explain herself. He had to be feeling the same way.

Ashley tried to summon her resolve, but she felt like dropping to the sidewalk and weeping. She was about to ask Landon how they were supposed to do this, how they might make the walk to their truck with arms so empty they ached, when a small four-door car pulled up.

Before Ashley could move or blink or take a breath, the guy behind the wheel jumped out, running around the front of his car and into the hospital foyer. Ashley and Landon watched him, and as they did, they saw the clear reason for the man's rush. Waiting just inside the glass double doors was a young woman in a wheelchair, her entire face lit up in a smile. Cradled close to her was a small bundle wrapped in pastel blankets.

A newborn, making that precious first trip home. The way Ashley and Landon's baby Sarah should've been making her first trip home. Ashley couldn't turn away. She watched the man take hold of a cart loaded with pink flowers and "It's a Girl" balloons and assorted gift bags. Watched the nurse push the wheelchair through the doors, chatting with the young couple, the three of them all smiles.

The man gently took the baby in his arms and carried her the few feet to the waiting car. He worked with great care, setting the baby in her car seat and gingerly lifting the buckle and straps over her head. The nurse helped the woman to her feet, and the new family, oblivious to Ashley or Landon or anyone but their precious baby girl, found their places in the car.

Ashley felt the tears before the family drove away. Her eyes blurred as Landon led her across the parking lot, up the ramp, and past two rows of cars to the Dodge truck they'd bought a week before the baby was born. Landon told her the truck was a way of looking past the impending birth and death of their daughter, a way of believing in the campouts and fishing trips that lay ahead with a household of boys.

But dreams of tomorrow didn't shine even a single ray of light on how Ashley felt now. She leaned her head back, closed her eyes, and felt a stream of hot tears slip down her face. Bloomington wasn't such a large place. If Sarah had lived, she might've wound up in the same kindergarten class as the baby girl they'd just seen. The girls might've played soccer together or been on the same cheerleading squad. They might've been best friends.

Ashley's heart hurt, and she pulled her arms in close around her middle. She hadn't gained much weight with Sarah, and her relatively flat stomach only made her feel worse. She slid down the bench seat and leaned against Landon. "I miss her so much." Her voice cracked. "I only held her for a few hours." She held her arms out from her body, remembering the feel of her infant daughter there just yesterday.

"God's so good." Landon's voice was thick. He hadn't said much but only because he was clearly struggling too. "She only had a few hours, but no baby was ever loved more in so short a time."

A smile lifted Ashley's lips even as more tears filled her eyes. "It was a miracle, how she looked so healthy, how everyone was there, surrounding us." She sniffed. "I'll always remember it."

"And God will use her life. We have to believe that."

Ashley nodded. She believed. No matter how great the heartache of losing Sarah, Ashley didn't doubt God. On several occasions during her pregnancy the Lord had reminded her to look for Him in the quiet whispers. And then in Sarah's final hour, there was her firstborn son, Cole, whispering to her about the picture he colored of Ashley's mother somewhere in heaven, holding tight to baby Sarah.

Even this morning, before Landon came to pick her up, Ashley could feel the Lord speaking to her. Sadder than she'd been since the death of her mother, she had taken her Bible from the hospital nightstand and flipped to Psalm 46. Partway through she stumbled onto a verse that had helped her a number of times, a verse she hadn't read in a long while. "Be still, and know that I am God; I will be exalted among the nations, I will be exalted in the earth."

In moments like this God wasn't asking Ashley to be victorious or walk through the door smiling. He was asking her only to stand, to be still, and to know that she didn't have to have the answers, because the Lord already had them figured out. *Be still, and know that I am God. . . ."* Yes, she still believed.

"Ash . . ." Landon's voice was unrushed and gentle. "We should get going. Cole and Devin are back at the house with your dad." He kissed the top of her head. "You okay?"

She nodded and used the backs of her hands to wipe her face. She straightened, and with what little energy she had, she pulled the seat belt across and snapped it into place. "When Mom needs a break from holding Sarah —" Ashley turned her wet eyes toward the man she loved so deeply — "you know who'll hold her."

"Who?" He slid the key into the ignition and waited.

"Irvel." Ashley smiled at the memory of the dear, sweet woman from the Sunset Hills Adult Care Home, Ashley's friend when she worked there.

Landon's grin lightened his expression. "You think so?"

"I do." She sniffed again. "Irvel and Mom'll share a cup of peppermint tea, and Sarah will be right there."

It was a comforting picture, and Ashley and Landon let the image stay between them, their linked hands all the communication they needed.

Ashley's dad must've known how difficult the ride home would be, because when they walked through the front door, the house was quiet.

Cole peeked around the corner of the kitchen and gave them a tentative smile and a halfhearted wave. "Hi." He stepped into view. "Papa put Devin down for a nap. He said that might be best. Plus, Devin was tired."

"How are you, Coley?" Ashley held out her arms. Silently she said a prayer that lasted only as long as it took for her to draw a breath, thanking God that her sons hadn't had anencephaly, that they were here and whole and healthy.

Cole came to her, a little slower than usual. He looked at Landon. "Is Mom okay? To hug, I mean?"

Landon uttered a soft chuckle. "She's fine. You can hug her, buddy." As he said the words, he looked at Ashley and a knowing passed between them. She wasn't fine, and neither was he. Maybe someday, but for now it would be a very long time before they could use that word and mean it. Still, it was important to get things back to normal for their boys, especially Cole, with his great sense of perception and concern for the people in his family.

Cole smiled, relieved. He put his arms around Ashley longer than usual. "Your tummy's almost flat again."

"Yes. Almost." Ashley smiled and ran her hand along the back of Cole's head. He hadn't been a baby for many years, but as he hugged her, she could remember what it felt like to hold him when he was. The feeling brought her some relief from the ache that had been with her all morning.

Landon moved closer and put his arm around Cole's shoulders. "Have you been sad today?"

"A little." Cole squinted up at Landon and then Ashley. "Sarah shoulda had a party today, and I was gonna be in charge of her so Devin wouldn't be too rough. I wanted to teach him how to be a big brother." He thought for a few seconds. "Babies are too young for heaven — don't you think?"

Ashley felt a lump in her throat, and with

her free hand she massaged it. "I do. Much too young."

"But —" Landon grinned despite the sadness in his eyes — "I bet you did a good job of being in charge of Devin this morning."

They heard steps from the family room, and Ashley's father came quietly around the corner. "He did a great job."

Cole lit up at the sight of his grandpa. "Tell 'em how me and Devin played with those giant LEGOs and built the biggest bridge ever!"

"Definitely the biggest."

"It was so big Devin wanted to climb on it, but I told him LEGO bridges didn't work like that." Cole stepped away from Ashley and grinned at his papa. "Right?"

"Right. You told him." Ashley's dad mussed up Cole's blond hair and cast a concerned look at Ashley and Landon.

"Hey!" An idea seemed to pop into Cole's head. "I'll go check on the bridge before Mom and Dad come see it." He darted off and ran halfway through the dining room before he stopped and quieted his footsteps, probably remembering that Devin was still asleep. "That was loud," he whispered. "Sorry!"

When Cole was out of earshot, Ashley's dad put a hand on her shoulder and then

Landon's. "I won't stay. You need your family time." He leaned close and kissed her cheek. Then he turned to Landon. "You can do this. Your faith will get you through."

Landon nodded. "And I have a feeling family's going to help a whole lot too."

When Ashley's dad was gone, Landon wrapped his arms around her and held her for a long while. They could hear Cole in the distant playroom, shuffling about, probably making sure every LEGO connection was firm and in place.

Ashley rested her head against Landon's chest. She was still so tired. In two days they'd have a small, private funeral, but right now even the thought of so much sadness seemed overwhelming. "Think he'll remember her?" She looked up. "A year from now? . . . Five years?"

"I don't know." Landon's eyes were deep, thoughtful. "But that little girl will stay with us, between us . . . a part of us until we see her again."

"Right there next to my mom."

"And Irvel."

Ashley smiled, and with that they followed the sound of Cole and spent the next ten minutes marveling at the bridge, which was bigger than Cole and Devin combined. Landon grabbed the camera and took half a dozen photos. Not long after, Devin woke and the four of them sat cross-legged on the playroom floor, taking apart the bridge and using the blocks to build a tower instead.

Every now and then, Ashley was painfully aware that amid the happy sounds of her family, one was most definitely missing.

The soft, precious cries of her newborn daughter.

The funeral service was brief and poignant — much like little Sarah's life. Ashley sat with Landon and the boys in the front row of the church, and the rest of the Baxter family surrounded them. Only Ashley's father spoke, quoting from Psalm 139 — the verses that talked about God knowing a baby before she was born and how He alone could knit a child in the womb of her mother. He also referred to Jeremiah 29:11, about God having good plans for His people.

"His good plans for Sarah will go far beyond this life." Her dad looked at the faces in the first few pews. His eyes glistened, but he smiled anyway. "We look forward to that glorious day when we are all together, at home in heaven, and we can see for ourselves the plans God had for our precious baby girl."

Ashley turned her eyes to the small white casket, covered in a spray of white roses and baby's breath. The delicately etched box was so small, so pitifully little. For the slightest, craziest moment, Ashley longed to cross the front of the church, lift the lid, and take her daughter into her arms one more time. She closed her eyes. *Sarah's not in there. I know she's not,* she told herself. *Help me, God. . . . Let me see her in Mom's arms the way Cole saw her.*

Ashley looked back at her dad. He was finishing, talking about God's mercies being new every morning. Then he stepped down from the podium and returned to his spot beside Elaine.

The church pianist played "Great Is Thy Faithfulness," and afterwards, when the funeral was over, everyone drove to the cemetery. The burial service took only a few minutes, and then — after hugs and quiet tears — the others left for their separate homes. Ashley had decided she didn't have energy for a dinner back at their house. The funeral was as much as she could handle.

Finally it was just Ashley, Landon, and the boys, standing near Sarah's casket. Landon had Devin in his arms, and without saying a word, he reached out and touched the edge of the wooden box. "Good-bye, Sarah," he whispered. Then he carefully took one white rose from the bouquet and brought it close to his face. For a moment he closed his eyes, and pain darkened his expression.

Ashley, too, took a rose and opened her other hand gently against the smooth casket top. "Someday, baby . . . someday we'll see you again." Ashley felt the tears on her cheeks, but otherwise her heart was numb. She wanted only to be home with her family, away from this terribly sad place.

Cole had been watching them, making circles in the grass with the toe of his shoe as if he wasn't sure what to do or say. But now he moved to the headstone adjacent to Sarah's plot. "This is where Grandma's buried, right? It says Elizabeth Baxter."

"Yes, Coley." Ashley touched his shoulder. "They'll be together here."

Cole nodded. He stared at the gravestone for a few seconds, then touched the lettering with his fingers. "Together, like in heaven."

"That's right."

Landon prayed, and the four of them stayed a few minutes longer. After that, they returned to the new truck and drove home.

Ashley didn't make her way to the nursery until after Landon and the boys were asleep. Earlier, Landon had urged her to take a nap, and she'd managed to get a few hours. But now she couldn't sleep. How different this night might have been, the hours spent rocking Sarah and laughing about their lack of sleep.

Ashley tiptoed down the hallway past Devin's room. Before Sarah's diagnosis, they had tossed around a couple of options for the baby's room. They could move Devin in with Cole — something both boys were in favor of. But the house was older, the rooms barely big enough for a twin bed and a dresser. Even bunk beds would've caused the boys to be crowded in one room.

Instead, they settled on turning Ashley's art room into a nursery. She usually painted at her dad's house, and she could move her paintings there. That way each of the kids would have their own space. Before she completed her third month of pregnancy, Ashley had pulled the bassinet from the garage and cleaned it, found the sheets and pastel skirt that her mother had given her when Cole was born. She boxed up her paints and put her easel in the closet and dreamed about whether the room would be blue or pink themed.

But after the news about her baby's birth defect — even when she told herself month after month that it was a mistake or that God would give her a miracle — Ashley couldn't bring herself to work on the nursery. As if some small part of her subconscious knew better. There were times when she went by the room and stopped, her eyes locked on the sight of the pretty bedding, her heart hoping beyond hope that her daughter would sleep there. When the truth about Sarah became painfully clear, neither she nor Landon found the strength to take down the bassinet.

The house was quiet. Still weary from the emotional cost of the day, Ashley entered the room and leaned against the inside wall. They'd planned to move the rocking chair from Devin's room into this one, since he could use the extra space for his toys. But that never happened, and now the room looked sparse and cold and lonely — all except for the bassinet.

Ashley went to it and rested her fingers on the frilly hood. Sorrow welled up inside her, and she slid her fingers down to the soft flannel sheets that covered the thin mattress. The spot where Sarah should've been sleeping this very moment.

I hardly knew her, God. Ashley stared at the empty little bed. *But . . . but I miss her so much. . . .*

Ashley closed her eyes, and her daughter's face came into view — her delicate features, her big blue eyes, her sweet baby lips. How long would it be before the brief image of Sarah, the one-day memory of her, faded into little more than a distant dream? She held her breath, and for a moment she could almost smell her daughter, feel her velvety soft skin.

I trust You, God; I do. But why her? Why Sarah?

The heartache tore at her because there was no way to bridge the distance between her and Sarah, not in this life.

Ashley gripped the side of the bassinet with both hands, and as she did, a voice sounded, clear and calm, like an intercom to every room of her heart. *Be still, My daughter, and know that I am God. . . .*

Relief flooded Ashley's soul, and with it came more tears. *Yes, Father, help me be still. Help me understand. . . .*

Again the response was distinct. *My daughter, I will be exalted among the nations, I will be exalted in the earth.*

Ashley let the words wash over her, stirring her thoughts and bringing a dawning of new understanding. She hadn't really focused on the last part of the verse, just the beginning, because what more did she need at a time like this than to know that she had only to stand, that God would be God, and that she was only responsible to be still?

But now the last part of the verse practically shouted at her with significance. The scene from the hospital room shone brightly in her mind. Her entire family gathered around her hospital bed and the certain feeling that Sarah's brief life and peaceful death had brought with them a number of changes in the people she loved — miracles that might otherwise not have happened.

In that time and place, the strain between her brother Luke and his wife, Reagan, had seemed gone entirely, the two of them holding tight to each other and their precious Tommy and Malin. The hurt feelings and distance that separated Ashley from her sister Brooke had faded with every photograph Brooke took, every minute of video footage, every teary-eyed look they shared.

And most of all, there was her newly found older brother, Dayne, and his wife,

Katy. Never mind what the tabloids and stress of celebrity had done to them in their first months of marriage. While they stood in a room full of family, sharing the precious life of little Sarah, Ashley had no doubt they'd survive. All of them would survive, and they would do so with love and laughter and the faith that every moment of life is precious.

That would be Sarah's legacy. But now, as the Scripture stayed in Ashley's mind, she realized it wouldn't only be Sarah's legacy; it would be the Lord's as well. Through the heartbreak of losing Sarah, God wanted all of them to understand something: He would be exalted. As relationships changed for the good around them, their heavenly Father would be exalted. In Dayne and Katy's case, if they survived the onslaught of media attacks bound to take place in the coming months, God would be exalted the whole world over.

Just like the verse promised.

Chills ran down Ashley's arms, and some of her sorrow was displaced by overwhelming joy and determination. Joy because of what God had started yesterday in the crowded hospital room. And determination because she suddenly knew how she'd survive the sadness of losing her newborn daughter. In the Lord's strength, she would play peacemaker to the relationships that seemed most touched by Sarah's few hours. She would make herself available and reach out as often as she could. She would pray for Luke and Reagan, for Brooke and herself, and for Dayne and Katy, and she would know two things for sure.

God would be exalted. And Sarah's death would not be in vain.

CHAPTER THREE

John woke up early Wednesday morning and rolled over in bed. He stretched his hand across to the empty place where Elizabeth should've been. Most days now he could get through the morning and not think about her and how badly he still missed her. But this was different.

Today would've been their thirty-ninth wedding anniversary.

Can You let Elizabeth know how much I love her? He stared out the window. The sky was deep blue, same as it had been all week. When he'd looked ahead to this day, he figured he'd take a trip to the cemetery, because her body was there, and somehow it seemed right that he pay his respects.

John sat up and stretched his back. The problem was, he didn't think of Elizabeth when he was at the cemetery. He thought of her here in their bed. Or in the kitchen, leaning against the counter with a cup of tea in her hands, a smile shining from her eyes. He thought of her in the rocker, the one next to his recliner in the living room across from the fireplace, with the mantel that held a framed photograph of each of their kids, including Dayne. He saw her across from him at the dining room table — no matter who was sitting in her chair — and he remembered her every time he walked along the path behind their house.

No, he wouldn't go to the cemetery to mark the day when he and Elizabeth had made the best decision of their lives. He would make the oatmeal she loved with the egg whites and fresh blueberries. Then he'd go out back and take a walk, take in the changes life had brought and the changes still ahead.

Later maybe he'd work on the scrapbooks for their kids. He wanted to hand them out at Christmas because a collection of letters from their mother was the best gift he could possibly give them. Of course, by then he and Elaine . . .

A suffocating sadness came over him, and he drew a slow breath and stood. He couldn't think about Elaine this morning. They had plans for tomorrow — breakfast out and a trip to the farmers' market. She had something wrong with her trash compactor, so later in the day he planned to go to her house and try to fix it. She would make her special lasagna, and the hours would be full.

But today belonged to him and Elizabeth. It wasn't something he and Elaine had talked about, but she knew it was his anniversary. Like last year on this date, she wouldn't call.

John glanced at the photo of Elizabeth and him on the dresser, but he didn't linger. Not at the picture and not at the top drawer that held a small velvet box he'd brought home one evening last week. He didn't want to think about what lay inside the box or what future anniversary days would be like if he carried through with his intentions.

Instead he made his oatmeal, and after he'd done his dishes, he pulled on a Colts cap and went in the backyard. For a few seconds he didn't move, didn't do anything but breathe in the sweet smell of morning and countryside and the hint of roses in full bloom from the garden where Elizabeth planted them some twenty years ago.

He started walking and lifted his gaze to the blue beyond the trees that rimmed the back of their property. "I know I shouldn't ask, God." He slipped his hands in his pockets and kept on. "But I still don't understand why. Why do You need her up there with You?" His voice was quiet, barely loud enough for him to hear. "She should be right here beside me."

And she should have been. They would've talked about Katy and Dayne and whether the pressures of the reality show and the movies they were making might be too much. They'd share their concerns about Luke and Reagan and their sorrow for Ashley and Landon. They'd celebrate Kari and Ryan's growing family and their gratitude about Brooke and Peter's healed marriage. And they'd pray that Erin and Sam might move closer.

Elaine cared about his kids, but talking about them with her would never be the same because Elaine didn't share their past. She had grown children of her own, after all. She hadn't been there to grieve with him when Dayne was given up for adoption, and she wasn't the one beside him rushing Brooke to the hospital for fifteen stitches the day she fell off her bike when she was in first grade. She hadn't been there for birthdays or first days of school, for graduations or great vacations, for broken bones or broken hearts.

He took the footpath over the bridge, the one he'd improved a year ago so he and

Cole would have a place to study the fish and catch frogs with the old net John kept in the garage. On the other side, he walked a little slower, following the path around a bend and out to the bench, where he and Elizabeth had sat together and talked more times than he could count.

Not only would he have to let go of the memories he and Elizabeth shared and the traditions that marked each holiday and the funny stories handed down over the years. But if he married Elaine, they'd have to find someplace to live. He sucked in a full breath and gripped the edge of the bench. As he did, he studied the back porch and windows of the old place. Elaine wouldn't want to move into the Baxter house. She couldn't compete with the memories of Elizabeth, and John wouldn't want her to try. He wasn't ready to move into her house either.

A wave of anxiety moved through his veins. He'd thought about selling the house before, and he always dismissed his concerns. But now, with the velvet box upstairs in his top dresser drawer, the time had come to think about the reality. They would have to live somewhere.

God, the whole thing makes me feel old and tired. He leaned back against the bench and closed his eyes. It would be easier to turn

Elaine away. Stay here in the Baxter house surrounded by his kids and grandkids and his memories. The memories most of all. *I had everything with Elizabeth, Lord. . . . Where am I supposed to go from here?*

John waited, and at first there was no answer, just the sound of a robin moving about in the trees overhead and the rush of water in the nearby stream.

But then, like the softest breath against his skin, John felt a verse come to life in his heart. *"Come to me, all you who are weary and burdened, and I will give you rest. Take my yoke upon you and learn from me, for I am gentle and humble in heart, and you will find rest for your souls. For my yoke is easy and my burden is light."*

The words felt like water to his soul, and they breathed life into his heart. Matthew 11 was a section of Scripture John had come back to many times in his life. When Elizabeth had cancer the first time and when Luke went through his rebellious season after the tragedy of September 11. *"Come to me, all you who are weary and burdened, and I will give you rest. . . ."*

The words expanded and filled his mind. There was always a reason why God placed a certain verse on his heart, and today was no exception. He was tired and weary. The burden of the decision before him was more than he could bear, especially on his anniversary.

He opened his eyes, and the message seemed clearer than the late-summer sky. If the thought of marrying Elaine was too much for him, then this wasn't the time to make that move. Instead he needed to focus on the Lord, on God's great and mighty power to lead and guide and grant wisdom wherever it was needed. To think about God's faithfulness. In doing so, he would be taking on the Lord's yoke and allowing God to dictate his next step.

For the most wonderful few seconds, John could almost feel Elizabeth sitting beside him. The memory of her was that strong. "Thirty-nine years . . ." He felt the sting of tears, but he blinked them back. A smile started in his heart and ended up tugging at his lips. Because when it came to Elizabeth, he couldn't do anything but feel the joy of all she'd been to him and the kids. *Thank You for her, God. I'm so grateful.*

He stood and gathered the strength he'd need to face the day. As he did, he heard the words once more. *"Come to me, all you who are weary. . . ."* He'd spend the day looking at pictures and calling his kids and reading the Bible, and he'd do it all with

Elizabeth's favorite CD of hymns playing in the background. But before too long, he'd do what he needed to do in order to be fair — both to himself and to Elaine. He'd call her and cancel their plans for tomorrow. Because until the Lord cleared up the questions clouding his heart, he had no right taking things further.

Even with the engagement ring sitting upstairs in the velvet box.

Katy was grateful for the going-away party at the Flanigans' house because it was a diversion. Rhonda Sanders — her longtime friend and assistant CKT director — was moving to Cleveland to be near Chad Jennings, who had filled in with the production of *Godspell* when Katy stepped down. The two were full of energy, in love, and excited about the future. They were leaving tomorrow, and Rhonda would live with one of the CKT families near the Ohio theater. The couple would work on two productions and then get married sometime next spring.

Katy pulled a package of frozen hamburger patties from the freezer and watched Rhonda and her fiancé, the way her friend's eyes sparkled when she looked at Chad and the way he hung on everything she said.

A hint of jealousy colored the moment,

63

and Katy looked away. Rhonda and Chad would have everything Katy and Dayne could never have. Anonymity and privacy and a world where the people who watched would cheer them on, believing in them and supporting them.

Dayne stepped out of the pantry with two enormous bags of hamburger buns. "Where does Jenny want them?" He was halfway to Katy when he must've seen something different in her expression. He set the buns on the granite countertop and came to her, gently touching her elbow. "What's wrong?"

She found a smile and looped her arm around his waist. "Sorry." She glanced at Rhonda and Chad again. In the living room someone was playing a song from *Beauty and the Beast* on the piano. By the sound of it, a roomful of kids provided the vocals. She let the noise around her fade. "Just wishing."

Dayne followed her gaze, and he seemed to understand at almost the same time. "That we could be them . . . ?"

"Not really." She turned back to Dayne. "For someday."

A dozen kids ran past, squealing and laughing and chasing a handful of others.

Dayne didn't seem to notice. He touched Katy's cheek, and a longing filled his expression. "It'll come."

"I know." Katy nodded, but neither of them seemed very convinced. She set the frozen meat on the counter just as Jenny hurried in from outside.

"The barbecue wouldn't light. Can you believe it? We must have the world's biggest grill out there, and with fifty kids waiting for burgers we couldn't get a flame." Jenny rushed by Katy and Dayne and washed her hands in the sink. "Jim had to get a match and light it the old-fashioned way."

Katy rolled up her sleeves and grinned at Dayne. Again she was glad for the chaos of the moment. "Well, if you've got a flame, put us to work."

"Take the tray from the bottom drawer and spread the burgers across it." Jenny looked slightly frazzled but brimming with joy, the way she always looked at one of her parties. She rattled off directions to Dayne, telling him where the condiments were and how many tomatoes to slice. "Once you're outside, I'm sure Jim could use your help. He likes a teammate for megameals like this."

The burgers were perfect that night, and the kids took their full plates and found places at the patio tables. Katy and Dayne sat on the outdoor sofa and watched the scene, how the veteran CKT kids blended with the younger boys and girls.

"Seeing them like this, I can almost picture them the way they are onstage, their costumes and lines. Everything." Katy set her burger down on her plate and gazed across the pool to the table on the other side where Tim Reed was sitting. He was a freshman in college this year. If the drama program had been able to continue, this would've been Tim's last year. There were other kids too. Bailey and Connor Flanigan, the precious brother and sister who had been family to Katy all the years she lived in their apartment over the garage. The Shaffers and the Picks, the Schneiders and the Larsons.

Katy shifted her attention and spotted Bethany Allen, CKT's area coordinator. Her life would also change now that CKT had no place to perform.

"I know what you're thinking." Dayne balanced his plate on his knees and put his arm around Katy's shoulders.

"Hmmm." She leaned against him. A breeze washed over the field behind the Flanigans' house and whispered through the maple trees that surrounded their property. She liked this, the way being here brought with it a relaxed intimacy, the sort of normal atmosphere she and Dayne never shared outside Bloomington. She smiled at him. "What?"

"How auditions should be taking place in a few weeks. How this'll be the first time in years that Bloomington won't have a fall CKT production."

"That and the kids." She narrowed her eyes. "CKT's been so good for them. What'll they do now? How'll they stay together?"

There was no answer, and Dayne didn't try to find one. Instead they both let the conversation stall, their attention on the kids and their laughter.

As they finished eating, a few kids jumped up, and someone turned on the soundtrack from *High School Musical.* The kids on their feet launched into a replicate version of one of the dance numbers from the hit teenage movie, and the others gathered around, singing every word.

What would give these teenagers an outlet now? They could hardly burst into song at Bloomington High, not without getting strange looks from the other kids. CKT had been a unique environment that allowed kids to sing and dance and feel good about their God-given gifts. A sick feeling tightened Katy's stomach. In comparison, working on a movie in England felt almost trite.

As darkness fell over the backyard, Jim and Dayne built a fire in the pit, twenty yards back from the pool and patio area. Everyone gathered blankets and folding chairs, and as the circle filled in, someone pulled out a guitar.

After Jenny passed out marshmallows and roasting sticks, she took a seat a little farther from the fire next to Katy. "You leave soon, right?"

"Next Tuesday." Katy stared at the fire.

Jenny pulled her knees up. "You worried?"

"Of course." Katy allowed a sad laugh. "*For Real* and all its slanted views debuts right after Labor Day. With the whole world watching."

A wisp of smoke curled their direction, and Jenny squinted. "You think it'll be that bad?"

Katy shook her head. "The previews have given one message loud and clear." She changed her tone. " 'Will America's favorite couple survive making a movie together? Look for the answers on *For Real.*' "

"I saw it." Jenny frowned. "I was hoping that was just the hype. To get people watching."

"Yeah, but then they have to *keep* people watching." Katy stared through the smoke at the trees near the back of the property. "I don't know why we ever agreed to it."

"I do." Jenny tilted her head, her expression softer than before. "You wanted to give them a window without giving them a door."

"Well . . . the plan backfired."

"How's Dayne feel?" Jenny's tone was too quiet for anyone else to hear.

"He's nervous. We get back to LA, then there's the premiere for our movie, and weeks later we'll be worlds apart."

Jenny was silent, maybe letting the reality of Katy's situation sink in. After a while she drew a slow breath. "Not exactly how you pictured it."

"No."

Again Jenny was slow in answering. "But you allowed it." Her tone wasn't critical or condemning. "You both did."

Her insight stayed with Katy long after the party was over, after she'd hugged Rhonda and Chad and promised to pray for them, and after she'd said good-bye to the Flanigans and a couple dozen CKT kids still hanging around.

On the drive home Katy said little. Jenny was right, of course. The movie and TV deals facing them were only happening because they'd allowed them. Katy gazed out the window at the night sky over

Bloomington. Dayne's movie had been set for a year, since way before their wedding. So what was she supposed to do? Sit home and count the days until he finished filming? When their director could hardly wait to see her in another movie?

Katy closed her eyes. They'd be gone at the same time, right? Keeping busy was the best way to get her mind off the fact that Dayne's costar for his upcoming film would be Randi Wells, who — despite Dayne's lack of interest — had already made her feelings for Dayne very clear. So what would it hurt if Katy was in London at the same time filming her own movie?

"You're not saying much." For an instant, Dayne took his attention off the road and glanced at her.

"Hmmm." She smiled, but she could feel it stop short of her eyes. "Thinking about what's next, how crazy it'll be."

For a few seconds Dayne didn't respond, but then he flexed his jaw muscles and nodded slowly. "More than we can imagine."

Once they were home, Dayne took a call from his director, and Katy went to their bedroom. She opened the patio door and was met by a sweet, cool breeze from the lake below.

Dayne was still on the phone when she

climbed into bed and turned on her side, facing the lake. It was too dark to see the water or even the outline of the distant trees. But the fresh air against her face reminded her that they were really here at the lake house and not in Hollywood with cameramen waiting outside for them to step onto their balcony.

She couldn't shake what Jenny said, especially now with Dayne deep in conversation about his next film. Every hairpin turn in the journey ahead was one they'd invited, one they'd not only allowed but welcomed. Was this really how they'd planned it when they stood on that Mexican beach and promised each other forever?

In the other room, Dayne raised his voice a notch. "The answer's no. Tell her we'll see each other soon enough." He sounded beyond frustrated. "I don't need a week to run lines with Randi. We've done this enough times. We'll be fine."

Katy pressed her face deeper into the pillow and closed her eyes. She wasn't worried about Dayne's feelings for Randi. They'd talked the situation through a number of times. Dayne wasn't interested — no matter what the tabloids said. But Randi was smooth. And she'd told Katy that she was interested in Dayne. Or maybe she was interested in the peace he'd found because of his faith. Whatever it was, Randi wouldn't miss an opportunity. Not with the two of them together in Mexico.

The place where not six months ago Dayne and Katy had experienced a wedding that was perfect. Hidden from the press and with only family and friends around, they'd had a few days singled out from the others. A time Katy would never forget.

She breathed in deep, and gradually she was there again. Standing in the bride's room at the beach resort, surrounded by her beautiful bridesmaids — Ashley, her matron of honor, Brooke, Kari, Erin, Reagan, and Rhonda. Katy could hear the excitement in their voices, see their stunning ankle-length dresses made of the palest pink satin and their elegant updos, compliments of a stylist brought in by the wedding coordinator.

Throughout the preparations, Katy remembered thinking how dreamlike every detail seemed. The love surrounding her, the beauty of her new family, even the fact that her parents had been well enough to come and add to the boundless joy of the event.

She could see again the way her bridesmaids gathered near the door, peeking through the crack and waiting for the signal. Their bouquets had been flown in, each of them a cascade of pink baby roses except for Katy's. Hers held white roses with several trails of baby's breath and baby white roses.

The guys looked beyond sharp in their black tuxes, white shirts, and pale pink vests and bow ties. Dayne wore tails, his vest and bow tie a crisp white against the black. But if she lived a hundred years, when she looked back on their wedding day, she wouldn't see his clothes. She'd see his eyes. The way he'd watched her as she came down the aisle at sunrise.

Katy pulled the covers up close to her chin and felt herself relax, felt sleep coming over her the way it did when she turned her anxious late-night thoughts away and focused on their happy times instead of the uncertainty ahead.

The wedding photos were breathtaking because they reminded her of the family she'd married into and how, if she and Dayne could only break free from Hollywood, maybe they would raise that same sort of family. In Katy's favorite group picture, the one with the entire wedding party, she and Dayne were at the center, with Ashley and Luke on either side. Luke had been Dayne's best man. Ever since Luke took over as Dayne's attorney, the two talked often. The others — Peter, Landon, Ryan, and Sam — were clearly proud to stand up for Dayne too.

Before the ceremony, John Baxter had pulled Katy aside. "We are the most blessed of all. Our family hasn't only gained a son in recent years. We've gained a daughter."

The images from her wedding stayed, but the sounds around her — the breeze from the lake, Dayne's movie conversation in the other room — faded. She wasn't lying in bed waiting for her husband, lost in a magical moment from their past. She was actually taking her first steps from the bride's room and Ashley was saying, "Okay, let's make this happen."

She was walking into the lobby, her white gown swishing along behind her, and she was whispering in her father's ear, "Remember, Daddy, all those times you told me I could be anything I wanted, have anything I wanted?"

Her dad was blinking back his tears. "Yes, baby. . . . I meant every word."

All the Baxter cousins were squealing and bouncing about in the lobby near the final door that separated them from the outdoor wedding. Then the wedding coordinator was opening the doors, and the sound of violins was filling Katy's senses. The coordinator was dismissing the bridesmaids and finally the children, saying, "Okay, now . . . don't walk too fast."

And the music was changing, and Katy was looking up at the frail man beside her. "Daddy —" she reached up and wiped the tear on his cheek with her fingertip — "I'm so glad you were well enough to come."

The notes began to form a song, and Katy recognized it and suddenly . . . a door opened a few feet away and a light pierced the darkness. Katy gasped and her eyes flew open.

"Sorry." Dayne came around the bed to her side and touched her shoulder. "I didn't mean to wake you."

"It's okay." She settled back into her pillow. "I was awake. Sort of."

He gave her a tender kiss and ran his knuckles lightly over her cheek. "I couldn't get off the phone."

Katy muttered something about how it didn't matter, and Dayne headed for the bathroom to get ready for bed. Only then did her mind clear enough to realize what had happened. In her desire to find a way back to the magic of their wedding, she'd fallen asleep. No wonder every detail had been so crisp and clear, so much like she was there again. The picture hadn't been a memory at all but a dream.

Suddenly she wanted to call Dayne back to her side, beg him to pray with her about the distance and temptation and glaring scrutiny their marriage was bound to get in the coming months. She leaned up on her elbow and stared after him. "Dayne?"

The sound of her voice died in the dark room, long before it might reach him. From deep within the bathroom she heard a faucet turn on. He hadn't heard her, and even if he had, praying together shouldn't have to be her idea, right? Dayne had taken the lead during their early months of marriage, so why not now?

Katy settled back onto the pillow and felt frustration throw itself into the mix of emotions smothering her. The dream had been so real, so vivid. And as she pictured herself again, the way she'd felt walking up the aisle toward her one true love, a horrifying thought hit her. With everything they would face in the coming season, maybe that's all their life together ever really was. A dream.

A fleeting, magical dream, from which it was inevitable that one day they would wake up.

CHAPTER FOUR

Long after the CKT kids were gone and after Jim and the boys and Bailey were in bed, Jenny Flanigan stayed up cleaning. Change was in the air, and Jenny wanted to mull it over, acknowledge it. The end of August always had this effect on her. Back when the kids were younger, each fall she would buy a calendar that covered sixteen months, because the year never began in January but when summer ended. Like her friends with kids, Jenny talked about the beginning and end of the year as it applied to her kids' school schedule.

This fall was no different. She and Jim had discussed home-schooling — something they had done before. But the boys wanted more time with their school friends, and Jim and Jenny agreed that it was important for their sons to keep those relationships. In another few years, maybe they'd come back home for their schooling.

The decision was the right one, but it still meant a quiet house during the day, a tight schedule in the afternoon when they would need to fit in homework and soccer practice. Connor had just decided to play freshman football at Clear Creek High, where he would be a part of Ryan and Jim's program. And Justin and Shawn had decided to take on flag football at their middle school.

Ricky, their youngest, said it best. "Mom," he'd told her earlier that day, "if I could freeze time, it would always be the last day of summer, and I would always be eight."

Jenny smiled as she dumped into the trash the remnants of barbecue potato chips from two large plastic bowls. She took the containers to the sink, turned on the hot water, and splashed in a few drops of soap. If only they could all freeze time. Because these days of busy schedules and homework and hurried dinners were the times they would remember, the moments that were weaving the tapestry of their lives.

Yes, the fall would be busy. But that wasn't the only change in the air this late-summer night. Jenny reached for a dish towel, and she caught sight of a framed photo on the kitchen counter of Bailey and Connor and a roomful of CKT kids after their final performance of *Godspell*. She leaned closer and looked at her two kids and then the others, at the light in their eyes and the invincibility in their expressions. They had believed then that somehow CKT would continue, that they would find a new theater and there would be a fall show — the way there had been a fall show every year since Katy moved to Bloomington.

Jenny's heart felt heavy as she grabbed one of the wet bowls from the sink. CKT was the greatest change facing all of them as September drew near. The kids who had delighted in singing and dancing and winning roles in one show after another would have an enormous void in their lives. Some kids would simply deal with their sorrow and move on to new activities. That's why Connor had decided to play football and Bailey renewed her commitment to take dance lessons after school.

But what about the kids who hadn't been blessed with social skills? CKT had provided a place for kids who were too big or small, too short or tall to fit in at school, kids who otherwise might not have found a peer group who accepted them. After one of the CKT shows, a girl admitted to the cast that she had been considering suicide before finding CKT. Others had been shy or awkward, but through CKT they'd found a confidence they would've missed out on.

Jenny studied the photo again. She had thought about asking the administration at Clear Creek High if they would allow CKT to operate out of their auditorium or maybe contacting one of the larger churches. But CKT's area coordinator, Bethany Allen, had already tried every possible venue twice. The old Bloomington Community Theater was about to be replaced with condominiums, and quite clearly they were out of options.

She dried the two bowls, but still she wasn't tired. Certainly she and Jim could continue their weekly Bible study with the CKT kids, but the numbers would likely dwindle without the theater to give them their common bond. Jenny looped the towel over the oven handle and was about to check her e-mail when she heard someone coming down the stairs.

"Mom . . ." It was Bailey's voice.

Jenny looked over her shoulder in time to see her daughter reach the last stair and stop. She was barefoot, and in her oversize Indianapolis Colts nightshirt, she looked younger than her seventeen years. Her face was pale, and her cheeks were tearstained. Maybe she was thinking about the same things Jenny was — how their lives would be so different without CKT.

Jenny went to her. "What is it?"

Bailey opened her mouth to talk, but instead she moved into Jenny's arms and buried her face. Jenny ran her hand along Bailey's back, and she could feel the slow, slight jerking of a series of quiet sobs. Suddenly it occurred to Jenny that maybe this wasn't about CKT. Alarm shot through her. "Sweetheart, did something happen?"

Bailey sniffed and wiped her eyes with the edge of her index finger. After a few seconds of struggle, she pulled back and looked at Jenny. Shame and hurt and shock colored her expression, and finally she seemed to find the strength to respond. "It's Marissa Young. I just found out."

Jenny's heart pounded against the walls of her chest, but she did her best to remain calm. "What happened to her?"

"I thought . . ." Bailey closed her eyes tight and let her forehead fall against Jenny's shoulder. Again she struggled to find the words. "I thought she was keeping her baby, that she'd talked to her mom about it. Remember?" Her eyes were pained as she looked up. "That's what Marissa told me. How she and her mom were going to work everything out and all that."

A sinking feeling hit Jenny. "I remember."

She didn't want to ask. "She didn't talk to her mom?"

"That's not it." Bailey sniffed again. "She had an abortion. She called and told me because she didn't want to lie to me. And she didn't want me to hear it from someone else."

"Oh, honey . . ." Jenny's knees felt weak. "I can't believe this."

She led Bailey to the barstools, and with the news still ripping through Jenny's mind, they each took a seat. Marissa was one of Bailey's friends, a girl she'd met at church when the two were in grade school. Several months back, when Marissa found out she was pregnant, Bailey and Jenny met with her at the Flanigan home. Marissa had reluctantly come, and Jenny had listened with a heart overflowing with sadness. That day she and Bailey prayed for Marissa, and they told her about the Bloomington Crisis Pregnancy Center. But in recent months the center had closed, and Jenny hadn't taken the next step.

She never spoke with Marissa's mother. Every time she made the call to Dotty Young, the woman was too busy to talk or unavailable. Jenny's messages were never returned and time passed.

Now Jenny felt like a truck had parked on

her shoulders. She anchored her elbow on the countertop and propped up her forehead with her clenched fist. "It's my fault." Weariness came over her, and she met Bailey's eyes. "I should've tried harder to reach her mother."

"No." Bailey shook her head fast and hard. "Her mother was avoiding you. That's what Marissa said." She hesitated. "Her mother *drove* her to the clinic."

Jenny couldn't have been more surprised if Bailey had said that Marissa's mother had kicked her out onto the streets. "Dotty drove her daughter to an *abortion* clinic?"

"Yes." Bailey's expression darkened. "Mrs. Young told Marissa an abortion would make it like it never happened."

Jenny moaned. "Was she really avoiding my calls?"

"I asked Marissa. She said her mom didn't want to talk to you."

Of course not, Jenny thought. Dotty Young knew exactly how Jenny felt about abortion. But until lately, Jenny had assumed that Dotty felt the same way. Now, though, when her daughter's future was on the line, she told Marissa to do something that went against their beliefs. Jenny put her hand over Bailey's. "Nothing will ever make it like it never happened. You know that, right?"

"Yes." Bailey gulped back another sob. "Marissa said she's been . . . she's been cutting herself."

"What?" Jenny forced herself to lower her voice. Kids were cutting, self-mutilating; that's what she'd heard from her friends. But Jenny figured kids acting out that way were the teens who were deeply troubled, kids who drank and did drugs and ditched school. Not kids like Marissa Young. Jenny controlled her racing heart. "Did she tell you why?"

Bailey exhaled long and slow, and the effect made her look defeated. "She said she deserves it after what she did to her baby." She bit her lip.

There were so many issues at hand that Jenny didn't know what to deal with first. "Marissa needs counseling right away. She should meet with someone at church."

"That's what I told her." Fresh tears filled Bailey's eyes. "She said she can't let anyone know. About the cutting. She's wearing long sleeves so her mom won't find out."

"She has to find out." Jenny kept her tone gentle. She gave Bailey's hand a light squeeze. "I have to call her. Even if she won't talk to me."

Bailey nodded, understanding. "Marissa'll be mad, but she needs help. Even if she won't talk to me again for telling you."

Amid the darkness of fear and guilt and deep futility, a ray of hope shone over the moment. Bailey was growing up. It wasn't enough anymore to tell Jenny what her friends were doing and then commit her to silence. Now Bailey understood that the safety of her friends was far more important than whatever that friend might think of Bailey for telling her mother secret information.

Jenny let her gaze linger on her daughter for a moment. Then she stood, went to the kitchen phone, and picked up the receiver. As it rang, she prayed Dotty would pick up. Seconds later she filled with relief as Marissa's mother answered. "I'm sorry for calling so late." Jenny leaned against the kitchen counter and closed her eyes. What would it be like to get a call like this about Bailey? She couldn't imagine.

"It's the weekend." Dotty sounded surprised by the call. "You know us; we're always up late."

"Right, well . . . I'm calling about Marissa." Jenny drew a quick breath and explained that she'd known about the baby and that she knew about the abortion. At first it seemed like Dotty might dispute the fact, but when Jenny told her that the information came from Marissa, Dotty fell quiet.

"Anyway, Marissa told Bailey something very serious." Jenny did nothing to hide the tired sound in her voice.

"Listen, Jenny." Dotty's tone changed. "What happens with my daughter is my business. I don't need you calling me, making me feel like I don't know my own child."

Jenny stifled a sad laugh. This was exactly the response she'd feared, the reason she hadn't ever contacted a parent after hearing the details of Bailey's conversations with friends. For the most part, people didn't want to know. When kids were using drugs or getting drunk, when they were breaking curfew or sleeping with their boyfriends, parents usually had some idea. But they chose to look the other way so they wouldn't have to deal with the reality. One friend had even told her that what she didn't know couldn't hurt her and that all teens veered a little off course now and then.

But Jenny wasn't letting Dotty deter her. Not when Marissa's life was on the line. She raised her voice just enough to express her concern. "Dotty, I'm sorry if you don't want to hear this." She launched into a brief but chilling description of the actions Bailey had told her about, the cutting and harm

Marissa was inflicting on herself. "She needs counseling. Please . . . get her in to someone at church tomorrow." She paused and did her best to sound compassionate. "Maybe you could go with her."

Dotty was quiet for several beats, and Jenny wondered if she was stunned or crying or even if she'd hung up. But then the sound of her sighing came across the line. "She actually told that to Bailey?" The anger was gone, and in its place was something closer to shock. "Marissa wasn't talking about someone else?"

"She was talking about herself." Jenny glanced at Bailey, who was still watching from her place at the kitchen bar. "I'm sorry, Dotty. I thought you should know right away."

Again there was a pause, and Jenny hoped maybe the woman would break, that she might cry out for Jenny's friendship and the chance to be honest about the heartache that had overcome them in recent months.

But Dotty kept her words brief. "I need to go." The heaviness in her tone said what she wasn't verbalizing. "I'll talk to my daughter. If she needs counseling, we'll get it. You don't have to worry about her."

After a terse thank-you from Marissa's mother, the conversation ended. Jenny replaced the receiver and sat back down next to Bailey. "That didn't go well."

"She probably doesn't believe you." Bailey rested her forearms on the counter. "But if she looks at Marissa's arms, she'll know."

"And maybe then she'll take Marissa for help." Jenny placed her hand over Bailey's again. "That's all we can hope for."

For a while neither of them said anything. Then Bailey angled her head, still sad but more thoughtful than before. "You know what I wish?"

"What, honey?" The house was quiet, except for the soft whir of the ice maker and a gentle breeze outside the open kitchen window.

"I wish the crisis pregnancy center hadn't closed. Marissa said it was shut down before she had her abortion." She narrowed her eyes, pensive. "I did a report on the center last year, remember? I had no idea it was closing."

"Me neither." Jenny felt sick about the way things had turned out.

"The center had an ultrasound machine, and they tell you information about what happens after an abortion, how damaged it leaves the mother." Bailey stood and shrugged. "It's too late for Marissa, I guess."

"Not if she gets help."

"I mean for her baby." Bailey's eyes glistened with sorrow. "It's just sad, you know?"

"For the baby and for Marissa." Jenny wanted to add that Marissa clearly was struggling with a broken relationship with God, along with everything else, but it was late. She stood also and put her hands on Bailey's shoulders. "Let's pray for Marissa, and then you get some sleep, okay?"

Bailey nodded and bowed her head. Jenny had expected to do the praying, but her daughter started in first, as if her heart was already overflowing with the things she wanted to share with the Lord. "Dear God, be with Marissa tonight." Bailey's voice caught, and it took a moment before she started again. "I can't believe she's hurting herself, that she'd feel so low she could do something like that. Please help her to be honest to her mom and lead them both so they can get her help. And please hold her little baby extra close. In Jesus' name, amen."

Jenny couldn't have put it any better if she'd tried. She hugged Bailey for a long time, then watched her trudge back upstairs to her room. When she was gone, Jenny sat down again and stared out the window at the dark, shadowy landscape outside. Her prayer came as naturally as her next breath. *Thank You, Father, for a daughter who loves me and shares with me. I know what we have is very special. And please give me wisdom so the bond between us stays.*

She was about to head to bed when an idea hit her. If there was no longer a crisis pregnancy center in town, then someone needed to reopen it. And who better than Ashley's sister? Brooke and her husband were both doctors, so they would have the connections and the means to get something started again.

Jenny's heart raced as the possibilities took form. She didn't know Brooke very well, but she could talk to Ashley. She could tell her about Marissa, how the only crisis pregnancy center in town had closed down, and how other teenage girls might choose abortion if they didn't have more information. And just like that Jenny could get the ball rolling toward a change for Bloomington, Indiana.

Maybe as early as tomorrow morning.

CHAPTER FIVE

Dr. Brooke Baxter West hung up the phone, snagged a tissue from her desk at the medical office where she had her practice, and dabbed at her eyes. *Not now,* she told herself. Tears would have to wait until later.

She checked her watch — 10 A.M., time for rounds at the hospital, a task that always required her utmost attention and focus. As a pediatrician, the kids in her care who needed a hospital stay were usually sick with things they would recover from — tonsillitis or pneumonia or severe croup. But today one of her patients was critically ill. Ethan Teeple needed her complete attention, no matter the ideas screaming through her mind.

The phone call had been from her sister Ashley. Proof that the differences between the two were behind them and that God was healing their hearts, bringing them back to a place of friendship. Brooke gathered her file of notes, slipped them into her briefcase, and headed for the door. The hospital was the next building over, and most days Brooke walked. On this late August morning the time outdoors would be especially welcome, a chance to think over the conversation with Ashley.

Apparently her sister had talked with Jenny Flanigan, one of the CKT moms. Ashley filled Brooke in on a situation that had happened with one of the teenage girls in Jenny's daughter's circle of friends. The girl had gotten pregnant and had an abortion because she had no other option, no other voice of reason. Not even the voice of her mother.

"The crisis pregnancy center closed just before Marissa would've needed it. Maybe it's time someone reopened it, Brooke." Ashley's voice was brimming with emotion. "Maybe that would be part of my Sarah's legacy."

The tears came quickly for Brooke as she pictured Ashley and Landon's tiny baby born with anencephaly and her short life before leaving this earth. From the time Ashley received the terrible diagnosis, Brooke had been opposed to her sister continuing her pregnancy. Medical training and prior experience had convinced Brooke that only one option existed when an un-born baby was diagnosed with anencephaly. Abortion. Eliminate the pregnancy, thereby saving the parents the trauma of carrying to term a child doomed to death.

But Ashley and Landon had done things differently, standing by their determination that God would bring a miracle out of their daughter's life — however brief.

The resulting birth and death of Sarah had touched Brooke like nothing before. It changed her. She had since come to realize that she could not suggest abortion to her patients. Not when the baby's ultrasound showed anencephaly. Not ever. But never until this morning had she thought about taking her new understanding of life a step further by reopening the crisis pregnancy center.

Brooke stepped out through the double doors of her medical building, and she could hear Ashley's voice the way it had sounded moments ago on the phone.

"Think about it," Ashley had told her. "Sarah proved that life is precious. She was loved as much in her few hours as she would've ever been loved if she'd lived to be a hundred. Shouldn't the babies of teen-agers in our city have that same chance? the chance to live?"

Goose bumps had run like electricity down Brooke's arms and legs. A crisis pregnancy center was crucial. It would give teenage moms or moms in crisis a chance to see their unborn children, a chance to recognize their pregnancies for what they truly were — lives that deserved a chance.

Brooke sighed and pushed through the doors of the hospital. She could think about the center later. For now she had to focus on the sick kids in her care. Especially Ethan. She took the elevator to the fourth floor, the one dedicated to children with serious illnesses. Down the hall and around a corner, she came to Ethan's room.

He was lying in bed, a precious bald child with huge blue eyes, but this morning he seemed more tired than usual. His mother stood next to him, holding his hand. She looked up when Brooke entered the room. Worry had creased her forehead and left dark circles beneath her eyes.

Brooke took gentle hold of Ethan's toes and shifted her attention to the small boy. "How's my favorite patient?"

Ethan's eyes lit up. Even on his sickest days he was a ray of sunlight in a hospital wing of sorrow and darkness. "I got my pictures." He pointed to a Mickey Mouse photo album on his bedside table. "The ones from Disney World!"

A lump tried to form in Brooke's throat, but she kept it at bay. "Photos of your trip. You'll have to show me."

"He had a great time." Ethan's mother found the hint of a smile as she reached for the photo album. She was opening it when Ethan's nurse Lindsay walked into the room.

"Dr. West, good to see you." Lindsay's eyes met Brooke's and there was an awareness, a sense that Brooke hoped Ethan and his mother couldn't see. The child wasn't doing well. His last surgery and rounds of chemotherapy hadn't stopped the cancer the way they'd hoped. The treatment he was getting now was his last chance.

"Did I tell you, Dr. West?" Ethan's voice was raspy, another sign of his struggle.

Brooke moved closer to the side of the boy's bed. She grinned at him. "Tell me what?"

"About Nurse Lindsay." Ethan beamed at the young brunette, who had moved to the other side of his bed. "Me and her are engaged. 'Cause when I get all grown up I'm gonna marry her."

"That's right." Lindsay's eyes shone with the sweetest sorrow. "Ethan's my little prince."

" 'Cept when I make her chase me . . . out in the halls."

Brooke giggled at the picture Ethan painted, and she walked to the chart positioned on the wall near the doorway. Her joy faded as she looked at Ethan's numbers. If his blood counts were a fair indicator — and they usually were — the cancer was still gaining ground.

Ethan took the photo album from his mother and began showing the pictures to Lindsay. "You can see them in a minute, 'kay, Dr. West? When you're done with the paper stuff."

"Okay, pal." Brooke didn't take her eyes from the chart. "I'll be right there." She flipped back a few pages and compared Ethan's blood levels, the steady downward progression of them. The numbers blurred, and Brooke sucked in a breath and held it. How strange life was. This cherished boy was fighting to live another day when every week women walked into the abortion clinic down the street and rid their bodies of a life that would've been just as special.

Brooke summed up the information in the report and jotted a few notes at the bottom of the page, just below the notes from his pediatric oncologist. The boy was sicker, no doubt. *But,* Brooke wrote, *he's as much a sunbeam as ever, a chatterbox with everyone who comes into the room — even if he's too tired to get out of bed. If anyone can win this battle, Ethan can.* She closed the file and placed it back in the holder on the wall.

Ethan's mother was watching her, the way parents of sick kids always watched, looking for a sign, a glimpse, a knowing that might show in a doctor's expression. Brooke kept her eyes from the woman as she moved back to Ethan's bedside and peered over his shoulder.

"See, Dr. West." Ethan was practically shaking with excitement. "That's me and Mickey Mouse! In person!" He pointed to a bright-colored photograph. "I got extra long time with him 'cause that's called Make-A-Wish! Isn't that great?"

"That is, Ethan." Brooke put her hand on his shoulder. "It looks like a wonderful time."

Ethan settled back into the pillow, exhausted from the effort of telling the story. His smile fell off a little, and he glanced at his mother. "Mommy says it was the time of our life."

Indeed, Brooke thought. She caught the attention of Ethan's mother on the other side of the bed. "Can we talk? Out in the hall, maybe?"

As Brooke stepped back, Lindsay moved in beside Ethan. "Show me the one with Dumbo again." Her voice was tender. "I love that ride."

"Yeah, me too!" Ethan's words were slower now, his eyelids heavier when he blinked. "You and me can go on it next time . . . when you come with us."

Brooke and Ethan's mother went into the hall. When they were out of earshot, Brooke studied the woman's face, the worry showing in the lines around her eyes and mouth.

"It isn't good, is it?" A desperation from somewhere deep inside her shone in her eyes. "His skin is paler than before."

"I noticed that." Brooke stared at the floor for a few seconds, and a sigh slid between her lips. "No, Mrs. Teeple, his numbers aren't good. We're going to increase his treatment dosage. But really . . . we're running out of ways to help him." She reached out and took gentle hold of the woman's hand. "You need to know."

Ethan's mother squeezed her eyes shut and gave a few quick nods. Brooke wondered if the woman might faint or drop to her knees from the sheer anxiety of the moment. Instead she opened her eyes, and in a voice choked with tears, she thanked Brooke. "I know you're doing all you can do." The corners of her lips lifted, despite her obvious pain. "We won't give up. Everyone we know is praying for that little boy." She glanced over her shoulder toward Ethan's room. "God does His best work when we're at the end of ourselves."

Brooke thought about her own daughter Hayley, who had nearly drowned and who — but for the miraculous power of God — might've been in a vegetative state at this moment and not attending school with her peers. "Yes." Brooke hoped Mrs. Teeple could feel her sincerity. "I believe that. My husband and I are praying for Ethan too."

They headed back into Ethan's room, and after a few minutes Brooke moved on to her next patient, a one-year-old recovering from a serious case of pneumonia. Things were on the upswing for Paige Tagliaferri, though, and Brooke expected this visit to have a much different feeling from the one with Ethan. She walked to the far end of the hall and turned down another corridor. Just past the nurses' station, she gave a light knock on the door and then stepped inside. Paige's parents had kept vigil at her cribside since she'd been admitted two days ago.

Now, as Brooke looked in, what she saw made her breath catch in her throat. Paige's mother, Megan, had climbed into the oversize hospital crib and was curled up beside little Paige. From a corner of the room came the soft refrains of classical music — Mozart, maybe. Brooke studied the picture they made, the young mother so concerned for her daughter that she had done the only thing she could do — place herself physically next to her child.

Brooke took quiet steps to the place on the wall where Paige's chart hung. She looked it over, and warmth filled her heart. Paige's last X-ray was much better. Her white count was normal, her little body responding to the antibiotics. If her exam went well, she could go home in the morning. Brooke replaced the chart and stared once more at the mother and daughter. Paige had been a patient since she was born. Her parents had spent years trying to conceive, trying every possible option before finally giving up. Only then, about a month later, did Megan find out she was pregnant.

Paige Tagliaferri was a beautiful child, with dark blonde hair, bright blue eyes, and the most delicate features. Every time Brooke saw her, she was smiling. Even after giving immunizations, Brooke loved her visits with Paige because her parents practically glowed with joy, as if having Paige and being parents was nothing short of a dream come true.

Brooke went to the side of the crib, gripped the edge, and whispered, "Hello, Megan. It's Dr. West."

The woman's eyes flew open, and for a moment she didn't seem to know where she was. Then she sat up, and a sheepish look filled her face. She leaned down and kissed Paige on the cheek before climbing out of the crib. "Sorry . . . I'm not sure I'm supposed to be in there." She reached back through the bars and stroked her daughter's hand. "She needed me."

"It's fine." Brooke smiled and pulled her stethoscope from her pocket. She slipped it on and moved in closer to the crib. "Her chart looks great. If she sounds good, she can go home tomorrow."

"I hope so." Relief filled Megan's voice. "We're taking her to California next week to visit my parents." A soft laugh came from the woman. "Like the rest of us, they can't get enough of her."

Brooke finished the exam, and as she expected, the baby's lungs sounded almost completely clear. She had finished making her recommendation that Paige go home and she was heading for her next patient when again the reality hit her. Ethan . . .

Paige . . . children who were wanted and prayed for and who, by their very existence, were walking miracles.

So what about the unborn babies of single mothers, babies of women who were frightened and not sure what to do next? The abortion clinic couldn't be their only option. Suddenly with a determination she hadn't felt since Hayley's accident, Brooke knew what she had to do next. She had to make a difference. Ashley was right; the town needed its crisis pregnancy center open again, and she and Peter had the resources and connections to make sure that happened.

Her heart kept time with the fast click of her heels against the tile floor. *I want this, God. I want to make a difference for girls who think their only choice is —*

She stopped short, and her prayer dropped off. To her left were a wall of windows and a door leading to a terrace, where visitors could find fresh air and solitude after a hospital visit. It was empty, and Brooke moved slowly through the door toward the far corner of the space. She grabbed hold of the railing and stared into the grove of trees surrounding that side of the hospital.

How many times had an abortion come at her recommendation when there was a poor diagnosis about a baby's health or when the mother was certain she didn't want a baby? Especially back in the days before she and Peter found the faith her parents had always shared. A parade of faces flashed in her mind, and she squeezed her eyes shut. *Forgive me, God, for what I've done. Forgive me . . . please.*

The prayer became a tortured echo, reverberating through her heart and mind and soul. Brooke could hardly move forward in an effort to protect girls from the choice of abortion without first recognizing the role she'd played in making them happen. She tightened her grip on the railing. *Lord, I didn't understand life until Sarah. If I could only take back every time . . .*

A warm breeze blew across the terrace, soft against her face. Only then did she realize she had tears on her cheeks. She swiped at them and hung her head. How could she put her name to a crisis pregnancy center when people would know her former stance on abortion? She had viewed it as a medical procedure, a woman's prerogative. Nothing more. She looked up through the trees to the blue beyond. *God . . . are You there?*

A stirring started, first in her heart and then in the depths of her being. There was no audible answer, but the presence of the Lord was tangible. She was forgiven, because that's what God's Word promised. Christ had died for her sins — even the sins of sending women to an abortion clinic. Now . . . now it was time for her to move forward.

Brooke took a long breath and then, with a new resolve from God alone, she turned and headed back into the hospital. As she walked to see her next patient, the feeling of God's Spirit stayed with her.

When her morning rounds were behind her, she walked back to her office and found a voice mail message from Ashley. "I had to call you back. I was reading the Bible, sitting in Sarah's room." Her voice was clear despite the heaviness of sorrow. "I stumbled onto Isaiah 43." She paused. "Brooke, I know you, and if you're considering my idea about the crisis pregnancy center, I know what you're thinking. You always expect perfection, and . . . well, you can be pretty hard on yourself. Anyway, read verses 18 and 19. I think they'll show you God's heart, the way they showed it to me." Another pause. "Love you. Call me."

There were years when Brooke wouldn't have considered keeping a Bible in her office. But after the tragedy with Hayley, Peter had given her a leather-bound edition with her name engraved on the front. She pulled it from the nearest shelf and ran her fingers over the engraved silver wording at the bottom. *Dr. Brooke West.* Peter's way of telling her he believed in her, that he would never again doubt her abilities as a doctor.

She set the Bible on her desk and flipped to Isaiah 43. Moving her finger down the page, she came to the verses Ashley had recommended. Starting with verse 18, she began to read. "Forget the former things; do not dwell on the past. See, I am doing a new thing! Now it springs up; do you not perceive it? I am making a way in the desert and streams in the wasteland."

Brooke blinked and read the verses again, more slowly this time. As she did, tears stung at her eyes. She really was forgiven. More than that, she was loved. Ashley's call told her that much. What were the odds that Ashley would read this passage today? Or that she would call and say so? Brooke touched the page and let the words wash over her one more time. Then she pulled a pen from her desk drawer and underlined the verses. *"See, I am doing a new thing!"*

On a day when she felt more conflicted than ever about her prior decisions, the verses seemed perfectly written for her. *God, is this Your answer?* She swallowed and imagined the crisis pregnancy center, the one Bloomington so desperately needed. The message from Isaiah was unmistakable. Let go of the past. . . . The Lord was doing something new in her life.

Streams of life across a wasteland of regret.

I hear You, Lord. I feel You. I won't miss this opportunity; I promise.

As she closed the Bible, as she glanced at her watch and collected herself for her next appointment, she became convinced of two things. First, she would talk to Peter later tonight about the need for the center. She would explain how God had led her onto the terrace and how He had forgiven her. And she would tell him about the verses in Isaiah.

And second, when the center was ready to open, when the first girls began seeking an option other than abortion, it would have the only possible name. A name that would forever memorialize the tiny baby who had changed everything.

The name would be Sarah's Door.

CHAPTER SIX

The moon splashed rays of light through the screen door in Dayne and Katy's bedroom. Dayne rolled onto his side. They had just two days left before reality would crash in on them, and Dayne couldn't sleep, didn't want to waste a moment of it. He turned his attention to the digital clock on Katy's bedside table — 11:15. Not that late, really. And the breeze off the lake was warmer than usual. An Indian summer night.

An idea began to form first in his mind, then deep in his heart, and Dayne couldn't shake it. He touched Katy's shoulder. "Hey . . ."

When she didn't respond, he tried again. "Katy." He kept his voice soft. "Baby, wake up."

Slowly she opened her eyes, and as she did, concern filled her expression. "Dayne —" she was breathless — "is everything okay?"

"Shhh." He ran his knuckles slowly against her cheek. "Wanna take a walk?" He could feel the pleading in his expression. They needed this, needed to soak in every moment while they were still in Bloomington. Before life rushed in and left them with nothing but memories of this time.

She was more awake now, and she rubbed her eyes as a smile began to lift her mouth. She propped herself up on one elbow and blinked a few times.

Dayne sat up and eased his fingers into her hair, cradling the back of her head. He kissed her long and slow, then breathed the question against her lips. "Please . . . walk with me, okay?"

A soft laugh came from her and she sat up too, squinting toward the patio door. "It's bright out."

"I know." He slid his feet over the edge of the bed. "I couldn't sleep, and then I got this idea."

"To take a walk?" She grinned at him, flirting with him in a way that said she was willing to find out what he had in mind. She checked the clock. "At 11:17 at night?"

"Exactly." He stood and reached for her hand. "It's the perfect time for a walk."

She climbed out of bed, and they slipped into jeans and sweatshirts. They tiptoed downstairs. Once they were outside, Dayne slid his fingers between hers and led her down the path toward the water. The moon was full and hung over the lake like something from a movie set. Dayne brought a flashlight, but they didn't need it.

As they reached the shore, he guided her toward the canoe tied to the dock. They'd found the old vessel through an advertisement in the local paper their first week back in Bloomington. Since then, they'd been out in it a handful of times, including one afternoon when they tried to miss a large rock and instead both wound up in the water.

But they'd never taken it out at night.

Katy hesitated and released Dayne's hand. "The canoe? Now?" Doubt sounded in every word. "Is it safe?"

"The lake's empty." He took her hand again. "We'll be fine."

In the splash of moonlight, he saw her fears ease. "You're crazy."

"I know." He led her to the dock and then bent down to untie the heavy rope that held the canoe. As he did, he looked back at her. "But in a few days we won't be able to be crazy without the whole world knowing." He gave her a crooked grin. "So why not now?"

She giggled, and the sound mixed with

the wind in the trees. "You have a point."

He helped her get seated, and then with a single push, he set the canoe in motion and settled in just behind her. He picked up a paddle and eased it into the glassy dark water. Again they were silent, surrounded by the gentle lapping of the lake water and the distant cries from a pack of coyotes. When they were fifty yards out, Dayne laid the paddle inside the canoe.

Katy gripped the bench seat and leaned back, her face toward the sky. Stars dotted the dark canopy but only the ones with the strength to stand out against the full moon. "It's beautiful."

"Mmmm. Yes." Dayne patted the spot beside him. "Come sit by me."

Careful not to rock the canoe, Katy shifted herself back so they were side by side on the middle bench.

He slipped his arm around her shoulders. "Can you feel it? The presence of God out here?"

She breathed in, slow and steady. "On the set . . . it was like I forgot He was with me, forgot to talk to Him and ask Him for help." She lifted her eyes to his. "Know what I mean?"

Dayne nodded. "We can't let it happen again."

"No."

He didn't have to explain himself. They'd talked about their faith and how desperately they'd need to cling to the Lord in the coming weeks if they were to survive the scrutiny that lay ahead. But out here, in the quiet of the lake, the truth of how much they needed God and each other had never been clearer.

"These past few weeks —" Dayne touched his lips to her cheek — "were like I dreamed it could be. I don't ever want to leave."

"Me neither."

They'd made the most of their final days in Bloomington. They took long walks around Lake Monroe, stopping at the same spots where they'd first fallen in love what felt like a lifetime ago. There were trips to the farmers' market with John and Elaine, and they made it to Cole's soccer practice a few times. Ashley and Landon were handling the loss of Sarah as well as could be expected. But they still appreciated having family around.

Dayne gazed into the night sky. Of course, no one wanted to be around family as much as he did. After a lifetime of loneliness, he finally had the kind of family everyone hoped for. If they didn't have to leave, he and Katy would have been on the sidelines for every soccer game and in the front row for his young nieces' dance recitals. They would've been there for Sunday dinners at the old Baxter house and each picnic at the lake.

"You're doing it again." Katy's voice was hushed, the barest of whispers.

"Doing what?"

"Borrowing trouble from tomorrow." She made a half turn and searched his eyes. "No one can take this from us. Not if we keep God at the center."

Dayne nodded more slowly than before. His lips parted, and he was about to ask her how they were supposed to keep God at the center when they'd be filming movies thousands of miles away from each other. They could keep God in their own individual lives, but at the center? The center of what? They wouldn't have anything but distance between them.

But he changed his mind. She couldn't know the answers any more than he could. Only by living out the next few months could they figure out how to survive. Whatever they did, though, she was right. Their faith would be key.

Doubts danced around them and mixed with the shadows that fell on the edge of the lake. Before Dayne could voice them, Katy put her arms around his neck and moved her face close to his. "I love you, Dayne. More than I ever thought I could love." She kissed him, a kiss that left no question about her intentions. "What happened a few months ago will never happen again. We learned our lesson."

He smiled at her and ran his thumb across her forehead. *Ah, Katy,* he thought, *it'll be harder than you think.* Again he didn't voice his concerns because all that mattered was her, the lake surrounding them, and the moonlight on her face.

He returned her kiss, and after a few minutes he forgot his fears completely. There was only Katy and his pounding heart and the gift of love God had given them. She was right. They'd survived the glare of the media before; they could do it again. Their love was stronger now. And as long as they could make it back to the shore of Lake Monroe, as long as they could remember who they were and Whose they were, they would survive.

Even if it took everything they had.

Dayne paddled the canoe back to the beach. When they reached the top of the path and stepped onto their deck, he turned and took Katy into his arms. "Thank you."

"For what?" She put her arms around his waist, and together they swayed ever so slightly. The passion from earlier was still in her eyes, still thick in her voice.

"For trusting me . . . that a canoe ride was the perfect way to spend the night."

A wisp of wind washed over her, catching her hair and freezing the moment forever in Dayne's mind. Katy framed one side of his face with her hand. With her other hand, she touched the place over his heart. "Whenever you're afraid . . . when you're somewhere on the beaches of Cabo, Mexico, and I'm on a bus in rainy London, remember this." She hesitated, her eyes looking to the deepest part of his soul. "Keep it here in your heart. So you won't forget what's waiting for us back home."

Somehow, still cloaked in the magic of the night, her words were enough to erase all fear, eradicate all doubt. He kissed her once more, and then he did something they'd done daily since they'd been back in Bloomington. He pulled her close, and in a voice clear and quiet, he prayed.

"God, guide us through the coming months. Help us avoid the headlines and focus only on what is good and right and true, whatever is excellent and honorable. The way Your Word tells us we should think." He held Katy a little closer. "Don't let anything separate us, Lord. And as we set out to our different locations, help us find You together, no matter how far apart we are. In Jesus' name, amen."

As Dayne finished, he looked at Katy for a long time, at the way the moon reflected off the water and sparkled in her eyes. "You're beautiful, Katy."

A shy grin played on her lips. "And you, Mr. Matthews."

Then, without saying another word, he led her back to their room. An hour later, after sharing with each other the love that would have to keep them through the next season, she fell asleep, her head on his shoulder.

Dayne's last thought was a simple one. They had much to look forward to once they survived the next couple of months: magical nights like this one and love without the glare of cameras, get-togethers with the Baxter family, and a regular place in church each Sunday. All of it would be waiting for them back home.

Now it was a matter of counting down the days until then.

Dayne felt sick to his stomach from the moment the private jet touched down in Los Angeles. It was just before two o'clock, the day after Labor Day, and Dayne had dreaded the coming night for months. This, after all, was the day he and Katy left Bloomington at least until Christmas. If that weren't enough, it was the day *For Real* debuted, the show that would take their already public lives and most likely make them a complete and utter spectacle.

A Town Car met them on the tarmac and whisked them off to their home in Malibu, the one they had kept closed for several months. It would be a busy week, not only because of the reality show and the buzz of attention it was bound to bring, but because this Saturday was the premiere for *But Then Again No,* the movie he and Katy had filmed together. The one where the camera crew for the reality show had mercilessly captured every offscreen moment.

They carried their things into the house with little fanfare. The paparazzi didn't know they were in LA yet, but they would. The movie premiere would be attended by every photographer in town. Not until they had unpacked and stepped out onto their back deck did Dayne realize how quiet he'd been.

He moved closer to Katy so their arms were touching. "I'm doing it, aren't I?"

"Borrowing trouble? Acting different?" Her eyes held none of the tension he was already feeling. "Yes, you're doing it. But I understand." A relaxed pause filled the space between them as she stared out at the Pacific Ocean. "The storm's just ahead."

Dayne followed her gaze and watched a series of waves break against the Malibu shore. The stretch of sand was dotted by only a handful of tourists and the usual surfers. He looked beyond the waves to the horizon, and something caught him by surprise. "There was a time when I didn't think I could live without this — the ocean view, the serenity of the beach." His voice was quiet, and a calm settled over the moment. "No matter what my day was like or how insane the celebrity thing got, the ocean was always the same." He lifted his chin a little, letting the feel and smell of the salty ocean air surround him. "It still is."

"Yes." Katy breathed in slowly through her nose. "I love it here." She smiled at him. "Until the cameras start clicking."

"It's amazing, for sure." He turned his attention toward her. "But the day my contract is fulfilled, I'll slap a For Sale sign out front and never look back. Malibu Beach can't compare to Lake Monroe." He put his arm around her shoulders and drew her near. "This will never be home after the last few months in Bloomington."

"There'll be snow on the ground by the time we get back." Katy sounded pensive. "By then we should've just been finishing the first CKT show of the season."

An ache spread through Dayne's chest. He hated that the theater had been sold and, worse, that there seemed to be nothing anyone could do to save the Christian drama group from dissolving. If only the timing had been different, he could've stepped in and purchased the building before it was gobbled up by developers. He ran his fingers along her arm. "You miss it."

"So much." She looked up at him, and a sudden layer of unshed tears filled her eyes. "Those kids need CKT." She blinked and looked back at the water. "But God allowed it to end. The theater, my directing career. I guess the end was meant to be." She stood a little straighter, as if she were steeling herself against the pain of the loss. "But, yes, I miss it."

They talked a little longer, and then Katy ventured into town for groceries since she was still the less recognizable of the two. She wore little makeup, old jeans, and a lightweight sweater, with her hair pulled back in a ponytail. She returned to the house with a carful of food and a report that no one with a camera had seemed to notice her.

Dayne barbecued chicken and grilled vegetables that night. But their conversation grew more strained as eight o'clock neared. Earlier that afternoon, he'd called his father, who reported that the entire Baxter family was tuned in, ready to see what the first episode of *For Real* might bring. They would see the show three hours before it was aired on the West Coast, but his dad said he wouldn't call until the next day so the family's feedback could wait until after Katy and Dayne had seen the show too.

"We're praying for you, Son." Kindness and deep concern marked every word. "Remember, this too shall pass."

"Thanks, Dad. I'll try to keep that in mind."

The hours passed slowly, but finally, at just before eight, Dayne joined Katy in the living room. The TV was already on, and she sat curled in the corner of the sofa, a pillow clutched to her middle.

"I'm shaking." She managed a weak smile. "Sit by me. Please."

He did as she asked, but frustration was building inside him. Why did they have to put up with this? They could turn off the television and catch the next flight back to Bloomington. Tell the producers they were finished with the movie industry. Let someone else play their roles in the upcoming films.

Dayne settled into the sofa and took hold of Katy's hand. As he did, he reminded himself of the reality of the situation. He was in a contract. If he broke the deal, he'd be sued, and worse, he would no longer be a man of his word. His word had always meant something to him, even back when he was living the shallow life of Hollywood parties and different women. But now that he'd given his life to God, his word meant even more.

When they talked about the movies Dayne still had to film, his missionary friend Bob Asher had agreed about keeping the commitment. "The answer isn't to bail on your promises," Bob had told him a few days ago. "It's to carry them out in a manner that pleases God. Do that and everyone will win."

Dayne agreed in theory. But now, with the first episode of *For Real* about to begin, he wasn't so sure about the winning part. Still, regardless of his desire to walk away from the movie industry, Dayne was committed to making good on his contract and his word.

Katy passed the remote to him. "In case

you have to turn it off." She flashed him a nervous smile.

The Chevrolet commercial on the screen ended, and at the same instant the reality show's techno opening filled the room. Dayne tightened his hold on Katy's hand. Images of Katy and Dayne flashed, one blending into another. A few of them were video clips when Katy had maybe been squinting into the sun or he'd been wiping his brow. But the way the clips were edited gave the appearance that the two of them were upset with each other.

"This is going to go from bad to worse." Katy uttered a sad laugh. "I feel like I should cover my eyes."

She was right, of course. The hour-long episode started with loving images of Katy and Dayne, but it changed quickly. Between video sections the program's announcers established that Katy and Dayne had come into the project as newlyweds, in love and ready to prove as much to the world.

"But by the end of the first week, the reality," the man's chipper voice told the viewing audience, "was something entirely different."

Just minutes into the program, the focus turned to the tabloids and rumors of spats between America's favorite new couple.

"Fighting and fury over the other women in Dayne's life," the announcer quipped. "But the worst was yet to come."

Halfway through the hour, Dayne was filled with rage, ready to have the show pulled from the air. But even as his anger blazed, he knew the truth. There was nothing he could do to stop the program. He and Katy had given the show permission, trusted the producers that the program would reflect the truth.

Instead, between the accusations and headlines flying wildly across the screen, the glow of new love darkened, and their relationship did unravel until the show's film crew almost had what would be perfect for their ratings — another Hollywood marriage on the rocks.

At the commercial break three-fourths of the way through, Dayne hit the Mute button. He tried to draw a full breath, but the tightness in his chest made it impossible. "We should've asked for a preview clause." He clenched his teeth and faced her. "Why didn't my agent think about that?"

"We didn't know." Katy leaned her head on his shoulder and nuzzled closer. She waved her hand at the TV. "We couldn't have seen this coming."

Dayne resisted the urge to snap at her,

because she was wrong. He'd seen it coming, and he knew better. He'd had much more experience with the paparazzi. It was Katy who had wanted the show, believing that if they gave the cameramen what they wanted on the set, they might leave them alone in their private moments. But even so, none of this was her fault.

He should've known better. A preview clause could've allowed them the chance to see the episodes before the public, a chance to pull the plug if the producers hadn't put together a package in keeping with the discussions they'd had months ago.

And there was no question now. The show was definitely going that direction. He dug his elbows into his knees. "I should've seen this coming."

"Dayne . . ." Katy sat up. Her voice was soft, filled with understanding. "It was my idea. This isn't anyone's fault."

"It is." He met her eyes, his anger suddenly gone. "I know this business. Of course they'd turn the thing against us." He touched her shoulder, searching her heart. Despite her fear, he could also see the strength that would have to carry them through in the coming weeks. "Happy couples don't sell."

"Hey . . ." Katy touched his face. Her

fingers were light against his skin, but even her body next to his couldn't shake the dread welling inside him. She sat a little taller and brushed her lips against his. "I'm here. Remember? With God we can get through this." She kissed him again, this time with enough desperation that her own fears were obvious. "That's gotta be enough, right?"

Dayne let himself get lost in her eyes. For the past month their relationship had been everything he had known it would be when he asked her to marry him. They were stronger than ever before, stronger in their commitment to each other and, more importantly, to God.

Even so, Dayne knew what was coming. The premiere — with every camera looking for the cracks in their marriage, for some sign that the strife that plagued them during the filming of *But Then Again No* might still be there or, better yet, that it might be worse. After the premiere would come their trips to different countries for filming their separate movies. Already the tabloids were hinting at the inevitable trouble ahead.

He ran his hand along her back. Fear would not win this battle nor would a world full of strangers hoping for them to fail. He pushed aside the fear that was all but strangling him and clung to her, held her as if by doing so he could keep anything and anyone from coming between them.

"Yes, baby." He pressed the side of his face against Katy's. "God and each other and our family. That has to be enough." Dayne repeated the words over and over in his mind. Yes, Katy was right. Of course she was. What they had together would be enough to pull them through.

Even if the rest of the world disagreed.

CHAPTER SEVEN

They were two days into the new school year, and Ashley missed having Cole at home all day. Three o'clock couldn't come fast enough, especially today. Landon had worked an early shift, and he was home in time to meet Cole at the bus stop.

Ashley moved a stack of mail off the dining room table, and on her way back through the living room, she grinned at Devin. "Daddy and Coley are coming, baby." She scooped him up and shifted him to her hip. "Let's go see!"

They reached the front door just as Landon and Cole were coming up the walk. Ashley opened the door and smiled at the picture they made — Landon in his navy uniform and Cole with his blond hair and bright red backpack.

Cole spotted her first. "Mom! We're doing a science experiment for school! I have a whole bag of mosquito eggs." He stopped, dropped his backpack onto the sidewalk, and unzipped the top. Then he pulled out a thick plastic bag half full of a murky substance. "See." Cole lifted the bag, a grin stretched across his face. "We get to see where mosquitoes grow best!"

Ashley took a step back. "Oh." She glanced from Cole to Landon. His eyes danced, and he had his fist pressed to his lips, trying not to laugh. Ashley raised one eyebrow. "The answer is outdoors." She pointed to the row of bushes a few feet from their front window. "Right there. That's where they grow best."

"But, Mom, that's the whole fun of it." He looked at Landon for backup. "Right, Dad? Plus, the teacher gave us containers, so the mosquitoes won't get out. Not even one!"

"Right." Landon shrugged, his expression innocent, as if he'd exhausted every possible option that might include keeping the mosquito larvae outside. "Cole needs five different environments."

"The refrigerator." Cole's eyebrows moved halfway up his forehead. "My teacher said that's a good place, 'cause it gives you something to compare."

Devin tossed his head back and laughed, as if he could understand the thought of mosquitoes in a refrigerator and the idea was the funniest thing he'd ever imagined.

"The outside fridge." Ashley motioned for Cole and Landon to follow her back into the house. "And nowhere in the kitchen, no matter what."

"Except the oven." Landon's look turned sheepish as he fell in beside her. He took Devin from her and kissed her as they walked up the steps to the house. "I told him he could put some in the oven."

Ashley moaned. "How long's the experiment?"

Cole came up along her other side and put his arm around her waist. "Just one week." He high-fived Landon as they headed into the house. "They take a couple days to hatch, but then some of 'em might not if they're not in the right environment."

"We definitely need the right environment for this to work." Landon gave Cole a serious look, then winked at Ashley.

As he did, Ashley felt her heart lighten. This was what life was about, the joy of raising their boys and helping them grow in their faith, cheering for them and taking part in their schoolwork. Even if it meant keeping mosquito larvae in the oven for a week. With Landon and the boys in her life, healing from the loss of baby Sarah was only a matter of time.

They ate spaghetti for dinner, and after-wards the four of them walked to the park at the end of their street. Summer was drawing its last gasp, the skies blue and the evening warmer than usual for this time of year. Devin had cut a tooth the day before, so he was less fussy than he'd been in a week, relaxed in his stroller and sucking on his pacifier. Cole was dribbling a soccer ball a few feet in front of them.

The moment felt wonderful, with Landon's presence beside her, the way his arm touched hers as they both pushed Devin's stroller. The only way the evening could've been better was if Sarah were with them.

Ashley looped her arm through Landon's. "Feels good, doesn't it?"

He smiled at her. "Definitely. Sometimes in the morning I have to remind myself . . . that this is really my life." He angled his head, his look curious. "This is the life Dayne wants for him and Katy. But after the other night . . ."

"I know." A heaviness settled over Ashley. "I talked to Katy yesterday. Hollywood can't stop talking about the show."

"I'm worried." Landon squinted at the bright western sky. "It's not worth it, making movies —" he met her eyes again —

"when they could have this."

They reached the park, and Ashley helped Devin out of his stroller. She held his hand as he walked to the baby swing; then she lifted him in and buckled the belt.

"Swing!" Devin raised both hands in the air, his exuberance limitless.

Ashley laughed and gave her son a soft push.

Thirty yards away, Cole ran to the far side of the grassy field. "I'll kick it to you, Dad. . . . Then you dribble it this way, and I'll try to steal it."

Soccer season was in full swing now, the first game coming up this Saturday. Cole liked basketball better, but soccer was starting to get in his blood. Ashley watched him kick the ball to Landon. "Come on, Dad. Don't let me steal it."

For the next half hour Cole and Landon worked the ball in a series of drills, and finally Cole took a turn walking Devin around the playground while Ashley and Landon sat on a nearby bench. Landon's eyes shone, and his cheeks were dark from the exhilaration of the play. The role of dad suited him, even more than the role of firefighter and hero. Ashley was sure he'd never looked more handsome.

"Catch me up on your family." He leaned

back against the bench. "Your dad seemed quiet the last time he stopped by."

"He is." Ashley eased closer to her husband and wove her fingers between his. "He's working on those scrapbooks for us, the ones with the copies of Mom's letters. But I think he's struggling."

"With Elaine?"

"With himself." Ashley kept her eyes on Cole and Devin, now walking around the back of the playground. "He's thinking about marrying her. I mean, he hasn't said so, but I can tell. It's a big decision."

"It is. But everyone figures it's going to happen."

"I guess." His statement stirred a familiar pain in Ashley's soul. Not because she had anything against Elaine at this point, but because her dad shouldn't be single. Her mom should be home with him. "Maybe that's why he's so quiet. Lots to think about."

Landon hesitated. "You're okay with it, right? Your dad remarrying?"

"Yes." Ashley's answer was quick. Her father's friend had reached out to her in a way she wouldn't forget. "Elaine's wonderful. But it's still weird, you know? My dad marrying someone else?" She stood and helped Landon to his feet. "Let's catch up with the boys."

They started walking, their pace slow. "I wonder if they'd keep the house."

Ashley stopped. "The Baxter house?" Her heart skipped a beat and then thudded into a faster rhythm than before.

"Yeah." Landon raised one shoulder. "Elaine might not want to make a new life with your dad in the house he shared with your mom."

A weakness hit Ashley at her knees, and she stared at the ground. After a few seconds she lifted her eyes to Landon's. "I . . . I never thought about that."

"I could be wrong."

But he wasn't wrong; Ashley was suddenly sure. The Baxter house represented her parents, John and Elizabeth Baxter, and every remarkable year while the two of them raised their family and shared that home together. Ashley tightened her hold on Landon's hand and started walking again. "He can't sell it."

"He might have to." Landon's tone was kind, but clearly he'd spent some time thinking about this. "Katy and Dayne are set, Brooke and Peter like the house they're in, and Luke wants to stay closer to Indianapolis. The rest of us couldn't afford it."

Another shadow fell over the moment.

"Luke isn't doing well."

"He and Reagan?"

Ashley frowned. They were closing in on the boys, and the sound of Devin's laughter filled the air. "Luke's traveling to New York a lot. Reagan says there's tension between them when he comes home. Luke's always on edge."

Landon seemed to mull over the possibilities. "You don't think . . ."

"He's having an affair?" Ashley shook her head. "He watched how it nearly destroyed Kari. I can't believe he'd take that route. No matter how strained things are at home."

When Cole spotted them, his face lit up. "Devin's walking good now." He stooped down and used his most encouraging tone. "Come on, Dev. Show Mommy and Daddy how fast you can walk!"

Devin laughed, and his eyes danced. He lowered his head and made two little fists. Then he took off across the field. Ten steps into the fast walk, he tripped and flopped face-first into the grass.

But it was a victory nonetheless. "You did it, buddy. Look at you!" Cole used the toe of his shoe to tap the soccer ball in his brother's direction. "You'll be playing basketball before you know it."

"Ball!" Devin pulled himself off the

ground and tumbled toward Cole's ball.

They played a little while longer, then helped Devin into the stroller and headed back home. Ashley was caught up in Cole's enthusiasm, but she couldn't shake the reminder about Luke. He had two kids, same as Ashley and Landon. This should've been a time when he and Reagan were enjoying the challenge of raising their family. Instead, Luke was busy traveling, and when he was home — at least from Reagan's perspective — he wasn't playing an active role with Tommy and Malin.

It was one more area where Ashley still believed Sarah's life might make a difference, where having seen how precious and brief life could be, the cracks in the rest of the family might be smoothed over. Katy and Dayne certainly seemed stronger after Sarah's birth and death. But Luke had always been strong-willed. In the months before little Tommy was born, he had nearly cut himself off completely from the Baxter family.

Ashley sighed as she and Landon found an easy pace along the sidewalk. She would have to call Luke and ask him what was going on. When they were kids, the two of them had been best friends. Even now, he was closer to Ashley than to his other sisters.

Maybe if she could get him to open up, things might improve between him and Reagan.

"So, Daddy, I was thinking a dark closet might be a good environment for the mosquito larvae. The teacher told us dark works good."

Ashley smiled, but her mind was still on her brother. Was it possible, what Landon had suggested? That Luke would consider having an affair? A shudder passed down Ashley's arms, and she made a mental note to call him tomorrow morning. In the meantime, she would act the only way she knew. The best way.

She would pray.

CHAPTER EIGHT

The premiere was one of the most antici-pated Hollywood events that year. Katy didn't need a lifetime of experience in Tinseltown to recognize that much.

Now, as their limo was about to pull up to the red carpet, she gave Dayne a weak smile. "I'm scared."

"Don't be." He looked calm and confi-dent, but something in his eyes gave him away. He was worried too. They wanted to believe they were a match for the publicity. But were they? Even with their faith? Dayne was sitting across from her, and he reached over and took hold of her hand. "Just be yourself. They'll see us for how we really are." His laugh seemed weaker than he probably intended it to be. "We're in love. The pictures tonight will show that."

Katy nodded. He was right. Every camera would be trained on them, and every re-porter would be looking for any sign of a problem. But that was just it. There were no problems, so none would be visible.

"You look beautiful." His gaze traveled the length of her. "So different from the small-town girl on that *Charlie Brown* stage."

He meant the words as a compliment, but somehow they hurt. They seemed a million miles and at least as many years away from that long-ago night when Dayne happened upon the Bloomington Community Theater and saw her for the first time. Katy pushed away the memory and smiled. "Thanks. You too."

He wore a tux, his blond hair cut short and conservatively styled, his face tanned from the last few days sitting out on their deck at the beach. No one would scrutinize his outfit tonight, but they certainly would be watching hers. This might be her first premiere, but she was very clear about the expectations. In addition to the story of Katy and Dayne, the next top bit of news to come out of the evening's event would be the dresses worn by the actresses. Katy was the leading lady, so hers would easily be the most talked-about gown of all.

One of the publicists from the studio had taken her shopping earlier that week, and somehow they'd avoided any paparazzi. Katy was happy with the results of the trip.

She wore a silver floor-length satin gown with a fitted bodice, a scoop neck, and three-quarter-length sleeves. Her blonde hair was curled in ringlets and pulled up just a few inches at the roots so it cascaded down her back and over her shoulders.

The limo came to a stop, and Katy peered through the tinted window. She exhaled through pursed lips. "Okay, then." She looked at Dayne. "Here we go."

"We'll be fine."

The limo driver opened the door. Dayne climbed out first, leaning back in to help her out. Katy had seen enough photos of premieres to know that the carpet was actually laid out for the celebrities to walk across and that it was truly red. But still the moment felt surreal. The click of cameras and the flash of lights along both sides of the roped-off carpet began even before she was out of the car. The barrage made Katy feel like they were suddenly and urgently under attack.

But Dayne had coached her, and now both of them were ready. Katy found her most gracious smile, and other than an occasional warm and sincere wave toward the crowds to her right and left, she moved gracefully down the carpet and kept her attention on Dayne, as if the two of them were sharing some sort of private joke, lost in each other's arms and too in love to notice the fuss being made about them. A few times she tipped her head back and allowed a ripple of laughter to tickle her throat. From the time they left the limo until they were inside and out of the glare of the cameras, they stayed together, showing the world the picture they'd practiced. That they were one, and nothing could come between them.

Once they were inside, Katy realized she hadn't exhaled the entire walk down the carpet. She did now, and for a moment she had to stop to catch her breath. Dayne had also warned her that though there wouldn't be as many cameras inside the reception area, there would be enough. Most of the major magazines would be represented as well as the top newspapers. They wouldn't be as quick to ask questions about Katy and Dayne's marriage in forty-eight-point bold headlines, but they would still be keenly aware of the current gossip, attuned to the doubts cast by the first episode of *For Real.*

Katy leaned in close to Dayne's ear. "How am I doing?"

"Perfect." He kissed her cheek and looked long enough into her eyes to make a perfect pose for a handful of cameramen who immediately rushed in and captured the moment. "I told you — we're going to be fine."

This side of the red carpet, Katy felt herself start to relax. They could do this. After all, they weren't putting on a show or faking anything. This was them, the way they'd be if they were in Bloomington, standing out on their back deck looking over a moonlit Lake Monroe.

Dayne led her to the tables lined with dozens of foods, most of which Katy couldn't identify. At the center of each table was an ice sculpture showing a pair of horses in full run — symbolic of the story line and setting of the movie. Katy was sure her surprise showed on her face, but she didn't care. The setup was astounding.

She was still admiring the spread, remarking about it in a whispered voice to Dayne when Randi Wells entered the building. The flashing cameras and commotion died down as someone shut the door behind her. Randi hadn't appeared in *But Then Again No,* so Katy hadn't expected to see her tonight. But her date was the movie's director, Stephen Petrel, a passionate man of virtue, who would also be directing Katy's next film in London. He and Randi were friends, and Stephen had often said that he viewed Randi like a daughter. Still, as Katy watched the pair, she wondered if Stephen had found something more than a fatherly relationship with Randi.

Then she remembered the dinner she had shared with the director during the filming of *But Then Again No.* Public pictures of Stephen kissing her on the lips at the end of the evening that night had nearly driven a permanent wedge between her and Dayne, though the director had meant nothing by the action. It was simply something people in Hollywood did — greeting each other with a kiss, whether they were coming or leaving a place.

"She looks stunning." Katy leaned in close to Dayne and turned her back to Randi so she wouldn't be caught looking. "She must be in the best shape of her life."

Dayne barely glanced in Randi's direction. "She's probably got designs on the supporting actor. Everyone says he's the next Brad Pitt." He kept his smile, but his eyes showed his disdain. "The way she comes on to her costars . . . it isn't professional." He took a small plate from the table and filled it with a skewer of chocolate-covered fruit. "After all the drama she's already caused offscreen, this'll be the last film I do with her."

A ray of sunshine dispelled Katy's lingering doubt. She was about to say that maybe Dayne's next movie could be something other than a love story when she heard a familiar voice drawing near to them.

"Dayne!" Randi squealed like a high school girl at a Friday night football game. Before he had time to respond, she reached him and threw her arms around his neck. "Just a few more weeks!" She laughed. "I haven't looked forward to a film this much in forever."

He inched free of her embrace and pulled Katy closer to him. "I was just telling Katy how —"

"You look amazing! A walking miracle, Dayne . . . I mean it." Randi still hadn't acknowledged Katy. Instead she placed her hands on either side of Dayne's face and tried to kiss him square on the lips.

But Dayne jerked his head just enough so her lips landed on his cheek.

Undaunted, Randi planted another kiss on his other cheek before taking a step back. Only then did she seem to notice that Dayne's wife was present. She gasped and gave Katy a perfunctory hug. "And look at you, the belle of the ball!" She sized up Katy's gown. "Gorgeous dress. Absolutely gorgeous."

With that she turned her attention back

to Dayne and let her gaze hold his a few seconds longer than necessary. Finally she winked at him, her eyes sparkly and confident. "Can't wait for Mexico!" She blew a kiss to Katy, turned gracefully, and headed once more toward the director.

Katy felt like she'd been run over by a freight train. If she didn't know Dayne so well, if she hadn't seen the depth of his love the last month in Bloomington, she wouldn't have made it through the premiere, let alone survive Dayne's upcoming time in Mexico. "She's unbelievable."

"I'm sorry." Dayne's tone was heavy with frustration. He clutched her more tightly to himself and guided her farther down the food table. "I'll talk with her." A cameraman was coming closer, video-taping them. Dayne's smile returned instantly, and he leaned in and kissed Katy tenderly. "Sometimes I don't think she realizes how she looks."

Katy reminded herself to keep up the smile. She stood a little straighter and caught a quick look of Randi joining a group of people milling near the theater doors. She was cozying up to the film's resident cowboy, the guy who had trained Katy on how to ride and who had hit on so many women on the set that he became something of a joke. "There you go," Katy said through her best smile. She nodded toward Randi. "He's more her speed."

Dayne glanced over his shoulder, chuckled lightly, and gave Katy what was clearly supposed to be an impulsive hug. The cameraman was closer now, just a few feet away. Dayne smiled in his direction, then steered Katy across the room. "If we can make it inside, we'll be free. The cameras aren't allowed in the theater tonight."

Another painful half hour of schmoozing passed. Stephen Petrel came toward them and again greeted Katy with his familiar kiss. This time Katy learned from Dayne, and at the last possible moment, she turned her head so his lips touched her cheek instead.

The director didn't seem to notice, nor did his actions seem inappropriate given his demeanor. He patted Dayne on the shoulder. "You two stay strong." His expression grew serious, and he nodded at Katy. "This town needs a lot more of what you two have." Passion blazed in his tone. "Don't let anyone take that away from you."

They talked for a few minutes about *But Then Again No* and Katy and Stephen's filming schedule in London. "No need to worry about her, Dayne. She's a good girl. There isn't a man alive who could turn her head, no matter what you read in the tabs."

As they moved in and out of conversation, Dayne stayed at Katy's side, never more than a few inches from her. He continually reached for her or drew her close for a hug or kiss. Katy learned quickly how to read him. He held her particularly close when someone came along who could possibly threaten them, someone the cameras would consider of interest — either to Katy or to Dayne.

The whole thing was exhausting, and by the time the theater doors opened, Katy felt like she deserved an Oscar for her performance. Which was strange, because smiling and being physically attentive around Dayne wasn't an act. Loving Dayne came as naturally as breathing. She was seated in the dark theater when a theory hit her. Maybe that's how relationships began to unravel with celebrity couples. Things might be great, but in the process of working so hard to prove that greatness to the public, the love itself became an act.

She closed her eyes and leaned closer to Dayne. *Never, Lord. Never let what Dayne and I share become something practiced and rehearsed.*

Often when Katy was in Bloomington,

whether she was alone working in the old community theater building or at the Flanigans' house in the garage apartment, she could sense the Lord's response to an urgent prayer. A prayer like this one.

But tonight just one feeling came over her as she lifted her words to God. The feeling of urgency. As if God wanted her and Dayne to be clear that they might survive Hollywood for a season, but they wouldn't survive it forever.

The future would depend on getting out before then.

Randi Wells stepped into the private bathroom and exhaled. She spent so much time being on that she wasn't sure anymore what it felt like simply to be herself. This much was certain — all eyes were on her and Dayne tonight. After all, they were costarring in his next movie, a love story set against the backdrop of a secluded Mexican beach. Nothing could be more seductive than that.

There was a knock at the door. "Hello?"

Randi jumped. "Uh . . . it's occupied."

"Oh, sorry." Then came the sound of the person moving on down the hall.

Randi stared at herself in the mirror. The magazines had been shouting about how great she looked, how Dayne's wife was bound to be worried with Randi and Dayne heading off to Mexico. Randi fixed her hair and grinned at her image. Just three months ago, the tabloids had criticized her for being ten pounds too heavy. She turned sideways and admired her figure. They had nothing to criticize now.

She was about to leave when her cell phone vibrated from inside her purse. She cursed under her breath, but the caller ID made her frustration fall away.

It was her mother.

Randi had been born and raised in Vancouver, British Columbia. She filmed her first movie in her early twenties, changed her last name, and quickly became a U.S. citizen. But her parents remained in Vancouver and stayed true to everything that had always mattered to them — their home, their community, and most importantly their faith. Randi had no delusions about the disappointment her mother held for her. The woman reminded Randi during their rare conversations that Randi's decision to live with this actor or that one was against God.

"I hear about you. You're living an immoral life." Her mother would cluck her tongue against the roof of her mouth.

"You've cast shame upon our family." There would be a heavy sigh. "We're praying for you, that you'll come to your senses."

It had been the same way with her mother since Randi filmed her first movie. Conditional love, unrealistic expectations, a concern more about the way Randi's actions might reflect on her mother than whether Randi was actually in need of help. Her mother might've meant well. But Randi had never been close to her.

Her relationship with her father had been entirely different. Louie Geer had owned a tour company, and he spent his days hosting groups of vacationers, telling people about Vancouver and its many sights, and doing so with a sense of dedication and humor that always brought people back for more. He'd been in his late fifties when cancer took him, but even before he got sick, he hadn't been worried about funding a retirement portfolio. He gave half his profits to charities in the area and had a way of living out his faith.

Randi felt the familiar sting of tears that came with remembering her dad. From the time she was a little girl, her father had delighted in the plays and amateur performances Randi would do on a school stage or around the house. "One day," he told her, "you'll perform on a stage so big, everyone will know you're a star!"

He'd believed in her when she was young and naive, and after she found great worldly success, he never questioned her. "We love you," he would say when they spoke on the phone. "Remember, honey, I'm here if you need anything." And when it came to the faith she'd been raised with, he made only gentle reminders. "God has a plan for you, Randi. Don't forget that."

During times the media had been particularly ruthless or when her husband walked out on her and their two young daughters, she'd had to fight the urge to run home and fall into her daddy's arms. Especially as he grew sicker. And now, with her mother living alone, Randi's long absences weren't right — no matter what tension remained between them. Her father wouldn't have wanted her to lose touch.

She'd told her mother as much when they talked a week ago. "After I'm finished in Mexico, I'll come for a visit, okay?"

"That would be nice, dear." Her tone was the usual mix of disapproval and a slight hurt.

Now the phone vibrated one more time, and Randi resisted the urge to answer it. Her father had loved her so much, no matter what she did or how far she strayed from her upbringing. But her mother would dampen her enthusiasm for the evening. She read the tabloids. More than once she'd warned Randi about staying away from Dayne Matthews. "He's a married man, Randi," she'd said at the end of their last phone call. "Respect that."

How could Randi explain that no one was really married in Hollywood? Not the way they were married in the real world.

Randi swallowed the lump in her throat and pushed her phone back in her purse. She snapped the clasp shut and took a final look at herself. *I'm sorry, Mom. . . . I'll call you later. I promise.* The thoughts comforted her, and she allowed herself to believe them. She had more to think about than a trip to British Columbia.

She'd been admiring Dayne from the sidelines for far too long. Katy Hart was a simple, country girl. She was no match for Hollywood's leading man. If Dayne hadn't figured that out already, then he would soon. Katy was a nice girl, but Dayne had made a mistake marrying her. Randi had always been the right choice for Dayne, the one who would've been his soul mate — marriage or not. Never mind that Randi had nearly befriended Katy after Dayne's accident. The truth was, Randi should've been the one helping him through his physical therapy. She'd known Dayne much longer than Katy, and Randi understood the pressures of the business. Katy had come out of nowhere and stepped into a picture where, truthfully, she didn't belong.

Randi found her smile again. One day, she and Dayne would be together; she was confident. Katy would be heartbroken at first, but then she'd move back to her small Indiana town and get on with her life. She'd marry some regular Joe, the way she should have in the first place, and she'd be fine.

It was Randi who wouldn't be okay without Dayne.

And she was about to have ten weeks on a Mexican beach to make Dayne feel the same way.

CHAPTER NINE

Reagan heard her son's piercing scream just as she laid Malin in her crib. The sound of it told Reagan there was big trouble, whatever had happened. "Tommy?" Her shrill cry woke Malin, but she left her daughter and raced down the hallway toward the sound of her shrieking son.

He was at the far end, where the wall became a railing system that led toward a winding staircase. The problem was instantly obvious. Tommy was on his knees, gripping two of the wooden spindles, his head stuck between them. "Help me, Mommy! I can't get out! Help me!" He tried to jerk his head free, but the spindles wouldn't let him, and he banged his head hard. He screamed again, this time clearly frantic. "Help me!"

Reagan dropped to the floor and put her hand on the small of Tommy's back. "Baby, stop screaming. You're okay. You need to be calm." But even as she spoke, she felt herself falling prey to her own panic. She reached through the spindles and tried to carefully ease his head in one direction, then the other, the way a person might try to separate two pieces of a 3-D puzzle. However he'd gotten his head wedged between the wooden posts, he was definitely stuck.

The entire time, Tommy's howling grew louder, and from down the hallway she could hear that Malin was crying too. "Dear God —" she uttered the prayer in a frantic whisper — "what am I supposed to do?"

"Call 911!" Tommy shouted, and even in his little-boy voice, his words made sense. "Tell them I'm stuck!" He let out another desperate wail and sucked in three quick breaths. He was crying so hard that he was beginning to hyperventilate. And from the room down the hall, Malin's cries grew louder too.

"Tommy! Calm down!" Reagan stood and took a few steps toward the bedroom she shared with Luke. "I'll call for help, but don't panic!" With her heart racing faster than her feet, she tore down the hall and into her room. The phone was on the table next to her bed, and she grabbed it. She had 911 dialed before she reached the door on her way back to Tommy.

"Nine-one-one," the operator said. "What's your emergency?"

Reagan was shaking so badly she could barely think.

Tommy let out another scream.

"My son," she shouted over the sound. "His head is stuck between the stair rails."

"Your son swallowed a nail?" The woman raised her voice. "Is your son breathing?"

Reagan wanted to yell at the woman. Of course he was breathing. He was screaming, wasn't he? Instead she covered her other ear and used her loudest possible voice. "Yes, he's breathing. He didn't swallow a nail; he's stuck. His head is stuck."

"Okay, ma'am. Someone's on the way. Stay by the phone in case we need to call you back."

She thanked the emergency operator and hung up.

In the distant places of her mind, Reagan thought that of course this would happen today, when Luke was away in New York City on business. Back when they lived in Manhattan, at least she would've had her mother around to help her with the kids. But here in Indiana, when Luke traveled she was on her own. They lived close enough to the Baxters to be a part of family holidays and birthdays, but too far for moments like this, when Kari or Ashley would've hurried over to help.

"Mommy, pray!" Tommy was panting now, making an attempt every few seconds to snap his head back through the space and harming himself each time. From the bedroom at the other end of the hall, Malin's cries were full-blown screeching.

"Baby, stop doing that; you're hurting yourself." Reagan dropped to the floor again. She rubbed Tommy's back and braced his head with her hand so he couldn't hit it against the spindles. "You have to be calm!" It took that long for her son's words to reach her heart. What had he said? Of course! They needed to pray. She leaned in closer. "Jesus, right now I beg You to be with Tommy. Help him be calm because help is on the way."

Almost in direct answer to her prayer, an idea hit her. "I know." She put her face as close to his as she could. "Let's pretend you're a baby dinosaur!"

Tommy let out one last wail, but it faded toward the end. "Wh-wh-why?"

"Because —" Reagan's mind raced — "you're a baby dinosaur and you're caught in a trap. And . . . and there's a T. rex downstairs looking for you."

His cries fell to a breathless whimper.

Help me, God . . . please. She searched her imagination. "And if he hears you, he'll come up here and get us both, so you have to stop screaming." She lowered her voice. "Okay, Tommy?"

"I'm . . . I'm not Tommy." He tried to shoot her a disdaining look as if clearly he couldn't be Tommy any longer. "I'm b-b-baby Ben, the brontosaurus."

"Right." Reagan turned toward the other end of the hall, where Malin was quickly losing what remained of her control. "You know what, Ben?"

"What?" Tommy was still struggling to catch his breath, but he was playing the game, believing there was a reason to stay quiet.

"Malin's being too loud for the T. rex." She gulped. "So I'll go quiet her down, and that way we'll all be safe."

"Wait!" He raised his voice, the panic back in a hurry. "How do baby dinosaurs get f-f-free?"

"Special dinosaur doctors come and help." She glanced out the window, but so far there was no sign of the paramedics. "And they're on the way, okay, Tommy?"

"Ben!"

"Right, sorry. They're on the way, Ben."

He held his finger to his lips. "Tell Ma-

156

lin quiet!"

"I will. Remember, stay calm!" Reagan was up and racing down the hall before her words were fully out. She reached Malin and found her daughter's face bright red, her nose running, and her eyes swollen from crying. "Mommy's here, honey. I'm so sorry." She lifted Malin from the crib and cradled her close to her chest. "Everything's okay now."

But Malin never calmed down easily, and she was still crying in Reagan's arms when the knock came at the door. Reagan raced downstairs and flung it open. A team of paramedics moved in as she pointed up at Tommy, his head stuck through the second-floor railing. "He can't get out."

"I'm a baby dinosaur," Tommy cried. "Look out for the T. rex!"

The rescue took only a few minutes and involved a paramedic carefully sawing one of the spindles in half and pulling it from the railing system.

The whole time Tommy entertained them with stories about baby dinosaurs. "I'm a baby brontosaurus. We hafta be quiet 'cause of the T. rex!"

One of the men made eye contact with Reagan, and the two shared a quick smile, the first Reagan had allowed since she heard

Tommy's initial scream. The paramedic was athletic-looking and younger than the others, probably in his midtwenties. Reagan noticed he wasn't wearing a wedding ring, and then she silently chided herself for looking.

"Quite an imagination." The guy's eyes sparkled. "I'll probably have one just like him someday."

Reagan still had Malin on her hip. "Good luck." She grinned again and brushed her bangs off her forehead.

At the same time, the other two paramedics released the protective hold they had on Tommy's head. "Okay, Ben, stand up nice and easy."

Tommy did as they told him, and when he was fully upright, he rubbed both sides of his head. He looked at Reagan. "Sorry, Mommy. I won't do that anymore."

Reagan leaned against the wall, drained from the ordeal. "Why *did* you do it?" She glanced at the young medic again. "We've lived here a year, and he's never tried this before."

"I was a lion!" Tommy crouched down and put both hands in front of him, his fingers curled like vicious claws. "I was at the zoo and someone tried to pet me, so I zoomed in to get 'em."

The medic let out a low whistle.

"Yeah." Reagan managed a weak bit of laughter. "Welcome to my world."

The two older paramedics were picking up the wood pieces left over from the stair railing and wrapping a long piece of rope around the remaining spindles to span the newly widened gap. "So we don't need to make another trip out here," one of them said.

While they worked, the other medic put his hand on Tommy's shoulder and stooped down to the boy's level. "Your head feeling okay?"

"Yeah." Tommy rubbed it again. "Dinosaurs get banged up." He looked at the man. "Hey, come see my room. It's got a million, trillion dinosaurs!" He grabbed the medic's hand, and off they went.

Reagan followed, and halfway down the hall she set Malin down so they could walk hand in hand. Her daughter was calm now, too distracted by the commotion to remember how angry she'd been just minutes earlier.

Tommy gave a one-minute nonstop monologue tour of his room and every dinosaur represented there. Then he grabbed hold of Malin's hand. "Come on, Mali. Let's go find your baby dinosaur game!"

The children hurried out of the room, Malin toddling along as fast as she could behind her brother, leaving Reagan alone with the paramedic. A strange feeling crept in with her other emotions, but before she had time to analyze it, the medic stuck out his hand. "I'm Eric. I've worked with the department for three years, and you have to know, I've never seen anything like this before."

Reagan took hold of his hand and felt the blood rush to her cheeks. She let go almost too fast and took a step back. Eric had blond hair and green eyes. He looked like he belonged in a calendar of men in uniform. She dismissed the thought and shifted her gaze to the floor. "The way Tommy is, we'll probably see you out here again sometime." She lifted her eyes to his once more.

And suddenly there it was. The unmistakable attraction in Eric's eyes, a look any woman could recognize, even if it had been months since she'd seen it. The way it had once been when Luke looked at her.

Eric glanced at Reagan's hand in a way that he must've intended to be discreet. "You and . . . your husband must stay busy with that one." He paused, and his expression told her he didn't mean to be too forward.

Again Reagan's answer was hurried. "My husband's away on business, but yes." She forced a laugh. "Tommy definitely keeps us busy."

"Well then." Eric shook her hand once more. His hand didn't linger, but his gaze did. "Maybe we'll see you around town."

Reagan's pulse raced, much like it had earlier when Tommy was stuck. Only now she was the one in trouble. "Maybe sometime."

Before she had time to wonder if what she'd said was wrong, Eric smiled at her. "Glad we could help." He tipped his head in her direction, turned, and headed toward the staircase.

She followed, and just then Tommy and Malin flew down the hall. Tommy had Malin's dinosaur game held high over his head, and Malin was toddling, arms outstretched, squealing at him. "Mine! Mine!"

The paramedics looked at the children, and Eric laughed. "We'll let you get back to your evening."

Reagan stepped into the path of her oncoming children and snagged the game from Tommy's hands. But all the while she looked at Eric. "Thanks . . . really."

They were gone and the moment was over before it ever really began. At least that's what Reagan told herself as she tried to restore order. She returned the game to Malin, then led the children downstairs. "Time for a movie," she announced. Both kids were too riled up for anything but a change of pace.

In a matter of seconds, she slipped in a Miss PattyCake video and moved to the front room. The fire truck with the paramedics was just pulling away. Eric was sitting against the window closest to her, and it might've been her imagination, but she thought she saw him look back at her house one last time.

Slowly she dropped to the sofa, her body half turned so she could see the truck drive out of sight. Only then did she grab a fistful of upholstery from the top of the sofa and close her eyes. What was she doing? Flirting with a perfect stranger? Making eyes at the paramedic who'd come to her house to rescue her son? In all the bumps and rocky places along the journey of her marriage, never had she allowed another man to turn her head. Not until now.

She released her hold on the sofa and let her hands fall to her lap. *What's happening to me?* The question rang through her soul with terrifying significance because she already knew the answer. Luke was traveling more than before — an aspect of moving to Indiana that neither of them had counted on. Luke could run Dayne's legal needs from the Indianapolis office, but he needed to meet with the main brass in New York at least once a month.

And that wasn't all. From practically the time they'd moved in, Luke had grown more and more distant, detached from her and the kids. They had their good times, of course. After Ashley and Landon's baby died, she'd seen a softer side of Luke, the tenderness she still looked for. He was also better after an hour of remembering his mother or when they talked about Elizabeth's ten rules of a happy marriage.

Reagan clasped her hands and stared at the floor. She couldn't remember the last time they'd read his mother's advice, but recently when Reagan brought it up, Luke dismissed the idea. "I know the secrets." He would sound tired, almost as if he was worn-out from trying to find the joy they once shared. "Knowing them and living them are two different things."

The strange thing was, neither of them could put a label on what they were feeling. He seemed bored and uninterested, and along the way she'd grown lonely. So lonely that even though it was wrong to think so, the encounter with Eric today stood out as the highlight of her week.

She hung her head and shielded her eyes. *I'm sorry. . . . I want those feelings to be for Luke only, Lord. Save us from where things are headed . . . please.*

The truth of her sudden feelings for another man horrified her and sent her scrambling off the sofa to the nearest phone. Marriage was sacred, and like Elizabeth had written in her letter, it took work. Reagan returned to the sofa, her fingers already punching in the numbers. It didn't matter whether he had a business meeting or was at a fancy dinner.

She needed to talk to her husband now, before another moment came between them.

Luke crossed the street at Broadway and 47th and headed toward 52nd Street and the August Wilson Theater. The city was fast and exhilarating. Days like this he missed it more than he remembered.

"How much longer?" Sandy, the young woman beside him, flashed him a smile.

"Not far." He grinned at her. "Besides, the walk's good for us."

"Wait a minute." From Luke's other side, James van Kelp III, in his late thirties and one of the firm's top attorneys, huffed along. "That's what Luke always says." He worked to keep pace with Luke and Sandy and the flow of pedestrian traffic on Broadway. "You fitness buffs are all the same! I say hail a cab."

"Ah, come on." Luke winked at him, then swapped a look with Sandy. "The firm encourages exercise. I get the memos."

"Okay, okay," James exaggerated a few huffs and wiped at his brow. "Five more blocks, right?"

Tonight they were seeing *Jersey Boys,* based on the music of the Four Seasons. The play had been James's idea, but only Luke and Sandy were willing to join him in the last-minute hunt for tickets. Now, with third-row seats in hand, they had just twenty minutes until showtime.

As they walked, Luke noticed the occasional half an instant when his elbow would brush against the arm of the woman beside him. He tried to feel bad about the experience, but the moment felt too good for regrets. Besides, he was doing nothing wrong. Sandy was the new paralegal at the office, and the two had struck up a friendship over Luke's last few business trips. She thought he looked like Dayne Matthews, and he felt bigger than life in her presence.

It was harmless, nothing he wouldn't have allowed if he'd still worked in New York. Sandy was single, but she knew he was married. As long as they stayed in group settings like the one they were in tonight, Luke couldn't find a reason to feel guilty.

"Anyone have a favorite Four Seasons song?" James was talkative, and tonight was no exception.

Luke exchanged a quick grin with Sandy. " 'My Eyes Adored You.' That's mine, hands down."

"Strange." Sandy's expression turned playful. "That's mine too."

"Ah, you gotta be crazy!" James gestured into the evening air. " 'Sherry' is the best, no doubt! And there's that one about December 1963, where . . ."

He was still going on about the song when Luke's phone rang. He pulled it from his pocket and saw it was Reagan. He could ignore her call, but that wouldn't make the evening out easier to explain. He held up the phone and his index finger; then he dropped back some from the others. "Hello?"

There was a pause at the other end before her voice finally filled the line. "Luke?"

"Yeah, hi, honey." A few feet away, a cabdriver laid on his horn, and another

166

responded. Luke tried to shield the receiver. "How's it going?"

"Not that well." She hesitated again. "Where are you?"

He had nothing to hide; he'd done nothing wrong. "Broadway. A few of us are headed to a show."

"A show?" She waited a few seconds before she released a laugh completely devoid of humor. "You're seeing a Broadway play?"

"*Jersey Boys* . . . remember? The story of the Four Seasons?" In the background, Luke could hear the sounds of Tommy shouting something about a game and Malin's shrill protests. He tried to sound upbeat. "What's going on?"

For a few seconds, Luke was sure she was going to lay into him. Instead, she uttered a weary moan. "Not much . . . now that the paramedics are gone. Tommy got his head stuck between the spindles on the stair railing."

Luke slowed his pace and brought his free hand to his eyes. "You've gotta be kidding me. How could that happen?" As soon as he said the words, he realized how they sounded. "I mean, I'm not saying you could've stopped him, but . . . why did he do it?"

"He thought he was a lion." Reagan's tone was colder than it had been only seconds ago. "Never mind. I'll catch you up later. Go enjoy your show."

Sandy turned around just then and moved closer to him. "Is it this block or next?"

"Next." Luke held his finger to his lips and tried to convey with his expression the importance of the phone call.

She mouthed, "Sorry" and slipped back alongside James.

"Who was that?" There wasn't a trace of understanding in Reagan's voice.

"Sandy, from the office. She's part of the group." He sounded defensive, and he worked to come across more relaxed. "James van Kelp had the idea. A bunch of us got tickets since I don't fly home until tomorrow."

"Great, Luke." Reagan raised her voice so she could be heard over Tommy's shouting. "That's my cue. Talk to you later."

Reagan hung up before he could say goodbye, and any feelings of guilt quickly became anger. What right did she have to be angry with him? He made the money, didn't he? It was his hard work that allowed her to be a stay-at-home mom and live in one of the finer homes on their block. And yes, that meant he had to travel now and then, but what did she expect? He should go back to his hotel room the minute work was done?

He closed his phone, shoved it in his pocket, and rolled his eyes. Then he picked up his pace until he was between James and Sandy once more.

"Everything okay at home?" Sandy's question held no guile, no hidden meaning. But it struck a nerve all the same.

Luke clenched his jaw and looked straight ahead. "As good as it can be."

"But not nearly as good as a live Broadway play!" James clapped a few times; then at the top of his lungs he began to sing, " 'Sherry, Sherry baby, She-e-e-e-e-rry ba-a-by . . .' "

Anywhere else James would've drawn at least a few disapproving stares. But not in New York City and especially not on Broadway. No one in the stream of people headed the opposite direction even seemed to notice.

James laughed. "See that! I shoulda been a Broadway star!"

The play was racier than Luke had imagined it would be. People his age thought of the Four Seasons as a group of sweet-natured teens whose innocent songs and stage presence represented their generation. But the show was riddled with cross language and references to promiscuity and adultery.

Leading up to the song "Oh, What a Night" was a reference to a one-night stand that a member of the group wanted to remember. Luke wasn't sure if it was coincidental or not, but as the song got under way, Sandy put her elbow up on the armrest against his. It took him several seconds before he moved his arm and longer to get his mind back on the play.

Later, when James and Sandy had caught a cab back to Midtown and Luke had returned to the hotel, he wondered about himself and the night with his distant coworkers. In the past, a play like *Jersey Boys* would've made him sorry he'd wasted his money. He would've been critical of any married man who took in a play sitting beside a single woman, even in a group setting. Which just went to show how far he'd come. Not necessarily how far he'd allowed himself to fall but just how different he was.

Because after he phoned the front desk for an early wake-up call, and as he hit the pillow that night, he wasn't plagued with guilt or regret or even a sense of uneasiness. He and Reagan were in trouble; he was aware of that fact. That's why he enjoyed himself so much tonight. He liked traveling.

The time away gave him a break from the tension at home.

In fact, Dayne had called earlier with some of the best news yet. Several weeks from now, a day of downtime had been scheduled on the set in Mexico — not enough time for Dayne to fly home but enough to get business done. Dayne's manager was meeting him on the set, and he wanted Luke there too. On the beach in Mexico.

Luke could hardly wait. At least he was doing well professionally. Only in his personal life did he seem to have the uncanny knack for disappointing people. Or maybe people simply expected too much from him.

"Why can't you be more like your dad?" Reagan had asked him before he left for New York. The question grated on his nerves and kept him awake. Was that what she wanted? For him to be just like his father? No one was as wonderful as the great John Baxter. Not even Dayne Matthews. Why couldn't she be happy being married to him, just the way he was, without heaping a mountain of expectations on his shoulders?

He would never be like his father. He'd already blown that opportunity. Not only on a chill fall night in September, the day before the Twin Towers collapsed, but in

171

the way he handled himself for a year afterwards. He would live with that truth until the day he died.

Luke sighed. Whatever. He and Reagan would work things out somehow. He would bring her a dozen roses from the airport florist, and they would remind themselves that having young kids was hard on any marriage. This season would eventually pass, and then they would find the love and laughter they'd left behind.

In the meantime, it couldn't hurt to see a play with friends who enjoyed his company. He yawned and rolled onto his side. He pictured Sandy, the carefree way she had about her, the sincerity in her smile. It was nice to hang out with someone who didn't resent him the way Reagan seemed to.

As he fell asleep, he reminded himself that he didn't have to recount the night for Reagan or apologize for his behavior tonight.

Why should he? He hadn't done a single thing wrong.

CHAPTER TEN

It was the third Friday night football game of the season and the first one at home. Like her friends who were in their last year of high school, Bailey Flanigan wore the school's blue and white colors and a T-shirt with the word *Senior* stenciled across the front. The game hadn't started yet, but even so, the air was alive, filled with an electric sort of giddiness. Clear Creek was the defending league champion, and tonight would be the most difficult test of the season.

The atmosphere was everything a Friday night game should be — the crash of the marching band cymbals, thick burgers on the grill in front of the concession stand, and the singsong chants from the cheerleading squad. But even with the excitement around her and despite all that was at stake for her dad's football team, Bailey could think of only one thing.

Cody Coleman should've been here.

If not on the field, then one of the team's best receivers in school history should've been on the bench beside her, cheering for Clear Creek and making plans for a late-night movie back at the Flanigans' house. Or down on the field next to her dad, watching the game from the sidelines and doing whatever he could to help out.

But definitely not sleeping in a tent in Iraq, worn-out from another day policing the streets in Baghdad.

"You okay?" Connor was beside her, scouting the stands for his friends. His freshman football team made a plan to sit together for the varsity games. "You seem sorta out of it."

"I am." She tried to smile, but it fell short. "I miss Cody."

"Oh." Connor nodded slowly and faced the field.

The team was warming up, the guys in three straight lines, with their dad and Ryan Taylor and the other coaches in their baseball caps and sweats walking between the lines, keeping the players on task.

Bailey tried to change the subject. "Think you'll play all four years?"

Connor narrowed his eyes, and at first he said nothing. He was a good-looking kid, with their dad's dark hair and broad shoulders and their mom's blue eyes. "Football's okay." He gave her a lopsided grin, but his eyes held a thoughtfulness that hadn't been there before. "It's not like CKT."

"No." Bailey stared out at the field. "We would have practice tomorrow, if . . ."

"If things were different."

"Yeah." She pictured the community theater, roped off with caution tape. An article in the local paper said the developer had plans to tear down the old building. "I still can't believe it's all behind us. The plays and auditions . . . the rehearsals. Katy. Even the theater." A sad, ironic laugh sounded on her lips. "It's like some kind of bad dream."

"Only every time we wake up it's the same thing." Connor breathed in deep and put his arm around Bailey's shoulders. "Maybe we're supposed to start it up again when we grow up."

"Maybe."

"Only . . . by then it'll be too late for our group." Connor slumped a little. "A bunch of the guys in the locker room were talking about Leslie and Lisa, the twins."

Bailey knew where this was headed. The girls were juniors, and until now they'd been very active in CKT. But without a place to stay involved, they'd changed their image

175

and become partiers. "They're getting around?" She winced as she waited for his answer.

"Yeah, a lot. According to the guys, anyway." Connor released his hold on her and looked again for his buddies. "Everyone cusses in the locker room. I hate that part."

Bailey sighed. "Does Dad know?"

"I talked to him. Cussing isn't allowed at the varsity level. Dad says it's a reflection on the coaches, so he's gonna talk to the freshman coach."

"Hmmm." Bailey studied him. "Definitely not CKT."

"No." Connor stood and pointed at a few guys one section down and two over. "There they are." He patted her on the back. "See ya later."

"See ya." Bailey felt a hint of sadness as her brother ran off. CKT had bonded them, turned them into the best of friends. It hadn't hit her until just now that she and Connor hadn't spent the same amount of time together. Connor hung out mainly with the freshmen, so their school friends ran in different circles. And by the time he came home from football practice each day, she was in her room doing homework.

Back when there was CKT, the two of them would congregate in his room or hers, listening to the current show's practice CD, laughing about the silly things that had happened at rehearsal, and guessing at whether they'd be ready by opening night. They shared none of that now. She and Connor would always be friends but not the way they'd been when their entire social lives were lived one show at a time.

Their close relationship was one more casualty, and suddenly Bailey felt the loss of CKT like never before.

A couple of her girlfriends scampered up the bleachers and filled in the spot where Connor had been. The conversation was shallow and full of drama. Who was planning to get drunk tonight and which of their friends was moving in on whose boyfriend. Bailey sat in the midst of them, but she said only an occasional word here or there. For the most part, she pretended to be focused on the close game, which Clear Creek won by a touchdown with a minute left.

Connor went to the house of one of the freshman players later for a team sleepover. By the time Bailey got home, the younger boys were lost in a Star Wars movie, and her mother was working on a magazine article.

When Bailey walked in, her mom pushed back her chair and rubbed her eyes. "Well?"

She smiled. "Did we win?"

"By seven." Bailey stuck her hands in the back pockets of her jeans. "Can you talk a bit?"

"Sure." Her mom stood and pushed the chair in. "Writing can wait."

"Thanks." Bailey moved into the kitchen. "I'll make coffee."

"Perfect." Rapid fire came from the television in the next room, and their mom turned toward the boys. "Let's turn it down a little."

"Yes, Mom." Justin was often the spokesman for "the brothers," as they liked to call themselves. "But we can't hear with you guys talking."

"We'll go in the dining room." Their mom smiled, but her voice held a no-nonsense tone. "But keep it down." She made a funny face. "It feels like a spaceship's landing on the roof."

All four boys laughed, and Justin did as she asked.

When Bailey and her mom both had a cup of coffee, they moved into the dining room and took chairs facing each other.

Bailey's mother tilted her head, her expression sympathetic. "Something happen at the game?"

"Not really." Bailey felt tears spring to her

eyes, and she wasn't even sure why. "It's just . . . everything feels so different."

"Hmmm." Her mom took a sip of coffee. "Seems to be a familiar theme around here."

"Yeah." Bailey settled back in her chair. "I guess I'm missing Cody. In his last letter he tried to hide it, but I could tell. He's worried about being over there."

"We're all concerned."

Bailey nodded. She was glad her mom didn't dismiss her fears. Bailey's faith wasn't wavering, and she would certainly continue to pray every day for Cody. But that didn't mean he would come home safely. War was dangerous; it was okay to be afraid for someone like Cody. "And I guess I'm a little mad at Katy."

"Why?" Her mom's voice grew slightly curious.

Bailey cupped her hands around the hot mug in front of her. The warm days had given way to cooler nights, and her fingers were still chilled from the game. She looked at her mother. "She didn't have to take that next movie. She could've stayed here and found someplace for CKT — don't you think? I mean, the Clear Creek auditorium might've been an option if she would've tried."

"Bethany tried more than once with the

administration. There wasn't room in the schedule." Her mom's tone was sympathetic. "CKT is *your* dream, sweetheart. Katy's dream is to try her hand at a film career."

"It isn't just my dream." Bailey's response was quick. "It's mine and Connor's and the other hundred kids in this town who need a Christian theater group."

"True." Her mom set her coffee cup down on the table. "So does that mean Katy doesn't have a right to her dream?"

"You saw *For Real.*" Bailey tossed her hands in the air. "Katy's putting her marriage on the line. She's risking everything and leaving us behind, and for what? For a shot at being famous?" She was talking too loud, and she stopped herself. "I'm sorry. It just doesn't seem right."

For a while they sat there, not speaking, taking an occasional sip from their coffees. Then her mom drew a slow breath. "I feel that way sometimes. And when I pray about Katy and Dayne, I have this sense — a very strong sense."

"A sense of what?"

"That God's still working on Katy." Her smile was warm, reassuring. "That the story of Katy and Dayne isn't finished yet."

Bailey let her hands fall on the arms of

the chair. "Yeah. I guess I never thought about it that way."

"But I understand. You and Connor are missing CKT." She reached one hand across the table. "You're missing sharing it together."

"Exactly." Bailey took hold of her mom's fingers. "Like I said, nothing feels the same."

They talked a few minutes longer, with Bailey catching her mom up on the kids at school, the ones who were out that very night drinking and making choices that could live with them forever. "One thing, though." Bailey felt her eyes light up. "The football team's not drinking. Dad's made a real impact with those guys."

"It's a year-to-year thing. Every group of kids needs the message." Her mom stood and cleared their coffee cups. As she did, she gave Bailey a half hug. "I love you, honey. I know it doesn't seem like it tonight, but God has a plan. Even with all the uncertainties."

Bailey leaned her head on her mother's shoulder. "I like to think so."

"He does, sweetie. That's the thrill of life — watching what amazing thing God's going to do next." She kissed Bailey's cheek. "For all of us." She nodded toward the TV room. "I'm going to go watch a little Star

Wars. Ricky saved me a spot."

"Okay." Bailey walked with her mom into the kitchen. "Thanks for talking."

"Always." Her mom grinned and then joined the boys. "I didn't miss the best part, did I?"

As Bailey headed for her bedroom, her mother's idea of watching and waiting for what amazing thing God was going to do next stayed with her. It was a good thought, a way of holding on when life seemed so unsure.

There was more in Bailey's heart than she'd been able to voice tonight, talks that would wait for another day. Like what she was going to do after she graduated and whether she would go to Indiana University or away to New York City or Los Angeles, where she and Connor sometimes dreamed of going. With applications to universities due in the next few months, Bailey and her parents had already discussed her options a number of times. Always Bailey came to the same conclusion. She would make her decision later.

But now that she'd started her senior year, later was right around the corner.

She dropped to her bed and reached beneath it for the box of letters Cody had sent her since he left. His words never came across as romantic. He made no promises and asked for none in return. But he cared about her. That much came across with every letter he wrote.

His latest note was on top. Bailey pulled it from the stack and eased it from its envelope. The letter started with a recap of basic training and how glad he was to be finished with the all-day drills.

We arrived in Baghdad a few days ago, and we're all set up. My bunk room has nine other guys pretty much right next to each other. But it's not so bad. Keeps you company when the nights get lonely.

Bailey smiled at the picture of Cody in a room with so many guys. It would've felt a lot like the locker room back at Clear Creek — the same smells and noises and easy laughter. In a house full of boys, Bailey could picture the scene well. Her eyes moved down the page.

The weird thing is not knowing what tomorrow brings. I mean, back at home none of us really know either. But out here, death is a part of life. So any day could be your last. It keeps you close to God — that's for sure.

Anxiety quickened her heart rate, and she directed her attention to the photo on her nightstand, the one of Cody and her the day before he left. She kept it close so she'd remember to pray for him. And maybe because it helped her remember how right it felt with his arm around her shoulders.

God, keep him safe. He needs You every minute out there.

She looked back at the letter.

I'll be home before too long, so save me a place at your house. You never know, I could be home sooner. Either way, pray for me. I need it. And, hey . . . I miss you. In case I haven't already told you.

Waiting for your next letter,
Cody

Bailey considered the meaning of his words. He could be home sooner if the war ended, if the president ordered the troops to pull out. That must be what he meant. But reading his words sent a strange feeling through her, almost like a premonition. He would also come home sooner if he was injured, or if . . .

She folded the letter and held it for a long moment. Cody would be fine because she was praying for him and God was with him. He wouldn't come home sooner unless everyone around him came home early too. She'd been holding her breath, and now she exhaled, hunching over her knees. By then she would've made up her mind about where to attend college. She might even be already gone, depending on her choice.

Whatever happened, Cody would come home at the right time, back home safe in Bloomington. He would help out with her dad's football team and take classes at Indiana University. Someday. She slid off the edge of her mattress, returned the letter to the box, and moved it back beneath her bed.

A yawn came over her. She crossed her bedroom floor to the adjoining bathroom and ran the hot water. For a few seconds she stared at herself and wondered how other people saw her. Was she Coach Flanigan's daughter? a drama girl who liked to sing and dance? a Christian? There had been no guys in her life since last spring, unless she counted Cody. And he was really more of a good friend, even if they'd both had feelings for each other before he left.

Tim Reed had called her last night while she was finishing her calculus homework in her room. He was in his first year at Indiana

185

University, taking a full load of classes and missing CKT as much as she was. "It wasn't supposed to be like this," he told her. His voice held a depth she hadn't heard from him in a long time, not since the days when they used to text each other. "I should be teaching a class for Katy, helping with the fall show, you know?"

They talked about Katy and Dayne, how tough it would be to live under that sort of public scrutiny, and about the CKT kids who were struggling without the theater group. The twins weren't the only ones getting into trouble. People were talking about a few of the kids who'd had lead parts in CKT shows but who were getting into drugs and partying.

"Let's face it. We need CKT." Bailey tried to keep the sadness from her voice. She didn't want every conversation with Tim to be about the loss of CKT. "Maybe you're supposed to get it going again."

"Hmmm. Someday." Tim laughed, but it sounded thoughtful, as if the idea wasn't out of the question. Before they hung up, he paused, almost as if he wasn't sure how to say whatever was coming next. "I miss you, Bailey. More than I say."

His comment touched her heart and took her by surprise. Last she'd heard, Tim was leading worship at his church a few miles away from the one Bailey and her family attended, and he was dating a girl who played keyboard Sunday mornings. He said nothing about the girl, and Bailey didn't ask. "Wow . . . I figured you'd kinda moved on."

"I couldn't really move on from someone like you." He kept his tone light. "I mean, come on. We wore tights together in *Robin Hood.* How many people have that in common?"

He'd ended the call by saying they should get together sometime. Maybe have dinner or catch a movie. Bailey agreed, but after she hung up, she realized they hadn't actually made a plan or picked a date. Typical of the Tim Reed she'd always known. Just interested enough to be mysterious, to leave her wondering about whether he might even be the guy God had planned for her.

But how did Tim really see her? She pulled a washcloth from the drawer and drenched it in the hot water. If he was interested, he'd set a date to get together. It was that simple. She pressed the steaming cloth to her face and held it there. Tim wasn't the one — not for now, anyway. Her daddy had always told her she'd know when the right guy came along because he would recognize her as the one-in-a-million girl she really was.

She wiped the washcloth over her face and rinsed it. A one-in-a-million guy — that's who she was holding out for. Whenever he came along, it would be worth the wait. In the meantime, without CKT, life would feel lonely. The girls at school were worse than ever — backbiting and gossiping about each other, stealing each other's boyfriends, and going to parties without telling Bailey. Even lonely was better than that.

When her teeth were brushed and flossed, she returned to her bed and slipped under the covers. It was after midnight already, but it felt later. Before she turned out the light, she pressed the Play button on her stereo and started up her favorite CD of the moment, the debut album by Mandisa. Something about the singer's soulful lyrics and deep emotion had a way of making Bailey feel closer to God. She turned down the volume and hit the light switch.

Her mom had taught her a long time ago that whenever she felt lonely, she could do something that would make her future love seem less far away. She could pray for that guy, whoever he was, wherever he was. "Because you know, Bailey, he's out there somewhere. He's already busy becoming the young man he'll need to be when the time's right for the two of you to meet."

The idea had helped Bailey more times than she could count. So as she closed her eyes, she felt a sense of hope ease the concerns in her soul. *You know all things, God, and if I'm supposed to get married someday, You know who the guy is and where he is. You know what he's doing and You're working to make him ready for his future . . . same as You're working to get me ready for mine.*

In the far reaches of the house, she heard the credits to Star Wars. The boys' movie was over later than usual.

Bailey rolled onto her side and pulled the covers up close to her chin. *Whoever he is, wherever he is, Lord, I pray that You'll protect him. Help him become the man of God You want him to be and keep him safe from the world. Thank You, Lord. . . . Thank You for letting me dream. In Jesus' name, amen.*

The call came just as Cody Coleman's division was headed out for a trek across Baghdad: Get to the office quick. Captain needed to speak to him.

"Oh, man! Come on, Coleman. You gotta be kidding." José, his bunkmate, rolled his eyes as he grabbed his gear. "No way you're getting out of this mission."

Cody frowned and checked his watch — 8:15 in the morning. He did the conversion in his head, the way he always did when he looked at the time. Just after midnight in Bloomington. He gave his bunkmate a mock look of helplessness. "Is it my fault I'm wanted just at the right — ?"

"Coleman! Get moving!" The order came from outside the tent. His platoon leader. "Captain needs you in the office. Now!"

"Figures." José pointed at Cody, his eyes full of laughter. "You clean the bathrooms this week. You gotta make it up somehow." He saluted Cody. "The other guys are already in the Humvee. Later."

"Later." Cody chuckled and picked up his pace, darting out into the daylight and jogging the fifty yards or so to his superiors' tent. This had happened last week too. One of the guys had an order to talk to a lieutenant, and in the process he'd missed a trip into the city.

But here, now, something seemed almost strange about the timing. Ten more seconds and he would've already been on the road to Baghdad, laughing it up with the other guys from his platoon, talking big and keeping the peace, trying to pretend they weren't all scared to death.

He pushed open the door, breathless from

the run, and his eyes met those of Captain Ray Rogers. Cody stopped in the doorway and saluted. "Sir. You sent for me, sir."

"At ease." The captain was a young guy, not quite thirty. He leaned forward and nodded at the chair across from him. "Sit down. Apparently you gained access to a building on the east side of the city yesterday."

"Yes, sir." Cody gulped. He still wasn't sure if he'd done something wrong. "I made it farther in than the other men."

"That's why you're here. Word just hit this morning that terrorists are using the building. We should've had that information before you went in. . . ." Captain Rogers pursed his lips. "But since you're alive to talk about it, we need everything, Coleman. Every detail you saw."

Cody exhaled. He wasn't in trouble. The army needed his information, and he was glad to give it. Whatever way he could help the United States finish off the terrorist cells in the city, he'd do it.

Twenty minutes later Cody was still talking to the captain, searching his mind for any possible details, when the phone rang on the captain's desk.

"Rogers here."

The call gave Cody a chance to think once

more about the building, what he'd seen and what might be helpful to the army now that they knew terrorists were using the place. But as he racked his brain, he watched the captain bring one hand to his face and heard him groan.

"You're sure? It was our guys?"

Cody's pulse pounded at his temples. Had something happened to some of their men? The captain probably had a couple hundred soldiers under him, and odds were Cody had eaten meals with just about all of them.

Captain Rogers muttered a few more words, then hung up the phone. He lowered his hand, and Cody could see that the man's complexion was ashen. His eyes were dry, but they were haunted by the worst kind of pain. "Somebody must've been praying for you, Coleman." His words were heavy with shock, slow and barely loud enough to hear. "They're all gone."

Cody's mouth was dry, and he shook his head, afraid to voice the most awful possibility. "Sir?"

"Your guys . . . they barely reached the city streets." He stood and turned, his back to Cody. "Roadside bomb. Blew the vehicle to bits." He turned again, an expression of horror written on his face. "They're gone. All of them." He breathed in sharp through his nose and stared at the ceiling. "I'm sorry, Coleman. Get back to your bunk and wait for orders."

Cody could barely think, let alone move. José and the others were gone? blown to pieces just like that? Their faces filled his mind. Guys who'd been vibrantly alive half an hour earlier. The random brutality of the killing was more than he could bear.

Cody staggered out of the office and back to his bunk. He flopped onto his cot and buried his head in the pillow. If not for the captain's request to talk to him, he'd be dead now. One more casualty on the streets of Baghdad. He felt sick to his stomach, terrified and furious and filled with disbelief.

Sobs welled in his chest, and finally — alone in his bunk — he let them come. Somewhere mothers were going about their day unaware that their sons were dead. Families, girlfriends, worlds shattered in an instant. *God . . . how could it happen? And why me? Why was I spared?*

At first there was no answer, nothing but the hollow senselessness of the terrible loss. But then, slowly, the captain's words came back to him. What he'd said had to be true because otherwise Cody wouldn't be here. There was only one possible reason that he'd been spared this morning.

Somewhere someone must've been praying.

CHAPTER ELEVEN

Ashley could barely keep Cole seated at the breakfast table Saturday morning, and several times Landon had laughed at their son's enthusiasm.

"A tree house, Mom!" Cole set his fork down and pushed his plate of eggs away. "I don't think you understand how big a deal this is." He traced his finger over the bare space in front of him. The sun was warm through the kitchen windows, and it cast a splash of light across Cole's face. "Me and Dad have it all planned out. Two stories! With a hideout at the top for treasures and stuff!"

Ashley couldn't contain her smile, but she raised her eyebrows at the same time. "Eat your eggs."

"I know. . . . I will." He pulled the plate back and flashed an exasperated look at Landon. "She doesn't understand."

When they'd checked the soccer schedule

and found that today was a bye, Landon suggested using the time to build a tree house. It was all Cole could talk about for the last week.

"It's not her fault." Landon winked at her. "Most girls aren't that into tree houses."

"But this'll be the best tree house ever."

"Juice!" Devin was sitting in his high chair between Ashley and Landon. He held up his sippy cup, slathered with egg bits and toast crumbs. "Juice!"

"Say please." Ashley snatched a napkin from the center of the table and wiped her youngest son's mouth.

"Peeeese." He gave her a cheesy smile. Then he shook his cup. "Juice, peeese!"

She hesitated and made a mental picture of the way Devin looked, eggs matted to his blond hair and smeared across his forehead and cheeks. Streaks of toast and butter on his pajamas. Someday Ashley wanted to paint him in a pose just like this one. She laughed. "I must really need to get back to the easel."

"Seeing pictures, huh?" Landon's look turned tender.

"Everywhere."

"Then start painting." Landon reached over the high chair and touched his fingers to her face. "But don't stop seeing pictures in a moment like this. I love that about you, Ash."

She felt his compliment deep inside, where she was still aching from the loss of Sarah. In the weeks to come, God would use her gift of painting to help heal her; Ashley had no doubt. But until this moment, the pain had been so suffocating she wasn't sure she even remembered how to paint. The fact that she was starting to see pictures in everyday life was a good sign.

"Know what I love about Home Depot?" Cole was balanced on the edge of his seat, his eyes wide. He looked from Ashley to Landon, but he didn't wait for an answer. "The superlong aisles and the stuff stacked to the ceiling, and every single piece is good for making things. Plus, it smells like a place for guys." He raised his fork for emphasis. "Right, Dad?"

Landon chuckled. "Exactly." He nodded to Cole's plate. "Hurry so we can get cleaned up and go."

Cole gave his brother a wary look. "You might want to start with him. He's gonna need a lot more cleanup time than me."

Ashley wiped Devin's cup with another napkin and filled it with juice. "This'll be Devin's first big building project." She leaned in and kissed the child on the cheek.

"Maybe he can help with the hammer."

"Probably not." Cole sounded serious. "We might let him haul in a few pieces of wood from Dad's truck." He checked with Landon for approval. "Because a hammer's too dangerous for him. He might smash in his face, right?"

"Well . . ." Ashley could tell Landon was trying not to laugh. He wiped his mouth and paused, gaining control. "I might have to help him . . . so he doesn't smash in his face. But he could maybe hit a few nails."

"Hmmm." Cole twisted his mouth. He tapped his finger on the table a few times. "I guess we could see." He leaned closer to Landon and whispered, "He's awful small still."

The debate continued a little longer. When they were done eating, Cole ran off to his room to brush his teeth and change into "work clothes."

Landon moved toward Devin's high chair, but Ashley stood and shook her head. "I'll take care of him. You go get ready." She put her hand around the back of her husband's neck and brought him close enough so she could kiss him. "Cole can't take much more waiting." Her eyes held his, and again she made a picture of the moment. Everyday moments — warm toast and orange juice, light shining hope and new life across the morning. All that and the love of her life to share it with.

"You're doing it again."

"I know." She lowered her chin and felt her smile turn flirty. "I might go to my dad's today and pull out the paints." She kissed him again. "Being with you makes me want to capture every minute."

He put his hand around her waist and held her at the small of her back. His kiss lasted longer this time. "Being with you makes me want to forget Home Depot."

Devin banged his high chair tray with both hands.

"Our baby's watching." Ashley giggled at Landon. "Go get ready."

A soft, exaggerated groan came from his throat. "Okay . . . the tree house first." He took a step back, but his eyes were still lost in hers. "We'll make something else later."

She gave him a suggestive look. "I'll hold you to it." She laughed again as she unsnapped the high chair tray and eased their messy son from the seat. "Now I've got two things to look forward to."

It wasn't until Landon had walked down the hall to their room and Ashley was alone that she realized something that filled her with hope. She carried Devin to the sink, took a clean, wet washcloth, and began wiping him down. Now that she was past the six-week mark, her doctor had said she could get pregnant again. And so, since losing Sarah, she and Landon had talked about their physical relationship almost as a necessary means to an end. A way to get pregnant once more and fill the void in their hearts.

But here . . . in the middle of a happy, chaotic Saturday morning, she and Landon had found time to laugh and flirt and look forward to intimate moments later tonight, all for one reason.

Because they loved each other.

It was another sign that God was carrying them, helping them through.

An hour later, after Landon and the boys were off to the hardware store, Ashley drove to the Baxter house and found her dad in the kitchen, kneeling on the floor, his head under the sink. At the sound of the door, he pulled back and straightened. "Hi, honey." His face lit up in a full smile. "I thought it might be you."

"Really?" She set her purse down on the kitchen counter. "How come?"

"Today's the big tree house day." He wiped the back of his hand across his forehead. "I knew you'd be looking for something to do." His grin held a hint of

200

sorrow. "I pulled your easel out and set it up in your room."

Ashley's heart melted. She moved slowly to the cupboard and pulled down two of her mother's favorite mugs and her old china teapot. "You and Landon . . . you both know me better than I know myself."

"It's time, Ashley. Ever since you were a teenager, nothing heals your broken heart like painting."

"Hmmm. So true." She filled the kettle with water and set it over a high flame. "What's wrong with the sink?"

"Leaky pipe." He leaned back beneath it. "Just needs a little tightening."

By the time the tea was ready and she'd poured two cups, he was finished with the repair. The tea smelled delicious. It had a hint of orange, and the sweet scent mixed with the steam felt wonderful against her face. Like fall and Christmas and cuddling near a fire, all in a single drink.

Her dad wiped the floor with a paper towel, washed his hands, and joined her at the kitchen table. "Good to have that done." He let out a long sigh. "Landon asked me to come over later. Asked me if I'd help out."

"Oh." Ashley went to the refrigerator and found the pint of cream her dad kept for her. As she splashed a few drops into her tea, she gave him a curious look. "Don't you and Elaine have plans?"

"No. Not this week. Not for a while now." He cupped his hands around the ceramic mug, and for half a minute he said nothing.

Ashley watched him. Something had changed, but she wasn't sure what . . . or why he wouldn't be seeing Elaine. She returned the cream to the fridge and took her seat across from him.

"Your mother loved these old coffee mugs." He smiled into his drink, his expression distant. "Bought them as an anniversary gift . . . at a craft fair at the university when you were still in middle school." He looked up and smiled again. "Never drank an ounce of coffee in them."

Ashley studied the container in her hands, turning it carefully one way and then the other. "She loved tea more than anyone I know."

"That she did." John blinked and his smile fell away. "You know, all you kids called me last month on our anniversary. Everyone but Luke."

"Luke . . ." Ashley stretched her legs out and crossed her ankles. "I'm worried about him." She gazed out the window at an old oak, its leaves dancing on the breeze. "I think he and Reagan are struggling more than they're letting on."

"Might be." Her dad was staring off to the side, his eyes fixed on nothing in particular. "Thirty-nine years. Feels like I married her just last week." A sad laugh came softly from his throat.

Thoughts about Luke faded, and Ashley searched her father's face. "I'm sorry. . . . We all miss her so much." She sipped her tea. Something was wrong with her dad, more than what came with the usual missing. "So, about Elaine . . . you didn't see her so you could build a tree house?"

He changed his expression, and Ashley nearly gasped from the pain she saw there. He hadn't looked so wounded since the months after her mom died. "I can't meet with her." He anchored his elbows on the table and seemed to gather his strength. Whatever he was about to say, he'd given it much thought. "I was going to marry her. I have the ring upstairs."

Ashley felt her heart thud erratically a few times. She tried to process the news without overreacting. The truth wasn't a surprise, really. She and Kari and Brooke and Erin had talked about the possibility for most of the last year.

Her dad brought his lips together tight

and shook his head. "I couldn't do it." He looked around the kitchen, glancing at her mother's framed photo sitting on the counter, at the old oversize stove and the window over the sink. Finally his gaze fell on the coffee mug in his hands. "I still see her everywhere." He shrugged, his tone empty. "I can't bring Elaine here to live with me. That wouldn't be fair to either of us."

Ashley resisted making a quick response. A year ago she would've been elated with the direction her father was leaning. Back then she had believed that no one could replace her mom, so why would her father even entertain the idea of remarriage? But a scene played again in Ashley's mind. She and Landon in the hospital room, not long before Sarah's birth. Elaine was the only person gathered that day who'd thought to buy Sarah an outfit. The soft pink clothes had built a bridge between Ashley and Elaine because the gift was something her own mother would've done.

Since then, she'd thought often about the possible marriage between her dad and Elaine, and she'd made peace with the idea. Even so, she agreed with him. How could he bring Elaine here to the Baxter house? How could there be room for new love in a house full of memories that went back decades?

Ashley felt a knot in her stomach. "I don't know, Dad. I mean, Elaine's become very important to you."

"She has." His expression fell. "It's complicated."

Ashley still wasn't sure what to say. "How's Elaine feel about all this?"

"I told her we'd talk later." He looked at the wooden clock on the wall. "Truth is, I have a lot to do. The pond's got weeds up to my knees around the edges, and I have to fertilize the flower beds."

"And the tree house." She smiled.

"Definitely the tree house." He grinned and crossed his ankle over the opposite knee. "I don't want to miss that. Cole told me it needs a grandpa's touch."

"I'm sure he did." Ashley finished her tea and kept her struggle to herself. She needed more time to think about her dad and Elaine. This wasn't the moment to jump in with whatever she thought was the best decision. Or maybe, for now, it simply felt good to think of things going on unchanged. Her father's place at the Baxter house, the familiarity of her mother's memory surrounding them, all the holidays and birthdays and get-togethers stretched out before them without someone new to change the picture.

She and her dad pushed back from the table at the same time. "My decision about Elaine?" He smiled at her but not quite enough to erase the sadness in his eyes. "In the end I think everyone'll be happier for it."

Ashley was still thinking about that when she went upstairs to her old bedroom, the one with a window overlooking the Baxter front yard. It would be a good day to paint outside, but she needed to sketch the image first. She waited until she was set up before pulling Cole's picture from a folder she'd brought with her.

She heard the still, small voice of God every time she looked at the image. In her prayers before Sarah's birth, she'd felt drawn to the Scripture about finding God in the quiet whispers. Then, the day of Sarah's birth and death, Cole had come to her side and whispered to her. He told her Jesus gave him a picture in his head.

Ashley smiled at the memory. The feeling was the same one she'd been having lately. Pictures in her head. Proof that her son maybe saw life's precious moments the way she did — worthy of capturing and framing.

Then he'd handed her this very picture. Across the top he'd written, *I love you,*

Sarah. Tell Grandma hi for me. Beneath that he'd drawn a picture of an older woman, smiling bigger than life. In her arms was a tiny baby girl, tucked safely in a pink and white blanket. When Ashley asked him about it, Cole said that God told him Sarah was going to be with his grandma.

It was this picture that Ashley had to paint before any other, while the details of Sarah's precious face were still fresh in her heart.

She lightly tacked Cole's picture on a worktable next to her easel. *Okay, God, help me bring the images to life.* She closed her eyes, leaned her head back, and breathed in slowly. In the distance, someone was burning a pile of leaves. The smoke hung faint in the air and mixed with the familiar smell of her paints. She opened her eyes and stared out the window. Clouds had gathered in the far sky but not enough to block the sun or rain on Landon and Cole's project.

Once more she studied Cole's picture, allowing his simple, child-like details to become the very real images of her daughter and her mother. With a fine-point charcoal pencil, she began sketching. Her mother's face first, then her dark hair and her slim, straight shoulders. The edge of the dark walnut rocking chair.

She filled in as many pieces of the picture

as she could before turning to the setting, where her mother's rocking chair would sit once the painting was complete. A field would be best because that's how Ashley saw heaven. A more spectacular picture of earth, with fields of lush green and flowers of every vibrant color possible. If that was the background, this painting would be more beautiful than any Ashley had ever created. A rocking chair set amid brilliant petunias and poppies and pansies, her mother and daughter surrounded by every sort of wildflower and vivid fields of green. She liked the idea. There would definitely be flowers because certainly heaven had . . .

Heaven had . . .

Gradually, almost in slow motion, she lowered her hand to her lap and stared at the canvas. It had been more than three years since her mother's death. She lived in heaven now . . . not here.

Ashley stood and walked to the window. She sat on the edge of the sill and looked out. A different sort of picture began to take shape. Dear Irvel living out her final years at the Sunset Hills Adult Care Home, certain with every breath that her beloved Hank was not dead more than a decade but merely out fishing with the boys.

Alzheimer's was a terrible, wicked disease.

But in some ways it had been a blessing to Irvel because the illness allowed her to live where she was most happy. In the past with her memories of Hank.

Ashley blinked and the picture disappeared.

What about her father? His memory was sharper than ever, which meant he had the blessing of remembering her mother. But also the certainty of knowing that she was never again going to walk through the front door. By choosing his memories over the life God had given him today, her dad would be cheating himself and Elaine out of countless years of joy and laughter, years of celebrating the here and now.

No matter what changes that might bring.

She walked back to her easel, set her pencil on the table with her paints, and headed downstairs. If her father married Elaine, the wedding would be bittersweet. She might cry through the whole thing. But she could embrace Elaine as her dad's new wife, and Ashley wanted to make sure she said so. Before her dad convinced himself to cut off all feelings for the woman.

She found him outside near the pond, wearing his old jeans and a denim shirt, a straw hat and work gloves. Already he'd cleared half the weeds around the pond. She stopped and watched him. Was this how he should spend the rest of his days? Tinkering around the house, doing odd jobs, and waiting for invitations from his kids and grandkids?

The notion felt all wrong to Ashley. Her father was social and outgoing, a conversationalist with a dynamic faith and a passion for life. Of course he should have the chance to spend his days with a woman who shared his interests. She walked out to him, careful to stay on the path. She couldn't afford a twisted ankle.

He looked up and tilted his head, shielding his eyes from the sun. "Everything okay?"

"No." Ashley let her hands fall loose to her sides. "Can you come in for a minute?"

Her dad set down his shovel, dusted off his hands, and peeled back the gloves. "You aren't sick, are you?"

She smiled, allowing warmth to shine in her eyes. "No, nothing like that."

His expression relaxed some, and he followed her through the closest door, into the formal dining room, where he had the scrapbooks laid out — six of them, one for each of his adult kids.

"Hey, look at this." Ashley studied the extent of the project. "You're really putting these together."

"You weren't supposed to see." He chuckled. "Of course, you were the one who first asked me to take this on."

The scrapbooks would contain a lifetime of wisdom, her mother's words compiled into one collection. There could be no greater gift when her dad finished putting them together. Ashley stared at the stacks of copied letters, and then — so she wouldn't get sidetracked — she turned her back to the project. She gathered her thoughts and took hold of her dad's hand. "I couldn't let another minute pass without saying something."

His smile looked deep into her heart, a smile that said he loved her and cherished her, the way he always had. "It must be important."

"It is." She fought a wave of nostalgia for what might've been had her mother lived. "Okay . . . so about Elaine. I think you're making a mistake by cutting her off like this."

It took a few seconds for her dad to clearly understand what she was saying. "You mean, you think I should still see her?"

"More than that." Ashley's voice was soft but certain. "I think you should marry her." She took hold of his other hand too. "Mom's gone." Tears sprang to her eyes and made her throat feel thick. "We all wish she were here, but she isn't. She . . . she wouldn't want you walking around this place like it's a museum." She smiled, even though her chin was quivering. "Mom would've wanted you to live. Even if that means getting remarried."

John's eyes grew wide, his surprise etched into the lines on his forehead.

Ashley realized she was trembling, her knees hitting each other. She'd taken a huge step, given her blessing to something that at one point she couldn't have imagined, let alone endorsed. She pursed her lips and blew out. "That's what I wanted to say." Then, as the tears in her eyes spilled onto her cheeks, she moved into her father's arms and held him. "I miss her too. So much. I still can't believe she's really gone."

For a long time they stayed that way, Ashley feeling the way she had when she was a teenager and her father would be the only one who really understood her, the only one who could hug away her hurt and confusion. She clung to him, and a few sobs caught her by surprise. She still wanted to turn around and see her mother sitting across the dining room table, smiling at her, telling her she was silly for being upset because she wasn't gone at all.

But she was.

Ashley laid her head on her father's shoulder. After her mother died, people had told her time would heal the pain. But it never did, and now Ashley was sure it never would. They would live with the loss of Elizabeth Baxter all the days of their lives, the way maybe they were supposed to live with it. So that when they were all reunited in heaven one day, there would be a completeness that could only come from being a part of eternity. But for now . . . for now they needed to get on with life — her dad especially.

She sniffed and pulled back. "Okay, Dad? Don't become a hermit on our account."

Questions and uncertainty and the hint of tears reflected in his eyes. He backed up a step and held Ashley's hands again. "I'm not sure. . . . I don't want to leave her behind."

Ashley released one of his hands and searched for the words. "You won't have to. Elaine loved her too. Remember?" She could hardly believe she was talking her father into growing his relationship with Elaine at a time when he was ready to let his friend go. But it was the right thing; Ashley was convinced to her very core. She stood on her tiptoes and kissed her father's cheek. "Live your life. That's what Mom would've wanted. Now . . ." She gave him one last smile, then glanced toward the staircase. "I have some painting to do."

Not until an hour later, when she was fully done sketching her painting, did she let her mind drift back to the idea of the scrapbooks her father was putting together. Each of them would have some of the same letters, of course. Like the one her mother had written about the ten rules for a happy marriage. But other times a letter might be directed just to the girls or to one or another of them. For instance, back before any of them knew about Dayne, her mother had written a very powerful letter addressed simply to her precious first —

Ashley gasped. Why hadn't she thought about this before? Their mother had written a very special letter for Dayne. Since he hadn't been raised by her, the letter was one of the only pieces of her Dayne would ever have. Ashley had found it in the box of letters in her parents' closet and thought it was for Brooke, the only firstborn they'd known up to that point. Instead, Ashley read it and realized it was directed toward a son, a brother she'd never known.

The letter had changed everything, but

until now it had never occurred to Ashley that the precious words from her mother were still tucked in their original envelope. She'd given it to her dad, and she'd watched him place it high on the top shelf of his computer desk. She'd known that one day her dad would give the letter to her brother, but it had taken months to find him. Along the way, she'd forgotten about the letter. Her dad might've forgotten too.

As she turned her attention back to her painting, only one thought comforted her. Dayne should've had the letter years ago, but maybe God knew better. Maybe the timing was such that this was when Dayne needed something from their mother more than ever. Ashley thought about that. Maybe it was part of the miracle Ashley was praying for where Katy and Dayne were concerned. More than in the past, their mother's heartfelt letter, her outpouring of love and concern and support for Dayne, would quite possibly mean everything to him now.

At a time when nearly all the world was against him.

Chapter Twelve

Katy and Dayne's good-bye rushed up on them like the final scene of a movie, one they didn't ever want to come to an end. Katy was impressed with how Dayne had handled the tidal wave of publicity that had slammed into them since the premiere. *But Then Again No* was bringing in more box office receipts than any other movie he'd made. Between that and the weekly episodes of *For Real,* Katy and Dayne were household names and living in a city where they were under constant watch.

Even with all that, Dayne had agreed to only the interviews their agent deemed mandatory. A few were local, but most required a quick round-trip to New York City. Dayne always made sure Katy was at his side, that they showed the world a united front, which was — they both insisted time and again — a very real picture of their love.

But even so, things felt strained. Their

relationship was so public at this point that any private time felt forced. As if the on-screen depiction of their relationship had done little more than transition to a quiet location. Sometimes they'd be talking on the back porch of their Malibu beach home, and Katy would catch herself sounding almost rehearsed. As if they were spewing nothing more than platitudes and cheap dialogue at each other.

Dayne had reminded her that high on the list of their enemies was the greatest enemy of all. The devil certainly did not want their marriage to succeed, not when they had made public note of being Christians, of trying to live a godly life. Katy was aware of that, but the knowledge didn't make their day-to-day visibility any easier to live with.

Now the time had come to go their separate ways. It was well after midnight, the second Friday in October, and Katy had a flight to catch early the next morning. She didn't plan to sleep. There would be more than enough hours on the plane for that.

"I think it's clear." Dayne had been outside on the pitch-dark porch, and he stepped into the kitchen. The lights were off inside too. It was their attempt to convey a simple message to the paparazzi: Katy and Dayne were asleep, so pack up and go home.

Katy was sitting at the kitchen table, drinking iced tea, staring into the darkness and going over in her mind the things in her suitcase. She felt Dayne come up behind her, felt his hand on her shoulder. She reached up and covered it with her own. "I can't believe we'll be apart till Christmas."

"Ten weeks." Dayne sighed. "Are you ready?"

"Packed, you mean? Yes." She stood and faced him. Her heart was pounding, and in the shadows she could see fear in his eyes.

"I meant ready to talk." He looked over his shoulder. "I haven't seen any activity down below for an hour."

She nodded and let her head fall against his chest. "I'm ready."

They had agreed a few days ago to take this walk tonight. The beach was so inviting, so peaceful. It was sad to live on the sand and never feel it with their bare feet. Dayne took her hand and quietly led her down their private back stairs, out the wooden gate. The late hour and the feel of his hand in hers, the gentle wind on her face, reminded her of their night on the lake in Bloomington.

But this wasn't a romantic walk in the moonlight. It was a chance to hold up everything good and right and true about their faith and their relationship and beg God that it would still be there when the next ten weeks had played out. There was no sense of adventure now, no feeling of wonderment or goose bumps. Just a weariness and a certainty that there would be rough seas indeed. They wouldn't navigate safely back to the harbor of each other's arms without seeking God and each other day to day. Hour by hour.

For nearly a minute, they stood outside the gate. Dayne knew the places where the cameramen usually hid, and now he studied each spot before shaking his head. "They're gone. We're alone."

The beach was empty as far down as they could see, though Katy was sure that around the curve of shoreline there would be the usual bonfires and surfers camped out. They weren't any concern because they came looking for waves, not Hollywood stars.

Dayne took the lead again, his steps quick until they reached the hard-packed, damp sand. "North?"

"Yes. North is good." Katy fell into place beside him. They both wore shorts and long-sleeved T-shirts. The night air was cool and damp, but it felt wonderful after being in the house all evening.

They set out, walking in silence, the sound

of the crashing waves the backdrop for their separate thoughts. North would take them by other large homes and away from the public access beaches. At this hour, once they got past their own gate, no one would know them from any other couple.

They walked a dozen yards before Katy realized how wonderful Dayne's hand felt, his fingers woven between hers. "I love you."

"I love you too." He smiled down at her. His jawline looked rugged and strong in the reflection of light off the water. Even here, his good looks were enough to take her breath. America's golden boy.

Katy turned her attention to the sandy stretch in front of her. She understood why the public wanted to know his every move, but where would it all end? She breathed in, feeling the heavy salt air fill her lungs. "Someday, right?"

"Hmmm?" They were down far enough from their house now, and Dayne stopped and turned to her. He took hold of her other hand, searching her eyes. "Someday?"

"That's when all the madness will stop, right?" She could feel the tears glistening in her eyes. "When we get out of the spotlight and make it back to Bloomington for good."

Regret changed his expression, and he slipped his hands around her waist, drawing her close. "I've thought about it a thousand different ways. We made these commitments." He breathed the words into her hair, his face brushing against hers. "We have to keep them."

"I know." Katy nuzzled against his neck. "I guess I just pray that it'll really happen." She lifted her chin and met his gaze straight on. "And that it won't always just be sort of out there. One year after another, chasing our dreams, making movies. Always waiting for someday to come around."

Dayne looked like he'd been cut through the heart. "Katy —" he put his hands on her shoulders — "this isn't forever, the movie life we're living. It'll end. I promise you."

"Maybe." She tried to smile, but the sadness weighing on her wouldn't let her. "You have two more movies to make after this one, and it'll be the same story. Publicity and paparazzi, previews and people tugging at you from all directions." She shrugged. "Why sit at home waiting for you back in Indiana? I might as well make movies too." Her back was to the ocean, and her bare legs felt the light mist from a series of breakers.

A stricken look came over Dayne, and he gave a few slow shakes of his head. "Don't

221

think about it like that. We'll find a way out of this. Nobody stays in the headlines forever."

"Except maybe you." Katy covered his hands with hers. "Dayne Matthews, America's heartthrob."

Dayne seemed like he wanted to respond, but instead he dropped his hands from her shoulders and took a few steps closer to the water. "You make it sound like a death sentence."

"No." She came up behind him and linked her arm through his so they were both facing the ocean. "I knew what I was getting into when I married you. I just didn't know so many other people would care. The last episode of *For Real . . .*" She winced and made a low whistling sound. "Talk about taking off the gloves."

He said nothing, but she could feel his arm and his posture tense. Immediately she felt sorry. The episodes had gotten worse each week, hinting that Katy and Dayne were fighting constantly and implying that their acting was certainly that. "You know it's Hollywood," the announcer had said last week, "when a pair of actors can convince you on-screen that they're really in love. Especially a couple with this much trouble surrounding them."

The tabloids were no better. Headlines screamed of a reunion between Randi Wells and Dayne on the beaches of Mexico. Katy had caught wind of so many "Trouble in Paradise" headlines she rarely even bothered to look. And maybe that was the best option anyway. She'd told herself before that the magazines were only damaging if she stopped to read them.

Dayne took another step farther away and crossed his arms.

Katy hadn't meant to upset him. She slipped in beneath his left arm, then put her arms around his waist and laced her fingers near his hip bone. "Sorry." She kissed his cheek. "It's not your fault."

"No." He relaxed against her but kept his face toward the water. "So that's it, huh?" He rested his chin on the top of her head. "You'll make more movies . . . and I will. And we never make it to someday?"

"It feels pretty far off." She inched her way around in front of him. "Hey . . . look at me."

Frustration deepened the small lines at the corners of his eyes. But after a few seconds he met her eyes. "I keep thinking of Ashley and Landon, the way they held on to each other in the hospital that day. They had every reason to be mad at God and the

223

situation, mad at the family members who doubted them."

Katy moved closer and felt the rise and fall of his chest against hers. "But they weren't."

"I remembered something tonight." He looked at the water again. " 'Consider it pure joy, my brothers . . .' "

Katy closed her eyes. " '. . . whenever you face trials of many kinds . . .' "

" '. . . because you know that the testing of your faith develops perseverance.' " Dayne's voice was quiet, heavy with emotion.

" 'Perseverance must finish its work so that you may be mature and complete, not lacking anything.' "

"Exactly." Dayne drew a full breath. "That was Ashley and Landon that day — a picture of the kind of faith that understands testing. Their baby girl was dying with every heartbeat, but they were smiling." He narrowed his eyes, clearly shaken by the memory. "They loved little Sarah with pure joy. Even in the very worst circumstances."

Katy felt a ripple of guilt stir the waters in her soul. She stepped back and let her hands fall slowly to her sides. "So, you're thinking if they can handle that sort of pain . . ."

"We should be able to handle this?" He took her in his arms and held her. "Yes. That's what I'm thinking."

For a very long time, neither of them talked.

Minutes passed while the realization spread an ever-dawning light across Katy's dark, self-pitying soul. Why had she been so shortsighted, so caught up in how bad her own situation was? Her troubles were so light next to Ashley's that the comparison made Katy feel nauseated, furious with herself.

Dayne was right, and Katy wasn't sure why she hadn't seen it before. Whatever lay ahead, the strife and pain wouldn't be as bad as losing a child. The days would be long and the separation great, but she and Dayne would be making millions of dollars filming movies and being catered to along the way. They would be adored by thousands of fans, despite the headlines in the tabloids or the targets on their backs.

Shame surrounded her, and suddenly she needed space from Dayne, needed to take this new understanding to God alone.

Katy turned and walked slowly toward the water until her feet touched the foamy white surf. With her hands linked in front of her, she looked out across the sea all the way to the shadowy gray horizon. *God, I've been so consumed . . . as if I were the only one in the world with troubles. How could I get this way?* She pictured Ashley and Landon, smiling as their baby died in their arms. She hung her head. *I'm sorry, Lord. Forgive me.*

She didn't hear Dayne come up behind her, but she felt him. Even before he touched her, she felt his warm breath against her neck.

His hands circled her waist, and the warmth of his solid chest sheltered her from the ocean air. "If they could get through that, then we can get through this."

"I know." She turned in his arms, and suddenly she was desperate for his kiss, his embrace. She moved closer to him, lifted her lips to his, and their tenderness quickly became a passion that left them both breathless. "I'm sorry." Her eyes searched his, and she saw the understanding she'd hoped to find. "I've been so negative, Dayne."

A smile started at the corners of his lips and then filled his face. "This is what I prayed for. You and I on the beach, celebrating our last night together — not arguing about it." He tilted his head back, and in a voice that competed with the crashing surf he yelled, "Thank You, God!"

They laughed together, something else they hadn't done much of lately. Then they walked hand in hand back to their house, free from the burden of dread they'd both carried since leaving Bloomington. Along the way they stopped every few yards and kissed, promising to call each other and to pray and to remember the message about joy. It took them half an hour to reach their home, and when they did, Katy felt like they'd been given a second chance not only to survive the coming months but to embrace them.

At the foot of their beach house stairs, Dayne held her close once more. "I'll miss you with every breath."

"When you close your eyes —" she touched her lips to his — "I'll be there. Always."

With that, they moved inside the dark house, up to the bedroom with the patio that overlooked the Pacific. For a long while, they prayed out loud, asking God to protect them and guide them and hasten the time until they could be together again. Then they found their way back into each other's arms and picked up where they'd left off down on the beach. Against the soft crash of the surf, and with Katy's flight just hours away, they shared the night in a fashion that could only be described one way.

With pure, God-given joy.

CHAPTER THIRTEEN

The dinner parties between Kari and Ashley and Brooke and their families were happening more often, and not just when their father asked them over to the Baxter house. With so many young kids between them and with the changes happening in their dad's life, Brooke was glad they were taking the time to get together.

Because when they did, like this October Saturday night, the love that filled Kari and Ryan's house was something Brooke and her sisters and their husbands cherished. The sort of love the Baxter family had always been known for. A love that was — even at this moment — being passed down to the next generation.

Dinner was over, and the three couples were sitting in the living room having coffee. Kari had a sleeping baby Annie in her arms, and Ryan was by her side.

"She's a daddy's girl." Ryan touched his

daughter's dainty chin. "But she's growing up too fast."

Brooke cast a discreet look at Ashley, but her sister only smiled at the comment. Ashley seemed to hold no sorrow over the life of little Anne Elizabeth. The baby's presence had to be a constant reminder of her loss, but Ashley never let on.

"She sure is beautiful." Ashley had her hand on Landon's knee, and she stood and crossed the room. For a few seconds she admired the sleeping baby, then smiled at Kari. "She looks like Mom."

"As long as she doesn't look like me." Ryan grinned at Ashley and then the others. "We don't need a little girl built like a linebacker."

"Although . . ." Peter lifted his finger. "I read in *USA Today* that more girls are getting full-ride soccer scholarships."

"Somehow —" Ryan leaned over his daughter and stared at her, clearly smitten — "I can't picture her playing goalie."

"You'd be surprised." Kari raised an eyebrow at her husband. "Pretty girls play soccer too."

"Yeah!" Maddie came tearing into the room. She put her hands on her hips and stuck out her chin. "I'm pretty, and I play soccer."

"Case in point." Peter leaned back into the sofa.

"Everything okay, baby?" Brooke slid to the edge of the couch and balanced her coffee cup on her knees as she peered at her oldest daughter.

"Actually, no." She gave Ashley an indignant look. "Cole's hogging the crayons, even though I told him that nice boys are supposed to share."

Ashley turned away from baby Annie and made a concerned face. "That's a problem."

" 'Zactly what I told him." Maddie gave a slight humph and tossed her head. "I said he was going to be in big, *biiiig* trouble when I told on him."

"She's nothing but a tattletale!" Cole's voice bellowed from the next room.

Brooke hid her laughter as did Kari, Ryan, and Peter.

Ashley exchanged a look with Landon, and without saying a word, he nodded and stood. "Son, come here, please."

Usually their time together wasn't without a few disagreements. Tonight, with all the kids spread out at a series of tables coloring autumn pictures to decorate their papa Baxter's house, there was bound to be some confusion. Even still, Brooke loved the tradition. For years now, the grandkids would gather at one house and draw pictures of pumpkins and harvest corn, trees with bright leaves of red and orange, and big tom turkeys. The pictures would be hung around the dining room at the Baxter house so the place would be decorated on Thanksgiving.

Now, though, Maddie pinched her lips together and waited for her cousin to enter the room.

Cole came in, eyebrows knit together, hands raised as if he couldn't be more baffled. "I'm coloring Indian corn. I need a lot of colors, so what's the big deal?"

"The big deal is, I'm trying to color my pumpkin but —"

"Shhh." Brooke held her finger to her lips and shook her head at Maddie. "Let Uncle Landon handle this."

Maddie seemed ready to argue, but then she nodded, more prim and proper than before. Every inch the persecuted victim. "Yes, Mommy."

"How many kids are out there?" Landon put his hand on Cole's shoulder.

Cole thought for a minute and began counting with his fingers. "Me and Devin, Hayley and Maddie." He said her name with extra emphasis and shot her a quick look for good measure. "Also Jessie and RJ.

'Course Devin's in his playpen, so that doesn't really count. Which makes five of us actually coloring."

"So if you've got all the crayons at your seat, is that fair to your cousins?"

Cole sneered at Maddie. "She doesn't need all those colors. She only needs orange. Pumpkins are orange."

"But the sky's got a sunset in my picture." Maddie took a few steps closer to Cole. "That's why. Sunsets have a million colors."

The adults in the room nodded, as if they could hardly disagree with that logic.

Landon lowered himself so his face was closer to Cole's. "We talked about this earlier, Son. The people in that room are your very best friends. The best friends you'll ever have."

Cole looked skeptical. "Better than Avery at school?"

"Yes." Landon stood to his full height again and shared a look with Ashley. "Better even than Avery."

Brooke turned her face into Peter's shoulder. The things their kids said . . .

Landon wasn't finished. "When you're eighty years old, your siblings and your cousins will still be your best friends." The adults had agreed long ago what came next. "Now you and Maddie go into the kitchen by yourselves and stay there until you can act like best friends."

Cole's expression fell, but he knew better than to argue. He nodded at Maddie. "Come on. Let's get this over with."

With a last helpless look at Brooke, Maddie followed Cole. Their voices faded as they turned the corner and moved down the hall toward the kitchen.

"Well done." Brooke beamed at Landon. "I love how that boy listens to you."

"He's a good kid." Peter chuckled. "Maddie just has a way of bringing out the worst in him."

"For now." Ashley took her place once more beside Landon. "One day they really will be best friends. All Cole's buddies will think Maddie's the cutest girl at school."

"It's so fun —" Kari kept her voice quieter than the others, since Annie was still sleeping — "watching them grow up and go to school together."

Again Brooke checked Ashley's expression, but her sister's smile didn't waver.

"I only wish Erin and Sam and the girls were here too. Dad would love it if we were all in one place."

"Speaking of Dad . . ." Kari glanced from Ashley to Brooke. "Has he talked to you . . . about Elaine?"

"He called me yesterday." Brooke took hold of Peter's hand and gave him a knowing look. "We weren't really surprised by what he had to say."

"We've been expecting it too." Ryan put his arm around Kari's shoulders and gave the others a sad smile. "I'm happy for him."

Only Ashley looked confused. She faced Landon. "Has he called us?"

"I didn't tell you? Sorry, Ash . . . I thought I told you." Landon cleared his throat. "He called to say he'd been talking to Elaine again, and as long as we didn't object . . . he was thinking of asking her to marry him."

Ashley's face went blank. She tossed her hands in the air. "Great. I'm the last one to know."

"Of course, you're usually the first." Kari grinned at her. "Remember how you knew about Dayne long before the rest of us."

"True." Ashley giggled. "Besides, I knew about this too." She paused, and her silliness faded some. "I had a serious talk with Dad a few weeks ago."

"Don't tell me you talked him into it?" Kari sounded as glad as she did surprised. "He's been moping around since his and Mom's anniversary. I wondered what changed his mind."

Ashley's expression grew tender. "I

235

couldn't stand the thought of him being alone for the next twenty years. That wouldn't bring Mom back."

"And she wouldn't have wanted that for him." Brooke's tone was kind, sympathetic. A year ago, this conversation would've been heated and full of emotion. But enough time had passed now. Their father and Elaine's relationship was something they'd all come to accept.

"So is this the weekend?" Ashley crossed her arms. "Since you're all up to speed on things."

"No." Ryan laughed. Next to him, Annie stirred in Kari's arms. "I don't think he'll move that fast. He told us he still has a lot to consider."

"I guess just the fact that they're dating again is something he wanted to run by us." Peter nodded. "We told him we're all okay with it."

From the kitchen, they heard Maddie giggling. "Stop it, Coley." The two kids appeared in the doorway, holding hands. "Okay, Mommy." Maddie flashed her sweetest smile. "Me and Coley are best friends again. Only he keeps tickling me."

Cole grinned at Landon. "Because making girls laugh is the best way to make up."

The guys in the room mumbled their

agreement.

Brooke pointed to the adjacent room. "Okay, how about you join the others."

"And this time she can have every shade of sunset she wants." Cole wiped his forehead with the back of his hand. "Girls are so much work."

"You got that right." Peter's response was quick. Then just as fast, he gave Brooke a worried look.

Everyone in the room laughed, including Brooke. She couldn't be upset with him. Instead she could only look at him and marvel at how far they'd come since the days after Hayley's near drowning. Back then she had been convinced that she and Peter would never again share an easy night of love and laughter like this one. It was proof that God hadn't only spared their daughter with the miracle of her life.

He had spared their entire family.

They were still laughing when the phone rang. Kari was sitting next to the end table, so she handed Annie to Ryan and reached for the receiver. With one hand pressed against her ear, she brought the phone to the other. "Hello?"

There was a pause on the other end. "Sounds like everyone's having a pretty good time without me." Happiness rang in Erin's tone, and she laughed too. "You have the whole gang over?"

"Pretty much." Kari motioned to the others. "It's Erin!"

A chorus of hellos broke out across the room.

"We had dinner together. Now we're refereeing for the kids."

"Ah . . . my full-time job!"

"Exactly." Kari laughed again. With all the noise, Annie stirred once more, and this time she opened her eyes. "Oops. I woke the baby."

"Glad to know I'm not the only one." Erin sounded easygoing and full of joy. "So . . . I have a question."

"Okay." The others quieted down. "Want me to put you on speakerphone?"

"Sure." Erin seemed like she could barely contain herself.

Kari pushed a button on the base of the phone, then hung up the receiver. "You're on."

"All right, here's my question." Erin hesitated. "If you have these big dinner parties next year, can you add another table for the kids?"

Kari met Ashley's eyes, then Brooke's. "Meaning what? You have us all on the edge of our seats."

"Meaning . . ." Erin let out a squeal. "Sam's been transferred to the office in Indianapolis — effective June 1, next year!"

She barely got her sentence out before the room burst into cheers and applause. Ashley and Brooke jumped up and hurried across the room so they could be closer to the phone.

"You're serious?" Ashley tucked her hair behind her ears and leaned over the table. "That isn't something to joke about."

"Of course I'm serious. I've been praying about this since the day we left!"

Ashley let out a happy scream, and she threw her arms around Brooke's shoulders and then Kari's. In the confusion of the moment, Annie began to cry, and that quickly became an all-out piercing wail.

"Well, I better let you go. We can talk more later." Erin's laughter rang out loud and clear on the tinny telephone speaker. "Couldn't wait to share the news!"

Despite Annie's cries, the room erupted into more shouts of congratulations.

Kari took Annie into her arms once more. "I have a hungry one. Be back in a little while." She cradled Annie against her chest and hurried down the hall to the bedroom she shared with Ryan. She enjoyed nursing her babies, and Annie was an especially good eater. She situated herself in the rocking chair near the window and helped Annie get comfortable.

Kari touched her daughter's cheeks. "God's working out all the details, little girl. Even the ones we can't see."

She thought about Ashley. Her sister was handling the absence of Sarah better than any of them could've imagined. She doted on Annie and was genuinely happy for Kari and Ryan. One day, if God so willed, Ashley would have another little girl. Kari prayed every morning for that to happen. She also prayed for her brothers — both of whom were struggling in different ways. But here was one prayer definitely answered. Erin and Sam were moving back to the area next summer!

Kari was so happy she had to blink back tears. Somewhere in heaven, she could only hope her mother might share in the joy of all that was happening. There were details that needed to fall into place, babies that were hopefully yet to be born, and marriages that needed some work. Maybe even a wedding somewhere in the future. But today Kari could do nothing but rejoice. Because though they didn't quite have the happy ending they were praying for, one

thing was very clear tonight.
It was within view.

Chapter Fourteen

Landon was playing hearts with three other firemen at the Bloomington fire station and trying to get off the phone.

"Come on, Blake," Seth, his buddy across from him, raised his hand in the air and let it fall to the table, exasperated. "You're on the phone more than a teenager."

Landon covered the receiver and whispered, "Wait a minute." Then he shot the other two a similar look. "I'm almost off!"

"Sure . . . sure." The fireman to his right set his cards facedown, stood, and stretched. "I'm getting a cup of coffee. Five o'clock puts me to sleep."

On the other end of the line were Ryan and Peter, Landon's brothers-in-law. The three of them were trying to work out the details of a fishing trip. John was joining them, but he'd already given his input. Any Saturday in the next month worked fine for him.

"I say we go this week." Peter laughed. "Otherwise it gets too cold for Ryan."

"Are you kidding?" Ryan was quick with his response. "I've spent half my life on the gridiron. You don't know cold until you've been laid out on a frozen football field."

"Okay, but we're not talking about ice fishing." Peter hesitated, and there was the faint sound of calendar pages turning. "Let's not take this thing into November."

Landon was about to say that he agreed with Peter. The coming weekend would work best, and if they made the trip later in the day, Cole could come with them. His soccer game was at ten o'clock, which meant they could be on the shore of Lake Monroe by noon with the whole afternoon ahead of them.

But before he could say anything, the fire alarm went off. The whir of the siren and its rhythm told them immediately what they were up against.

"Structure fire, gentlemen." One of the guys at the table dropped his cards and pulled his radio from his pocket. On the other end a dispatcher was already giving out the address.

"Gotta go." Landon shut his phone and hurried with the others out the door and into the garage, where their turnouts hung on hooks adjacent to the fire trucks. The call was for both units, so at the same time four firefighters from the other side of the firehouse were streaming into the garage.

Landon was the designated paramedic tonight, and even though so far the call didn't involve medical, he would need to be one of the first at the scene. His fingers moved nimbly, securing his uniform and tightening his chin strap. He climbed into the driver's side as the heavy-duty garage door lifted. "Where are we going?"

Seth took the seat beside him. He was the lieutenant on duty, the one in charge of corresponding with dispatch and making sure they knew where they were headed. "Walnut south toward Ruel Highway." They had a GPS, but the firefighters at the Bloomington station had worked there for years. They knew the roads faster without punching in the address.

Already the siren was blaring, and Landon whipped the fire truck west down 4th Street. He was turning left on College when Seth barked a few more questions at dispatch. Then he turned to Landon. "It's one of the old farmhouses on Dillman Road. Make a left just before the highway."

Dillman Road? Landon's heart skipped a beat, then slammed into double time. The

Baxter house was on Dillman Road. But it couldn't be. . . . The old road had dozens of homes on acreages. There was no reason to think the call was for —

Seth rattled off the street number and stopped short. "Blake, that's the Baxter place. I'm sure of it."

The address was still screaming through Landon's mind. "Yes. It is." The Baxter house, the one Ashley and her siblings had grown up in, was on fire. At this hour, John Baxter might be home. Ashley might even be inside, working on her painting. If she was, the kids would be there too. Downstairs watching TV, no doubt. *Dear God, help us.* He tightened his hold on the steering wheel and did the only thing he could do without actually being on the scene.

He prayed.

John's shift at the hospital had been lighter than usual. Mondays were rounds at the hospital and only a handful of patients in the office. A flu was going around, and a few newborns needed checkups. At the hospital he stopped in to see Brooke's patient Ethan Teeple. The boy was still in grave condition, but his smile always warmed John's heart. If anyone could fight leukemia, it was Ethan. John prayed for the boy often.

He headed out of the hospital parking lot and turned east on 2nd Street. He was just reaching College when two fire trucks tore through the intersection headed south. John pulled over, waiting until the emergency vehicles had cleared the path. *Be with them, God. Please be with them.*

He'd always prayed for the city's firemen because they needed all the help they could get. But he prayed especially now that he had a son-in-law who worked for the department. He tried to remember if Landon was on duty today.

The traffic moved back into the various lanes, and John turned right on College. He settled into a steady pace and stretched his left leg out. The weekend had been nice — better than he could've hoped, really. He and Elaine had gone out to dinner both Friday night and Saturday. He smiled at the memory. She forgave him. Maybe that was the strangest part of all.

After Ashley's talk, he had called Elaine and explained that he was sorry. "I'm confused. There's no other way to say it," he told her.

John held the steering wheel with one hand and stayed even with the traffic around him. The fire trucks and sirens were too far ahead to be seen. Again he smiled to himself. He still couldn't believe Elaine's reaction to his apology that night. One other time he'd tried to back out of their friendship, and she'd reacted the same way. That time it had also been Ashley who found a way to bring them together during the final stages of the project to bring Katy and Dayne's house up to par.

Since then, things had been great until his and Elizabeth's anniversary. "I guess I started second-guessing myself," he told Elaine.

Instead of being angry, she had nothing but compassion in her tone. "I understand. I would wonder about you if you weren't second-guessing yourself. You've already loved so fully in your life. Maybe once is enough." Her empathy filled his heart and doubled his feelings for her.

John kept his eyes on the road, enjoying the familiar drive. It wasn't dark yet, and the leaves were brilliant oranges and reds. Against the blue sky, the picture was stunning. Only then did John notice a plume of black smoke in the distance.

He kept on, past Winslow Road, and as he neared Rhorer, he could see the smoke more clearly, in the direction of his house. He felt the first ripple of concern. Was it

247

one of his neighbors? The black plume was thick enough that it was most definitely a house fire. John had seen a few of them over the years, enough to recognize the volume and height of the rush of smoke.

He drove by Church Lane, and as Walnut curved to the right, he kept his peripheral vision on the billowing smoke. *Dear God, protect the people inside. Please . . .*

But there was no comforting response this time, only the pressing urgency to drive faster, to get home and see how close the fire was to his house. He took the shortcut down Empire Road and turned left onto Dillman. What he saw then took his breath. The fire trucks were barely visible, up the road a quarter mile or so. But there was no mistaking which house was on fire.

It was his.

He pressed his foot harder on the gas pedal and sped into his driveway in time to see red flames pushing through the roof near the back of the house. Two fire trucks were angled into the end of the driveway, and as John drove up and parked, he saw that half a dozen men were dousing the house with water.

His heart thudded against his chest, pounding out a rhythm of barely controlled panic. In his role as doctor, John had been in too many emergency situations to count. But here . . . with his house and all he held dear going up in flames before his eyes, he could barely breathe as he raced up the driveway.

He was halfway to the house when Landon came running toward him. He ripped off his helmet, his face stricken. "I can't reach Ashley. I've already been through the house, but I can't find her."

"She isn't here." John was certain. He'd talked to her half an hour ago. "She's at the mall getting clothes for Devin."

Landon's body sagged with visible relief, but his face was grim. "I need you to stay here by your car, okay?" He lifted his helmet and took a few backward steps. "We're doing the best we can. It looks like it's contained in the attic." He hurried off toward the others.

Please, God. John's prayer was more of a desperate cry. *Help them save the place.* He stared at the house, at the thick, dark smoke pouring out of the far section of the roof. That was the area over the garage, so maybe . . . maybe the structure could be saved.

His eyes never left the building, but he wasn't seeing his house in flames on a perfect fall evening. He was seeing it the way it would always look — alive and warm with light and laughter and conversation. With Elizabeth and him walking around the back near the creek and Cole stooping low near the pond catching tadpoles. With a Christmas tree in the front window and carols being sung from the living room.

John had no idea how much time passed, but with every minute the flames lessened and then finally disappeared altogether. Still the firefighters poured water on the roof, two of them from positions high on ladders that extended from their trucks.

From the time he and Elizabeth bought this house, they'd been grateful for the fire hydrant. There weren't many along Dillman Road, but the one the firemen were using now sat right at the end of his driveway. Without it, the firefighters would've had to connect hoses from two or three houses away, and they would've certainly lost the Baxter house in the process.

One after another his kids began arriving. Ashley must've called Kari and Brooke, and in no time the whole family knew, the way they always knew about any event that affected one of them. The looks on their faces broke his heart. They huddled in a small bunch — Ashley and the boys, Kari and Ryan and their kids, and Brooke. Peter had stayed home with the girls, and Luke was away on business again. Reagan called, though, and John promised to let her know how things turned out. Ashley took care of calling Dayne and Katy and Erin and Sam and leaving them messages.

"Has anyone been inside?" Ashley had tears on her cheeks. "Tell me we can still save it."

Smoke hung thick in the air, and before John could answer her, Landon trudged over. He had smears of soot along both cheeks, and his eyes were bloodshot. "God was with us. I could feel Him today."

John was afraid to ask, but Brooke stepped up and searched Landon's face. "Is any of it salvageable?"

"Yeah, Daddy." Cole had his arm around Ashley's waist. His eyes were wide with fear and admiration for his father. "You saved it, right?"

Despite the exhaustion in his expression, Landon's face lit up with the most wonderful smile. "We sure did, buddy." He turned to John. "We contained it completely. When the house was built, someone used firewall material to separate the attic from the garage." He wiped his hand across his brow and coughed a few times. "It was an inferno in the attic, and the garage is flooded. But

251

the rest of the house only has minimal smoke damage."

The words washed over him. *Minimal smoke damage?* The entire place had looked like an inferno when he pulled into the driveway. John wanted to close the distance between himself and his son-in-law and wrap him in a big hug. But Cole and Ashley and Devin surrounded him, and Landon was already backing up, needing to return to the other firefighters. Instead John stuck his hands in his pockets and grinned at Landon. "You know what this means?"

"Yeah . . . I get first dibs on bait this Saturday."

John laughed. "Exactly."

After the fire trucks left and the other family members had gone home, John and Landon went into the house and moved from one room to the other, opening windows. Miraculously, Landon's assessment was accurate. The smell of smoke was strong in the house, but nothing was charred and there was no permanent damage.

"You can get a cleaning crew out here, and the place'll be as good as new."

"That and a new roof and attic." John shook his head, astounded at all the firefighters had salvaged. "Who made the call?"

"The neighbor on your right. Mrs.

McCarry. She was canning blueberries when she looked out the window and saw smoke."

John reminded himself to visit Edna McCarry and thank her.

Landon was explaining the rest of the story. "If she'd been another few minutes later, we would've lost the whole house. It was that close."

"What caused it?" John couldn't imagine how a fire would've started in his attic. He hadn't been up there for a year at least.

"Looks like a wiring problem. Probably a few squirrels in the attic. Once they start gnawing at wires, the situation gets danger-ous pretty quickly." Landon directed John back outside and around the house to the side where the damage was the greatest. "You'll need new siding on most of this wall, but mostly because of smoke and water damage to the exterior. Of course, you'll need a new interior on your garage."

"But the insurance will cover that."

"Tell you what . . . how about you get your things and stay with us tonight. You'll need a few days for the smoke to clear from the inside."

Emotion welled up in John's chest, and he studied Landon, overwhelmed. This time he hugged him hard, the way men hugged each other after surviving a battle together. John had cared about Landon long before Ashley let down her guard enough to love him. Suddenly as he held tight to Landon, John could see the young man again the way he'd looked in the hospital room years ago, the day he went into a burning house and saved the life of a little boy. Landon had nearly died, but God had other plans — plans for Landon to marry Ashley, to be a father to Cole, and to raise a family with her.

And even plans for him to save the Baxter house.

John stepped back and found his voice again. "You go ahead and join your family. I'll be over in half an hour."

When Landon was gone, John stood outside and studied the section of his roof that had been destroyed by the flames. In a month, with new paint and roofing, new drywall in the garage, no one would ever know the fire had happened. Tears stung his eyes for the first time that night, and he covered his face. *Thank You, God. You spared my home, my memories.*

A voice clear and distinct whispered deep inside him, *My dear son, all good things are from God. . . . Your memories are not contained in a building. They are a gift you carry with you.*

Gradually, a certainty filled John's soul, and he stayed there, his face covered, while the answer worked its way through him. He'd been fretting almost constantly about his home, wondering how he could move forward in his relationship with Elaine when to do so might mean giving up the old Baxter house.

But now, on the evening when the place almost burned to the ground, God had given him wisdom to understand what the walls and ceilings and flooring really meant. He dropped his hands to his sides and moved to the edge of the house. Then he put his fingers against the siding and ran his thumb along the rough painted exterior. Wood and cement and glass and roofing tile. That's what the place amounted to.

He gripped the piece of siding and closed his eyes. God wanted him to understand something today. His memories did not need a house in order to stay vibrantly alive. They would live inside him as long as he had a heartbeat. If the Baxter place had burned to the ground, his memories would not have gone up in smoke. They might lose photographs, but the pictures Elizabeth had trained him to take — the mental pictures — would live on as long as he had the ability to remember.

No kitchen table was needed to see the look on Elizabeth's face when she returned from taking one or another of their kids to their first day of kindergarten. And John didn't need the front door to see her breezing into the house, her arms full of groceries, her eyes dancing with light and life. The house was warm and lovely, and he was fond of it the way he might be fond of a best friend. But suddenly, with every cell in his body, he knew he didn't need the wood and beams to be happy.

He needed his children and grandchildren. And he needed the woman who had become his dearest companion. He patted the piece of siding and took a few steps back. He would ask Elaine to marry him. Then, if she said yes, he would do what he'd been dreading for months.

He would put the Baxter house up for sale.

CHAPTER FIFTEEN

Dayne had been in Mexico for nearly two weeks when the one-day break in action happened. Now he was in a rented Suburban, driving back from the airport with Luke riding shotgun next to him. His brother was in high spirits, and Dayne was looking forward to their time together.

"This is the life." Luke's window was rolled down, and he breathed in deep. "You can smell the ocean air from here."

"It's so much warmer than it is in LA." Dayne felt a lazy grin tug at his lips. "Makes me want to bring Katy back here when the movie wraps."

Luke leaned back in his seat. "Yeah, how are things with Katy? I mean, really?"

"Not as bad as the tabloids want you to think." The laughter left Dayne's voice. It was like this every time he had a conversation with someone he knew well. Especially family. Everyone wanted to know what truth

— if any — was in the stories dominating the headlines. Trying to convince everyone all the time got old, like everything about his role as a celebrity.

"I sort of wondered." Luke made a nervous face. "I mean, it can't be easy telling Randi Wells you're not interested."

Dayne lowered his brow. Luke's comment seemed strangely out of place. After all, he was a Baxter. He'd been raised to be a man of God, a faithful husband. "It's pretty easy when you know where your priorities are." Dayne glanced at him. "Put yourself in my place."

Luke shook his head and gave a dramatic huff. "That's what I mean. I wouldn't want to be in your place. Way too much temptation."

Dayne kept his eyes on the road ahead, but he had a sinking feeling that Luke and Reagan might be in even more trouble than he'd guessed. Before he could bring it up, Luke asked another question, keeping the attention on Dayne. "So how often do you talk, you and Katy?"

"The goal is several times a week." Dayne was distracted by Luke's attitude. "It's tough because it's seven hours ahead in London. I finish shooting for the day, and it's usually the very early hours of the morning there. By the time she's up and moving around, I'm usually in bed."

"But she's . . . you know, she's okay with all the stuff people are saying about you and Randi?"

Dayne was beginning to feel irritated. "Let's get one thing straight." He peered out the window at the blue sky and puffy white clouds, at the swaying palm trees and expanse of ocean. "This might feel like a paradise island, but to me it's a movie set. Randi and I have nothing going on." He allowed a sarcastic laugh. "The director's worried we don't have *enough* chemistry."

"But . . . you and Randi . . . you used to date, right?"

"That was a lifetime ago." He held his breath and released it in a rush. "The tabloids think this movie shoot will be the death of my marriage. But it won't be. Katy and I are stronger than ever."

"The magazines run photos of you and Randi every week."

"Of course." Dayne laughed so he wouldn't yell at Luke before their visit even really got started. "We're starring in a movie together. Every time we stand next to each other someone takes our picture." He lifted one eyebrow. "That doesn't mean we're having a thing."

259

Luke stopped the rapid-fire questions after that. The ocean came fully into view, and the warm, humid air from the gulf washed over them. "I could spend ten weeks here, no problem."

Dayne gave Luke another strange look. "If I closed my eyes, I wouldn't believe that was you beside me."

"Don't close your eyes." He nodded at the road ahead of him. It was a single lane and gravel. "That wouldn't be good for either of us."

"I'm serious." Dayne could hear an edge of anger in his voice. "Maybe the better question is, how are you and Reagan?"

The sound of the Suburban's tires crunching over the gravel was all they heard for more than a minute. Finally Luke exhaled like someone utterly defeated and looked at Dayne. "We aren't good."

"Yeah . . . I had a feeling." Dayne patted his brother's knee. His anger faded. If things weren't good between his brother and his wife, then no wonder Luke was acting so strange. "Tell me about it."

The gravel road opened up to an unpaved parking lot. Dayne pulled the Suburban into one of the first spots and killed the engine. He turned so he could see Luke better.

"I don't know." Luke wore sunglasses, so

there was no reading his eyes. But his tone sounded more heartfelt than it had since Dayne picked him up at the airport. "I want things to be like they were, but . . . with the kids and our hectic pace, it doesn't seem like there's any way back."

"You said you were traveling more?" This was strange to Dayne because Luke worked exclusively on Dayne's interests. The job shouldn't have required much travel, unless Dayne needed him during times like this.

"It's the higher-ups in New York. They treat me better since you're my client. I get invited to seminars and big meetings, that sort of thing."

Dayne rested his elbow on the steering wheel. "Trips like that are optional. You should know that."

"Not really, not if . . ." Luke's voice trailed off. He removed his sunglasses and stared at Dayne through eyes that looked dead and closed off. If the eyes were windows to the soul — and Dayne knew they were — then Luke's windows were sealed shut. He turned his gaze to the windshield. "You're right. I don't have to go."

"Is that what you tell Reagan?" Dayne hated where this was headed. "Because that's not fair, man. I mean, she's probably wishing I'd cut you some slack."

Luke said nothing in response, which told Dayne he was right.

"Look, I'm sorry things aren't great." Dayne put his hand on Luke's shoulder. "We can talk about it more tonight, okay?"

Already it was nearly time for dinner, and Dayne had to check back in. He was finished shooting for the night, and he had tomorrow off, but there were always dailies that needed viewing. The director was working with Randi in the afternoon, but she'd asked if she could meet Luke. Apparently since her divorce, her husband had kept their attorney, and she needed a new one.

Dayne had planned to introduce them over dinner. The catering company was barbecuing chicken on the beach tonight. But as they walked into the camp, Randi was talking to the director, and she turned and spotted them. She wore a peach-colored bikini top with a flimsy white gauze shirt unbuttoned over it. Her black shorts were skintight and just long enough to not be considered part of her bathing suit.

While they walked, Dayne caught a glimpse of Luke checking out Randi in a way that even a single guy shouldn't. "Put your eyes back into your head," he said quietly. "I'll introduce you; then I'll show you to your room."

"Sounds good." Luke swung his overnight bag onto his shoulder and stayed at Dayne's side while they went down the path toward Randi and the director.

"Dayne! You've been gone too long. I have a hundred questions for you." Randi ran to him and gave him a quick hug and a kiss on his cheek. She glanced over her shoulder at the director. "You have questions, right?"

The young man was from Spain and had a brilliant eye for making unforgettable films. He looked at his clipboard and flipped a few pages. "Not really." He winked at her. "You answered all of them." He moved up the path a ways to a group of assistants.

Dayne knew that Randi had noticed Luke the moment they stepped out of the Suburban. But she waited until now to turn her attention to him. A look of surprise crossed her face. "Dayne, you didn't tell me your brother was a twin. Introduce me already!"

"Right." Dayne felt suddenly awkward. "Randi, this is my brother, Luke Baxter."

"My, my." Her smile was demure and subtle, but her interest in Luke was clear. "You're sure a sight for sore eyes."

Dayne studied his brother, watching for inappropriate behavior. Thankfully, Luke didn't react overtly to her flirting. Instead he nodded politely. "And you're Randi

263

Wells." His eyes held hers maybe a beat too long, and he smiled. "Nice to meet you."

"Yes." Randi shook his hand and kept his fingers tucked in hers. "Tell me you're a new addition to our cast." Then she raised an eyebrow. "Wait! You're the lawyer Dayne's been talking about!"

Luke smiled, as if he were used to receiving this attention from Hollywood stars. "I am." He kept his cool. There was no gushiness, none of the awestruck fan attitude he'd exuded earlier in the SUV. Now he was calm, beyond collected. "I handle Dayne's affairs."

"Lucky you." She sent a teasing look Dayne's way. "I've tried handling Dayne's affairs a number of times." Her tone took on a mock disappointment. "But he won't let me."

Dayne was sure Randi wasn't talking about legal affairs. She was too bright to make that innuendo unintentionally. He averted his eyes and kept all his attention on his brother. "Luke's a good lawyer. Handling everything just fine."

Randi looked from Luke to Dayne and back again. "You two seriously could be twins." She touched Luke's arm. "Hang around here very long and they'll make you a body double for Dayne." She tilted her face, studying his features. "You might even be the better-looking brother, Luke Baxter."

A slightly strange silence followed, and Dayne could read the interest in Luke's eyes, even if he wasn't saying anything.

"Well —" Randi crossed her arms, her eyes still locked on Luke's — "let's sit together at dinner. Give me your best pitch. Maybe you could handle my affairs too." She touched Luke's arm once more, and her eyes held a deeper meaning. With that, she took a few steps and waved at Luke. "See you in an hour . . . out on the beach, okay?"

Luke shrugged, uncertain, but his face lit up with his smile. "Sure. See you there."

After she was gone and out of earshot, Luke set his bag down and let his shoulders slump forward a little. He breathed out, as if he'd been holding his breath since she walked up.

Dayne started walking down the path again. He wanted to scream at Luke, tell him he'd looked way too friendly, too inviting. But he swallowed his frustration. "Come on. I need to get you to your room."

Luke hadn't really crossed any lines. Besides, Dayne wouldn't let Luke out of his sight, so there was no real danger anything would happen between him and Randi.

Even so, this was one more bit of trouble Dayne hadn't asked for. One more trial. No question, before he went to bed he'd need to do something he hadn't done in a week.

Reread the verses about joy.

If he was honest with himself, Luke hadn't thought about Reagan or the kids more than a few passing times since he arrived at the set. He'd been excited about meeting Randi Wells — mostly because she was a beautiful celebrity, and now he — Luke Baxter — had access to that world. But he hadn't counted on Randi being interested in him. Not in his wildest dreams.

It was after nine o'clock, the sky long since dark, and he was seated between Randi and Dayne at what had become a beach bonfire. He was barefoot and wore khaki shorts, a white T-shirt, and Dayne's Baja California baseball cap, the one he'd borrowed earlier when the sun first started setting. Dayne had told him to keep it. The cast and crew had all received a hat when they checked into their rooms at the beginning of the shoot.

Luke pushed his toes deep into the sand. It was hard to believe this was really his life, practicing law from a beachfront movie location somewhere in Mexico. Away from home, things were better than he ever could've dreamed. He surveyed the others gathered in groups of two or three around the fire. A few members of the cast were roasting marshmallows, lost in quiet conversations. Dayne was talking about the TV show *For Real* and how it should be against the law to produce something so false and call it reality when they were approached by the movie's director and one of the producers, guys Luke had met earlier.

"Matthews, we were looking at dailies from earlier this week. Brilliant stuff, man." The director put his hand on Dayne's shoulder.

"You got a minute, though?" The producer nodded toward the beach bungalow that was serving as the editing room. Luke had heard about it in a tour of the set before dinner. The producer made a concerned face at Dayne. "We want you to see something. The way the lighting's falling on you, we might want a few retakes from the other day."

"Or maybe you'll like it." The director started walking up the beach. "Come take a look. It'll just take a minute."

"You got it." Dayne glanced at Luke. He leaned closer so no one else could hear him. "Don't do anything I wouldn't do."

267

Luke laughed, and he managed to sound relaxed. He gripped both armrests of the chaise lounge he was stretched across. "Come on." He kept his voice low. "Be serious." On the other side of Luke, Randi was talking to someone else.

Dayne stood and gave Luke a wary look. "I am serious," he mouthed. He waved his thumb in Randi's direction and whispered, "She's trouble."

Another ripple of easy laughter came from Luke. "Go get your work done."

The men were already several yards ahead of Dayne, headed to the bungalow. Dayne held Luke's eyes a few seconds longer. "Be right back."

"Okay." Luke turned toward the fire and tried to believe this was really happening, that he was really here rubbing elbows with top movie stars. More than that, he wasn't a visitor or a fan on the set. He was part of the crew — the lawyer for Dayne Matthews.

It was heady stuff but not nearly as heady as what had happened during dinner. Dayne had been talking to a few of the other crew members, and Luke was in line getting his chicken when Randi had walked up. She stopped inches from him and leaned close to his ear. "Sit next to me at the bonfire, okay?" She gave him a look that could only be described as direct. "You intrigue me, Luke Baxter. I want to get to know you better."

That was all, nothing more until someone lit the fire and a few guys set canvas chairs around the circle. Luke was walking over, Dayne right beside him, when Randi came up and linked arms with him. "Don't forget, Luke. I've got the seat beside you."

But since they'd circled around the fire, Randi had seemed distracted by another conversation until Dayne left. Even before he reached the bungalow, Randi turned to Luke. She leaned her head back, and for a while she smiled at him, her face lit by the glow of the flames. She was sipping what was maybe her third glass of wine, and she looked a little more than relaxed. "We should've met a long time ago." Her voice wasn't slurred, but it was softer than before, meant for only him.

"We should have." Luke wasn't sure what to say or how to take her. Was she coming on to him, or was this part of her act, how she treated everyone on the set? Or maybe her interest was just her way of making him feel welcome. He focused on the reason he was here. "As legal work goes, this is a great place for business." He studied her face. "Dayne says you're looking for a new attorney."

"I am." Some of her over-the-top giddiness disappeared, and she looked more like a lost little girl than a famous movie star. She crossed her arms and stared into the fire pit. "That's not what I meant."

A strange swirling began in Luke's stomach. Butterflies tickled at his insides and made him shift in his seat, suddenly uncomfortable.

He didn't have to squirm long before Randi turned to him again. "Walk with me." She held out her hand, and her expression was utterly innocent. "I meant what I said. I'd like to get to know you better." She stood and gave him a gentle pull until he was on his feet. As she did, she looked over her shoulder toward the bungalow where Dayne was getting in a few minutes of work. "Don't worry about what your brother said." Her smile was sweet and a little shy. "I won't get you in trouble. I just want to hear more about you."

Luke's head was spinning, but he could hardly argue with her. After all, she wasn't making any hidden or overt suggestions. She was merely asking him to take a walk. Her hand in his sent chills down his legs, and he thought about Reagan. "Well . . ." He released Randi's fingers and casually wiped his palms on his shorts. He could take a walk with her, but he couldn't hold her hand. Dayne could come out of the bungalow at any minute. If he saw Luke holding Randi's hand, he'd chase them down and drag Luke back to his chair.

They walked toward the water and headed up the beach to the right, where the stretch of sand was pitch-dark.

When they were well out of visibility from the people around the fire, Randi hugged herself and slowed her pace. "We could walk for miles this way and not run into anyone." She lifted her face to the sky and the millions of stars that were visible now that they weren't near the light of the fire. "The location guys did a great job with this one. We're supposed to be in the middle of nowhere." She smiled at him, and again she looked shy. "And we are."

Luke swallowed. "It sure feels that way." A part of him screamed that he should turn around, lead her back the other way, where they'd at least be closer to people. But a more compelling part wanted to play this out, to see what Randi wanted to talk about and why she felt the need to walk where the beach was more remote.

They were another fifty yards down the beach, Randi making small talk about her

271

love of Mexico and the warmth of the people, when the cell phone in her jean shorts rang. She stopped, and a concerned look flashed on her face. "My mom's been trying to reach me. I better take this." She pulled the phone out, snapped it open, and turned toward the water. "Hello?"

For a few seconds, Randi stayed frozen that way, listening. Then she brought her fingers to her mouth and gave a few quick shakes of her head. "No, Mama, you can't be." Her breath caught in her throat, and she uttered a slight cry. "No . . . I can't leave here this week. You know that. . . ." She managed a few more short sentences before she hung up and dropped the phone back into her pocket.

Luke crossed his arms and hesitated, not sure what to say. "You wanna be alone?"

"No." She hung her head, her body still facing the water. "My mom . . . she has cancer. We lost my dad to it more than a year ago, and now . . . I can't believe it." She lifted one shoulder. There were tears in her voice when she tried to talk this time. "My mom says it's very fast moving. She only has a few weeks. I have to get home as soon as possible."

An image of his mother lying in bed those last days before her death filled Luke's mind. "My mom died of cancer." He kept his distance, but he wanted her to feel his comfort. "It's a terrible thing. She was in her fifties. Way too young to die."

"My dad was the same. Just fifty-seven."

Luke groaned. "I'm sorry. There's no easy way to get through something like that."

"But you've been there." Randi turned to him, studying his face as if she might find some answer to the pain in her heart. "You know what it's like."

"I do." He couldn't help but move closer to her. She was hurting, racked by a type of pain Luke knew too well. With his thumb he brushed her blonde hair back from her face. "You and your mom are close?"

"Not really. I was closer to my dad. He was the best man in the world." She smiled at him, but her eyes glistened with unshed tears. "Strong believer, great family man." Without making any obvious move, she seemed to be closer than before, just inches from him. "Before he got sick, he could always make me laugh. Even in the midst of my marriage falling apart." She blinked and a pair of tears slid down her cheeks. "I always figured I'd get closer to my mom later, when we were both older. Only now . . ."

Without giving his actions any thought,

without meaning anything other than a show of comfort, Luke pulled her close and hugged her. "I'm sorry, Randi." He allowed their embrace to continue, and as he did, she began to cry. The wine might've affected her emotions, made it easier for her to break down. But the moment wasn't about being drunk or about a one-night stand or even a bit of flirting. It was nothing of the kind. Luke was merely there for her at the right time, right place. Offering Randi the very thing he had needed when his mother was dying.

Someone who understood.

Dayne wasn't gone ten minutes, but as he returned to his place around the fire, his stomach fell to his knees. Luke was gone. Randi too. He didn't want to draw attention to the pair, didn't want some gofer to hear his concerns and alert the paparazzi. People on the set felt no guilt in passing tips to cameramen. The tabloids paid big money for insider information, and photographers representing all the major magazines were staying at a hotel a few miles away.

No, Dayne couldn't bring attention to the matter. Instead he walked slowly toward the water. What was wrong with his brother, anyway? The thing he loved about the Baxter family was that they were the kind of people Hollywood knew nothing about. They loved God and their families, and they found a way to make everyday life something worth seeking after, something worth finding, whatever the cost.

But here was Luke Baxter, off somewhere with Randi Wells, while his wife and babies waited for him at home in Indiana. Dayne kept walking until he was out of the glare of the bonfire. Then he peered down the beach in either direction. But even as his eyes adjusted, he saw nothing, no sign of them.

God, stop him from doing anything he'll regret. Dayne breathed the prayer, but as he walked back up the sandy slope toward the fire, he felt more defeated than he had all week. He missed Katy. Tonight he would stay up as late as he had to in order to find a few minutes when they could talk. Dayne considered how the evening might go, and he realized a late night might be just what was needed. Not only for the precious few minutes with Katy, but so he could babysit his brother.

He frowned as he dropped into his beach chair. Of course, that was providing Luke and Randi even found their way back to the bonfire at all.

CHAPTER SIXTEEN

John had been this nervous only a handful
of times. He and Elaine were driving to Red
Lobster — nothing overly fancy, but John
had reserved their favorite booth, the one in
the corner of the back room. That way
they'd have more privacy. But he wasn't going to ask the question there of all places.
After dinner he would take her to the
Indiana University campus, and they'd
walk. Somewhere along the way, he was
praying God would give him the nerve to
make his move.

As he drove, he remembered how different things had been decades ago when he
asked Elizabeth to marry him. By then
they'd been through so much together, they
felt like they'd been married five years. Elizabeth had gotten pregnant and had a baby,
and she'd been sent away and forced to give
up the child without either of them having
a say in the situation.

By the time she came home and they were allowed to be together again, the marriage certificate was more a formality. Nothing could've made them closer than the consequences of their actions already had.

Tonight was entirely different.

John was in his sixties, and a small voice kept insisting that the idea of remarriage at his age was ridiculous. But every time his thoughts took that turn, he remembered what Ashley had told him: *"Mom would've wanted you to live. . . ."* And then his mind would drift to one of the letters Elizabeth had written to him.

He'd read it so many times that he knew the important parts; they played in his heart one more time as he focused on the road ahead. *We're not as young as we once were,* she'd written, *and I want you to know, whatever happens in the years to come, you must choose life. We both must. Every day we wake up with another twenty-four hours.*

"Lots on your mind?" Elaine had her hands folded neatly over her purse, which lay on her lap. She wore dark slacks and a pretty wool sweater woven with fall colors. Her hair looked nice, as usual, but he had a feeling she'd done something special with it today.

"I guess so." John reached out and took

hold of her hand. His voice was gentle, and his heart beat hard in anticipation of all the night held. "You look pretty. I don't think I told you yet."

She smiled, and with his hand in hers, she seemed to relax a little. "I had my hair done today."

"I thought so." He surveyed her. "You don't look a day over thirty-five."

"Credit the darkness for that." She laughed and looked out the window. As her laughter faded, she turned to him again. "How are the repairs coming?"

"It's been eleven days since the fire." John liked this, the diversion from the velvet box in his pocket. He focused on his answer. "A construction company's already gutted the garage. Took it down to bare beams. Then a few days ago I had an electrician in. He's rewiring the attic and the garage walls, but he's checking the whole house too."

"It was squirrels, right? That's what they found?"

"Yes. There was a vent on the back side of the house a few feet from one of the old maple trees. Apparently there was a family of squirrels in the tree that probably got in through the vent last winter."

John explained how the electrician had taken him up into the attic and shown him the animal droppings and matted fur and the gnawed wires not far away. "It could happen to anyone. The electrician said people with attics should check them for animals a couple times a year."

"I need to have mine checked."

"Anyway . . ." They were almost to the restaurant, and John switched lanes. "They gave me an estimate of mid-November."

"Really?" Elaine sounded surprised. "That's pretty fast."

"The main contractor's a friend of mine. I helped his daughter when she had pneumonia a few years back." He turned left into the Red Lobster parking lot. "He says this is his chance to make it up to me."

"That way you can have Thanksgiving with your family, everyone gathered at the Baxter house."

"Yes." John fell quiet. Elaine had meant nothing deep by her comment, but it reminded him that this would be the very last time they would all gather at the Baxter house for Thanksgiving. He pushed away the thoughts, but they left a sting of sadness that stayed until he and Elaine were seated. Then, the way he'd done so many times lately, he reminded himself of the lesson God had given him the day of the fire. Memories didn't need a house in order to be real. They could celebrate Thanksgiving just as easily in a new house, the one John intended to buy for himself and Elaine. If only he could get up the nerve later tonight to pull the ring box from his pocket.

"You're invited, you know. For Thanksgiving."

Elaine's smile was shy and maybe colored with a hint of anticipation. As if she possibly had an idea about what might be coming after dinner.

John couldn't put too much thought into what she was thinking. It was all he could do to focus on the menu and order his dinner.

When they were finished eating, when they were back in the car, John took a quick breath and rubbed his hands together. "It's cold."

"Colder than it's been. But not too bad."

John realized he probably sounded like a nervous teenager, but he couldn't help himself. He was shivering more from nerves than the weather. "Remember that pathway across the campus I told you about?"

"The one that stays partially lit all night long?"

"Right. Lined with trees all decked out in reds and yellows." John blew on his hands. "If it's okay, let's take a walk out there."

Elaine hesitated long enough to smile. "Okay. I brought my coat."

"Me too. And I have a couple scarves in the back. In case it's windy once we get on campus."

Her eyes danced. "You're the most thoughtful man I know, John Baxter."

They drove to the campus and parked in the lot on the south side, near the entrance off 3rd Street. John climbed out and circled the car for Elaine. "Here." He opened the back door, reached inside, and pulled out her long coat. "Get this on."

"At least it isn't windy."

"No, but we can use the scarves anyway." Anything to ward off the chills he was feeling. He grabbed the two red scarves from the backseat and handed one to her. "I picked these up downtown a few years ago."

"Mmmm. So soft."

Their hands touched as he helped her with the collar of her coat. John realized that his palms were sweaty. *God, could You help me here . . . please? I feel like a kid on a first date.*

My son . . . I know the plans I have for you. . . .

The verse whispered across his heart and allowed him to exhale. How good God was, caring about his nervous prayer in a moment like this. The Scripture was the exact one he and Elizabeth had shared with their children so often through the years. God had plans for them, good plans.

Now the Lord was reminding him that the words didn't apply only to his children, but to him too. They applied to the new life with Elaine that would start on this very night.

With that in mind, John's tension eased. As they set out on the path, he offered Elaine his arm, and she took hold of it with both hands. They wound their way up a small hill and then out onto the lower end of campus. "See . . . isn't it nice here?"

"It is." Elaine stood a little straighter and breathed deeply. "I love the smells of fall. The crisp air, the colors. All of it." Her smile stayed with her. "The kids and I used to debate which was the best season in Bloomington. The warm summers, with the frogs and crickets and late nights at the lake . . . or the serene beauty of fresh fallen snow in the winter."

"I think that's my favorite. At least through Christmas." He felt his eyes twinkling. "January and February are a bit long."

"Yes." She laughed, and it added an intimacy to the moment.

"Ashley loves spring, when the flowers show up and everywhere she looks she sees a masterpiece ready to be painted."

"Spring is beautiful." Elaine glanced at the different trees that lined the path. "But for me it's no contest. There's nothing like fall in Bloomington."

"I agree. It's probably tied with winter for me." He thought about summer and spring and chuckled. "Or maybe I just love living here any time of the year."

They were well along the path now, and suddenly John remembered why he was here, why he'd wanted to take this walk tonight. He gulped and opened his mouth, but he couldn't think of what to say.

"I may not have told you." Elaine slowed her pace, and even in the dim light from the path, he could see the sincerity in her expression. "I'm glad you wanted to start seeing me again, but I'm grateful you were honest about your feelings, back when you thought you might've changed your mind."

"About seeing you?" His words sounded stiff, as if they were struggling to make it past his throat.

"About us." She stopped and faced him. "I would never want you to be uncomfortable." She took her time, showing none of the nervousness that was creeping back into his heart. "If you chose to live the rest of your life and never call me again, I could

283

understand. Remember?" The look in her eyes was deep, sentimental. "I've been there. It's just been longer for me; that's all."

John was quiet for a moment. Elaine's husband had died ten years ago, but that didn't mean she hadn't suffered some of the same doubts and hurt he was still working through. "Sometimes I think that's what drew me to you in the first place." He lowered his hands and cupped them around hers. "You'd found a way to survive. Just being around you told me that it was possible. If you'd come out okay on the other end, still able to get up in the morning, maybe I could too."

Elaine was quiet for a few beats. "Your kids are doing better. I could see that in their faces the last time we were together. Especially Ashley."

"You made a connection with her at the hospital that day." John would always be grateful for the simple token of kindness, Elaine's decision to stop at the store and buy a baby outfit for little Sarah. "Ashley's told me a number of times how that was something only a mother would do."

"Elizabeth and I were very good friends. Different, yes. But we thought about life the same way." Elaine's eyes reflected the familiar pain, the kind that never quite went away. "I'm not sure if the gift was what any mother would've thought about. But it was what Elizabeth would've done."

John's heart filled to overflowing. The woman before him was exactly what he needed for the next part of life's journey. She was the centerpiece of the good plans God still had for him. Even now in his sixties. He released her hands and cleared his throat. If he didn't make his move now, he might faint from sheer anxiety.

Elaine watched him, a mild curiosity mixed with the tenderness in her smile. "You feeling okay?"

"I am." He allowed a nervous laugh. "Great, actually." He reached into his coat pocket and lifted the velvet box from inside. As he brought it out, Elaine seemed to realize what was happening.

Her gaze fell on the small box, and she breathed in sharply. "John . . . what's . . . what are you . . . ?"

With every heartbeat, fresh confidence replaced the anxiety he'd been feeling over this moment for months. Elaine was his friend and companion, the woman he wanted to spend his life with. He opened the lid and pulled out a simple but stunning yellow-gold diamond ring. At the center was a squared-off solitaire, and on each side were rows of smaller diamonds.

He lifted his eyes from the ring to her face. If they'd been younger, she might've been giddy with excitement, bouncing on her toes even. But here, alone on the quiet path at the center of Indiana University, Elaine only looked at him, deep inside him to the places of his heart that had already belonged to another. Tears shone in her eyes, and she struggled to speak. "I'll never . . . replace her." She looked at the ring, then back up at John. "I wouldn't dare try."

"I know." John took the ring from the box and eased it onto Elaine's finger. "That's what I love most about you. You'll let me keep Elizabeth." He touched the fingers of his free hand to the place over his heart. "You'll let me keep her in here and know that I still have room enough for you too."

Elaine uttered a sound that was more cry than laugh. "I'm sorry." She crooked one arm around his neck and pressed her forehead to his chest. "I'm sorry either of us had to walk the path it took to get to this moment." She drew back and smiled at him through her tears. "But here we are."

"Yes." He held her hand, running his thumb over the new diamond ring again and again. "I want to spend the rest of my days with you." He felt tears on his own cheeks now, because this was the most bitter-sweet of all happy moments. "Marry me. Make a new home with me. Please, Elaine."

She dabbed at her cheeks, and this time her laugh was filled with all the promise the future suddenly held. "Yes, John . . . I'll marry you. And together we'll allow for times when yesterday's losses are so great all we can do is get through the day." She wiped another tear. "But we'll do it together, and we'll be stronger because of each other."

"We will." John kissed her, a warm kiss full of promise and new love. But also full of an appreciation that he couldn't begin to express. Because Elaine understood him like no one else ever could've after the death of Elizabeth. She understood, and now she would stand beside him the rest of his days. Their love would not replace what they'd known in their younger years. Rather their love would complement it. And in that way they would find life again. Vibrant, abundant life.

The kind Elizabeth had asked him to find.

CHAPTER SEVENTEEN

Rain started falling well before sunup. Ashley would've made a day of staying home and pushing Tonka trucks across the family room floor with Devin, but during breakfast she noticed they were almost out of milk.

"Looks like we'll be taking a quick trip to the store." Ashley sat at the kitchen table, adjacent to Devin's high chair, and tickled his chin.

He giggled and slapped his hand against the Cheerios scattered across his tray. His hair was just as blond as Cole's but it was curly, and in the mornings it stuck out in a dozen different directions. Devin used his whole hand to slip two pieces of cereal into his mouth. When he succeeded, he grinned. "Big tuck!"

"Yes, big, big trucks. We'll play when we get home." Ashley stood and cleared her own bowl. "First we get an adventure to the store! In the rain!" She laughed quietly to herself. Her mom had taught her how to laugh at rainy Mondays. "Life's only as fun as you make it," she would say. The sentiment was something Ashley wanted to pass down to her kids as well.

After breakfast, Ashley dressed Devin in his most snuggly sweatshirt and jeans. She dug out her favorite coat, and they headed for the market.

Twice between the display of Jonathan apples and the milk shelves at the back of the store, she ran into people she knew. A mom with a boy in Cole's class and the receptionist at her hairstylist's studio. Both women seemed nervous when they saw Ashley, unwilling to maintain eye contact. Instead they hurried on with their shopping.

The first woman made just one statement. "It must be hard for your family, with Dayne Matthews always in the news."

Ashley smiled and shrugged. "It's the nature of his business." She thought back to the time when she and her siblings had made the tabloids, after the paparazzi found out that Dayne had reunited with the family he'd never known. "I think we're getting used to it."

Ashley filled her cart with two gallons of milk, a few loaves of her favorite wheatberry bread, a pound of sliced turkey, and a bunch of bananas — Cole's favorite. Then she headed to the front of the store.

She saw the cover of the magazine even before she reached the checkout. There for all the world to see was a full-size photo of a woman who was clearly Randi Wells, sharing a passionate kiss with a man who from the side certainly appeared to be Dayne. The headline read, "Dayne Matthews Caught Red-Handed!"

Ashley's head began to spin, and a rush of adrenaline coursed through her veins. Her heart slammed into double time, and she gripped the cart handle so she wouldn't fall to her knees. What in the world was Dayne doing? She removed one shaking hand from the cart and reached for the magazine.

That's when she noticed it wasn't the only magazine with the picture. Each of the five tabloids had the photo in one form or another, and all with a similarly condemning headline. "Dayne Matthews Moves On!" or "Randi Wells Has Her Way!" or "No Saying No to Randi!" Ashley grabbed one of each and slipped them onto the conveyor belt ahead of her food items.

The checker was an older gentleman, one Ashley had seen often when she shopped. He was making silly faces at Devin. "Cutest little boy of all our customers combined."

The man put the magazines in a bag and put the bag into the cart. He seemed to make no connection that the story on the front covers involved Ashley's brother.

Ashley was grateful because she couldn't have talked about the picture. Not when she could barely catch her breath. Her heart raced, and she fought panic the entire way home. She managed to get Devin inside and into his playpen and the groceries into the kitchen before she took the bag of magazines to the nearest sofa. She pulled out the one with the biggest color photo on the cover.

"Dayne . . . what did you do?" she whispered. Her shock and disbelief left no room for sadness. Not yet.

She stared at the profile of her brother and the way his baseball cap was pulled low over his face. The shot was taken at night, so the cap seemed to be more about Dayne hiding his identity. That fact and the photo's poor lighting made it clear the picture wasn't taken while the two were filming their movie. Ashley scrutinized the image of her brother. Because of the kiss, Dayne's face wasn't entirely visible. If Randi's face weren't so clear in the shot, there could've been a question about the guy in the picture being Dayne. But everyone who followed celebrity gossip knew Dayne and Randi were a few weeks into a movie shoot on a remote beach in Mexico. There was no need for a full shot of Dayne's face for the truth to scream from the cover of the magazine. Only one possible explanation existed.

Dayne was having an affair with his co-star.

Ashley's shock was wearing off, and now her sick feeling was being edged out by anger. If Devin weren't sitting a few yards away, she might've taken the magazine and hurled it at the wall. How could Dayne do this? Why spend all those years wooing Katy if he wasn't finished playing the field?

Her heart ripped in half at the thought of Katy. She might be in London, but she would find out about the photo. Someone would tell her or print it off the Internet, and her world would crash in around her. Not only that, but she wouldn't have a private place to grieve.

Ashley gritted her teeth and flipped through the pages until she came to the spread on Dayne and Randi. Again the headline mocked Dayne's status as a married man. "No Chemistry Problem for Dayne and Randi," it read in bold letters over a layout of half a dozen photos. Dayne was pictured laughing with Randi, sitting near her at a picnic table eating what looked like barbecue chicken, and standing with her, their arms touching, while a man the magazine identified as the director spoke to them.

In each photo Dayne and his costar seemed beyond relaxed and friendly. Combined with the picture on the front of the magazine, they looked like they were falling in love.

Ashley noticed something else. In the cover photo Dayne wore a navy baseball cap and a white short-sleeved T-shirt. The same as in the interior photos, where his face could be seen clearly.

Her mind raced. She should contact Katy and catch her before she could see the horrible photos. Ashley didn't give the idea another minute's thought. She set the magazine next to the bag, rushed to the kitchen table, and grabbed her cell phone from her purse. She'd picked up an international plan for the length of the shoot, and twice already she'd gotten through to Katy for an update.

Ashley punched in Katy's number and waited. Their last conversation ran through her head.

"My costar's a single guy," Katy had told her. "Sometimes I think he might be trying to hit on me, but he knows I'm not interested. Calls me sis now, which is much better." Her voice grew pensive. "Somehow my marriage gets a whole lot less scrutiny in London. They're still more focused on a possible conspiracy with the death of Princess Diana. The pace is slower, not as much pressure." Katy was quiet for a moment. "I've learned something. Making a movie is a job, and I'm going to finish it to the best of my ability. But I'm counting the days, Ash. I can't wait to be back home with Dayne."

Ashley cringed at the memory. *How could you, Dayne? Why?* The phone rang three times, four . . . five. Then it went to Katy's voice mail. When the beep sounded, Ashley opened her mouth to say something, to express her outrage and hurt and to let Katy know she had a right to be angry and that she, too, was furious with Dayne. But all she said was, "Hey, Katy . . . it's Ashley. Call me."

She snapped the phone shut and stood there, not sure what to do. What else had Katy said the last time Ashley talked to her? Had there been a sign? a warning that her marriage was on the brink of utter disaster? Ashley tried to remember every detail. She had asked about Dayne, how he was doing, how often they were talking.

Dayne's location was more remote, Katy had said, so reaching him was difficult. "We don't talk as much as we'd like, but Dayne's aware of the position he's in . . . you know, filming a movie with Randi Wells." She had sounded tired. "He's careful what he says, how close to her he stands, and whether his body language might be taken wrong. Even then he's afraid things will get misconstrued."

No, there had been no warning — not as far as Katy had let on. Ashley returned to the sofa and looked at one of the magazines again, at the way Dayne was holding Randi, how they clung to each other, lost in the kiss. Ashley's anger faded to sorrow, because in the short time she'd been aware that Dayne was her brother, she had actually come to believe that she knew him, that she understood the heart that beat inside him. A single tear fell onto the photo, just below Dayne's elbow. How sad that plastered on the cover of a tabloid was the real truth. He was like many of his peers in the glare of Hollywood's brightest lights — swayed by any wind of temptation. It was a devastating revelation. Dayne Matthews wasn't the man she'd thought him to be.

He was nothing more than a self-absorbed celebrity.

■ ■ ■ ■

Dayne dragged his feet in the surf as he ran down the stretch of sun-drenched sand. Twice he looked back over his shoulder at Randi, and he laughed. "See?" he shouted, out of breath, exhilarated from the chase. "You can't catch me! I told you!"

"Watch me!" She wore a bikini top and a sheer gauze skirt tied at the waist — a cover-up for her bathing suit bottom. "I'll catch you if I have to chase you the rest of my life!"

Dayne ran full-out, down the sand and into the crashing waves. He wore shorts and a white T-shirt, and as the water hit him, the shirt clung to his ribs. He spun around and faced her again. "You're crazy — you know that?"

"Because I love you!" Randi ran to him, splashing and laughing. When she came within a few yards, she stopped.

Suddenly, with the admission of her feelings, the moment changed. His laughter faded first, and then their smiles dropped off and their hands fell to their sides. Their eyes held, chests heaving from the run.

"I do love you." The wind whipped her hair sideways and back, away from her face, and tears sprang to her eyes. "I always have." She took a step closer. "So why won't you let me?"

"Why?" Dayne stared at the surf and gave a slow shake of his head. "You know why." When he lifted his face again, he felt rage and frustration screaming from his eyes. He clenched his hands and lifted his face to the sky for a few beats before finding her eyes again. Behind him another wave crashed and sent white water rushing against his lower body and hers. "Does it always have to be so hard?"

"No!" she shouted with all the pent-up emotion and desire she'd held for him over the years. Like a magnet drawn to steel, she began to move toward him slowly, almost trancelike. "It doesn't have to be so hard." Tears spilled onto her cheeks, but she ignored them. "Don't leave me. . . . Please . . ."

He took a few steps toward her through the knee-deep water, angry and confused, the conflict in his heart great, his desire greater. They came together slowly, Dayne fighting the moment until he was in her arms. He trembled as he framed her face with his hands, working his fingers into her wet hair. The kiss was inevitable, marked with equal amounts of passion and anger, sorrow and exhilaration.

They were fifteen seconds into it when the command came from up on the beach. "Cut!" The director pumped his fist into the air. "Perfect! Perfect lighting, perfect backdrop, perfect emotion."

"Perfect kiss." Randi's eyes danced. "Like I've said, that's the trouble with you," she whispered close to Dayne. "We're so good together there's no need for retakes."

Dayne put his hands gently on her shoulders and eased free of her embrace. He smiled, but the simple act took as much effort as the previous scene. "All in a day's work."

The assistant director yelled his name, and Dayne was grateful for the reason to walk away. He resisted the urge to wipe Randi's kiss from his mouth. "Coming." He turned from Randi and jogged up the sandy slope. The movie had only two kiss scenes, and this was the first. Dayne didn't want them in the movie, but this was a compromise from what the script had originally called for when Dayne was first linked to the picture. He'd won the battle on no between-the-sheets action, nothing with less clothing than the scene they'd just shot.

But still . . . he felt cheap and dirty and guilty. He'd never hated being an actor more than he did right now. He pictured his wife, so many thousands of miles away, and he missed her so badly he could hardly draw a breath. *God, please let me reach her. I need to talk to her.*

As he finished his prayer, the director announced a thirty-minute lunch break, and assignments were given for where the principals needed to be next. Dayne was thrilled. He did the math and knew it was evening in London. Still time to call Katy. He talked with the assistant director about wardrobe changes for the next set of scenes. Randi was busy on the other side of the set, though more than once Dayne saw her glance his way. Her relentless attempts to lure him were making him angry. She continued even though he'd done everything possible to let her know he wasn't interested.

He was in love with his wife. Period.

When he finished with the assistant director, he headed for his gear bag, changed from his wet T-shirt into a dry one, and then jogged farther up the beach toward the catering table. Just as he reached the food line, the refrains of the *Robin Hood* theme came from deep inside his bag. The song was the one he'd sung for Katy at their wedding — "(Everything I Do) I Do It for You" — and Dayne had set it as his ring tone before leaving Los Angeles a few weeks ago.

His heart soared as he unzipped his bag and grabbed his phone. In a hurry, he held it to his ear. He could already hear her voice. "Hello?"

"Hey, friend . . . it's Bob."

Dayne felt the disappointment grate against his soul. *I need to talk to Katy . . . especially after a scene like that one.* "Just a minute." He snagged one of the baseball caps from his bag, worked it low over his eyes, and took the nearest chair. When he was several yards from the catering area, he dropped down and exhaled hard. "Hey, Bob. Caught me at a good time. We're on a break."

For a few seconds Bob was silent, and Dayne wondered if the connection had been lost. "Bob . . . you there?"

"Yeah, I just . . . I wanted to call as soon as I could."

Dayne hadn't noticed before, but Bob seemed more serious than usual, the way his boyhood friend almost never sounded. Then Dayne remembered. He was supposed to call Bob last week and he forgot. Bob and his wife were missionaries in Mexico City, and they'd invited Dayne to come for dinner. So far neither of their schedules had allowed them the time. That must be what this was about. "Hey, about our visit . . . I might have a free day next week, Tuesday or Wednesday."

"That's . . . not why I called." Bob's tone was strained, almost abrupt.

The sand felt warm against Dayne's feet, and he stared out at the gulf. "Okay." He pulled the bill of his cap down lower still, squinting against the sun. The air was warm and gentle against his skin. "Why'd you call?"

"You must've seen it by now, right?"

A flicker of alarm flashed through his mind. "Seen what?"

Bob let out a low groan. "The cover of the tabloids. The ones that hit this morning. I saw them on the Internet." There was an uncomfortable pause. "What are you doing? How could you let her — ?"

"Bob!" The beach beneath Dayne's feet felt like quicksand, sucking him into a place so deep he might never escape. He covered his other ear with his free hand. "I have no idea what you're talking about."

"Paparazzi followed you to the shoot. You have to know that."

"Of course. They come and go, but that's it. There's not much to shoot, really."

"Dayne . . . whatever's happening with you and Randi, you can tell me the truth.

You need to talk about it." Bob paused. "Before you lose everything." His tone suggested that maybe Dayne already had lost everything.

Dayne pinched his temples with his thumb and index finger. "Buddy, call me crazy, but I'm being honest here." He didn't want to ask, but he had to know. "Tell me what you saw."

Bob drew a slow breath. "You and Randi, full embrace, locked in a lovers' kind of kiss if ever there was one. I called a friend back home and had him check. The picture takes up almost the entire cover of every tabloid."

Dayne had to stand so he could force his lungs to breathe. He took off his baseball cap and worked to keep from yelling. "That's impossible. We just finished shooting our first kiss scene." He looked behind him; a few people milling near the food table seemed to be listening. He slapped the hat back into place and stormed off toward an empty stretch of beach.

"The picture's pretty clear." Bob's tone was just short of accusatory. "No one else around, poor lighting. Definitely not a movie scene."

"It wasn't me!" He clenched his jaw and tightened his fist. "You believe me, right? I'm telling the truth here." His mind raced, and his stomach tightened into a knot. How could this happen? He'd done everything possible to keep his distance from Randi. He covered his face with his free hand. "I can't believe this."

Bob waited, clearly wanting some sort of explanation. "I'm looking at the picture right now. The headline says you were caught red-handed."

"No . . . this isn't happening." Dayne wanted to scream or lay into the person responsible for this. His mind raced, turning circles around itself and making him so dizzy he could barely stand. "Tell me this . . . how do you know it's me?" It was the only thing Dayne could think to say. No matter what Bob was looking at, the picture wasn't him and Randi. It couldn't have been.

Bob hesitated. "Well, you're wearing a white T-shirt and a blue baseball cap. Says something about Baja on it."

Dayne jerked the hat from his head again and stared at it. The same hat he was wearing right now. He flung it toward the water and paced farther from the set. He clenched his teeth so tight he could hardly get the words out. "The whole cast and crew got those hats."

"The front page picture isn't the only one.

There are others — you and Randi standing together, laughing, sitting near each
other." Bob sounded confused, but at least
his tone didn't sound as doubtful.

"Yeah." Dayne laughed, but there was
nothing funny in the sound of it. "Are we
playing Frisbee in one of them?"

"Uh . . ." Bob paused. "Yeah, you are.
Definitely."

"Of course we are." He paced the other
direction, back toward the catering area.
"Those are from the set. Scenes from the
movie."

"Wait, I think . . . yes, it says that in small
print beneath those pictures. 'Dayne and
Randi carry heat from the film into real life.'
That's what it says, friend. The problem is,
in each one you're wearing the same shirt
and baseball cap."

"The scenes we're working on happen all
in one afternoon at the beach. Of course
I'm in the same shirt and baseball cap."
Dayne kept his tone in check. The news was
horrific, the worst since he and Katy had
started dating. But the facts weren't Bob's
fault.

"No, Dayne, not the same in the shots
from the filming. The same there and on
the front cover, in the shot with you kissing —"

"It wasn't me!" He shouted this time. "I'm sorry, but please. You have to believe me. I haven't kissed her, not until today." He wanted to run toward the sea, jump in, and swim until he reached someplace sane and normal, a place where the truth was told and tabloids didn't exist. He stopped pacing and faced the water. "I promise; I'm telling the truth."

Bob hesitated. "I don't understand it . . . but I believe you." He made a slow sound, as if he was breathing out through gritted teeth. "Man, you need to talk to Katy."

Dayne pictured his wife somewhere on a set in London and getting the news. Worse, maybe seeing the tabloids for herself. He walked a few feet to a palm tree and leaned against the rough trunk. If he had to work this hard to convince Bob, how would Katy take the news? "I hate this."

For a minute his friend said nothing. Again Dayne wasn't sure if they'd lost their connection. But then Bob continued. "Think, buddy. Who else could it be? Someone on the set who looks like you, maybe? A body double?"

Yeah, that was it. Dayne felt the smallest sliver of hope. "Right . . . exactly. Like I said, we all got those hats." He stood and paced toward the water again. "And everyone's wearing T-shirts. It's the beach, after all."

"So give it thought." There was the sound of a magazine's pages being turned. "Actually, you can't really make out your full face in the cover photo. The profile looks like you, the build, the hair color."

"But it has to be someone else." Dayne felt worn-out, defeated. He still had half a day of shooting left, but he felt like telling the director he was through. Forget the movie and everything else about Hollywood. He wanted to be on the next flight to England. The impossibility of his situation rose before him like the most treacherous of mountains. "Bob, I need to go. Thanks for calling."

"I'm glad it isn't you. I really thought . . ."

"Wow." Dayne kept the bitterness from his tone, but there was no hiding his hurt. "You really thought I'd come here and have an affair with Randi Wells?"

"You're human, Dayne." Bob sounded kinder than before, more understanding. "Any of us could fall. That's why we need a Savior. I just . . . wanted you to know I was here for you . . . if that had been you on the front cover."

The depth of Bob's friendship eased Dayne's hurt. How great a friend Bob Asher was. He hadn't called to condemn or belittle but to stand next to Dayne, if indeed he was in the process of the biggest fall of his life. And Bob was right. People fell. "Well, this time I'm still standing. But thanks for being there."

After the call was over, Dayne kept his distance from the others, his heart thudding against his chest. Should he call Katy and try to catch her before she saw the picture? Or had she already seen it?

He was about to dial her number when he heard the director's voice. "Places, everyone . . . break's over!"

Dayne swallowed hard and stuffed his emotions deep inside him. His anger and betrayal by the media, his hurt and frustration and fear, all of it would have to wait until after the day's filming. They had a schedule to keep, and even a few hours of missed time wouldn't be tolerated by the director.

He returned to his gear bag and dropped the phone inside. As he strode across the sand for his next scene — an argument between him and the actor playing Randi's mother — he scanned the cast and crew. Who had done this to him? Who had slipped off with Randi for a clandestine make-out session and let him take the fall? He pondered the idea all afternoon between takes. He was sitting alone on the sand when he realized the guy — whoever he was — wasn't the real problem. Randi was the one sneaking off with a guy who somehow was a dead ringer for —

Dayne grabbed a quick breath. He ran his fingers through his hair and tried to remember how to exhale. All afternoon he'd gone through the list of men on the set, but none of them had his look, his exact build.

None of them except the one person he had never considered until now. A guy who looked just like him. Dayne had hoped that when he figured out who was really in the picture, his heart would settle into a normal rhythm and the pain inside him would ease. But now, as the pieces fell into place and the truth consumed him, Dayne's pain didn't ease.

It doubled.

CHAPTER EIGHTEEN

It was the day before Halloween, and all Katy could think about was that back home — if CKT had still been together — tonight would've been the group's annual fall festival. The kids gathered every October 30 and staged a carnival on the theater grounds. CKT members would wear friendly costumes from a previous show and have game booths where kids could win candy.

The event never raised much money, but it gave the CKT kids another reason to get together, a place to bond. Katy checked the clock tacked up on one of the set pieces. Fifteen minutes before the afternoon shooting was set to begin. It was only seven o'clock in Bloomington, but Jenny Flanigan would be awake.

Katy took out her cell phone and found Jenny's number on her speed dial. She completed the call and waited.

Jenny answered on the third ring, her tone upbeat. "Katy, I can't believe it's you!"

"Hi." Tears stung at the corners of Katy's eyes. She felt like she'd entered another world here in London. Life at home seemed forever away. "I had to call. It's the thirtieth."

"I know." Disappointment crept into Jenny's voice. "Bailey and Connor were talking about it last night. The first year in a long time without a CKT fall festival."

Katy felt a lump in her throat. "How are they . . . Bailey and Connor?"

"They miss it; I won't lie." Jenny sounded compassionate. "But they understand this is what you want. And they don't have a theater even if you were here." She sighed. "It's just one of those hard seasons in life. They're still asking God for a miracle."

The picture made Katy even sadder. Her two favorite teenagers, begging God for a miracle that could never happen. "What about the others — the Shaffers and Picks and Larsons? . . . Are people talking about CKT?"

"They are. A bunch of them met at our house a few days ago because Bailey and Connor invited them. The goal — like every time the kids get together — was to think of a way to stop the developers from tearing down the theater." Jenny didn't seem very optimistic. "In the end they mostly sang praise songs and prayed, asking God to bring CKT back, however He might make it happen."

Katy felt her sadness worsen. "I miss it so much. If I could come home right now, I'd step in front of the wrecking ball and beg the developers to change their minds."

"Land is valuable downtown." Jenny made a slightly defeated sound. "The old theater's probably worth twice what they bought it for."

A tear fell onto Katy's jeans, and she dabbed at her eyes. "What else? Anything in the tabloids?"

"I'm impressed." Jenny's tone grew lighter. "You're actually staying away from them. Well, good for you."

"I take it you aren't reading them either?"

"Definitely not. If I want the truth, I'll talk to you. Besides, it's not healthy for the kids to get caught up in the whole celebrity-crazed world of the tabloids."

"No, probably not." Katy peered across the asphalt to the place where Stephen Petrel was busy handing out directions, setting up the next scene. "Listen, I don't have long. I guess I just wanted to hear your voice. A year ago . . ." Her emotions swelled, and she couldn't finish the sentence.

"I know. . . . You didn't picture things going like this." Jenny had always known just what to say. Her friendship was one more thing Katy missed about Bloomington.

She struggled to find her voice. "I never wanted the kids to lose CKT."

"Pray for them." Jenny's tone was filled with a smile. "They asked me to ask you. Bailey has a sense about this whole thing. That if everyone's praying, maybe they'll find a solution, a way to keep the group together."

"I'll pray." Katy bit the inside of her lip to keep from crying. "Tell them I love them."

When the call ended, Katy spotted Ian Walters, her costar, heading over to join her. Katy tucked her phone into her bag and sat up straighter. "Hi." She found a friendly smile. She wasn't in the habit of sharing her personal life with Ian, and now wasn't any time to start.

Keeping things on a surface level with other men had been Jenny's idea. "Guard your heart," her friend had told her. With all that was at stake in Katy's marriage, she had welcomed the advice.

Ian took the chair across from her. He had a paper plate with a sandwich and three cookies. He held one up. "Hungry?"

"No." She smiled again. Her heart was breaking from missing her theater kids. She was hardly hungry. She kept her tone light. "Thanks anyway."

"You look pensive." Ian slid his chair closer so their feet were nearly touching.

Katy felt self-conscious for a few seconds, until she remembered that there were no paparazzi on the set today. She could have her feet a few inches from her costar's without anyone assuming she was having an affair. She kept the walls in her heart firmly in place. "Just missing home."

"Mmmm." His eyes flirted with her. "Not me. I rather like being here across the pond with America's number one sweetheart."

"Yes, well . . ." Katy grinned at him. She tucked her feet beneath her chair. "My husband appreciates your brotherly kindness."

Ian rolled his eyes in mock disappointment. "Yeah, yeah . . . tell him I'm happy to oblige."

"Sis?"

He did an exaggerated sigh. "Fine. Sis."

This was the relationship Katy and Ian had found together on set. Yes, they had chemistry, and when they needed to, they could ramp it up a few notches. But the film wasn't a passionate love story. It was the

313

story of a woman battling depression and her husband's quest to help her. The brotherly kindness thing worked both offscreen and on.

They were talking about the scenes that had to be shot yet today when Katy caught Stephen Petrel in what looked like a deep conversation with his assistant director. A few times, Stephen glanced over his shoulder to where Katy and Ian were sitting.

"There you go again." Ian was playing with her. "Too distracted to have a real conversation with me."

Katy shook her head. "Sorry. It's just . . . Stephen. He looks upset."

"Stephen's always upset." Ian chuckled. "The guy's such a perfectionist. I'm surprised he ever finishes a film."

Stephen took a large manila envelope from the assistant, then turned and walked toward them. By the time he approached, Katy didn't have to ask if there was a problem. The answer was heavy in Stephen's eyes. He put his hand on Ian's shoulder. "Walters, I need to talk to Katy for a minute."

Katy's heart skipped a beat. What could've happened? The scenes were going along well; they'd had to reshoot only a couple, and that was mostly because of lighting issues. For a moment she wondered if someone was accusing her of having an affair with Ian. It was something she'd talked about with the director because she needed all the help she could get. "I can't have the press thinking Ian and I have a thing," she'd told him. "So help me out, okay?"

Stephen had been mildly amused by her concern. After all, only a few photographers from the U.S. were working the shoot. "You aren't the story," he told her. "No one cares about you and Ian Walters unless you give them a reason to care."

He was right of course. The story was Dayne and Randi, and so far Dayne had taken great pains to keep things as platonic as possible with his costar. But maybe it was something with the reality show. *For Real* was still taking stabs at them, showing the world how poorly she and Dayne got along and how precarious their marriage really was. If somehow the photographers had caught Katy in what seemed like a cozy moment with Ian, they'd be thrilled to run the pictures.

Ian collected his plate, winked at Katy, and sauntered off toward the food line again. A few members of the cast were gathered near the coffee table, including one young starlet who was making her debut in the film. Katy had a suspicion that Ian was interested in her too.

Katy turned her attention fully to her director. "Stephen?"

He was one of the warmest men she knew, but now his face was so serious he looked almost gaunt. "Step over here for a minute, will you?"

She stood and followed him to a patch of land just behind one of the trailers. It was a spot where they were out of sight from any of the other cast or crew. "What is it?" Katy felt her face grow hot, and her hands began to tremble. Something terrible must've happened for Stephen to look the way he did.

"You haven't seen yesterday's tabloids yet?"

Katy's heart sank. "Don't tell me. . . ." She clenched her fists and stared at the ground. "I've done everything I could to keep away from him. The idea of Ian Walters and me having anything but a working —"

"It isn't you and Ian." Stephen lowered his brow and put one hand on her shoulder. "I can't believe no one's said anything. Probably because we've been so focused on the shoot."

The ground beneath Katy's feet felt soft and unsteady. She braced herself against the back of the trailer and waited.

Stephen reached into the envelope and pulled out three color images. He held up the first one. "I'm sorry. I wish you didn't have to see this."

Katy stared at the image, and her mind went into a self-defense mode. It took several seconds for the photo to make sense, for her to understand what she was seeing. And even then it took seconds more for the damage to start detonating deep in her soul. The picture was of Dayne and Randi Wells, the two of them locked in each other's arms, kissing as if . . . as if they were madly and passionately in love.

"No . . ." Katy felt herself start to drop, but Stephen caught her.

He put his arm beneath hers and steadied her. "You can't fall apart. I've seen this too many times in this industry." He spoke to her like her father might've. "You and Dayne need to talk. But you'll get through this."

Get through it? Katy stared at the picture again. The words across the top yelled, "Dayne Matthews Caught Red-Handed!" She felt dizzy and sick to her stomach. Black spots danced before her eyes, and she could no longer hear what Stephen was saying. Something about affairs being common-place and temptations often too great to resist. How it was possible to move on and that she couldn't put a lot of stock in a location affair because those things happened.

Katy closed her eyes and tried to keep from passing out. *No,* she wanted to shout at him. *They don't happen to me.* She wasn't like that. She believed in truth and faith, loyalty and fidelity, and that a person didn't get married without at least intending for those things to happen. All of which was what Dayne believed too. At least that's what . . .

She felt the blood leaving her face. "Stephen . . . help me." Something was happening to her, and she couldn't figure out what. She was falling, spinning, and someone was catching her, and a loud rushing sound filled her ears, and a searing pain cut through her heart. *Dayne . . . you didn't. . . . You couldn't have. . . .* Her thoughts scrambled and began to fade.

Then there was nothing but cool, damp darkness. In the depths of inky blackness, Katy still had the wherewithal to ask herself the only question that mattered.

How could it happen? . . . How could it . . . ?

And then she could no longer ask the question, no longer form the words. The spinning and the dizziness stopped, and there was only the pain and a terrible empty feeling, worse than anything Katy had ever known.

As if her entire world had come to an end in one single, devastating moment.

Stephen was standing over Katy when she came to. That much she understood. But where was she? And why was she here with the director when . . . ?

In a rush, it all came back. Stephen walking toward her, the concern on his face. And the picture. The photograph that told the whole story, even if every important detail was missing.

"You passed out." Stephen carried a wet washcloth to the sink, rinsed it, wrung it out, and brought it back to her. He set it gently across her forehead.

"How . . . how long was I down?" Katy tried to sit up, but nausea hit her like a wall.

"Not long. A few minutes, maybe."

Katy looked around and understood. Stephen had helped her into the trailer they'd been standing by. Now he and the assistant director were watching her, clearly worried.

"You're getting some of your color back." Stephen stayed at her side. "How do you feel?"

She looked deep into the older man's eyes,

and then she crooked her arm and placed it over her face. How did she feel? Her husband was having an affair with Randi Wells. She felt shocked and terrified and humiliated and furious at the same time. But with every passing minute, she felt something else too.

Clarity.

She lowered her arm back to her side and took a long breath. If Dayne was abandoning her, she would have to find a way to survive. Not because affairs were commonplace, as Stephen suggested, or because this sort of thing was bound to happen in their business. But because she had her faith. And with Christ she could do all things.

Even survive this.

Katy propped herself up on her elbow. *God, be with me. I can't do this alone.*

My daughter, I am with you . . . even to the end of the age.

The response swayed across her soul like a life rope. Her heart still pounded against her chest, but she could breathe now. She sat up on the edge of the cot and looked at her director. "Let me see the envelope." Her voice held a calm that hadn't been there earlier. "Please, Stephen."

The man swapped a look with his assistant. "I don't know. . . . I think maybe you need time to —"

"You were right, what you said before." The ground felt firm beneath her feet now. "I need to face this. So, please . . . let me see it."

With a look that said he still wasn't sure this was a good idea, he handed her the envelope. She removed the three pictures inside and set them on her lap. She could tell from the lighting and quality that the first photo was almost certainly not taken during a moment of filming. She held her breath and shifted the top page to the bottom, until she'd looked carefully at each of the pictures.

Same shirt, same hat . . . the story left the reader no doubt whatsoever. In addition to the carefree, happy moments Dayne and Randi were sharing on the set, they were definitely taking part in an offscreen affair.

By the time she reached the top photo again, her shock was wearing off. She stared at the image until her tears blurred it. *Dayne . . . how could you?* Whatever Randi had done to trap him, the decision ultimately was his. He had allowed her to lure him away. He and Katy had been married for less than a year, and already their time together had been marked by rumors and gossip and hints at infidelity. And now . . .

Now in a sudden, sad moment of clarity, she saw her marriage for what it really was — an impulsive act, doomed from the beginning.

Katy wiped her tears with the back of her hand and sniffed once. She would finish her film, return to Bloomington, and find a way to get on with her life. She would lean on God because He alone could help her survive the pain radiating through her. Somehow she would teach again, because this . . . this world of celebrity and failed commitments could never be where she belonged.

The facts were clear now, and she looked up at Stephen. "I'll need the rest of the afternoon."

"Fine." He touched her shoulder. "We'll work on other scenes. The rest of the cast doesn't know what happened. They think you're sick."

She nodded. It wasn't a lie. She *was* sick, and in that moment she wasn't sure if she'd ever be well again.

When the directors were gone, Katy found her phone. *I have to call him. He has to know that I've seen the picture.* Her hands shook as she dialed Dayne's number, but after four rings his recorded voice came on, asking her to leave a message.

For a few seconds she opened her mouth and tried to think of something to tell him. But in the end she hung up just as a series of sobs overtook her. There was nothing to say, really. The picture on the cover of the tabloid had said it all. She wept until her body convulsed with sorrow. She squeezed her eyes shut and begged God for understanding. *How could it happen, God? I believed in him!* The realization grew. The rumors and hints at infidelity, the problems the reality show had picked up on . . . maybe they'd been true all along. If Dayne was capable of this, then how could she believe anything he'd told her?

This time there was no answer, and slowly, as her tears subsided, Katy understood. The knowledge was deep and sure. It tripled her pain and made her feel like she was drowning in an ocean with no surface to swim up to. Because the photograph of Dayne and Randi didn't mean her brief marriage was on the rocks.

It meant it was over.

CHAPTER NINETEEN

Luke saw the fire truck as soon as he turned onto his street. After what happened with his father's house, panic hit sure and fast, and Luke picked up speed. He saw no smoke, and Reagan hadn't called, so there couldn't be anything seriously wrong . . . unless whatever it was had just happened. He was suddenly grateful he'd left work a few hours early today. He screeched to a stop and was turning off his engine when Reagan and a blond fireman came out of the house together.

His relief was short-lived. "What in the . . . ?" Luke sank back into his seat and watched his wife.

Reagan was talking to the firefighter, apparently so caught up in the conversation that she didn't notice Luke parked across the street. She smiled and gestured toward the roof of the house and then toward the open front door. Whatever she said, both of them laughed, and after a few seconds of conversation, their smiles faded. The fireman nodded, intent on whatever Reagan was saying. Reagan shrugged, dainty and flirtatious. At least it looked that way to Luke.

Anger shot a rush of blood to his face. What was happening here? He grabbed the door handle and was about to burst from his car and demand an explanation when the firefighter stepped closer to Reagan and hugged her.

It wasn't a long hug or one marked with intimacy. No kiss followed. But still, Luke's mouth hung open. Was Reagan having an affair? Was that what this was? He watched the guy wave to Reagan and then jog to his fire truck. He climbed inside and drove off, all while Reagan never even looked in Luke's direction.

He opened his car door before Reagan had the chance to go back in the house. At the sound, she turned toward him. The guilt and surprise on her face were unmistakable. He hurried across the street, his eyes glued to hers, his steps pounding out a rhythm only slightly harder than his beating heart. When he was halfway up the walk, he stopped and stared at her.

"What was that?" Luke waved his hand at

the fire truck, now almost to the end of their street.

"Don't yell." Reagan shut the front door and took a few steps closer. "You'll wake Malin."

Luke huffed at her. "Maybe I don't care about waking Malin." Disbelief was working its way through his mind. "I pull up earlier than usual and some firefighter is giving you a hug, and you tell me not to yell?" If there'd been a wall nearby, Luke would've punched it. Instead he willed himself not to lose control. "You wanna tell me what's going on? When a fireman stops by for an afternoon hug?"

She crossed her arms and stared at some spot near her feet. When she looked up, there was a coolness in her eyes that he'd seen only one time before — on September 11, 2001, the day her father was killed in the Twin Towers. "He's a friend." She blinked, but still the coolness remained. "He listens to me."

A ripple of fear shook Luke, but he dismissed it. "You made friends with a firefighter who listens?" His tone mocked her, but his mind was racing. How had this happened, and how long had they been friends?

"He was one of the guys who responded when Tommy got his head stuck." She sighed long and slow, as if she didn't have the energy to fight with him. "He's been back a few times, checking the wiring in the attic, making sure the house is fireproof."

"Yeah." Luke uttered an exaggerated laugh. "Somehow I don't think the wiring in our house is the problem here." He walked by her, pushing through the front door and hurrying past the living room, where Malin was sleeping on a blanket on the floor. He didn't stop until he reached their bedroom. Only then did he put his briefcase down, loosen his tie, and move to the window that overlooked their spacious backyard.

Reagan followed him but not quickly. He heard her walk in and quietly shut the door behind her. He turned in time to see her sit on the edge of the bed. She had a magazine in her hands.

"Why'd he hug you?" Luke realized he was shaking — more from anger than hurt. No matter how far his work had taken him, regardless of the situations he'd gotten himself into, he never once considered that his wife might be back at home having an affair.

The walls in her eyes fell a little. "I told him today was the anniversary."

Luke furrowed his brow, searching his

memory for what she was talking about. "Anniversary?"

"The day they found my dad's remains. It was six years ago today."

Even with his anger and shock, the truth hit him. A picture flashed in his mind — Reagan and himself on the eighty-ninth floor of the north tower of the World Trade Center, sitting in her father's office, chatting with him. Making plans to see *Riverdance* in New York City that night. Reagan had been her father's princess. Clearly she carried the pain of his death with her still.

Luke shifted his weight. What was he supposed to do next? Tell her, oh well, then . . . the fireman's hug made perfect sense in light of what day it was? A part of him felt sorry for her, but that didn't change what had happened. He was about to ask exactly how many times the firefighter had been over when Tommy's screams pierced the silence. Luke made a sound that expressed his frustration. "Can't that kid get through a day without screaming?"

"He's probably looking for me." Reagan stood just as Tommy ran into the room.

He wrapped his arms around her legs. "Malin's sleeping with my blanket!" His voice wasn't as loud now, but it was the worst possible whine. "I told her not to, but she is, Mommy! And it's mine!"

"Listen." Luke took hold of Tommy's shoulder. "Go to your room!" He pointed down the hallway. "You're too old to scream about a blanket!"

Tommy stared as if he couldn't believe Luke was serious. Then his expression collapsed in a heap of sorrow. He turned and ran from the room, crying as he went. "Nobody loves me! Nobody . . ."

"Oh, brother." Luke looked at Reagan, but she averted her eyes. "That's not acceptable. Him talking to us like that."

"Maybe if you were home more often, you could help me figure out a way to teach him." Her answer was quick and sharp. Anger flashed in her eyes, then faded just as quickly. "Never mind." She held out the magazine in her hand. "Looks like we're not the only ones having trouble, huh?"

He looked down at the cover, at the photo and headline. It took a few seconds, but the reality of the picture hit him square in the chest like a runaway locomotive. His lips parted, but no words came out. His mouth went dry, but before he could look at his wife, before he could dare consider the most horrible possibility, she shoved the magazine at him and walked away.

Before she left, she looked back once. "I

guess finding girlfriends on the road runs in the family." She held his gaze a few seconds, then spun around and marched down the hall toward Tommy's room.

Luke stood there frozen. His pulse slammed into overdrive, and a layer of sweat broke out across his forehead. Reagan knew. That had to be the reason she'd shown him the magazine. She knew and now she felt free to do whatever she wanted.

He looked at the picture and at the headline above it. Slowly, a realization began to dawn in his mind. Maybe she didn't know. She might've meant exactly what she said. Finding girlfriends on the road ran in the family. In other words, like anyone else who looked at the photo on the cover of the tabloid, Reagan might actually believe that Dayne was having an affair with Randi Wells.

Suddenly he remembered the text messages. He pulled his phone from his pocket, flipped it open, and clicked a series of buttons until he had emptied his phone's inbox and out-box. There. That would help. He ran his tongue along his lower lip and looked at the magazine cover again. If Reagan believed what the world believed, then he was in the clear . . . at least for now.

The phone in Luke's pocket rang, and he

jumped. He pulled it out and stared at the caller ID, his heart skipping a beat. It was Dayne. He gulped and flipped the phone open. "Hey." He kept his tone appropriately somber. By now Dayne would expect he'd seen the picture.

"Listen, I don't have long." Dayne sounded mad, his words like a series of rapid-fire bullets. "Tell me what happened that night with you and Randi on the beach."

"Me and Randi?" Luke searched for something to say, anything to make Dayne believe he wasn't having an affair with Randi. He managed a weak laugh. "Don't tell me you think I'm the guy in the picture?"

"Well, it isn't me. That's all I know." Dayne's voice was laced with anger, but it was obvious he was working to keep it from being heard. "My life's falling apart over here. Tell me the truth."

"I am." The laughter in Luke's voice was replaced with a solid confidence, a convincing assurance. "I promise you, that isn't me in the picture. You're asking the wrong guy."

There was a pause. "Okay." Dayne seemed at a loss for words. "Thanks. I had to ask."

When the call was over, Luke looked at his hands. He was shaking hard, his heart thumping erratically against his ribs. He put the phone back in his pocket and stared out the window. Dayne would find a way out of this mess; he always did. But then what would happen? Someone was bound to figure out the truth.

Luke studied the photo, the way Randi looked lost in the moment. The guy . . . the guy was someone he no longer even recognized.

Dear God . . . what have I done? Who am I?

There was no response, no comforting answer. Guilt came down around him like the claustrophobic bars of a prison cell, guilt like Luke had never felt before — not even back when he left home and cut ties with his family. This was guilt strong enough to destroy him. Luke could feel it like poison in his blood. Because no matter what story the picture told and no matter what lies Luke was willing to tell . . . even if the whole world believed otherwise, Dayne wasn't having an affair with Randi Wells.

Luke was.

John stared at the magazines spread across his office desk. Ashley had called yesterday and told him about the tabloids, right after she learned the news. Now the door was

332

firmly locked, and John had half an hour before his next appointment.

Funny how it was, raising a family, being a father. Babies came and parents did the mental math: twenty years and the house would be sadly quiet again, the children out on their own, making their way in life. John leaned closer to the magazines and studied the picture of Dayne and Randi, and a deep sadness pierced his soul. The truth was, parenting never really ended. Here was his oldest son — a young man he hadn't even met until a few years ago — caught publicly making the worst mistake of his life.

But all John could think was, *Hey, that's my son!* He would've flown to Mexico that afternoon if he thought Dayne needed him. He'd called him, of course, but their conversation was brief. Dayne denied kissing Randi and explained that the photo had to be of someone else.

"What about Randi? What's she saying?"

"She isn't talking. I told her it wasn't me in the picture, and she only said that it should've been." Dayne sounded exhausted. "I talked to Katy but only for a few minutes. She had to run — something about her film. But I could hear it in her voice. She doesn't believe me."

John frowned. To be honest, Dayne's

denial sounded pretty flimsy. Still, Dayne was his son, his firstborn. Whatever his trouble, John wanted to be there for him. Even if in the end Dayne came clean and admitted the whole thing. This wasn't the time to abandon him.

He cleared his throat. "I'm sorry, Son. This is terrible." He tried to think of how he could offer encouragement, but no words came to mind. Dayne ran in a different world, and John knew little about how to navigate it. In the end, he offered the only help he could. "Let me know if there's anything I can do."

"There is." Dayne's voice was thick with emotion. "Pray, will you? Just pray for us."

Now, in the quiet of his office, John was grateful to have some tangible way to help, a way he could keep being a dad for his fully grown son — even at a time like this.

John's thoughts shifted to Luke, and his heart ached with a heaviness he hadn't known in years. Ashley had spoken to Reagan a few times in recent weeks, and finally Ashley had talked to him about their conversations.

"Reagan thinks Luke's having an affair." Ashley sounded heartbroken. "He's in New York much more often than before, and several times he's been out to see plays with some woman from the office." A cry sounded in her voice. "We have to do something, Dad."

John sat very still, the pain of his sons' choices sharp within him. Both his sons, struggling in their marriages . . . both dabbling with outside relationships that threatened to destroy the commitments and promises they'd made. Anger toward the enemy of their souls rose up inside him. Dayne and Luke were Baxters, after all. It wasn't the Baxter way to disregard marriage, to treat so cavalierly the bond between a husband and a wife.

So John would do what he'd done so many times in the past — he would fall to his knees and beg for God's help, for His Spirit to intervene and His life and light to reign in the situations with both sons. John stood, pushed in his chair, and lowered himself to the carpeted area between his desk and the sofa against the wall. As he hit his knees, he remembered key times when he'd done this before.

A decade ago, when Ashley left for Paris, a rebellious young woman searching for thrills she couldn't find in Bloomington, and when she came home, pregnant and alone, so ashamed that John and Elizabeth wondered if she'd ever connect with their family again.

He'd fallen to his knees when Kari's first husband moved out to live with one of his college students and again when a jilted boyfriend of the young woman stalked Kari's husband and killed him. Kari was weeks away from delivering Jessie, and without seeking God, without prayer for strength, John was certain none of them would've survived with their faith intact.

He had prayed this way after the tragedy of September 11 and again when it became clear that Reagan had lost her father in the collapse of the Twin Towers, and he'd prayed when Luke chose to leave home and live with a girl who was opposed to everything that had once mattered to him.

Always John took his pain and fears and brought them to this place, his private office. Here, on his knees, he could feel the Spirit of God beside him, sense His presence and know for certain that his Lord would answer. One way or another, He would answer.

John took a deep breath. *I'm here again, here on my knees, humbled before You. My sons are struggling, Father.* He closed his eyes and pictured the photograph on the cover of the magazine. Dayne could deny what was happening between him and his costar, but the picture told the story. He sighed. *I think Dayne's in denial, Lord. He's so far from family, so far from the kind of support that could help him in his faith. Open his eyes and let him see that what he's doing is wrong and that by denying the truth he'll only make things worse. And Luke, Lord . . . convict him of his actions and bring him back to a right life. Help him make amends with Reagan. Please, Father, hear my cry today.*

He stopped because over the years he'd learned one very important lesson whenever he sought God this passionately, this fervently. He needed to do more than ask; he needed to listen. He hunched over his knees, waiting. Listening.

Then in the stillness of the room, a Scripture came to him, filling his mind with truth and peace. The verse was from Colossians, something John had read a few days ago. *"In him lie hidden all the treasures of wisdom and knowledge."*

My son . . . heed My words. I know all things. . . . I will show you in time.

A holy presence came over the room and the place where John was kneeling. What did the Scripture mean here, in light of John's troubled heart for his sons? He let the words run through his mind again and again, and finally a picture began to take shape. Today things with his sons and their wives seemed hopeless, beyond repair. But God alone knew all things. His wisdom and knowledge were indeed very great treasures.

John wasn't sure what hidden wisdom and knowledge might come from the incident with Dayne and Randi or with Reagan's suspicions, but suddenly he had no doubt. Some truth was going to come to light, and when it did, healing could begin. That was what God wanted him to understand, and the realization flooded John's soul with an indescribable joy.

No matter how great his love for his sons, God loved them more. And God knew all things, which meant John could lean on the Lord and know that Dayne and Luke were being shaped and molded by God alone — however terrible things seemed at the moment.

He spent another twenty minutes kneeling on the floor, praying about his daughters and their families, asking God to protect their marriages and to strengthen their faith. As he was nearing the end of his prayer, God granted him another piece of wisdom, making one thing very clear: John needed to send the scrapbooks to his children as soon as he was finished with them so their mother's message of love, her words on marriage and commitment and family, would reach them as soon as possible.

Before it was too late.

CHAPTER TWENTY

Her mother's funeral was over, and Randi was trying to find the strength to make her way out of the church. She walked next to her daughters, gripping every other pew as she moved up the aisle toward daylight, toward the rest of her life without either of her parents.

She was home now, in British Columbia, where it didn't matter that she was a famous American movie star. Two more days and she'd be back on the set, back in the place where she was praised and held up as an icon of fame and celebrity. But here, people were far more taken by her parents and the legacy of faith and community involvement they'd left behind. The packed church this morning was because of her mom's friendship to others and because of her father's generosity, his quick smile and helping hand. If someone needed something, they could turn to Louie Geer and know that he would come through.

"Put God and family first, little girl, and all the rest will fall into place," he used to tell her.

Randi's youngest daughter tugged on her jacket. "Mommy . . ."

"Yes?"

She tilted her face up, her brow furrowed. "Is Grandma gonna stay in the pretty box?"

Randi took hold of her hand, then turned to the side and reached for her older daughter. She could feel the truth from her childhood rushing into place. She gave her little one a sad smile. "Grandma's not in the box, baby. She's in heaven. With Papa."

When they walked out into the bright midmorning, Randi put her sunglasses on. Across the street from the church was an old park, with a grove of evergreens and a number of stunning aspens. It was the last day of November and the leaves had long since fallen, but that didn't matter. In a single glance Randi could see the way the park looked in any season. The place called to her, offering the familiarity she was longing for.

"Let's go to the park." Randi waited for a clearing in the traffic and then crossed the street.

The girls were quieter than usual, but

once they reached the swings, they skipped off together and started playing.

Randi sat on the nearest bench, and a million memories danced to life. Here, after church, was where she'd sit with her daddy when she was too tired to swing, when her sisters, Jamie and Kelly, were busy playing on the slides and Randi simply needed time with her father. Even back then she was a daddy's girl. That's why today was so hard. She didn't have more than a handful of really good memories with her mother, and now she was gone.

Randi leaned back against the park bench. The memory faded, and she stared up through the barren branches to the sky beyond. "How can you and Daddy both be gone?" She'd cried so much already; she wasn't sure she had more tears left. But now, alone with the past, her eyes filled once more. Her voice was a broken whisper. "How am I supposed to live without you?"

The answer came over her slowly and brought with it a shame Randi had denied ever since leaving home for Hollywood. Her parents had taught her to love God first, no matter what. A mountain of guilt pressed down on her shoulders and made her squirm in discomfort. She had taken none of her parents' advice, and still they had loved her. Right to the end, in their final conversation, her mother had stressed only one concern. "I don't know how you really are, sweetheart, but please come back to Jesus." Her skin was clammy and pale, death only hours away. "I love you, Randi. . . . I don't want to be without you."

Now the words washed over and over Randi again.

The possibility that maybe she had misunderstood her mother all these years grabbed hold of her and pressed in against her chest. She tried to fill her lungs, but she couldn't draw a complete breath. As loving as her father had always been, as much as Randi and her sisters had been his princesses, her mother had loved them too. If Randi didn't find her way back to the Lord, she would miss out on heaven. That was the message of the Gospels, after all. Randi remembered that much.

A shiver ran over her arms, and her teeth chattered. She was having an affair with a married man. She and Luke Baxter had come together quickly and passionately on the beach that night, as if there were no one else in the world but the two of them. In the five weeks since then, they'd sent each other text messages and shared quiet conversations. When she returned to Los Angeles, they had plans to meet up once a month, if possible.

And Luke was hardly her first detour from the path her parents had lived. She couldn't count the number of men she'd been with — all of them connected to the entertainment industry one way or another. Some were married; some weren't. During her own brief marriage, she'd been faithful until she caught wind of her husband's outside interests. After that, neither of them had been faithful.

A sob caught in Randi's throat, and she felt consumed with a new and sudden fear. If she died today, the Lord wouldn't recognize her. He could hardly welcome her into heaven to spend eternity in the place where her parents were.

Randi stared at the bench and ran her hands over the smooth wooden slats. For the first time in a decade, she could see herself for what she was — filthy and wretched and without hope. She was walking down a path of destruction, and if she didn't let the death of her mother change her, nothing ever would. She gripped the arm of the bench and closed her eyes tight.

I'm sorry, God. I've failed You in every possible way. I'm dirty and tired and ready for a change. Right here, Lord. Forgive me and make me clean in Your sight.

She wasn't sure whether to expect an answer or not, and there was no audible response. But as she finished praying, she remembered something else her father had told her. "Whenever you're ready, whenever you let go of yourself and grab hold of God, He'll welcome you with open arms."

The mountain lifted, and her next breath filled her lungs with a new peace and assurance. There was no time to waste on making her next move. She had chosen Luke because he looked and acted so much like Dayne. But how wrong she'd been. She couldn't have Dayne or Luke, and maybe God wanted her to be alone, without a man at all. Maybe the Lord wanted to be the only one in her life for a while. She steeled herself toward the possibility and pulled her cell phone from her purse.

The entire country had seen the photo of her and Luke, and they'd pinned the indiscretion squarely on Dayne's shoulders. Immediately after the picture ran, Dayne had confronted her about it. "You know that isn't me!" He seethed with anger and fear she'd never seen in him before. "You can clear this up, Randi." His eyes had been wildly desperate. "Call the tabloids. Tell them the truth." He threw his hands in the air. "How can you not care? My marriage is on the line."

Randi had only mumbled something about how the guy in the picture should've been Dayne, and then she'd walked away. In the weeks since then, Dayne had been the consummate actor, professional in all things as they continued shooting the film. The director had never even once asked if things were okay between them, never mentioned the possibility that their chemistry had taken a blow. But it had, of course.

Randi figured Dayne could handle the heat; he was used to it. Luke was a private guy, she told herself. It was more important that his identity be kept a secret when it came to their affair.

The wind rustled through the evergreens in the small park. Luke needed his privacy? Was that the only thing that had motivated her? Randi felt disgusted with herself. She couldn't lie anymore — not to herself and not to the world. Her real hope had been that the photo might break up Dayne's marriage, and then . . . finally . . . she would have a chance to win him over, the way she'd always tried to win him over.

Again she felt dirty, but then she remembered her prayer and the certainty of God's forgiveness. With that in mind, she had no time to waste. She punched in a series of numbers on her cell phone and waited, her breathing quick and shallow with anticipation. This was the first of several calls she needed to make, but this one was the most important.

It was a call she should've made five weeks ago.

Katy was tired nearly all the time, and twice she'd talked to Stephen about how she was feeling. She had no symptoms, really. Nothing other than a lack of energy and a struggle with getting out of bed each morning. Her director pegged the problem right away, since what else could be wrong with her?

She was depressed, and if not for the distraction of the movie, she might've tumbled into the throes of a depression so great she'd need to check in to a facility. That might come later. For now she had just a few weeks until they wrapped up the movie, a few weeks until she could return to Bloomington.

Katy was in her trailer, searching for the energy to get back out to the set. Their break would be over in five minutes, and there wouldn't be another chance to rest until lunchtime. They'd been working since six this morning because they needed sunrise shots. Now it was eight o'clock, and Katy would've been happy to sleep another ten hours.

She and Dayne talked every few days, but their conversations were always short. Early on, he'd told her that he had a suspicion about who the guy in the photo might actually be.

"Come on, Dayne." She didn't raise her voice. It was too late for that. "Who else could it be?"

He told her he'd had an idea, but then that fell through. "So maybe it's a stuntman or a lighting guy." His tone pleaded with her. "It wasn't me; that's all I know."

In the weeks since then, the magazines had taken the story and run with it. There were reports of partying on the set, beer flowing freely, and a romance between Dayne and Randi that couldn't be denied. One week a popular tabloid headline took Dayne's approach. "Dayne Doesn't Remember Affair!" it shouted in big, bold letters. Katy had read the article late at night in the privacy of her hotel room.

"So much drinking and partying is happening on the set of Dayne's current film," the story started out, "that Dayne doesn't remember his wild affair with costar

Randi Wells!"

Dayne denied that also. He hadn't drunk anything on the set, and he'd definitely never acted without knowing what he was doing. "We need to talk, Katy. Let me fly there so we can have a day together. Please."

"No." Katy didn't want to talk about the affair here in London. The tabloids would go wild over the idea of a confrontation on the set of Katy's film. "It can wait. We don't need to make any decisions yet."

In that way, she was able to keep him from flying out to see her. They were both busy, both shaken by the events surrounding them. The best choice was to lie low, finish their films, and return to Bloomington. There, on the deck of their lake house, they could talk about what the future held.

And what it didn't hold.

She heard a group of people walk past her trailer, their conversation loud, their laughter bright and cheerful. Katy moved to the small mirror on the wall near the trailer door. How long had it been since she'd laughed? She thought about what day it was, and she knew the answer.

Stephen had talked to her several times about taking a break, leaving for a few days, and working things out with Dayne.

But she had refused the offer. "What

would it help?"

"I don't know." Stephen seemed frustrated with the changes in his leading lady. "He's telling you he didn't do it. Maybe you should hear him out face-to-face."

Even Ian Walters encouraged her to go. But she couldn't leave the set now, not when she was a part of nearly every major scene in the film. Besides, her personal life hadn't spilled over into the movie more than a couple of times.

Right after she first saw the photo of Dayne and Randi, Katy had struggled with getting back into character.

Stephen had pulled her aside and explained her choices. "Either you take a break and get some help, or you find the strength to make this your best performance yet."

The story was about a woman battling depression, whose sorrow was so great it nearly sent her over the edge. Stephen had a point. If Katy could transfer what she was feeling about Dayne to the character she was playing, then not only would she give a strong performance, but she could delay dealing with her real life until she and Dayne could be together again.

When they would sort through the pieces of their broken marriage and figure out a way to move on alone . . . in their separate lives.

Katy touched the dark circles under her eyes. No matter what the future held, the pain in her heart was doing the very thing Stephen had hoped it might do. It was working for the film. She not only owned the part, she lived it. Breathed it. With her limited sleep and torturous alone moments, she even looked the part.

Stephen had stopped talking to her about taking a break. If Katy wanted to work through her pain and depression by taking it out on the set in fourteen-hour workdays, so be it. Her director had told her he was there for her if she needed anything. But he wasn't where Katy was finding the strength to make it through each day.

She was finding that in her phone calls home to Jenny and to her sister-in-law Ashley. Most of all she was finding it in her well-loved, much-read Bible.

As it turned out, a few members of the cast were interested in Scripture and what it taught about life and death and living right. Katy could hardly believe it, but three times a week before the first shots of the day were filmed, the group met in her trailer to study God's Word. Since a few of them had never been exposed to Scripture, Katy started where she herself started anytime she wanted to reconnect with God. In John chapter 1. So while her heart was ripped in a hundred unrecognizable pieces, her soul rejoiced at the changes happening in the people around her.

"There's something about you I haven't seen before," one of her female costars told her after the first Bible study. "Whatever it is, I want it too. The thing that makes you beautiful isn't something you can buy on Rodeo Drive or win at the Academy Awards."

The compliment had touched Katy and given her purpose. God was carrying her through the pain and confusion, holding her in His arms until she and Dayne could talk in person about their failed marriage. Not only was the Lord holding her up, but He was using her to bring others to Himself. As much as she hurt, she couldn't ask for more than that.

She was about to step out of her trailer when her cell phone rang. It was well after midnight in Mexico, but still she had a feeling it was Dayne. As she reached for the phone, she saw his name in the caller ID window. Most of the time she took his calls. Partly because she wanted to keep the communication between them open so they wouldn't feel like complete strangers when they met again in Bloomington.

And partly because she missed him with every breath.

Now, though, she stared at her phone, and then, with it still ringing, she walked out of her trailer and back to the set. She still loved Dayne. With everything she had, she loved him. But he was lying to himself and lying to her, and if this was what it meant to be married to Dayne Matthews, Katy couldn't take it.

She couldn't spend a lifetime like this.

No, she would only talk to him every day or so, and eventually — when December was almost over — they would finish filming and return home. Katy would have some time alone, because after Dayne was finished in Cabo, the cast and crew needed a few weeks in LA to wrap things up. That was fine with Katy. She would continue her Bible study, searching for wisdom and hope and a reason to go on. She would beg God for the grace to forgive Dayne and the wisdom to know how to move on from here.

But she was very sure of one thing. This was her last movie. When she was finished filming, she would return to her home in Bloomington, where she would spend the rest of her days.

With or without Dayne.

CHAPTER
TWENTY-ONE

Dayne snapped his phone shut and slid it back into his jeans pocket. "No answer." He planted his elbows on the small wooden kitchen table and stared at his friend Bob. With the death of Randi's mother, the cast and crew had been given a few days off. Dayne had asked Katy if he could fly to London and spend his break with her.

But she'd turned him down. "I'm busy, Dayne. We're filming early morning till late at night. The talking can wait until we're together."

So Dayne had done the only other thing he knew to do. He'd come here, to Bob Asher's house in Mexico City, where a few years ago he'd given his heart and soul to God.

"What was her attitude last time you talked?" Bob sat across from him, his expression colored with deep concern.

"Same as it's been." Dayne made a fist and leaned his forehead against it. "She doesn't come right out and call me a liar, but she's different." He let his hand fall to the table and looked at Bob again. "It's like she's resigned herself, like she's already decided we're finished."

Bob sat a little straighter and seemed to concentrate, as if he had something sensitive he wanted to bring up. "Tell me about the picture again."

They hadn't mentioned the tabloids once since he showed up at Bob's house. Dayne hated thinking about the cover photo, let alone talking about it. He realized how bad the circumstances looked and how much he seemed to be the man in the picture. Talking about it only brought to life the fact that even the people closest to him — his wife, his father, and his friend — doubted him.

Dayne let loose a shaky sigh. "It was taken at night, so at first I thought about who would've been off with Randi after dark." He held his hands out, palms up. He hadn't told anyone about his initial suspicion, but maybe it was time. "The only person I could think of was my own brother, Luke."

"Luke was in Cabo?"

"Yes." Dayne allowed a sad laugh. "No one really knows that but the people on the set. And here's the thing. Luke and Randi did take a walk alone on the beach the night he was there."

"Well then . . ." Bob's eyes shone with new understanding. "Maybe that's the answer."

"That's what I thought." Dayne pictured the way Randi had looked when he brought up the possibility a few days after the photo ran. "I talked to Randi about it, and she was horrified. 'Absolutely not,' she told me. She said Luke wasn't the one she wanted." Guilt crept into his tone. Somehow her attraction to him had to be his fault, one way or another. "She wanted me; that's what she said. The guy wasn't Luke."

"So you believe her? That's that?"

"No, I called my brother. I asked him if anything happened on the beach that night." Dayne could still hear Luke's sincerity. "He promised me it wasn't him."

"Hmmm." Bob studied the table for a few seconds, as if he was trying to get a handle on the possibilities. "And you've been through the rest of the cast and crew?"

"There's nearly a hundred people working on the set." Dayne sat back in his chair. "Caterers, security, camera guys. I've begged God for the answer and talked to a few who seem a little more friendly with Randi." He clenched his jaw. "The thing is, she knows the truth and she won't talk."

Bob shook his head. "I can't imagine

working with her every day since then."

"Yeah." Dayne stood and walked toward the window of the Ashers' small house. There were still lights on along the busy street. Life going on as it did in Mexico City, where celebrity was not the all-consuming force it was back home. He raked his fingers through his hair, his back to Bob. "Before this break, she pulled me aside. Told me she's sorry. She was drunk, and she honestly doesn't remember." His sad laugh rang through the room. "She even had the nerve to ask me, 'Dayne, are you sure it wasn't you?'"

"And you . . . you weren't drinking, right?" Bob sounded hesitant, as if he didn't want to accuse Dayne of any wrongdoing. But the facts mattered greatly to the story.

"No." Dayne turned and looked at his friend again. "I wouldn't dare have a beer on a set with Randi Wells. Someone would take a picture, and there'd be the proof." He pretended to paint a headline in the space in front of him. "'Dayne Matthews Boozes It up on the Beach!'" He returned slowly to the table and gripped the back of his chair. "The thing is, someone kissed her. Someone stood on that beach and made out with Randi Wells." Again he struggled with the rage inside him. "Whoever he is, he's letting me take the fall." He sat down, defeated. "Me and Katy."

Bob was about to say something else when Dayne's phone, still sitting on the kitchen table, vibrated to life. Like always, the song from *Robin Hood* rang out, a painful reminder of all Dayne had at stake. Maybe it was Katy. Maybe she'd thought things through and realized he couldn't possibly have started an affair with Randi. He was far too in love with Katy for anything of the sort.

He reached for the phone, glanced at the caller ID window, and just as quickly hit the silence button on the side and dropped it back onto the table.

"Who is it?" Bob had his arms crossed, his face still pensive. He'd promised Dayne he would help clear up the situation if at all possible, but so far they were getting nowhere.

Dayne felt tainted even saying her name. "Randi. Naturally. Her timing is always like that."

A shadow fell over Bob's face. "She's home for her mom's funeral, right?"

"That's why we got the break."

"And she calls *you?*" Bob raised his brow. "That's not good. I mean, buddy, that woman has it out for you."

"I know. If I can just finish up the film and get back home . . . maybe when Katy sees me in person, she'll understand I'm telling the truth." Dayne rested his arms on the table and leaned forward, too battered to continue the conversation. Why would Randi call him? Wasn't it enough that they had constant contact on the set? He'd made it abundantly clear that he wasn't interested, and now . . . now what was Bob supposed to think?

Katy hadn't accused him of lying, but she hadn't talked to him about the incident either. Her lifeless tone and short sentences told him what her words did not. The last time they talked, she'd admitted that her feelings for him had changed.

"Of course they have," she'd told him. She sounded tired constantly, as if she didn't have the energy to fight the battle surrounding them. "I guess I'm rethinking whether I want this life, every transgression and misstep plastered over the tabloids."

"That's not fair. You knew what you were getting into." Dayne had tried not to sound desperate, but that's usually where he wound up by the end of their conversations. "What about our walk on the beach that night? Faith and each other, remember?"

"Things changed. What else can I say?"

So, no . . . she didn't come out and accuse him of lying. She didn't need to. Her attitude and responses told him everything he needed to know. Whenever he pressed her, when he asked her directly whether she believed him or not, she always answered the same way. "We'll talk about it in person. Let's get our movies finished first."

Now Dayne was practically crazy with fear over what Katy was planning and how differently she actually felt about him and their marriage. He pushed himself back from the table and got a glass of water. He poured one for Bob too.

When he returned to his chair, he met Bob's eyes and saw a knowing that was familiar with his friend. As if Bob finally had a game plan that might make a difference for Dayne.

"Your marriage is on the rocks, Dayne. You see that."

There was no need to respond. Dayne only let his gaze fall to his clenched fists there on the tabletop. Moments like this he wondered if he was having some kind of wild nightmare and at any moment he might wake up to find that he and Katy were happily in love, doing their separate jobs and counting down the days until they could be together. "Yes . . . my marriage is on the rocks." He felt the pain of his words with every syllable. "No argument here."

"Then now's the time." A new energy filled Bob's voice. "You have to do whatever you can, whatever it takes to restore things with Katy."

"I need a miracle."

"Good!" Bob reached across the table and covered Dayne's hand with his own. "Because we serve a God who is in the business of making miracles happen. Your situation looked so grim that I was starting to forget that."

Dayne wasn't sure whether to allow a glimmer of hope or feel further defeated that even Bob Asher — his friend of unending faith — thought the situation looked grim. He looked up and saw the determination in Bob's face. Almost in response, Dayne felt a fight rising in him as well. " 'With God all things are possible,' right? Isn't that what you taught me?"

"Right. But it didn't come from me." Bob was actually smiling now. "It came from the Bible. That means it's a promise."

They talked a few minutes more, and then Bob prayed. He asked God to move heaven and earth on behalf of Dayne's marriage, and he begged that the truth — the full and complete truth — would become miraculously known. That lies would cease, and webs of deception would be broken — wherever they existed.

A power came over the room, power and peace and a certain sense that God was moving, that the prayers being lifted in this very place would not go unanswered. That even now, God Almighty had a good plan for Dayne and Katy.

Dayne prayed next, choking out the words through a throat tight with hope and sadness. "Please give me a sign, Lord. Show me the truth and let it become clear to everyone involved." He felt a sob lodge in his chest, but he worked past it. "I can't lose Katy. She's . . . she's everything to me."

His cell phone began to ring again as he uttered the final words. "In Jesus' name, amen."

Dread hovered in the balance as he looked at the caller ID. The name in the window caused Dayne to hesitate. He looked at Bob as he moved to open the phone, and even before he said hello, a strange understanding came over him. Maybe this call would contain the answer he'd been looking for. The call wasn't from Randi, and it wasn't from Katy, either.

The call was from his brother, Luke.

■ ■ ■ ■

Luke had wandered from one side of Times Square to the other, moving aimlessly north along Broadway and then south again on the other side of the street. He felt terrible about what he'd done, and now he'd heard from Randi. She wanted to break things off immediately.

"My parents wanted one thing from me," she told him. "I have to try to find it. That means this is the last time you'll hear from me."

So Randi had found the strength to move on, but still neither she nor Luke had reached Dayne with the truth. He hadn't even tried. Luke stuffed his hands in his pockets to ward off the chill in the air. The city had received its first snowfall a week ago, and now a bitter cold moved in between the high-rises that made up the Theater District.

He'd seen another play tonight — *Mary Poppins* — with more free tickets from the office. But this time he didn't take Sandy or any of the others. If they wanted tickets, they could make their own plans. He needed to be alone, needed to contemplate his life and his future without the temptations he usually surrounded himself with.

The sets were unbelievable — more elaborate than anything he'd seen on a Broadway stage, even at the production of *The Lion King*. But it was the story line that grabbed his heart in a strange and unexpected way. The story showed George Banks so caught up in his job and his self-importance that he spent a decade missing out on the treasures of life — his wife and kids. Sure, they shared a house, but George was no more invested in the lives of his family than he was in the lives of the strangers who came and left his bank each day.

In the end, through the intervention of Mary Poppins, George saw his family and his life in a new way — before it was too late.

Luke crossed 43rd Street and continued north. So what about him? He and Reagan were barely speaking to each other. He had a suspicion that there was more to her friendship with the firefighter, and certainly she suspected him of having a girlfriend here in the city. The truth seemed shady and intangible for both of them, and so far they had avoided having any deep discussions on the matter.

It was enough to come home at the end of the day and deal with Tommy and Malin without also making time to do surgery on his marriage. The main reason he hadn't pulled Reagan aside to talk to her, though, was because of his great and consuming guilt.

He'd asked God for help, told Him he was sorry and that he didn't recognize himself any longer. He was sure his mother would've been heartbroken by the person he had become. But in order to come clean with Reagan, he would have to admit the affair with Randi. Somehow he believed that telling her would make things worse. They could continue on the way they were, with neither of them any wiser about whatever was going on behind the scenes. And that way, they could still have a semblance of faithfulness and commitment.

A police car screamed down the street, followed by two others. Cabdrivers slammed on their horns, urging pedestrians to get out of the way. No one stopped and stared. No one looked alarmed. Another night in New York City.

Luke pulled his scarf tight around his face and braced himself against the wind. It was the same way with him. His life was in crisis mode, sirens blaring through his heart and soul. But no one noticed him or wondered about the pain he was carrying any more than they would wonder about any other pedestrian walking the streets of Times Square.

The pain was his own. The guilt, too.

But if he didn't deal with it, he would wind up exactly like George Banks. Married to his work, with only the shell of a life outside the office. That was if Reagan didn't leave him first. This wasn't the life his parents had hoped for him. His actions weren't the result of anything he'd learned from growing up a Baxter.

He reached 48th Street and the hotel where he was staying. The doorman smiled politely as he walked past and into the elevator. His room was twenty-nine floors up, and with each number that passed, Luke became more sure of his next move. Whatever the fallout, whether Reagan could understand and learn to forgive him, or if it meant she wanted to move on without him, he had just one choice if he wanted to turn things around. He needed to tell the truth.

The moment he walked into his room, he dropped to the edge of the bed and dialed Dayne's number. *Okay, God . . . after this there won't be any turning back.* He gulped back his fear, and as he did, he caught a glimpse of himself in the mirror that hung over the bureau. He wasn't the guy he'd

367

once been, the cocksure twenty-one-year-old who had known he would be everything John Baxter was and more. His eyes were empty and fearful, but maybe after today, they'd reflect something he'd been needing more than his next breath.

Forgiveness.

He sent the call, and on the second ring Dayne answered. "Hello?"

Luke squeezed his eyes shut. "Hey, Dayne . . . it's me, Luke."

"I know." Dayne seemed impatient but not angry. Almost certainly he had no idea why Luke was calling. "What's on your mind?"

Luke's heartbeat pounded in his temples so loud that he wondered if Dayne could hear it through the phone line. "I owe you an apology."

For a few seconds, silence weighed heavy in the space between them. Then there was the sound of Dayne drawing a long breath. "Okay . . . go on."

"I lied to you." Luke opened his eyes and massaged his brow. He wanted to change his identity or move to another planet where the truth would no longer matter. But there was no such place. He breathed in and held it. "It was me in the photograph. Randi made me promise not to say anything, and

I . . . I didn't want Reagan to find out." He exhaled through clenched teeth. "I'm sorry."

Again silence, and then something that sounded almost like a stifled cry. "You're serious? You were the guy?"

"I was. Randi had been drinking, but we weren't drunk. She just didn't want people to know. Me either. For very selfish reasons." Luke felt sick. He wouldn't blame Dayne if this was the last time they ever spoke. And something else he hadn't thought about until this moment — Dayne would probably fire him. How could he trust Luke with his legal affairs when Luke was a liar willing to let Dayne go down in flames over a tabloid photo?

"You and Randi . . . is there still something between you?"

"No. It's over. I want to make things right with Reagan." Luke stood and went to the window. His head pounded, and he only wished for the call to end. "Things are terrible between us, and she doesn't even know about Randi." He leaned against the window frame. "I'll have to tell her, of course. But . . . I had to talk to you first."

Dayne must've heard the pain and desperation in Luke's tone because this time he didn't hesitate. "I don't know what to say." His voice wasn't angry the way it should've been. "I asked God to show me the truth, and you called at almost the same minute."

"Yeah . . . well, I don't blame you if you're through with me. I'm just about through with me too. Mom wouldn't recognize the man I've become."

Dayne's joy was clear even over the phone. "We can talk more later, but I can tell you this . . . I'm not through with you." The happiness in his tone mixed with a love that defied logic. "I didn't work so hard to find my family only to write you off now. I forgive you. I mean it."

Luke braced himself against the window and tried to catch his breath. Had his brother actually just said those words? He forgave him? Luke had betrayed Dayne's trust in every possible way, and in return he was being given a kind of grace he'd known just once before. When his parents welcomed him home from his rebellion after 9/11.

Peace washed over him. Peace and a sense that he couldn't possibly accept his brother's forgiveness. But then, the grace Dayne was offering him was supernatural, the kind that came from faith in Christ alone. Luke wanted to tell him no, that forgiveness wasn't necessary because Luke didn't deserve it. But he couldn't get the words past his lips.

"I know how you're feeling." Dayne's tone was rich with compassion. "I've made lots of bad choices in my life. It's a matter of untangling the knots and moving forward." He seemed suddenly in a hurry to get off the phone. "Does Randi know you're telling me?"

"No. But something's changed in her too." Luke realized there were tears on his cheeks. He wiped at them and coughed to clear his voice. "I'm not sure what's happening, but God's doing all the work."

"Yes." Again there was a smile in Dayne's voice. "That's exactly what it is." He promised to call Luke again soon, and then the call ended.

As Luke tossed his cell phone back on the bed, he pictured Reagan, the way she'd looked that long-ago September 10, when he stopped by her Indiana University apartment before her softball game. He was supposed to go with her that day, but instead . . .

Instead they'd stayed alone in the apartment and watched Monday Night Football. Reagan had fallen asleep on the couch beside him. What happened next changed the course of their lives.

Luke turned his back to the window and moved to the bed. In some ways, the consequences from that day were still playing out six years later. He and Reagan had gone against God's plan, and in the year that followed they'd been little more than strangers. The same way they were now.

Luke stretched out on the bed and closed his eyes. He wasn't tired, but he needed to make a plan. And then in a rush he could see the obvious truth — there was only one plan to be made. That way, after tonight he could move ahead with not one less lie choking the life from him but two less. With that he didn't hesitate. He picked up his cell phone and dialed the one person he'd hurt most with his decisions.

His precious wife, Reagan.

It was all Dayne could do to keep from calling Katy right then and there. Bob clearly knew something dramatic had happened, and when Dayne hung up the phone, the details tumbled out.

"I wanted so much to believe you." Bob pulled him into a hug. "After you explained yourself that first time we talked, I never really thought you were lying."

"I know. It's okay." Dayne wasn't angry at Bob or anyone else who might've doubted him — whether for a brief time or to this day. He was a movie star; of course he would be a candidate for having an affair with his leading lady. But the truth was out, and Dayne could hardly wait to share it with the world. He felt like a wrongly convicted prisoner who had finally and completely been set free.

"The timing." Bob laughed. "I mean, is God great or what?"

Dayne smiled, and he felt it to the center of his soul. He had done what Bob had trained him to do — relied on God's promises and taken the painful situation straight to the throne room of heaven. Along the way, God had met him right here. This very night.

He wanted to call Katy before another minute passed, but it wasn't even four in the morning in London. So for the next two hours, he and Bob talked about Luke and his life and then about the dreams Dayne had for that far-off someday when he could leave acting behind and live out his days in Bloomington, on the shore of Lake Monroe, surrounded by his family.

Finally, when it wouldn't be too early Katy's time, Dayne excused himself, stepped outside, and stood against the doorframe. Luke's reputation and marriage were on the line, so Dayne wanted to be careful who he talked to about the truth. After all, people were used to seeing his name in the headlines. But Luke's name? If the public found out the truth, the affair with Randi would stay with Luke the rest of his life. With Dayne, though, the tabloids were always taking potshots, looking for dirt. What the public thought of him didn't matter. No, Dayne wouldn't reveal the information, but he needed Katy to know.

The call went through, but after a number of rings it went to her voice mail. Dayne hesitated but decided against leaving a message. This was the sort of news he wanted to tell her himself, not through a recording. He hung up and looked at the time on his phone. She was probably in the shower, which meant she might not see she missed a call from him until late in the day.

She had less than three weeks of filming left, so it was crucial he talk to her before she went home. Otherwise she'd make the trip to Bloomington without knowing the truth. In that case she was bound to feel farther from him, more intent on returning to her former life without him.

He pressed his lips together and clicked his phone shut. He'd get the word to Katy somehow, even if he had to change his filming schedule to reach her. For now he could only pray for one more miracle.

That Katy would believe him until then.

CHAPTER
TWENTY-TWO

Ashley drove through Bloomington in a daze, trying to focus on her MapQuest directions and not the terrible conversation she'd just had with Reagan. She was meeting Brooke and Kari at the site of the crisis pregnancy center. Ashley loved the name Brooke had come up with for the center, and they all agreed. Sarah's Door would honor the brief life of Ashley and Landon's little girl.

From the beginning, the prayer of Ashley, Brooke, Kari, and their friends and families who had joined in the effort was always the same. That whoever walked through the doors of the center would find life and choose life. At that moment of crisis and forevermore.

Now, though, Ashley could've prayed a similar prayer for Luke and Reagan. Of course she'd known there was trouble. They'd all known. Reagan had hinted about it before, but not until a few minutes ago did Ashley understand how critical the situation really was.

"Mama!" Devin was in the back, strapped in his car seat. He caught her attention in the rearview mirror and grinned, pointing out the window at a semi in the next lane. "Big tuck!"

Ashley's heart melted. His joy was so complete, so innocent. "Yes, buddy, big, big truck." Each week it seemed Devin got a little more like his older brother. A little more adventurous than Cole but with the same tender heart. A reflection of their daddy and their heavenly Father.

Devin gasped, his eyes wide, and this time he pointed at a dump truck.

Ashley checked the directions once more at the stoplight. When the light changed, she drove another half mile and made one final turn. She stayed focused until she pulled up in front of the closed-down storefront site of the previous crisis pregnancy center. Brooke had already signed a new lease for the space. They had scheduled a few workdays for cleaning and painting, and then when the new furniture and equipment came in, they could celebrate the re-opening.

Ashley turned off the engine and settled

back in her seat. Brooke and Kari weren't here yet, so she gave herself permission to think once more about her conversation with Reagan, the one she'd had on the drive here.

"Things aren't good," her sister-in-law had told her. "Luke moved out this past weekend. He took an apartment a few miles away."

Ashley had to work to maintain control of her van. "What? How did that happen?" She thought about turning around and heading straight for her brother's house.

"He told me the truth about the picture in the tabloids." Reagan hesitated. "The guy in the photograph wasn't Dayne. It was Luke."

Dizziness swept over Ashley, and at that point she pulled into the parking lot of a convenience store. "Are you serious?" She had never even considered the possibility. Here all this time . . . all this time she'd been worried sick about Katy and Dayne, deeply disappointed in her older brother for his inability to be faithful. When all along the problem was Luke's.

Reagan explained that Luke had gone to Cabo for a couple of days to help Dayne with contracts. Luke and Randi had taken a walk on the beach that night. The picture on the cover of the tabloids told the rest of the story.

A sinking feeling grabbed at Ashley, and for a moment she let her head rest on the steering wheel. "I can't believe it." She wanted to feel happy for Dayne and Katy, but the sorrow of Luke's mistake was too great.

Reagan explained that Luke had started drinking during his business trips, and he'd connected with one of the women from the law firm. "So it isn't just Randi." Sarcasm colored her tone. "Luke's making moves wherever his work takes him."

"Does Dayne know?"

"Yes." She sighed, but the bitterness remained in her voice. "When Luke was finally willing to come clean, he called Dayne first. As far as I know, though, he hasn't gotten ahold of Katy yet."

Despite the bad news, hope flooded Ashley's heart. If Dayne knew, Katy would know eventually. At that point she'd have to allow for the fact that a misunderstanding had happened. Someday not too far away, the relationship between Katy and Dayne would be restored to what it once was.

But Luke and Reagan . . .

Her sister-in-law explained that after Luke came clean, the two of them slowly realized the sad truth. There was nothing left of their marriage. "It's not altogether a bad thing, Luke getting his own apartment. There's a lot of anger between us right now." Her tone softened for the first time. "Maybe one day we'll be ready for counseling. But until then, the kids deserve more than us fighting all the time."

Ashley was kind but urgent. "It isn't better for anyone. Get counseling now before the two of you convince yourselves to move on."

But Reagan had her mind set. "Sometimes life doesn't give you a storybook ending, Ashley."

The call had ended, and Ashley pulled back into traffic.

Now Ashley still couldn't believe the news and how far her brother had fallen. She looked at Devin. He'd fallen asleep, his curly blond head nestled against the padded side of his car seat. She reached back and stroked his chubby hand. No one needed to tell her about storybook endings. If she'd been writing the story, Sarah would be sitting in the backseat next to Devin, healed and alive. But in the course of losing her daughter, Ashley had been convinced of one promise from God. The miracle of Sarah's life would happen in the lives around her. In the relationships that made up the Baxter family. The verse that had spoken to her in the days after coming home from the hospital with empty arms still stayed with her. Not only should Ashley be still and know that God was in control, but the Lord would be exalted!

Tears filled her eyes. So how was God being glorified now?

She searched the street again for signs of her sisters. She was early but only by a few minutes.

Yes, Sarah's life had to count for something, and that sad, joyous day at the hospital, Ashley had looked at the faces around her and known that the miracle would be increased love all the way around. Already her father had acted on his desire to love much and to make the most of his days. He had asked Elaine to marry him.

Afterwards, he'd called each of his kids and told them the news. Their dad and Elaine wanted a summer wedding, which meant that Erin and Sam would already be back living in the area when the celebration happened. No matter how bittersweet the announcement, Ashley cared for Elaine. She was happy for her dad, glad that he wouldn't live the rest of his life alone. There was glory for God in that.

But Ashley had never imagined that the one living alone before Christmas would be Luke.

Ashley made a mental note to call Luke immediately after meeting with her sisters. As she did, Brooke pulled up. Kari was with her, and the two of them looked happy, laughing about something. Kari's car was probably parked back at Brooke's medical office, since parking downtown, where the center was located, was always at a premium. They climbed out of the van, Brooke holding the hand of Kari's three-year-old RJ and Kari with little Annie's baby carrier looped over her arm.

Ashley hated to ruin the mood, but they needed to know. She took her still-sleeping Devin from her van, walked around, and leaned on the passenger door.

Kari noticed Ashley's tears and the look on her face first. "What is it?" She set down the baby carrier and came to her. "What happened?"

"Let's go inside." Ashley dabbed her fingers at the wet trail on either cheek.

Brooke looked at her a moment longer, clearly worried. Then she pulled a key from her purse and unlocked the door, and the three of them and their kids moved in where it was warmer.

For the next ten minutes Ashley explained the dire straits Luke and Reagan were in. The news was sobering to all of them, and not until Brooke checked her watch did they remember the reason they had gathered.

"I hate to change the subject, but I have to get back to the office." Brooke frowned. "Let's take a look around. We can talk about Luke after that."

The space was bigger than they'd hoped for — mainly because their dad had pulled strings with the building's owner, a friend of his from both the hospital and church. Rent for the building would be half of what it might've been otherwise.

"We'll put sofas along those two walls," Brooke said, "and office furniture in each of the smaller rooms."

"When'll you be ready to open?" Kari shifted the baby carrier to her other arm. "The notice for volunteers has been running in the paper for a month now."

Brooke smiled, even though the concern about Luke remained in her eyes. "We've got two retired nurses who are best friends and want to make this their full-time mission. A number of senior high school girls are willing to put in a few hours a week as part of their community service work. Bailey Flanigan is one of them." She thought for a second. "Then, of course, you two will be on call, in case we need to cover for our regular staff."

"What about ultrasound equipment?" The machines from the previous center had been sold when the center closed. Now they were the most critical item needed before they could open. "Did Dad's contact come through?"

"He did. Between our families, CKT, and a few donations from church friends, it looks like we'll have one here the day we open."

Ashley could hardly believe how successful they'd been. Only a few months ago, reopening the center had been nothing more than a possibility, a distant idea. If Bailey Flanigan hadn't said something about her high school friend, Ashley might never have heard about the need from Jenny. She certainly wouldn't have called Brooke with the suggestion. And now, people from church and the community had pulled together to answer the need. It gave Ashley hope about every aspect of the future — even where it concerned her extended family.

Brooke held out her hands to Ashley and Kari. "Let's pray."

This was the real reason they'd come —

to dedicate the space to God and to ask Him to bless every woman who might ever walk through the doors.

They formed a small circle, and RJ tugged at Kari's sweater. "I pray too, 'kay, Mommy?"

"Okay, sweetie." Kari smiled at him. "Pray that lots of babies will be helped by this place."

"I like babies." RJ shifted around her and stood protectively over his little sister. "Annie likes me too."

"Yes. Very much."

Devin was awake now, still in Ashley's arms. He put his fingers in his mouth as he watched his cousins. RJ patted Annie's head, and for an instant, Ashley felt the pang of deep loss and maybe even a little jealousy. Her boy should have a baby sister to protect too.

She sniffed and met the eyes of her sisters. This wasn't the time for regrets, and she could see that Kari and Brooke were watching, weighing her reaction to the poignant scene. Ashley smiled. "It's okay. Let's pray."

They thanked God for the idea of reopening the center and for providing the space and people and equipment.

With tears in her voice, Ashley finished the prayer. "May every girl who walks through Sarah's Door know the loving touch from You, our Father, and may they make a decision for life, both for themselves and for their babies. So that Sarah's legacy, a legacy of the value of life, however brief, will live on."

She held tighter to Devin and leaned her head against his. "As for our brothers, Lord, they need Your intervention now. We beg You. Help Dayne and Katy clear up their misunderstandings, and convince Luke that he needs to be home to work at his marriage. Let Luke and Reagan see that they need counseling, and they need it now." Ashley paused. "Teach them that no one wins by walking away."

When the prayer was over, the sisters hugged before Brooke and Kari piled back into Brooke's van and headed out.

Ashley wanted a few more moments. She switched Devin to her other hip and pressed her free hand against her flat abdomen. She could still remember clearly the gentle kicks and turns, the sweet rolling sensation that Sarah had brought throughout her pregnancy.

Before Ashley left, she turned the lock on the inside. Then, for a while, she stood out front staring at the newly painted front window and the sign that hung on the door.

This was the first time she'd really focused on it. Sarah's Door — A Crisis Pregnancy Center.

Gratitude swelled in Ashley's heart and she felt overwhelmed by the goodness of God. He hadn't planned for death to be a part of life. But it was because they lived in a fallen world, where eventually everything and everyone would die. Even so, God's promise was that He would make good come out of any situation. Any heartache. Sarah's Door and all it would mean to the community of Bloomington for months and years to come was proof that the Lord would keep His promise. Because of Sarah's death, He would be exalted in Bloomington, at the very least.

Now Ashley could only pray that God would make good come out of Luke's and Dayne's situations too.

CHAPTER
TWENTY-THREE

The task of putting Elizabeth's letters into
scrapbooks for his kids had been far more
draining than John ever could've imagined.
Not the copying and sorting and adding
pages to the scrapbooks, but the emotional
drain of reading each of Elizabeth's letters
many times over and making sure the
personal ones wound up in the proper
books and that the ones written to him or
with general thoughts for her family wound
up in each.

John knew he couldn't make plans for his
upcoming wedding without putting this
project behind him. And now — finally —
at just after nine o'clock the second Monday
in December, he was finished. He stood
back and admired the six books spread
across the dining room table. They smelled
faintly of smoke but were otherwise undam-
aged by the fire.

He'd found photos of Elizabeth for the

covers, each one special for the son or daughter it belonged to. For the five youngest Baxter kids, he'd made a collage of Elizabeth with each of them. On Brooke's, for example, was a picture of Elizabeth standing next to Brooke just inside the doors of Clear Creek Elementary School on her first day of kindergarten. Next to it was a picture of Elizabeth and Brooke dancing in the living room and one of the two of them on Brooke's graduation day and again on the day Brooke married Peter. Maybe the most precious was the photo of Elizabeth with Maddie and Hayley the day Hayley came home from the hospital after her near drowning.

Elizabeth had been there through so many milestones, so many key moments in the lives of their children. The photos were similar for Kari, Ashley, Erin, and Luke.

Only Dayne's was different. On the cover of his, John had used just two pictures. A photo of Elizabeth as a young college girl, the way she'd looked when Dayne had been born. It was the same picture she'd left with Dayne's adoptive parents, the one that Dayne had used to find Elizabeth several years ago.

Next to it was a favorite picture of Elizabeth that John had taken after one of their big family outings to Lake Monroe. Elizabeth was sitting in a beach chair, her sun hat shading her face. The lighting had been just right, and John had grabbed the camera and snapped her picture. It wasn't often that a photograph captured a person's eyes in such a way as to get the exact feel of her heart. But this one did. John hoped Dayne would treasure it.

He was grateful for Ashley's reminder about the letter Elizabeth had written specifically for their firstborn. It was the one Ashley had found when she'd pulled down the box of letters from John's closet back when he hadn't been sure how to tell his kids about their older brother. Or even if he should tell them.

The letter was the reason Ashley had become driven to find her brother, but more than that, it was something deeply personal that belonged to Dayne. A letter he still hadn't seen or read. John opened the front cover of Dayne's scrapbook. Yes, everything about the book was bound to touch Dayne in a most special way. More than the others, maybe, because though Dayne carried inside him Elizabeth's sentimental spirit and love of family, he hadn't had the privilege of knowing her. Not for more than an hour, anyway.

John looked to the far end of the table, to the place where one much smaller scrapbook lay. The seventh book. On the cover was a series of four photographs of John and Elizabeth, each taken during a special season in their lives. When they were very young, when they were in the throes of raising toddlers, during their kids' teenage years, and again when their kids started having families of their own. The photos represented love personified. John and Elizabeth connected for all time — mind, body, heart, and soul.

He hadn't planned on making an album for himself, but in the end he'd had no choice. There were things Elizabeth had written to him that would encourage him, push him to be his best for the rest of his days. John wouldn't keep the scrapbook on his bedside table. But he would pull it out every now and then. Elaine would understand.

He flipped open the front cover of his book and let his eyes fall one more time on the first letter inside. It was brief and to the point, the way Elizabeth had rarely been when she put pen to paper. But it spoke volumes to his heart every time he read it.

My dearest John,

He stopped and caught his breath. The tears didn't come as easily or as often now, but here, with the project finally completed, his eyes grew watery. Just the act of reading those three words made Elizabeth's voice ring clear in his mind. *My dearest John . . .* They were words she said often, sometimes when she was being silly or when she was tired at the end of the day. "My dearest John, I'm exhausted. I believe it's time for me to turn in." Or "So . . . my dearest John, how was work for Bloomington's best doctor?"

He let his eyes linger on the words, and when he could see clearly, he continued reading.

You just called and told me about your patient, about how you were at his bedside and how you played a role in saving his life. As we hung up, God brought something to mind, and I had to write it now, had to tell you in case I forget or I never get the chance again.

You're a brilliant doctor, John. The life you saved today wasn't your first, and it won't be your last. But you should know something, my loving husband. You saved my life first. My parents had rejected me, dismissed me as a lost cause and an embarrassment. God used you to redeem me, to show me the redemption He had planned for my life.

For our lives.

Just remember that when you set out for work each day. I sit here, mom and wife, lover and friend, because you breathed life into me. I'll love you with every heartbeat, my darling.

Now and forever yours,
Elizabeth

God had used him to save her. Until he'd found the letter a few weeks ago — near the bottom of the box — he hadn't remembered ever considering such a thought. Elizabeth had been intelligent and confident, a natural born counselor with a knack for understanding God's wisdom in relationships. He had always believed she did him a favor in standing by him through their troubled early years.

But now he saw that she felt otherwise. It was fitting, really. They had always complemented each other, and now — even into death — they would complement each other in this. That each of them would spend their days knowing they'd become the person they were because of the other.

John blinked, and for a few seconds he

considered heading outside into the dark, walking along the path and finding the familiar bench where he and Elizabeth had spent so many wonderful hours talking about their family, praying about the day-to-day challenges of life.

But it was late, and he had something even more important to do before he turned in. He needed to box up the scrapbooks and deliver them to the houses of his kids. Brooke's, Kari's, and Ashley's would be easy. They lived within ten minutes of him. He would drop Dayne's in the mail in the morning and overnight it to the set in Cabo so Dayne would have the words of his mother as soon as possible.

But the one he was sure mattered most was the one that would take him nearly an hour out of Bloomington before the night was through. That was okay. John would've driven all night to get the book into the hands of his youngest son.

Ashley had told him the latest, and the news had driven him to double his efforts on the project. Luke had been particularly close to Elizabeth, and maybe . . . maybe her death had hurt him more than the others. It was something he hadn't considered until the last few days. Luke had been through a lot in recent years, so perhaps it wasn't any surprise that he was struggling with the task of being the man everyone expected him to be. No amount of hurt or loss would excuse his behavior, of course. But if anyone could use a reminder of his mother's love, it was Luke.

Even if — by all indications — the message was coming too late to make a difference.

Ashley didn't want to read her scrapbook yet. Not until she'd spent an hour working on the painting of her mother and baby Sarah. She laid the boxed scrapbook on the bed in the corner of the room and set about finishing the field of flowers. Never had the brilliance of color so taken her breath as it did in this painting. With God's help it felt like she'd actually captured a piece of paradise — the beautiful, alive way that heaven would have to look with her mother there.

It was early Tuesday afternoon, and Landon was home with the boys. It was his day off, and ever since her dad dropped the scrapbook off the night before, he had known Ashley was anxious to break away by herself and read it.

"Will you go to the cemetery?" He'd put his arms around her this morning in the kitchen.

He didn't need to clarify himself. She knew what he meant. Her eyes got lost in his, and she smiled sadly. "No. I thought I'd spend a few hours on my painting. Then maybe sit by the window in my old room and look at it there."

Landon nodded. "I like that." He kissed her gently. "Take as long as you need."

Now, with the field of flowers just about finished, Ashley had the strangest sense that her mother was actually in the room with her. The memories of yesterday were alive and tangible. The smells of the old room. The sound of a gentle wind through the trees outside. Winter in the air and Christmas around the corner.

As she worked, she could almost hear her mother downstairs calling to her. *"Ashley, I'm putting on the kettle. Want some tea?"*

Yes, Mom . . . I'd give anything for one more cup of tea with you. Tears blurred her eyes, and she blinked them back. There was something about the end of another year, something that had a way of putting distance between the vividness of her memories of her mother and the reality of life without her.

Her mother was gone. Life had moved on, the way life always had the nerve of doing.

But here in this room a few feet behind her was a reminder of her mother's words, her heart and love for Ashley and each of her siblings. Because of that, she could almost see her mother in the doorway, smiling at her, watching her paint. *"I love your paintings, Ashley. . . . You have a gift from God. I hope you use it for Him always."*

A stream of tears left a hot trail on each of her cheeks. *God, am I doing that? Is my gift helping anyone get closer to You?*

God gave her not an answer but a picture. That was how the Lord often talked to her, how He showed her precious moments and glimpses of life. The picture was of a large playroom. Cole and Devin were on the floor building LEGO villages, and in the distance there was a little girl — maybe two years old — with golden hair. Ashley could see only the back of her, but she seemed to belong in the picture somehow.

There on the wall of the playroom was the painting, the very one she was working on right now. Ashley had the strongest sense that the painting gave her children peace and certainty of God's love and the reality of heaven. Where they would all live forever one day.

The picture consumed her, giving her purpose and renewing her energy not only for finishing this painting but for putting the other pictures in her mind on canvas. Where they would leave a legacy for her kids, if not for the world. She put the final accents of deep purple into the field of flowers and then set her brush in a jar of cleaner.

Okay, God . . . help me get through this. Ashley turned and faced the book. Suddenly she felt none of the fear or trepidation about the sweet sorrow that would certainly lie ahead in the coming hour. This was a chance to spend a little time with her mother. There was nothing frightening about that, no matter how bittersweet.

Before she started, she did what her mother would've done. She went downstairs, made herself a cup of tea in her mother's favorite mug, and then returned to the head of her old bed. She set the cup on the sill in front of the window that was opened just enough to allow fresh air to clear the paint fumes.

It was colder today, and snow was in the forecast for the first time that winter. The weather experts were calling for a white Christmas and more snow than in recent years. Ashley was glad. She loved the idea of being in front of the Baxter fireplace, celebrating Christmas with everyone gathered in one place.

Carefully, because the contents were the closest thing to having her mother here with her, she lifted the lid off the box and pulled the scrapbook out and onto her lap. She had known the book would contain her mother's letters, but she hadn't expected the photographs.

She had many pictures of her mother, and over the years she'd scanned them into her computer so she had a digital library of the most precious ones. But it had been months since she'd looked through them. So here, laid out on the cover of the scrapbook, they gripped her heart in a way that caught her off guard.

There was a photo of her mother pushing her on a swing at the park and another of Ashley and her side by side, pulling weeds from the flower garden behind the Baxter house. The garden was still there, and her father was diligent about keeping the weeds at bay.

Her eyes shifted to the next picture, one of Ashley and her mother at a corner of the old kitchen table, two cups of tea in front of them, the teapot her mother loved placed between them. Of all the pictures of them, she would forever be grateful to her father for taking this one. Sometimes the everyday moments in life were the ones no one captured with a camera.

But because of this very picture, Ashley would always have a vivid memory of the way she and her mother would gather so often over tea, the way they used that time to talk about the struggles that were so prevalent for Ashley — at least through her early twenties. She smiled at the picture. What would she have done without her mother back then?

The next picture was of her mom cradling baby Cole. She was sitting in her rocking chair, and Ashley was crouched down on one side. Her mother had her arm around Ashley's shoulders, her body language giving a very clear message. *This is my daughter, no matter what her past mistakes. And this is her child, whom I love with all my heart.*

Ashley studied her son's face, the way it had looked years ago. How long would it be before he forgot about his grandma Baxter? He still talked about her, still referred to her being happy in heaven or taking care of Sarah. But he would be ten before they knew it, and then fifteen, and then a senior in high school. The years would fly by, and his grandmother would be merely a fading light from his boyhood days.

It was why Ashley was sad about turning the calendar pages, about welcoming in a new year. Because it placed one more day between the reality of her mom and the memory of her.

Ashley bit her lip and opened the front cover. The first letter was one she remembered. A letter of joy and love and congratulations because after a year of virtually no contact with her family, Ashley had returned from Paris. She tried to imagine how she'd feel if Cole deserted them after graduation. If he jetted off to a foreign country and came back having compromised himself and his faith. Would she have the grace to write such a letter of love to him only a week after his return?

She read the letter again and knew the answer instinctively. Yes, she would have the grace because her mother had extended that same grace to her. Funny, because from what she'd gathered from her dad, her mother hadn't been given the same grace by her own mother.

But then, she'd had the love of John Baxter. And that had made all the difference.

One by one Ashley read through the letters, finding treasures and bits of wisdom she'd never seen before and cherishing the familiar notes or letters she'd read when she found the box in her father's closet. Along the way she cried because of the tenderness of her mother and because with her words so alive in Ashley's heart, it made the missing almost unbearable.

At one point, she stopped and sipped her tea. Then, with her free hand, she reached out to the empty spot beside her and willed herself to remember what it was like when her mother had sat there. Her mother would've wept over the death of Sarah, and she would've made certain to spend extra time with Ashley just to be sure she was surviving the loss.

Ashley grabbed a few quick breaths and lifted her eyes to the painting a few feet away. That was the only comfort, really. The fact that the painting wasn't some sort of dreamy notion. It was reality. Her mother and her daughter truly were together in heaven. Cole had seen them there, the way only a child can see things.

Over the next half hour she finished reading the book. She made a point of reminding herself that next time it might be better to take the collection in small sections so she could savor each letter. With tender care, she closed the cover and eased the book back into its safe place inside the box. She covered it with the lid and finished her tea.

With that, she returned once more to her

painting, and again the image of the play-room came to mind. Only this time the details were clearer than before, and Ashley realized something strange. The playroom wasn't the one set up at their current house. It was bigger and full of a sort of love and history that they hadn't yet attained there.

A gasp slid across Ashley's lips, and she brought her fingers to her mouth. Suddenly she knew exactly what room she was seeing. It was big, with full light from the westerly windows. Of course, it wasn't possible that she'd ever see the image the way it looked in her mind, because sometime next sum-mer the old place was going on the market. Her father was moving on, and the rest of them would have to move on with him. No more creek behind the house, no more frog pond or path around the house. No more garden with more fragrant memories than flowers.

Even still, the image shone in her heart and soul, vivid because it was the place where she and her siblings had played and done puzzles and learned to write their alphabet. If only the picture could be a sign of things to come, a sign that somehow their father would change his mind and hold on to the place. Because the brilliant picture in her mind wasn't at her current house at all.

It was downstairs.

In the house that — even after it was sold — would forever belong to the Baxters.

CHAPTER
TWENTY-FOUR

The only contact Dayne had managed with Katy was two messages — one from him to her and one from her in response. Now it was the twelfth of December, and he'd had a talk with the film's director. When the filming on location ended in less than a week, he would need to return to Bloomington until after Christmas. The Los Angeles work could wait until January. Otherwise he was pulling out.

"Dayne . . ." The director seemed stunned by his request. "I didn't realize things were so bad."

"They are." Dayne wasn't as worried as before, but still . . . until he had some time with Katy, there was no telling what she was thinking. Even with the truth about the picture in hand, Katy might have convinced herself that she couldn't stand the scrutiny or the pressure of being married to him.

The director didn't hesitate. He'd called a

break so Randi could attend her mother's funeral. Certainly he could call off further production until after the holidays. "Just get things figured out, okay?" He patted Dayne on the shoulder. "I know how tough this business can be on the home life."

Now Dayne was piling a plate full of fruit and sliced lunch meat, ready for some solitude on the beach during the lunch break, when one of the gofers hurried toward him with a package in his hands.

"Mr. Matthews!" The young guy seemed anxious to catch Dayne before he walked away with his plate of food. "Wait up!"

Dayne stopped and allowed him time to arrive with the package. "For me?"

"Yes." The kid grinned, as if making an important delivery to Dayne Matthews was the highlight of his day. "It's marked urgent."

"Thanks." For a moment, Dayne wished he had more time. He would've liked to ask the guy's name and how he'd wound up working the shoot. Maybe encourage him to enjoy his anonymity while he still had the chance — provided he was aiming for a career on the screen, like most of the young people on the set.

The package was heavier than Dayne expected, but he was still able to tuck it under his arm, carry his plate of food, and move down the beach to the chair he'd set up beneath a palm tree. By now it was understood among the cast and crew that Dayne Matthews ate his meals alone. Not because he thought too highly of himself or because he couldn't be bothered to mix with the rest of the cast. But because his personal life demanded he find peace somewhere. Even if it was only during a lunch break between scenes.

He set his plate on the sand and rested the package on his bare knees. Even in December, the weather this far south was warm and inviting. Shorts and a T-shirt were still the only wardrobe any of the guys needed.

He checked the return address and saw that the package was from his father. He ripped open the mailer and pulled out a box from inside. Dayne knit his brow, confused. Was his father sending his Christmas present two weeks early? And all the way to Cabo, Mexico? It seemed unlikely.

Dayne lifted the cover off the box, and what he saw melted his heart in as much time as it took to draw his next breath. Inside was a scrapbook, and on the front were two pictures of Elizabeth Baxter. A small note was attached to the top corner of the book: *Thought you could use this now rather than later. Love you, Dad.*

Even with all he'd been through, this wasn't a feeling he was familiar with. His father's love for him spread through his chest and filled him with warmth and assurance. How incredible to think that thousands of miles away in Bloomington, the busy John Baxter had taken time from his own life to put together this book.

With his inability to reach Katy eating at him a little more each hour, this gift couldn't have come at a better time. Dayne didn't have to open the front cover to know that much. Still, he could hardly wait to see what was inside. He lifted the book and moved the box to the sand on the other side of his chair.

Dayne opened the front cover and there, protected by sheer plastic, was an original letter, handwritten and addressed to:

My dearest firstborn, my son . . .

Dayne's heart hesitated and then skittered into a strange rhythm. What was this? He gently pulled the letter from the protective sleeve and looked past the first page to the signature at the end. It was signed simply, *Your mother, Elizabeth Baxter.*

What? Dayne's head spun and he stared at the letter, not believing it was possible. Then, slowly, a memory took shape. When Ashley found him, the first time she called to make contact, she'd told him something about a letter. Yes, a letter that their mother had written to him. In the excitement of meeting his family and connecting with each of his siblings, Dayne had forgotten about the letter.

Until this very moment.

He sucked in a quick breath and returned to the beginning of the letter. It occurred to him that these were the pages Elizabeth had held; the ink on the page was ink she had placed there. Somewhere years ago, she had taken the time to sit down and put her feelings into words. And now those words would remain with him forever, one of his greatest treasures.

He started at the beginning, reading the first line once more.

My dearest firstborn, my son,

If you are reading this, then you have found me. Or you have at least found the others. Son, I have prayed for the chance to tell you this information in person, but time is running out. I can't go peacefully to be with the Lord until I make every effort to reach you. Even if the only way I can do that is through this letter.

Your father and I have thought about you with every passing year. Every birthday and Christmas, the fall when you must've started school, the year you would've graduated. You were always in our hearts, just a mention away. We had no choice about what happened, dear son. My parents sent me away, and a woman took you from me even when I screamed for her to bring you back. This is the part you must know. We never wanted to give you up. Never.

Dayne stopped and looked out at the gulf. How must Ashley have felt after reading those two paragraphs? She and the others had gone all their lives not knowing about him, and then — in the time it took to read the beginning of a single letter — everything about her life and the lives of all the Baxters changed suddenly and permanently. He found his place and rubbed his thumb absently over the slightly faded paper.

After you were gone, they told me to forget about you. They said I'd be better off if I convinced myself you had never been born. Your father and I prayed that you would be adopted by a Christian family, people who would raise you to share the faith that has always been so important to us. We tried to convince ourselves that you belonged to God, that He had found a family for you, and that somehow the social workers had been right. You were never ours in the first place. But we were wrong. My deepest regret in all my life is that I didn't fight harder to keep you.

Her deepest regret? He read the words again and a third time. If he and Katy didn't fight harder for their marriage, the words could be his someday. His deepest regret would be that he didn't fight harder to keep the woman he loved. If these were the only words from his mother, written specifically for him, then he needed to gain whatever wisdom he could from them. She hadn't intended that last statement to apply to his marriage, thirty-some years later. But it did. He began reading once more.

The way you felt in my arms the day you were born is something I will never forget. Your fuzzy blond hair and blue eyes, wide and alert, as if you knew our time was short. I didn't think I'd ever know that feeling again, the warm weight of my newborn son against my chest. But God gave us more children. Five more. And last of all He gave us a son, a boy we named Luke.

A strange feeling stirred in Dayne's heart. He forgave Luke, and even with the frustrating lack of communication with Katy, he couldn't hate his brother over what had happened. Still, who would've thought that decades after Elizabeth wrote this letter, it would be Luke who would wind up causing him such pain, such damaging hurt? He dismissed the thought.

Watching Luke grow up has always filled my heart with a mix of joy and sorrow. Because he looked just like you. When he turned one and learned to walk, I knew what you would've looked like as a toddler. It was the same when he lost a tooth and learned to ride a bike and graduated from high school. Every milestone was a reminder of all I'd lost with you. All I'd missed.

And so I've begged God for just one thing. That somehow in the midst of my final days I might have the chance to see you again, to hold you one more time. One last time.

Sadness and gratitude mixed and flooded his soul. God had answered Elizabeth's prayer, because against all odds he had found his mother's hospital room. They'd shared only an hour, but he had indeed hugged her and told her the answers to the questions she had. It was then that she'd told him the importance of faith and how very much she wanted him to know the love of their Savior. So they could share eternity together.

There was no going back, no undoing the past or living it over again. But if there had been, Dayne was certain he and Elizabeth would've been very close. The way they felt in the brief time they shared together. He looked at the pages in his hand again. She talked about hoping he had been placed in a warm, loving home and about her curiosity over whether he had a wife and kids.

Then she talked about the first time she had cancer.

I was sick one other time, and I tried to find you. The records were sealed, and we were turned away. So I know that it'll take a miracle now, but that's okay. The

God we serve is in the miracle business. Our lives have been a testimony to that.

My prayer for you is that you would know God, that you would have a relationship with Him. Also that you would know the love of family — our family. You might belong to other people, but you will always belong here with us too. Because whenever I think of my precious children, I don't see five — I see six. I always will. I love you, Son. If I don't get the chance to hold you here, then I have to believe God will let me hold you in heaven. And there we won't ever have to say good-bye again.

Your mother,
Elizabeth Baxter

For a while Dayne remained still, staring at the pages, trying to imagine the way she might've looked when she wrote these words to him. He flipped through the book and saw that it was a collection of letters — each of them from Elizabeth and written to her children, of whom he was one.

Then, careful not to damage the pages, he slipped the letter back into the plastic sheet and closed the book. He couldn't look at another page, not now, when his heart was so consumed by the words he'd just read.

He set the book back inside the box and covered it with the lid. His food forgotten, he walked out toward the surf, his eyes on the horizon. A part at the end of her letter stood out. The part about their God being in the miracle business. It was something he'd heard his siblings say often in the few years he'd known them, and he realized what a gift they'd been given. All of them, and him most of all because his adoptive parents had loved the Lord also. As a result, they'd had parents who believed the truth — that with Christ all things were possible.

It was one of the first Bible verses Bob had told him to memorize. "You'll come up against some tough times in life. That's when you have to know the truth. With God all things are possible."

God was still working miracles. That's why all things were possible.

He'd seen proof of that even in the last two weeks. First with the phone call from Luke, exonerating Dayne fully and completely from the unfaithfulness the world had accused him of. And even in the change he'd seen in Randi. She was a different person since her mother's funeral. They'd talked about it once, over another beachside barbecue at the end of a day of filming.

She'd taken the place across from him,

and at first he'd tensed up, scanning the beach for cameramen.

But she spoke before his discomfort got the better of him. "I'm sorry, Dayne." For the first time since he'd known her, the eyes America loved held no guile, no ulterior motive. "I pushed too hard, and I made a fool of myself." She stared at her plate, and for a while she seemed too ashamed to speak. "I won't try to make it up to you, but just know it's over. Losing my mom . . . well, it changed me."

"I didn't get to tell you." Dayne wanted to be more of a friend, especially in light of Randi's loss. But the attention surrounding both of them dictated that he keep his distance. "It's too bad, about your mother."

"Yes." Her expression held the sadness that had made her on-screen performances nothing short of brilliant since her return to the set. "She was a great woman. When I die —" she looked beyond the beach to the far mountains — "I don't want people to say I was a great actress." She looked at him once more. "I want them to say I was like my parents."

He nodded. "I understand."

After that, she'd said a polite good-bye and moved her plate to another table, with a group of cast mates who were much less well-known. Since then, she'd been friendly to Dayne but never more than that. She kept her distance unless they were working on a scene.

Nothing was impossible with God if Randi could have a change of heart. It was a truth that wouldn't have surprised Elizabeth Baxter. She had taught her children to believe in the impossible, to look for God's redemption in all people, all the time. And now, she was passing the lesson on to him.

Lunch was almost over, so Dayne did what he did every day. He pulled out his phone and called Katy. Again the line rang and rang, and again the call was transferred to her voice mail. He sighed as the beep rang out. "Katy, it's me. I have something important to talk to you about. Please, baby . . . please call me. I'm going crazy without you."

Before he snapped his phone shut, he replayed her message, the only one he'd received from her since learning the truth about Luke. Her voice sounded distant and strained in the squawking way messages often sounded on voice mail.

"Dayne, it's me." Pause. "Sorry I haven't been more available. Stephen wants to let us go home earlier than planned, so he's added a few hours to every day of shooting." Another pause. "I know you want to talk, and I do too. It feels like . . . I don't know, like everything about our relationship was maybe a little too rushed. Anyway, we'll talk when we're back in the States or maybe when we're both in Bloomington." Only then did her voice turn tender. "No matter how bad things are, I miss you. More than you know." She hesitated. "Talk to you later."

That was it, the only communication he'd received from her in more than a week. Dayne gathered his determination and thought again about Elizabeth's message. In addition to her strong belief, she was clearly concerned about Dayne's family life — both the one he'd been raised with and the one he was creating for himself now that he was an adult.

He pressed his toes into the damp sand and longed for his return to Lake Monroe. How kind of his father to send his Christmas present early in case he needed his mother's words more now than later. The present reminded him of the power in a gift, how sometimes the best way to express love to another person was through an action.

The director shouted that the break was over. "Places, people. . . . Take your places!"

But Dayne couldn't move, couldn't respond at all. An idea had begun to form and grow — first in his mind and then deep in his heart. He laughed, and the sound danced and mixed with the crashing of the surf. Why hadn't he thought of it before? The Christmas gift taking shape would be his best ever. The thought of giving it filled him with a joy he hadn't felt in weeks.

"Matthews . . . now! We have a lot to do!"

Right. He laughed again, the smile on his face so full and complete it felt foreign. But he picked up his pace because they did have a lot to do so they could finish filming and get home. Katy didn't know about his director agreeing to delay the wrap-up work in Los Angeles until January. She wouldn't be expecting him back for another week — just a few days before Christmas.

Instead, he would make it home before her by a day or two. Just enough time to set his plan into motion. Dayne could hardly contain himself, because the gift he was going to give her wasn't any ordinary present. It couldn't be wrapped or placed under the tree. Rather, it was a gift that would take them back to the very beginning. When his mother had been granted the one thing she'd wanted before she died. A chance to meet her oldest son.

Now, if Dayne could hold on to his mother's belief in miracles, he and Katy might both find their way back to that amazing time. So the message from Elizabeth would live on the way she'd prayed it would.

The message that nothing was impossible with God.

CHAPTER
TWENTY-FIVE

Despite the fact that she was completely absorbed in finishing the filming of her movie, Katy's waking hours were consumed with two main thoughts. Getting closer to God and getting home again.

She didn't feel well, and though the film benefited from her sadness over the situation with Dayne and her longing to speak to him in person, she worried about what it would mean once she returned to Bloomington. Depression wasn't something she'd ever experienced, and combined with her failed marriage and the loss of CKT, the future seemed cloudy and uncertain.

Katy was sitting in one of the director's chairs, studying her lines for the scene they were about to shoot. Five more days and they'd be done.

Stephen said he loved the dailies, and he often pulled her aside to show her how nicely the film was turning out. "You're bringing everything you can." He smiled at her in the fatherly way he had about him. "You won't be sorry."

Her job was easy, really. Wake up every morning and play herself. She'd learned a long time ago in school that the best acting happened when a person wasn't acting. Katy could vouch for that theory personally. She read through the lines once, then went over them in her head, with her eyes focused on the tops of a grove of nearby trees. Her part was smaller in this scene; the lines were already firmly in her mind.

She shut the script but kept her eyes on the trees. *God . . . I love that You're here in London, same as You are in Bloomington. Thank You for that. . . .* The other day she'd read in the book of Romans that people had no excuse for not believing in God because the proof of His existence was in the created things. Like the trees and the sky and even the gray, dreary clouds overhead.

God was with her, holding her. No matter what happened with her marriage, she wouldn't lose her love for God, her need to be close to Him.

Her cast mates were gathered around the food table or sipping coffee a few feet away. But Katy was lost in thought, the way she often was.

Stephen had talked to her about her future yesterday. "There's a lot of interest, Katy. Studios would love to have you star in another film. Frankly, I'd be honored to work with you again. You're a natural, a real pro."

Katy smiled because she appreciated him and how he believed in her ability. She had wondered once upon a yesterday if she was capable of acting at this level. Stephen Petrel was one of the top directors in the business, and he left her no doubt. "Thank you." She placed her hand on his shoulder. "If I was going to stay in the industry, I wouldn't do films for anyone but you."

The disappointment in his eyes told her he knew where the conversation was headed. "But . . ."

"But I'm finished." There was no hesitancy in her voice or her determination. "I'll wrap up this film and do whatever you need me to do for the premiere. But then I'm done." A sad laugh tickled her throat. "I can't wait, really. After doing this for a while, all I want is my life back."

She thought about those words now. She could certainly return to Bloomington, but there was almost no hope of getting her life back. If she could, she would return to the days when CKT was flourishing and she was caught up in life at the Flanigan house. Back when she wondered about Heath the sound guy or the attorney with the strange compulsion to criticize her food choices. Or Manly Stanley, the rock-paper-scissors champion. At least then life could make her laugh.

Her past ran through her mind like a short film. She had willed herself to learn something from her days of dating Tad, the drama student she'd met in high school. When he got pulled to the top of Hollywood's A-list practically overnight, she wasn't surprised to hear he was doing drugs. But when he died of an overdose, she grieved privately and with purpose.

Never again, she'd told herself. She wouldn't date an actor, and she wouldn't wind up working in the industry. She would teach kids and stay in a small town. Anything to avoid the fate of someone like Tad. Yet here she was, married to America's top Hollywood actor and hunted by paparazzi rabid to catch her in a less-than-perfect moment.

She squinted against the painful glare of yesterday's compromises. She loved Dayne Matthews. He had come into her life and taken hold of her heart in a way she was helpless to resist. Not because of who the world thought he was. Because of who she knew him to be. Even now, with the dozens of tabloid stories on his unfaithfulness, she loved him.

Whether he ever came clean about the picture of him and Randi, she didn't care. She would never doubt the truth: she'd gotten to know the man he really was, the Dayne no one else understood. She swallowed so the sadness inside wouldn't overtake her minutes before she needed to be on. The problem wasn't that Dayne had lied to her all along. It was that after a lifetime of playing the role of celebrity, all too often the real Dayne disappeared from existence.

Katy had hoped otherwise, prayed otherwise, but these last few weeks had given her the answer she'd dreaded. Dayne would always have a weakness for women like Randi Wells, actresses who threw themselves at him and convinced him that the love story on-screen should go on long after the cameras stopped rolling.

Since seeing the picture of Dayne and Randi, Katy's feelings for her husband had changed. She wasn't sure they would ever be what they'd once been.

She pictured Dayne, heard the earnest sound in his voice when he left his last message. Strange how they couldn't connect.

She wasn't avoiding him, even though he clearly thought she was. She was merely focused on the task at hand and driven to spend time in God's presence when she had a down moment. Truthfully, she didn't want a list of excuses from Dayne. She wanted to look into his eyes, past the surface explanations to the private places of his heart. Only then would she know what had really happened, how he had ended up on the cover of the tabloids with Randi Wells in his arms.

Ten yards away, Stephen was motioning for people to take their places.

As Katy started to climb down from the chair, her cell phone rang. She smiled. Seemed like it was always this way. Dayne would call just when she had no time left to talk. She pulled her phone from her bag, opened it, and held it to her ear without checking the caller ID. "Hello?"

"Katy?" The voice belonged to Ashley. "Oh, I'm so glad I caught you. I have to talk to you right now."

"Okay." Katy covered her other ear and tried to focus. Her sister-in-law didn't sound angry or frantic but rather almost excited. "What's going on?"

Ashley took a fast breath. "So here's what happened. I just hung up the phone with my dad, and he said he talked to Luke about

Mom's letters and the scrapbooks, and then Luke told him that so far Dayne hasn't been able to tell you." She paused barely long enough to grab another breath. "Are you following me?"

"Um . . ." Katy tried to absorb everything Ashley was saying, but she was lost almost from the beginning. "Not really."

"Sorry. I'll start over."

A smile started at the corners of Katy's lips. Same old Ashley. So intent on making things right, on helping the Baxter family communicate and find peace with each other. She laughed, and the sound of it lightened her mood. Whatever the reason for this call, Ashley thought it important enough to place right away. She sat back in her chair and nodded toward Stephen. She'd be there as soon as the call was finished.

"Katy? You there?" In the background, she could hear a child's voice. Probably Devin. "Tell me I didn't lose you."

"No, Ash, you didn't lose me." Again she laughed at the strangeness of the call. "Maybe you should start at the beginning. . . ."

Ashley noticed Landon the minute she hung up. She placed the receiver back on the phone base and met him halfway across the kitchen.

"How'd it go?"

"Good, I think." She felt exhausted and grateful and on the verge of tears. "She listened. I mean . . ." Ashley slipped her arms around Landon's neck and rested her head on his chest. "She wasn't shouting for joy or anything, but she was interested at least."

He stroked her hair, her back, swaying slightly and not forcing the conversation.

"This is so hard." She didn't want to cry. The boys were in the playroom, Cole ready for Landon to take him to school. It was a bright, sunny morning with six inches of fresh snow on the ground. She held Landon a little more tightly. "It's twelve days till Christmas, and I wanted only one thing this year."

Again Landon knew her well enough to stay quiet, to let her finish. He kissed the top of her head and waited.

"I wanted to be absolutely sure of Sarah's miracle, of the difference she'd made." Ashley pulled back. "Remember? There in the hospital room, how it seemed? Luke and Reagan looked happy, and Dayne and Katy. Especially those four."

"And now . . ." Landon understood. His

eyes mirrored her disappointment.

"Now it seems like everyone's forgotten what it was like, standing there and watching life come into existence and be snuffed out — all in a few hours."

"Daddy, I'm ready!" Cole's voice sang from the other room. "Plus, Devin needs a new diaper."

"Thanks, honey." Landon said it loud enough for Cole to hear, but he kept his attention on Ashley. "But *I* remember." He kissed her again, this time on her lips. "And you remember. She taught us life's a fragile thing. Every day's a gift."

"Exactly." Ashley was so frustrated with her brothers. "So what about Luke and Dayne and their wives? Don't they see how the lives they're living cheapen the message of Sarah's life?" She took a step back and released him. He needed to leave, and there wasn't much more she could say. "It's just . . . I wanted her life to count for something right here in our own family."

Landon held his hand up to her face and looked deep into her soul. "That's the beauty of life . . . the reason you and I are here today."

She covered his hand with her own. "What do you mean?"

"Remember the Bible verse that meant so

much to you after we came home from the hospital?"

"Yes." Ashley felt a calm come over her at the thought of the Scripture. " 'Be still, and know that I am God.' "

"Exactly." He cared so much for her. His tone, his touch . . . She was grateful every moment for the chance to love Landon Blake.

Ashley liked where this was going, but she still wasn't sure how he was applying the verse at a moment like this. She searched his face. "Meaning what?"

"Meaning . . . God works in His own timing. Maybe — where your brothers are concerned — He simply isn't finished just yet."

Landon's kind words stayed with her, comforting her long after Landon had taken Cole to school and gone off to the fire station. She could only hope he was right, that what she was seeing now wasn't the completed picture.

Ashley cleaned up Devin and then laid him down for a nap. Afterwards, she opened her Bible and let the words of the Scripture fill her soul. Yes, that had to be it. God wasn't finished with the miracle of Sarah's life. They could still come together the way she'd wanted them to, because there was

still time.
Twelve days, to be exact.

CHAPTER TWENTY-SIX

The humidity was gone. That was the first thing Dayne noticed when he woke up Monday morning, but it took a minute before he remembered where he was. Then with a burst of action, he tore out of bed and stared out the patio door. His heart pounded, and another few seconds passed while he cleared his head.

He wasn't in Mexico anymore; he was home in Bloomington, at the house on Lake Monroe. Snow covered the ground, and more was predicted for the next few days. Dayne slid open the door and breathed in deep. The rush of cold air felt wonderful, as if it alone had the power to bring his tired heart and soul back to life.

It's so beautiful here. He slid the door shut again and took hold of the doorframe above him. He stretched and then looked back at the small clock on his nightstand — 9 a.m. He'd slept longer than he planned, but that didn't surprise him. He hadn't gotten in from the airport until midnight, and then — with details of his Christmas plan consuming him — he hadn't fallen asleep until sometime around two.

He wasn't trying to call Katy any longer. She'd left him another message, this time explaining that she would be home on Wednesday, six days before Christmas.

"You'll still be in LA, but the minute I'm home I'll call you." Her tone was unreadable, distant. "You're right. We need to talk as soon as possible."

Dayne smiled and headed for his closet. The fact that he was home before her would be her first surprise. But if he was going to pull off the other one, he needed to get moving. He had a lot to do and only a day or so to make it happen. He caught his reflection in the mirror as he passed by their walk-in closet, and he barely recognized himself. Not just the tan he'd picked up after two months in Cabo but something about his eyes.

He was halfway through a bowl of oatmeal and bananas before he realized what it was. He looked happy. The shoot had worn on him, dragged him down. He hated being away from Katy for so long and detested the lies splattered across the headlines. A more somber expression worked for the troubled relationship scenes in the film. But now that he was here, nothing could take the smile from his face.

When he finished breakfast, first on his list of errands was a stop by the Monroe County Building Department. He'd gone online when he was in Mexico, so he knew exactly where he was headed. The Monroe County Courthouse that stood tall and proud at the center of the town square in downtown Bloomington. Room 310.

Dayne hummed the refrains from a hymn he'd heard during the weeks of services at Bloomington Community Church. "Great is Thy faithfulness, O God my Father, there is no shadow of turning with Thee. . . . All I have needed Thy hand hath provided — great is Thy faithfulness, Lord, unto me!"

The tune played again and again as he drove into town, careful to take the corners slowly since he wasn't used to driving in these conditions. The streets were clear of snow, but there was still ice in spots. He wore old jeans, work boots, and a bulky brown winter jacket. The baseball cap for the day was not the navy one with Baja California embroidered across the front. It was one that read simply Bloomington

Hardware. No one knew he was returning early, so he expected to get through the morning without being recognized.

If he was careful, anyway.

Dayne parked at one of the metered spots adjacent to the town square and stepped carefully from the 4Runner. His breath hung in the air in front of him as he navigated to the sidewalk. Only then did he realize how beautiful everything looked around him. He stopped, mesmerized.

Christmas lights hung along both sides of the street. The place looked like a winter wonderland. Katy had told him about Christmas in Bloomington, how each year a designated Santa flipped a switch and ignited something the town called a Canopy of Lights. Now, anchored to the sidewalk, Dayne could see how the display got its name. From the dome of the courthouse, strings of twinkling white lights draped over the town square and across the bordering four streets, forming a canopy. The bare sycamore trees surrounding the courthouse were also covered in lights.

Standing there, with only a few people making their way to and from the old building, Dayne felt like he was on the set of a movie too good to be true. He inhaled deeply, filling his lungs with the cool, clean air. *I'm home, God. This is where I want to live.*

He remembered what he'd come to do, so he hurried to the front door of the courthouse and went inside. He had so much energy, so much joy bursting inside him, that he jogged up the stairs to the third floor, the song in his heart once again. When he reached room 310, he moved inside soundlessly, the bill of his baseball cap low over his eyes, the collar of the jacket turned up.

Behind a counter decorated on either end with vibrant poinsettias was a pleasant-looking woman with gray hair and a red and green Christmas sweater. She was filing paperwork, but when he walked in, she looked up and smiled. Dayne hesitated, but she showed no signs of recognizing him, none of the usual gasps or fluttering hands. Just a warm Bloomington, Indiana, smile.

Dayne relaxed and adjusted his baseball cap. "Hi. I had a few questions about one of the buildings in downtown Bloomington."

"Okay." She set down her files and came up to the counter. As she moved closer, Dayne noticed the stencils on her office window. Right across the center it read, "Merry Christmas" and "Christ Is Born."

Dayne could hardly believe the atmosphere in the public building. Apparently through most of Bloomington, people celebrated Christmas as Christ's birthday.

The woman reached the spot opposite him and set her hands on the counter. "Do you have an address?"

"I do." Dayne liked the sparkle in her eyes. She looked like someone who would sit in the front row at Bloomington Community Church, embracing the message and the moment, singing louder than anyone else and maybe a little off-key. He pulled a piece of paper from the pocket of his jeans and handed it to her.

She barely glanced at it before a look of recognition appeared in her eyes. "The old theater. Your questions might not matter. Let me check something."

Dayne had driven by the community theater late last night. Before they left to film their separate movies, Katy had kept him informed about the delays on the building project intended for the theater's site. The developers had dealt with far more red tape than usual because the theater was so old. A state senator had filed papers proposing that the theater be listed as a historical landmark. That battle went on for months before the decision was made. The theater was a few years too young. It didn't qualify. At that point, the developers' plans were finally put through at the Monroe County planning office.

He hadn't heard that the building had been torn down, but he wanted to make sure. As of midnight, it was still standing, still surrounded by yellow caution tape. Now, though, panic grabbed hold of him. He swallowed, waiting while the woman took her time moving back to the filing cabinet.

She checked the fronts of the drawers, then pulled open the third one down. A few more seconds of sorting and she lifted a file. Again she moved slowly back to the counter, staring at the contents while she walked. "Mmm-hmm." She gave a sad shake of her head. "That's what I thought."

"What?" Dayne wondered if she could hear his pounding heart.

"Today's the day." She looked at him. "People don't appreciate a landmark anymore. New construction and condominiums." She gestured back at the filing cabinet. "Twice as many applications for building permits in the last six months as in all last year combined."

"I'm sorry." Dayne was frantic to understand. "Today's the day for what?"

"Demolition." She pushed the thick file across the counter and gave it a single tap. "It's all right here. This morning the wrecking crews will reduce that old theater to a pile of rubble."

This wasn't happening. Dayne couldn't catch his breath, couldn't think straight. He hadn't made it back to Bloomington early and rushed down to the courthouse only to find out he was too late, right?

Dayne opened the file and saw a simple document on top with only a few lines of text. It was an approval from the Monroe County Building Department, granting permission for Hanson Development to begin demolition of the Bloomington Community Theater, in preparation for a condo project slated to begin in February. At the bottom of the document, the last line read only this: *Demolition to begin Monday, December 17, at 10 a.m.*

Dayne looked at the clock on the office wall. It was 9:47. He was already halfway to the door, nodding at the woman as he went. "Thank you. Merry Christmas."

"Merry Christmas and a happy —"

He didn't wait around long enough for her to finish. He flew down the wooden stairs and out into the cold morning. Again he was careful of ice, but he had no time to waste. *Please, God . . . not yet. Delay them just a few minutes longer. Please.*

A sense of urgency came over Dayne like nothing he had ever experienced. He slid into his SUV and drove as fast as he safely could, down College, over to 3rd Street, and down Woodlawn toward Bryan Park. The theater stood across the street.

At least that's where it had stood last night.

Bailey could hardly believe it had come to this.

She and Tim Reed and two dozen kids from CKT and many of their parents gathered at Bryan Park, across the street from the theater, the one where they had spent countless hours rehearsing and performing and bringing stories to life for the people of Bloomington.

They shivered and tugged their winter coats tighter around themselves, but they were helpless to do anything other than what they were already doing — gathering together to pray for a miracle.

Bailey held Connor's hand on one side and Tim's on the other.

One of the girls who had played an ensemble role in CKT's version of *Narnia* was praying. She had tears on her cheeks, and her nose sounded stuffy as she begged God for intervention. "Don't let them tear down our theater, Lord. We know You're here and that You see us."

When she finished, a middle school boy to her left took over, asking God with a clear, calm voice to save their theater from demolition.

Bailey tilted her head up just a bit, opened her eyes, and stared at the building across the street. Two police officers stood guard on either side of the structure. It was protocol, according to the article in yesterday's *Bloomington Press*.

Her parents had encouraged the prayer circle. If God didn't choose to intervene with a change of heart on the part of the developers, then He must have another plan. The same way He'd had another plan for Cody. That's what her mother said, but here in the freezing wind, her feet stuck in snow, Bailey wasn't so sure. Cody still wrote to her every week or so, but he was missing home badly. How could that be the plan God wanted for him?

Same thing for the kids of CKT. They needed the theater if they were ever going to start performing again, and the talk among parents was that they would find a way. Even if it meant having parent volunteers act as temporary directors.

There was more yelling across the street, more instructions being shouted through the megaphone. Trucks were moving in closer.

Bailey looked up at the ominous gray steel ball hovering from a solid chain, right next to the theater. *God . . . please. There has to be a way.*

She glanced to her left and saw that her mother had her eyes open too. She looked at Bailey and shook her head. "I'm sorry," she mouthed.

At that moment, there was another shout from the man who looked to be in charge, and someone at the controls set the wrecking ball in motion, pulling it back and into the air. It was a matter of minutes now, maybe seconds. When they released the ball, it would tear through the theater and that would be that.

The end of an era.

Bailey couldn't watch. She hung her head and squeezed her eyes shut. She could already imagine what it would sound like — the crushing of brittle wood and windows, the collapse of the building. But that wasn't the sound that filled the air. Instead there was the squealing of tires as a vehicle pulled up across the street, followed by the slam of a door.

The boy praying stopped midsentence, and everyone opened their eyes and looked.

By then, the man had his back to them, flying from the SUV, holding up his hand as he ran toward the wrecking crew. "Stop! Wait!"

The workers continued as if they couldn't hear the man or didn't care.

Still the man ran toward the theater. Soft gasps came from the members of the prayer circle. Parents put their arms around the shoulders of their kids, and a couple of moms covered their mouths, too surprised to speak.

Bailey watched with the others. She was shivering harder than before, stunned at what she was seeing. Both police officers went into alert at the sight of a man running toward the site. They met him near the curb, and an animated conversation broke out.

Bailey held her breath. Whispers came from her friends and their families surrounding her. All of them wanted to know the same thing. Who was the man, and why did he think he had any control over the demolition? A minute passed, and one of the police officers escorted the man to the lead worker, the one with the megaphone.

Another conversation took place, and the man in jeans pulled a small piece of paper from his pocket. For what seemed like forever, the supervisor stared at the paper the strange man had given him. Then he waved at his fellow workers, calling them over and creating an impromptu group conference.

"What's happening?" Connor leaned close to her.

"I don't know." Bailey moved forward, making the circle smaller so she could draw from the warmth of Connor and Tim on either side of her.

"The guy looks familiar." Tim was shivering too. "Don't you think?"

"Maybe he's an angel." Connor squinted, trying to see what was happening.

Around the circle, the adults began speculating in whispered voices. Whatever was happening, it had put a sudden and dramatic end to the actions of the wrecking ball. Another minute passed and the supervisor nodded. Even from across the street, Bailey could see that the guy was smiling as he shook the stranger's hand.

The supervisor lifted the megaphone to his mouth and pointed at the man behind the controls of the wrecking ball. "Lower it! We've got a change in plans."

Almost immediately, the controller set to work on a panel in front of him, and the huge ball lowered harmlessly to its original position.

Passersby seemed to sense something big was happening. People stepped out from local businesses, and a crowd formed along the sidewalk across from the theater.

The group of kids and parents erupted into a mass of cheers and shouts and spontaneous hugs. God had granted them the miracle they'd asked for, and Bailey couldn't stop the tears from falling onto her freezing cheeks. Whatever had happened, the theater wasn't going to be torn down — at least not this morning.

One by one, the men in hard hats climbed into their trucks and cars and drove off. The stranger stayed, still talking to the supervisor. A few minutes later, the supervisor left, and after that, the wrecking ball was backed off the theater grounds and loaded onto a flatbed truck.

As the truck pulled away, Bailey looked at the spot where the man's SUV had been parked. "Hey . . ." She felt her head start to spin. "His car's gone."

With the crowd gathered and the traffic slowed to a crawl around the theater, Bailey hadn't noticed the stranger leave the site and return to his vehicle. Now his SUV was gone, and they hadn't gotten the chance to talk to him or thank him. She looked at the faces around her. "Did you see him leave? Did anyone see him?"

Tim shook his head, and a few of the parents exchanged looks of astonishment. Whoever he was, he'd come at just the right time and taken part in a dramatic answer to their prayers.

Across from Bailey on the other side of the circle, her father cleared his throat. "Let's thank our God."

Again they held hands, this time with an electric excitement pulsing through the crowd. Some of the passersby wandered in their direction. An old woman wrapped in a wool coat and scarf, a group of young businessmen, and a family who'd been driving by moved closer to the circle, and as Bailey's dad bowed his head and started to pray, the strangers around them prayed too.

"God, we have no way to thank You for what just happened. We don't understand it." He paused, and Bailey could tell he was choked up. "We only acknowledge that without You, the theater would be gone by now. So we thank You. In Jesus' name, amen."

Then, as easily as they drew their next

breaths, the CKT kids began to sing. Softly at first, with shaky voices, and then with a sound that rose confidently toward heaven, filling Bryan Park and drawing more people closer. " 'I love You, Lord . . . and I lift my voice to worship You . . . O my soul, rejoice! . . . Take joy, my King, in what You hear. . . .' "

The song built and grew, and the people of Bloomington who had stopped to listen joined in, some with tears in their eyes. Something very special had just happened, and though none of them knew exactly what or whether the demolition might still be rescheduled, they knew this:

God reigned.

The CKT group gave one another one more round of hugs and smiles before heading for their cars. Bailey and Connor walked together, their parents a few feet in front of them, talking with the Shaffers. Tim Reed had driven his own car and parked it on the other side of the theater, so he was no longer with them.

"You know what I think?" Connor looked over his shoulder at the theater.

"What?" Bailey wasn't shivering anymore. Her heart felt light and free, as if anything truly was possible for those who believed. She reached up and put her arm around

Connor's shoulders. He was taller than her now, but he'd always be her little brother.

Connor turned back to her. "I think he was an angel." His expression was intently serious. "I mean, he shows up out of nowhere and stops the wrecking crew." He snapped his fingers. "Then poof . . . just like that he's gone."

Bailey gave him a look that said maybe. Angels were real, after all, and what had happened this morning defied any earthly logic.

Bailey brought it up on the way home, and her parents acknowledged that yes, the Bible confirmed the reality of angels.

"There's a verse in Hebrews." Her father glanced at them in the rearview mirror. "Thirteenth chapter. It says be careful to entertain strangers, for by doing so, some people have entertained angels without knowing it."

"Wow!" Connor slid to the edge of his seat and gripped his dad's shoulder. "That's the coolest thing. I never heard that before."

Bailey had read it sometime a few years ago, but she'd never given the Scripture much thought. The idea sent a new kind of wonder over her, and by the end of the day — after getting to school late and taking her math test, after coming home and learning that the whole town was buzzing about what seemed to be a change of plans by one of the city's top developers — she could do nothing but believe that maybe angels didn't wear flowing robes and have golden wings.

Maybe they wore blue jeans and a baseball cap and drove an SUV.

CHAPTER
TWENTY-SEVEN

Ashley hung up the phone and gave a victory shout so loud that Devin responded with one of his own. Ashley laughed. "That's right. . . . Thank God for answered prayers!" She caught her breath and tried to decide what to do first. Landon! Of course! She needed to see him right away, needed to tell him about the conversation before she forgot a single detail.

"Devin, baby, let's take a ride." She swept her son out of his high chair, kissed his forehead, and hurried to the closet for his coat. She grinned at him as she fastened his zipper. "Our first big Christmas present just came through."

Fifteen minutes later, in a swirling cloud of snow, she pushed through the doors of the fire station and carried Devin to the back room. Landon was sitting by himself on a worn sofa, reading a magazine, but when he looked up and saw Ashley and

Devin, he jumped to his feet. His face was suddenly marked with fear and concern.

Ashley held up her hand and laughed. "Nothing's wrong. It's okay." She set Devin down, walked to Landon, and hugged him long and hard. "You aren't going to believe this! I had to tell you in person."

Landon looked dazed, as if Ashley had suddenly and certainly become a crazy woman. "You drove through a snowstorm?"

Ashley glanced out the window and dismissed the weather with a flip of her hand. "It just hit. It's not that bad." She gripped his shoulder and took hold of Devin's hand with the other. Together the three of them sat down on the edge of the sofa. "This is huge, Landon! God wasn't finished yet, remember? Like you said the other day."

Devin moved from her lap onto Landon's. He stuck his fingers in his mouth and stared at Ashley. "Happy!" His singsong voice was slurred, but clearly he was enjoying the moment.

"Yes, baby . . . Mommy's very happy," Ashley cooed at him. If only her mother could see what a darling little boy he was growing up to be.

"No one could ever accuse you of lacking passion, Ash." Landon was used to slowing Ashley down, and now he grinned at her, shaking his head. "Wait, so who'd you talk to?"

"Reagan called me this morning. You won't believe it."

Landon tucked his arm around Devin's waist and settled back into the sofa. His eyes were warmer than a summer day on the lake, but they were also laced with humor. "I'm sure I won't."

Ashley could feel her eyes dance, but she ignored his teasing. Instead she plunged into the story, starting at the beginning, the way she'd had to with Katy the other day. "Okay, so I'm making Devin breakfast this morning and Reagan calls. Apparently Luke finally opened his copy of the scrapbook with Mom's letters. He took it home to his little apartment, sat at the kitchen table, and read the whole thing. Cover to cover."

The details spilled out, with Ashley taking only the necessary breaths. Reagan's voice had been tearful, and it took half an hour for her to get to the point, but Ashley didn't mind. This was about her brother, one of her best friends in the world.

After Luke finished reading the scrapbook, he'd gotten in his car, driven straight to his house across town, and knocked on the door. When Reagan answered, she saw him on her front step crying. Weeping, even.

"He told her he was so sorry and that he wanted them to get counseling." Ashley's eyes were wide. "He told her he needed help but he needed her too, and guess what she said?"

"What?" Landon was bouncing his knee, keeping Devin entertained.

"It wasn't altogether good, but it was better than silence." Ashley pushed her dark hair back from her face. "She told him she hadn't been innocent either, but she'd been thinking about little Sarah. She didn't want to waste the days and months and years in her life hating Luke or being haunted by bitterness." She held out hands. "Can you believe that? From a woman who a week ago wasn't willing to make a phone call to save her marriage."

Landon smiled, a joyful knowing on his face. "That's amazing."

She explained how Luke didn't hesitate, even when Reagan admitted that she'd been guilty too. Instead he hugged her for a long time, with snow falling around them. "Reagan told me they weren't ready for happily ever after, but get this. . . . Luke's moving back home this weekend! Isn't that so great?"

"He is?" Landon stood and let Devin down on the floor. Their toddler beelined across the room, with Landon hurrying after him. "That's half of what we prayed for, right?"

"Right." The reminder cast the slightest shadow over the thrill of the moment. Luke and Reagan were back under one roof, but Ashley still hadn't heard anything from Katy and Dayne. Even if they were trying to fly home from their separate locations, they might not make it. The Indianapolis airport was predicting a shutdown sometime tomorrow because of the blizzard moving in. Ashley frowned as she watched Landon and Devin chase each other across the floor of the firehouse. *If they're trying to fly home, please, God, let them make it. They need to be together.* Then and there Ashley committed herself to praying all day and into the next for her older brother and his wife. Whatever it took, because she believed so completely in seeing Sarah's miracle take place. The entire miracle. Which meant they needed to keep praying until they heard from the couple.

Because Christmas was only one week away.

Katy's was the last plane allowed into Indianapolis before the blizzard shut down the airport to all travelers. They touched down at five in the morning Wednesday, and Katy caught a Town Car back to Bloomington. She was grateful, and as she climbed inside, she prayed for safe travel. She had to reach Dayne, even if it meant walking through snowdrifts.

She was practically bursting with the news, but she wouldn't call him in Los Angeles until morning his time. That would give her the chance to get home, unpack, and catch her breath. The whirlwind of emotions that had surrounded her since Ashley's phone call was something she would have to work to put into words.

Getting out of the airport was an ordeal, and Katy winced as the driver swerved and nearly hit someone in the adjacent lane. She closed her eyes, exhausted and anxious. *God . . . get me home. That's all I want now. Please get me home.*

I am with you, daughter. . . . Fear not.

The words came right from Scripture, from a number of verses where God wanted His people to be comforted by the most obvious truth — He was with them in the storm, the way He'd been with His disciples on the stormy lake or when all hope seemed lost at the house of his friends Mary and Martha. He was with Katy and she needn't be afraid. Even here, on a wintry ride across

Indiana.

Katy sank back into the plush leather seat and pulled her Bible from her bag. She wasn't sure what was happening, why Dayne hadn't tried harder to reach her or how she could've missed the signs. But God was up to something big, and Katy had resigned her pride on the matter. If Dayne was innocent, so be it. They needed to talk and make a plan.

But she couldn't write her marriage off that easily. Especially not in light of the news she'd just learned.

She turned to 2 Chronicles 20. Growing up a Christian, Katy had many times heard people tossing around the idea that the battle belonged to the Lord. A nice thought, she used to tell herself. It gave her a picture of handing her troubles over to God and letting Him deal with them.

But when she was in college, she stumbled upon 2 Chronicles and the Bible story behind the wonderful truth. Jehoshaphat and God's people were in big trouble, facing the most terrifying battle of their lives. In many ways, it seemed that they should give up, turn themselves over to the enemy, and pray for fewer casualties that way. But God told them otherwise. Katy's favorite part of the story came in verse 15: "Do not be afraid or discouraged because of this vast army. For the battle is not yours, but God's."

Wasn't that exactly how she felt? The media and public opinion formed a vast army directly opposed to Katy and Dayne. But the two of them belonged to God, which meant they didn't have to fear the outcome. God would fight the battle for them.

Katy read past the battle scene to the most exciting part. While the people were singing and praising God, He set traps for the approaching army, and the enemies of His people were defeated. That last part always struck her, maybe because of her years with CKT, performing musical theater.

She closed her eyes and pictured the way her CKT kids used to gather in the basement of the theater before each show, holding hands and singing "I Love You, Lord" a cappella. The group had accomplished some remarkable feats — forgiving the young drunk driver who had taken the lives of their friends and forming friendships that defied stereotypes.

And of course. Because God's Word made it clear that His people can find victory in the praising and singing.

Katy stared out the window at the rolling snowdrifts on the side of the highway. The victory came through praise, but why was that? The question stayed with her. How did the act of praising God set a person free from the battle she faced? She pondered the possibilities, and as she did, she began to hum her favorite hymns quietly, so only she could hear them. "Amazing Grace," "How Great Thou Art," and half a dozen others, until finally the answer presented itself clearly.

While she hummed, while her mind was taken up with the lyrics of the old hymns, she was unable to worry or doubt or fret in any possible way. A truth rose to the surface of her heart. Praising God was an act of trust, a way of putting aside the cares and troubles of this world and looking to God alone. No wonder that's where the battle was won.

She returned to the Bible, switching to the Sermon on the Mount in Matthew 5. The words seemed to move straight off the page and into her soul, as if by reading them she could rid herself of every sad and lonely moment from the past few months. She drank in the Scriptures like a person dying of thirst — every truth restoring a little more life to her.

The trip took three hours, much of it spent at barely a crawl. By the time they reached the city limits, the sun was out and highway workers had cleared the major streets. Katy straightened in the backseat and savored the familiar sights of Bloomington, even though it was buried under three feet of snow. *Thank You, God. . . . Thank You for getting me home.*

Christmas lights were strung along the streets, wreaths tacked to the doors of most of the businesses leading into the city. She could hardly wait to see Jenny and Jim and their kids and to begin soul-searching about what was next for her now that CKT didn't have a theater.

The thought pierced her heart with a fresh sadness. Why hadn't she and Dayne tried harder to keep the place from closing down? Okay, so the theater wasn't a moneymaker unless it was torn down and replaced with condominiums. But did everything have to make a profit in order to be worthwhile?

Katy narrowed her eyes, wishing she could ask the driver to take a detour past the downtown area where the theater had stood. But she couldn't bring herself to ask the question. Jenny had told her that the demolition was scheduled for Monday. Katy figured it might be a month before she had the courage to drive by the empty lot.

The roads leading up to their lake house

were more slippery, and again the driver took his time. When he finally pulled into the driveway, she felt a rush of relief. Not that she'd been afraid — after God had breathed the reminder of His peace and presence into her soul, she had no fear. No, the relief came only because she was finally where she belonged.

Home on Lake Monroe.

She paid the driver, and he helped her get her bags to the front door. If he recognized her as Dayne Matthews' wife, he didn't say so, and she was again grateful. She wanted only to get inside and start thinking about what she'd tell Dayne first, how she'd let him hear her news without breaking down midway through the first sentence.

Dayne was in LA now, where he'd be until Christmas Eve. That meant she would wait until ten to call him — seven his time. Hopefully he'd be up by then.

She lugged all three of her bags inside. With the winter storm, she'd expected the house to be freezing. After all, it had been months since either of them had been home, and they hadn't asked anyone to open the place while they were gone. They had no pets to feed or plants that needed watering.

But as soon as she drew her first breath,

Katy smelled fresh coffee. "What in the . . . ?" She set the last bag down and moved toward the smell. She rounded the corner and stepped into the spacious kitchen; it was empty but the coffeemaker was half-full. She might've just been blanketed with peace, but the idea of someone breaking into her house and brewing coffee was enough to make the blood drain from her face.

"Hello?" she called as she walked to the coffeepot. It was warm to the touch. Someone had indeed been here and made coffee. She looked up, her pulse thudding through her body. There were only two options — either they were still here, or they hadn't been gone long.

She opened a drawer at the end of the granite counter and snatched a small can of pepper spray. Dayne had given it to her for when she might be out here at the lake alone and need some way to defend herself. She twisted it into position and held it straight out in front of her.

Slowly, cautiously, she tiptoed down the hall. "Hello . . . who's here?" Her voice echoed against the walls, then faded. The house was deathly silent. "Hello?"

Katy reached their bedroom and aimed the pepper spray sharply around the corner.

When no one jumped out or grabbed her, she poked her head into the doorway and peered around the room.

It was empty. But there, on the neatly made bed, was a piece of white paper. Katy blinked and lowered the pepper spray. What was this? Had someone broken in, made coffee, and left her a note? The idea seemed ludicrous. She crossed her room with steps that were more normal, less like something from a horror flick.

She picked up the note and the room tilted. It said, *Katy, meet me at the theater. Dayne.*

What? She blinked and read the note again. He was home? He was supposed to be in Los Angeles, unless somehow she'd lost a week. As she stared at the note once more, confusion rocked her soul. If he'd been home, why hadn't he called her? And why would he want to meet her at the theater, when the building had already been torn down? She lowered herself to the bed to stop the room from spinning. Was this happening? Had he really come home before her?

The truth settled into place gradually, and the pieces began to come together. The coffee was Dayne's doing, not the work of a stranger. But was he serious? He wanted her to drive through the snow and meet him at the place where the theater once stood? What was he up to?

Then the reality of his nearness overwhelmed her. Dayne was here! Home in Bloomington! And in just a little while she could see him again, hold him. Yes, they had differences to work through, but she understood now, and suddenly she couldn't wait to see him, to tell him what she'd found out. She stood and grabbed a pair of boots and her thickest coat from the closet. Her car was in the garage. If Dayne wanted her to come, she would come.

Now if she could only make it to the theater.

CHAPTER
TWENTY-EIGHT

Dayne sat at the center of the old wooden stage, the same place where Katy had been the first time he saw her. He'd contacted Stephen Petrel yesterday and learned that Katy was flying home today, arriving early in the morning. Dayne tracked her flight online and knew that she'd landed safely. He wasn't sure how long it would take her to make it to Bloomington, but this was where he wanted to be when they first saw each other again.

Here, at the Bloomington Community Theater, where it all started.

His idea had come off without a hitch, and ten times an hour he asked himself why he hadn't done it sooner. The reason, of course, was that he and Katy weren't going to be around. Without Katy there to run CKT, if the theater was sold, then maybe it was God's way of shutting a door. Ending a season.

The place was drafty, and in the hour since he'd arrived here this morning he'd walked around and found a long list of things that needed upgrading or replacing. No investor would tell him he'd been given a deal on the place, but Dayne didn't care. He folded his hands and rested his forearms on his knees.

He could still see the face of the lead developer when he ran up and asked the crew to stop. At first the police had been angry, thinking him an insane citizen or some maniac intent on stopping progress. It took only a few seconds for them to realize who he was, and once he was able to explain himself, the police officer had introduced him to the developer.

"It's about making money, right?" Dayne looked intently at the guy.

Hanson Development was well liked and respected throughout town. The organization donated to every charity in Bloomington and was a huge supporter of the local schools. No one blamed the developer for wanting condos where the theater stood. The townspeople were the ones who should've risen to the occasion long before now. If the city would've held an emergency meeting and purchased the building as a landmark, the situation never would have gotten this out of hand.

The developer had given Dayne a hesitant smile. "I'm a businessman, Mr. Matthews. Of course it's about making money. But look . . . our plans are already in motion. We've invested a lot of money into making this project happen."

"I realize that. I want to buy the theater." Dayne took his checkbook from his pocket. "I'll cover any of your expenses also."

The man's mouth hung slightly open, and it took a while before he summoned his team around. They agreed that if Dayne was serious, they could put off the demolition and move the meeting somewhere warm and dry. At least to talk about the possibility.

Dayne smiled at the memory. They'd come to terms before lunch, not only on the theater but on the buildings that stood on either side that were also slated for demolition. The price tag was high but nothing compared to what Dayne made per film. In the end, the developer was actually glad to have the theater off his hands. The paperwork had been a nightmare, and now Hanson Development was cash poor. With money from the sale they could start acquiring property for a new housing tract.

"We were about to be the bad guys," the

466

developer had told Dayne as they finished their meeting. "I couldn't have asked for a better ending to the day."

Now Dayne was beginning to dream up big plans for the buildings, ways for the adjacent spaces to house tenants and make money so that the theater could be self-sufficient. A fifties diner on one side and a coffee shop on the other, maybe. They would widen and pave the parking lot to connect all three sites, and by the time they were finished, the price would feel like a bargain.

Dayne hadn't stopped dreaming about the project since the developer handed him the keys. He straightened and pulled them from his pocket. Keys were a funny thing; an entire world could be opened with the right one. He slid his fingers over the cool metal and was putting them back in his pocket when he heard a car pull up outside.

Normally, with the traffic from downtown, he wouldn't have noticed. But today, everyone in Bloomington was home getting ready for Christmas, enjoying the snowstorm and making the most of a day inside. Everyone but the one person he couldn't wait to see. Dayne sucked in a quick breath and stared at the back door of the theater, the one Katy always used.

Suddenly he wasn't alone on the wooden stage. He was in the back row, a baseball cap pulled down over his forehead, a hooded sweatshirt hiding his identity. He was gripping the armrests and staring at the kids onstage — Charlie Brown and Lucy and Schroeder — all singing at the top of their lungs: *"Happiness is . . . three kinds of ice cream . . . having a sister . . . coming home again."*

The show was ending, the parents and families in the audience giving a standing ovation, and there . . . there she was, a blonde vision with an innocence Dayne had never seen before. She was walking onto the stage and the kids were surrounding her, calling out her name. *"Katy . . . Katy . . . Katy . . ."*

There was a sound at the door, someone opening it.

"Katy?" Dayne's throat swelled with emotion, and his tears made it hard to see. He stood and waited, and it occurred to him that the rest of his life hinged not on his career or the way his newest movie was received or what the tabloids said about him.

But on what happened in the next few moments.

■ ■ ■ ■

The surprises hit Katy one after another, like a series of tidal waves in which every one took her higher and higher to a place of joy she'd forgotten could exist. She crept through town, certain that the only reason Dayne had called her to the place where the theater once stood was so he could console her, tell her how sorry he was that the building was gone.

Not until she pulled up out front and stared at the theater for half a minute did she actually believe her own eyes. The building was intact, standing just as it had always stood, year after year after year in the heart of Bloomington. She felt tears spring to her eyes, and she brought her hand to her mouth, shocked at what she was seeing.

What had happened? And what role had Dayne played in keeping the old place up another few days? This was where he'd proposed to her, so maybe he wanted one more chance alone with her, a chance to sit together and remember every wonderful moment that had happened here.

She climbed out of her car, and that's when she saw the glass-covered marquee where CKT would proudly promote whatever show was in progress. Only now . . .

Her eyes had to be playing tricks on her. She walked closer and shaded her eyes. The glare from the new-fallen snow made it hard to read until she was a few feet away, and then . . . she was right. She began to shake, more from the shock and joy exploding in her heart than from the cold morning.

The sign read, "CKT Presents *Charlie Brown.*" Exactly what it had read years ago when CKT performed its first-ever musical here in this very building. The way it read when Dayne Matthews happened to be driving out of town and stopped in for the final ten minutes of the final show in the run.

She was breathing faster now, dizzy from the possibilities that suddenly lay before her. Her steps were slow and measured, her boots sinking into nearly a foot of snow with each stride. But finally she reached the back door and tried the handle. When the door opened, she trudged inside and shook the snow from her feet.

Only then did she look up and see Dayne watching her from a folding chair at the center of the stage. He was tan, and the stress of the last few months showed around his eyes. But the look on his face was the one she had longed for with every passing day.

He stood, his eyes never leaving hers. "Katy . . ."

She took a few steps toward him and then stopped and looked around. The rows of seats, the balcony sections on both sides of the theater — all of it was exactly as it had been the last time she saw it. "How did . . . ?" She turned to him again, and this time she saw tears on his cheeks.

"Dayne . . . how can you really be here?" She practically floated the rest of the way to the stage and up the stairs. And then they came together in an embrace that dissolved the miles and months between them in so many seconds.

Dayne was breathing hard, clearly fighting his emotions. "Don't ever leave me." He clung to her, holding her close and nuzzling his face against hers. "I can't live without you."

"I'm sorry." Her tears came harder now, flooding her eyes and making her nose stuffy. "How could I have doubted you?"

Dayne drew back slowly, his expression lined with disbelief. "What?"

"I know. I was going to call you today when I got home." A cry that was part laugh crossed her lips. "Ashley told me." Katy lowered her chin and allowed the remorse in her heart to show on her face. "But that wasn't her job." She searched for the right words. "If the tables were turned, I would've flown to Mexico to convince you I'd done nothing wrong. But I denied you that chance."

Dayne's eyes were still damp, but his voice was calmer and laden with a deep sadness. "I had hoped you might believe me."

Katy wanted to defend herself, tell him that the picture had tricked the whole world, so why not her? How could she have known Luke might stop by and visit Dayne in Cabo or that Luke would have the gall to make out with Randi Wells on the beach? But every possible excuse felt lame against the one piece of evidence she hadn't considered.

Dayne's word.

She moved close against him again and pressed her head to his chest. "I was wrong." Her voice was muffled against his pullover. "I was a world away and believing the tabloids, and I was wrong." She looked at him. "When Ashley told me the truth about Luke, I would've chartered a plane to see you, but we had to wrap up the film. I figured I'd call you when I got home and tell you how sorry I was."

"You were ready to throw it all away." It wasn't a question, and the hurt in his voice would stay with her forever. "After all we've been through? Would I have been that easy to walk away from?"

"No." Katy shook her head, and more tears rushed into her eyes. She slid her arms around his waist and grabbed fistfuls of his sweater. "Even if it was true, I couldn't leave you. God made that clear . . . in the last few days. Before I talked to Ashley."

With that bit of knowledge, she felt him relax against her. "It doesn't matter anyway. We're here. I love you, Katy." Dayne brought his lips to hers slowly, the way he'd kissed her that first time up in the bleachers of Indiana University's football stadium. This wasn't a moment for passion but for finding their way back.

Katy stared at him, her heart slamming hard inside her. "So, what's all this?" She glanced around again. "Why are we here?"

A smile started in Dayne's eyes and quickly filled his face. He took a step back, and as quickly as it had come, his smile faded. "I had to be here." He looked straight into her heart. He turned to the back row of seats and pointed to a spot in the middle. "That's where I was, remember? The first time I saw you."

Her chin quivered as she looked. She nodded because she couldn't speak.

"And here." He tapped his foot a few times on the wooden stage. "Here is where I found you lying beneath a plastic Christmas tree."

Katy sniffed. "The day you asked me to marry you."

He came closer to her again, his fingers cupping her face with the most gentle touch she'd ever known. "The day you said yes." He kissed her again, longer this time, slower.

When she looked at him again, her quiet giggles warmed the air between them. "That's why we're here?" She gave him a wary look. "The place was supposed to be leveled the other day. That's what Jenny told me."

"It's a long story. I'll tell you later." Dayne backed up, and as he did he reached into his right pocket. Katy heard the sound of keys before he pulled them out and held them up for her to see. "It's yours, Katy. The theater is yours." His eyes shone with anticipation. He handed the keys to her. "Merry Christmas."

She shook her head, not believing him. Not believing she was even standing here when a week ago she'd been half a world away, ready to give up on him. A cry came from her and she searched his face, trying to make sense of what he'd said. "Dayne?" Her voice was little more than a shocked whisper. She held out her hand, and he pressed the keys into her palm. "Are . . . are you serious?"

"Yes. You can start CKT up again as soon as you want."

"Tomorrow?" Katy laughed and brought her hands to her face. It was more than she could imagine, almost too much to believe. The theater was hers? They could be presenting their next show as soon as spring? She lowered her hands and worked them around his waist. "I must be dreaming. I mean, can it really be happening?"

"It's real, love." The smile was back in his eyes. "I should've done it a long time ago. Maybe we would've spent the last few months together instead of . . ." He brushed his knuckles against her cheeks, her brow. "Come sit with me. There's more."

Good thing he wanted to sit. Katy's knees couldn't hold her up another minute, not with the way life was changing before her eyes, growing more wonderful with every heartbeat. They took seats in the front row.

Dayne turned to her. "I bought the buildings on either side. They're yours too."

Her mind raced frantically, pulling up images of the buildings that anchored the theater. "I can't believe this." If he'd purchased those too, then he wasn't giving her the theater as an impulsive Christmas gift. He'd thought this through. But what did that mean about their future? He still had movies left on his contract and . . . and . . .

"I love you, Katy. I hope you never doubted that."

Her thoughts shifted, and guilt rained down on her. How could she have doubted anything about him? What twisted lie had seeped into her soul that she would believe that photograph — even if the picture looked exactly like Dayne? She closed her eyes for a few seconds. *God, what did I ever do to deserve the love of a man like Dayne Matthews?*

Remember, daughter . . . I know the plans I have for you . . . to give you hope and a future.

The tears came again. *Thank You. . . . Thank You, Lord.*

Katy hugged herself. "I love you too. I'll spend the rest of my life proving that to you."

Only then did his entire story pour out. He explained how he'd been in Mexico, deeply affected by the scrapbook his father had made him. "I realized that sometimes a gift says more than words ever could." When he smiled at her, he looked like a schoolboy who was young and in love, with a world of possibilities spread before him. "The right gift, anyway."

Dayne shared his vision of a diner on one side of the theater and a coffee shop on the other. But it wasn't until he'd pointed out the obvious things they should upgrade in and around the theater that the real crux of his plan came to light.

"I talked to my agent." He was more serious than he'd been since she walked through the door. "I told him I need a few years off. After that I'll do one movie a year, until I've finished the two films left on my contract." Anger flickered in his eyes. "I told him he could forget casting me in a love story. I'm finished with that."

Katy tried to remember how to breathe. Dayne hadn't missed a single detail. "Me too. I've filmed my last movie." She was still trying to take it all in, grasp the reality of what tomorrow held. She remembered one important question. "How did you . . . Why aren't you in LA?"

"We'll finish up after the holidays." He took her hands in his. "I want you to come with me. We can stay indoors whenever I'm home if you want, but I don't want to be alone. We're a team, okay?" He made a silly face. "Then we come back here and I apply for the job I've always wanted."

She picked up on his humor, and her laughter filled the theater. "Set builder?"

"Exactly." He gave her a look of mock concern. "Of course, I'm up against some tough competition."

"Yeah —" Katy leaned in and kissed him — "but you're sleeping with the boss."

Some of the silliness left his eyes. "I will be, anyway. After tonight."

She savored the sensation of his hands in hers and willed herself to remember this moment. The feel of the wooden seat beneath her, the musty smell of the old theater, the look in his eyes. She wanted to remember it not just next week and the following months and years, but when she was old and gray. Dayne had given her the greatest gift of all — a gift even better than the theater and the chance at a normal life. He'd given her his forgiveness.

With that, the future was bound to be nothing but bright sunshine and brilliant sunsets.

Dayne didn't want to move, didn't want anything to interrupt this precious time with Katy. His plan had worked, and now he rejoiced with her that yesterday was gone

478

and a sea of tomorrows spread out before them. He and Katy, together in Bloomington, making plans for the CKT kids and whatever musical they might do next.

That was something else wonderful yet to come — the announcement that Dayne had bought the theater and together they would reinstate Christian Kids Theater. Already Dayne had talked to a reporter from the *Bloomington Press.* The man needed more information from the developer and the county office. He figured the story might run sometime next week.

Dayne looked around the theater, and with an increasing sense of excitement he detailed some of the projects they could have done immediately. They would hire someone to replace the roof and restore the brick that made up the exterior of the building. The old marquee worked, but it needed a new case and improved lighting. "There're the windows of course —"

Suddenly Katy sat a little straighter and held up one hand. "Dayne, wait —"

"We'll restore every one of the windows to their original condition, and —"

"Hold on. . . ." She was speaking, but he didn't really hear her. "I have something to —"

"A new furnace, maybe a whole new

HVAC system depending on the . . ." A nervous chuckle sounded in his throat. "Sorry. I guess I got carried away." He gave her a sheepish grin. "You were saying?"

Tenderness softened her expression, and a dreamy look sparkled in her eyes. "I was saying . . . I forgot something." Her purse was on the floor beside her; she reached inside and pulled out a small, flat bag. "I picked this up at the airport."

Dayne studied her. He had a sense that something big was happening. Otherwise why would she be in such a hurry to give him an airport souvenir? He took the bag, reached inside, and eased the gift out. It was a tiny white T-shirt, and across the front in colorful letters it read, *I'm a Bloomington Baby.* Dayne smiled at it and then at Katy. The gift was adorable and so appropriate, especially since they had both reached the decision at the same time — that Bloomington, not Hollywood, was where they wanted to be.

"I like it." He held it up in Katy's direction. "We should frame it and hang it in the kitchen."

Katy giggled. "We can't frame it. What good would it be behind glass?"

What good would it be? He stared at the shirt again. And then like the gradual light from an early morning sunrise, a thought began to dawn on him. He looked slowly back at Katy. "You mean . . . we have a reason to *use* it?"

Her cheeks were more flushed than before. She slid closer to him, and the truth was in her eyes. "Our baby does." She blinked back tears and seemed to struggle to find her voice again. "That's who the shirt's for."

Dayne breathed in sharply and rushed to his feet. He looked at her, not sure what to do next. "Our baby? You're . . . you're . . ."

"I am." She stood and pressed her hand to her stomach. "I found out yesterday when the shoot ended. I bought a test at the drugstore."

He breathed in and willed himself to exhale. This was no time to hyperventilate. "Katy, you mean it? You're pregnant?"

She laughed. "Ten weeks, if my calculations are right."

Dayne let his head fall back and shouted, "I'm a dad! I'm going to be a father!" For a moment he remembered that he should already have one child by now. His former girlfriend had gotten an abortion without ever talking to him about it. But that sad story belonged to the past. He raised both fists in the air and jogged from one end of the theater to the other and back again. "I

481

can't believe this. It's the best news ever."

"I know. I couldn't wait to tell you, but then —" she motioned to the walls surrounding them — "you gave me the theater." She put her arms around his neck. "I didn't remember about the little T-shirt until now."

"All this time . . ." The truth of the situation was beyond his full comprehension. They had been thousands of miles apart in separate foreign countries, believing their marriage had fallen apart when . . . "All along God's been knitting together our firstborn child."

Katy slipped her arms higher around his neck and pressed the side of her face against his. "Can't you just see it?"

"I can see it a lot better now." He was still breathing hard, still trying to grasp the fact that in less than seven months he would be a father. This was everything he had ever hoped for, everything he and Bob had prayed about that night at Bob's kitchen table in Mexico City.

Slowly, tenderly, Katy swayed in his arms, and he sensed that they were both holding tight to this moment. "Can't you see her walking between us on the path around Lake Monroe?"

He pulled back just enough to catch her

smile. "Her?"

"Or him." Katy shrugged. "It doesn't matter."

She was right, of course. The only thing that mattered was that God had blessed them with a child. Dayne eased Katy's head against his chest.

It was ironic, really. Ever since his first Hollywood break, people had said Dayne Matthews had it all. They cited the usual list — looks and athleticism, fame and more money than he knew what to do with. Cars and women and invitations to the right parties. But the fact was, all that had been meaningless and empty.

Now he would have a future with Katy here in Bloomington, where in time people would come to forget his former life. He would be known for his development of the theater project and for helping Katy with CKT, for being the best husband he could be and for taking his family to church each Sunday. And one day, not too far from now, people would see him in the role he'd always wanted — the role of being Daddy to his child.

The world could write Dayne off, complain that he had walked away from a brilliant career and more fame than a person had a right to. But in this moment the label people wanted to tack onto him was right in every possible way. Dayne truly had it all, for one wonderful reason.

Someday was finally here.

CHAPTER
TWENTY-NINE

Ashley nestled back into her father's sofa and surveyed the chaotic Christmas Eve scene taking place around her. Everyone was here, including Erin, Sam, and the girls. At the last minute, Sam had gotten permission from his boss to take a trip to Indiana to figure out where they would live once they moved here in June and to spend a few days meeting with the management in the Indianapolis office.

The timing couldn't have been better. Last week's storm had left a blanket of white across Indiana, and even now flurries added to the magic of the night. During dinner, her dad announced that he and Elaine had set their wedding date for the last Saturday of June, six months from now.

Ashley looked across the room to where her dad and Elaine sat at the dining room table, catching up with Erin and Sam on all the excitement surrounding their impending move. At the far end of the kitchen counter was an enormous bag of wrapping paper from the gift exchange they'd had before church.

And stacked on the counter next to the bag was today's newspaper, with the article that had run on the front page. CKT was back in business. Katy had reported that nearly all the kids had contacted her, thrilled with the news. Auditions had been set for the last part of January, after Katy and Dayne returned one last time from Los Angeles.

All the pieces had come together, everything Ashley and Landon had prayed about. Now she couldn't think of anything better than watching the snow fall outside the window and seeing her entire family gathered together for Christmas. Everyone except Luke and Reagan.

The house fairly shook with the sounds of love and laughter, the way the Baxter house was supposed to sound. Ryan, Landon, Peter, and Dayne were in the TV room, watching the NFL highlights from the week. Every few minutes one of them would let out a shout or a loud "Can you believe that?" The guys were close friends, and Ashley was sure that Sam was looking forward to being part of the group again.

They'd all gone to the Christmas Eve candlelight service together, even Luke and Reagan. But afterwards, Reagan had told Ashley that they needed to run an errand before joining the others. Ashley passed the word on to her dad and the others, and she figured her brother and his wife would be here any minute. She smiled at the picture they'd made earlier today at church and a few weeks ago when the entire Baxter family had caravanned to Indiana University for the Chimes of Christmas, the annual choir production that half the town turned out to see.

When their voices joined for a haunting final refrain of "Silent Night," Ashley surveyed the faces around her and hoped — as she'd done so often before — that her mom had a window. The way Christmas was coming together would've made her mother so happy.

Ashley looked around the room, from the warm flames dancing in the fireplace to the spots on the floor where her sisters were playing a card game of spoons with the older cousins. Ashley was too tired to play this round. Now, snuggled beneath an old throw her mother had crocheted twenty years ago, she found herself glad for the quiet.

"Coley has s-p-o-o." Maddie gave him a concerned look. "It's not seeming that good for you."

"I can still win." He raised his brow at Kari. "Right?"

"You can." Kari and Brooke swapped a quick smile. "It just means you're out of chances."

The hand began with cards passed around the circle at record speed. Ashley watched as Brooke quietly took the first spoon from the pile in the middle. Maddie took one next, and then Clarisse, Chloe, and Jessie grabbed one apiece. Kari and Katy were the last ones to get spoons, maybe half a second before Cole shot his hand toward the middle. With no spoon left to grab, he dropped his cards and shrugged.

"You lost, Coley." Maddie used her sweetest voice. She tossed her long honey-blonde hair over her shoulder. "Sorry 'bout that."

Ashley's sisters tried equally hard not to laugh. None of Cole's cousins loved him as much as Maddie did, but none of them teased him as much either.

Cole studied Maddie, and he seemed to understand — maybe for the first time — that he could still walk away a winner as long as he downplayed the importance of the victory. A smile suddenly replaced his frown. "Oh well; that's okay, Maddie. Now I get to sit with my mom."

Maddie looked confused, as if she should make some kind of retort. But she only frowned and turned her attention back to the game.

Cole giggled. Then he popped up, crossed the room, and snuggled on the couch beside Ashley. "Can I share the blanket?"

"Of course." Her heart melted at the way her little boy was growing up, how his legs hung over the sofa and onto the floor now. She fanned the blanket out so they each had half. "How's that?"

He rested his head on her shoulder. "Perfect."

"Good." She ran her hand over his hair.

"Whatcha thinking over here, anyway?" He reached out and took hold of her hand.

"I don't know, about Christmas and family. How blessed we are."

"Oh." He sounded pensive, the way he sometimes got. "I thought maybe you were thinking about Sarah."

The grief that was never too far away poked at Ashley's heart. She swallowed, curious about what was on Cole's heart. "How about you? What are you thinking?"

"About Sarah. How much I miss that little sister." He snuggled closer. "Especially when Annie's around."

The tears in Ashley's eyes were more from joy than sadness. How wonderful that for now Cole remembered Sarah, that her brief life had made a difference to her oldest son.

"I know." Ashley looked across the room at the baby swing set up in the corner. Annie was tucked inside, nuzzled against her blanket, sound asleep. "Annie makes me miss Sarah too."

"But at least we have Annie." Cole peered at her. "Plus, Sarah's safe with Grandma in heaven."

"Right."

Cole relaxed against her again. "I think I'll go see if Papa wants a piece of chocolate from the candy dish."

"Papa or you?" She tickled his ribs, and the sound of his laughter erased the sorrow from a minute ago.

"Okay . . . okay." He stood and kissed her on the cheek. "Maybe both of us." He waved at her as he turned and scampered off. "Love you."

"Love you too." Ashley stood and stretched. The younger kids were at the kitchen table coloring their Christmas story books with the pictures of Mary and Joseph and baby Jesus in a manger. Already her dad had gathered all the kids around and shared the Christmas story from the book of Luke, the way he did every Christmas Eve.

She wandered into the kitchen and came up behind Devin. He was using oversize baby-safe crayons, coloring long lines of red across the three wise men. He looked up and grinned at her. "Mama, see!"

"Yes, baby. Very nice." She moved around the table admiring the pictures being created by RJ, Heidi Jo, and Amy. Last she came to the picture Hayley was working on.

It defied odds that Hayley was alive, let alone sitting at the table coloring within the lines. She smiled at Ashley. "Hi." Her eyes were bright and innocent, the way they always would be. Every few months she reached another milestone. This year in school she was writing her alphabet, learning to spell words, and making her first attempts at reading. Things no doctor — even Ashley's dad and Peter — ever thought she'd be able to do in the early days after her near drowning.

"Hi." Ashley put her hand on Hayley's shoulder. "Tell me about your picture."

Hayley was coloring the manger scene. All the animals were brown, and the people were blue, the lines not quite neat and tidy. But the sky around Bethlehem was a brilliant, solid yellow. She talked about each of the animals and about Mary and Joseph and Jesus. Then Hayley pointed to the yellow sky. "A miracle happened that night, Aunt Ashley. So that part's all goldy."

Ashley could hardly argue with the logic. She was about to ask if any of them wanted another Christmas cookie when she heard the front door open.

"We're here!" Tommy burst into the room. He was wearing glasses now, and combined with his short, spiked haircut he looked like an adorable cartoon character. He raised his hands and curled his fingers in his best impersonation of a dinosaur. Then he let out a roar that filled the house.

"Yes, we're definitely here." Reagan blew at a wisp of her bangs as she carried Malin into the room. "Nothing says Christmas like the roar of a T. rex."

Conversations broke out across the house, and everyone gathered near the Christmas tree.

Brooke waved her hands until she had everyone's attention. "You know what time it is, right?"

Ashley grinned at Kari, and a few of the men rolled their eyes.

"That's right, all you scrooges out there." Brooke's voice was lighthearted, the joy in her expression undimmed by the slight sarcasm from the guys. "It's time for the cousin photo!"

Every year they tried to find a way to put all the Baxter grandkids into one picture. This time, Ashley had a feeling it was going to take all the adults working together to pull it off. The men moved a few chairs close to the tree, while Ashley and her sisters fussed over their kids, making sure hair was in place and vanilla icing was rubbed off their sticky cheeks.

The older kids stood behind the chairs, their backs to the tree. Elaine stepped in and helped arrange the little ones in the chairs in the front. Annie was awake now, and Kari set her gently in Jessie's arms. When it looked like everyone was in place, Ashley and the others darted out of the picture and grabbed their respective cameras.

For the next few minutes, each of them took a handful of shots. If they were lucky, there might be a single image between them with every one of the kids open-eyed and smiling.

With the photo behind them, the kids were ushered into the TV room for the traditional showing of the cartoon version of the Grinch. Once the movie was going, the adults returned to the living room.

Ashley and Landon were the last to join the others, and a hush fell over the room. Ashley looked at the faces surrounding them. She wagged her finger at them, teasing. "Okay . . . stop telling secrets."

Reagan stood and walked to her. In her hand was a small red gift bag. She smiled, but there was something very deep in her eyes. She handed the bag to Ashley and gave her a long hug. "Luke and I had one more gift for you. Something I made for you. Of course —" she smiled at Luke — "our life being what it is, we didn't get a gift bag until half an hour ago."

Landon looked puzzled. Ashley had to assume that he too was in the dark about this unexpected gift. All eyes were on her as she took the bag and gave Reagan a tender smile. "You didn't have to do this."

"I know." She motioned for Luke to join her, and he did, carefully dodging the crowd around the room and making his way to Reagan's side.

Then he pulled Ashley into a hug. It took her back to their growing-up days when the Baxter house had only a fraction of people around the tree on Christmas Eve. Back to the days when her little brother was her best buddy. He eased back to his place by Reagan and locked eyes with Ashley. "It's something we both wanted to do."

Ashley didn't waste any more time. She pulled the tissue from inside and handed it to Landon. Then she lifted out the most delicate Christmas ornament. It was handmade, with precious white lace and a single red ribbon woven around the circle. In the center Reagan had embroidered the words *Our Little Miracle* and beneath that the year.

"Turn it over." Reagan moved a little closer to Luke.

Ashley did, and tears sprang to her eyes instantly. On the other side was a photo of baby Sarah. A beautiful shot, one that captured her perfect features and her precious blue eyes. Ashley looked at Reagan. "How . . . how did you know?"

"I just thought you needed something on your tree." Her voice cracked. "So no one ever forgot about her at Christmastime."

"No, but . . . how did you know that's what we were praying for? That God would work a miracle out of Sarah's life?"

Reagan's face went blank and she shrugged. "I didn't know that part."

Happy tears spilled onto Ashley's cheeks. Of course Reagan hadn't known about the prayer she and Landon had lifted to God every day since Sarah's birth. But God knew.

Ashley pulled Reagan, Luke, and Landon into a group hug, and beside her she could feel tears on Landon's face too. "Thank you, Reagan," she choked out in a strained whisper. "I'll treasure it forever."

The others stood and circled around, waiting to pass the ornament and remember again the face of the baby they'd known for such a brief time. The scene reminded Ashley of the way they'd shared Sarah for the few hours of her life, passing her from one to another.

This, then, was the final part of the miracle of Sarah's life. Not only had God used her to soften the hearts of Dayne and Katy and Luke and Reagan, but none of them would ever forget the tiny daughter and granddaughter and cousin who had not lived long enough to share a Christmas with the Baxter family. And in that way she would live on, not only in heaven with their dear, sweet mother, where someday they would all join her.

But here in their hearts.

Ashley realized that she hadn't completely let go of Sarah, hadn't reached a point of thanking God for her short life when what she had really wanted was for her daughter's life to outlast her own.

At the far end of the circle, Ashley's father slipped his arm around Elaine's shoulders and began to sing. " 'O Lord my God! When I in awesome wonder . . . consider all the worlds Thy hands have made . . .' "

It was a praise song like none other, and Ashley met the eyes of Katy standing next to her. Katy had told her the revelation God had given her, about how victory was found in singing.

The ornament was back in Ashley's hands, and she looked down at it, at the sweet face of her little girl.

Around the room, a few others joined in the singing, with her father's voice the loudest and steadiest of all. " 'I see the stars, I hear the rolling thunder . . . Thy power throughout the universe displayed.' "

As they reached the chorus, everyone in the room sang, " 'Then sings my soul, my Savior, God, to Thee . . . how great Thou art! How great Thou art! . . . Then sings my soul . . .' "

Ashley closed her eyes and sang for all she was worth, praising her God and King for the miracle of Sarah's life and for the goodness that He alone had provided. He had been exalted through the miracle of Sarah, after all. Not just for her and Landon but for all of them.

As the song ended, Ashley felt a release, and she knew deep within her soul what it was. The battle was over; Sarah belonged to God fully, completely. She reached out and joined hands with Katy. This was the beauty of the Baxter family, that they came together in times of great sorrow and times of great joy and that they were stronger because of each other.

Ashley didn't want to think about next Christmas, when the Baxter house would likely belong to strangers. Her father was right. They didn't need walls and windows to be part of the Baxter family. They needed God and each other.

The song ended, and in the other room came the faint refrains of the Whos in Whoville singing without any presents at all. Ashley smiled. Dr. Seuss had gotten the message right. Victory came in the song.

In the years ahead, when they got together they would laugh and look back at the years gone by. And always they would sing praises to their mighty Savior, and when they did, they would win — no matter what defeat they'd faced that year. They'd have victory because with God they could stand up to any battle that came their way. And someday in heaven they would experience the greatest victory of all.

A reunion like none of them had ever dared dream about.

A WORD FROM
KAREN KINGSBURY

Dear Friends,

What an emotional journey it's been, trying to bring to a close my series on the Baxters. Especially this installment, which was written in the weeks after my dad's death. My dad always told me that one day everyone would know what a wonderful writer I was. But having him in my life made me know for certain that life was about so much more than writing.

My dad was a firm believer in life. I told you that last time. But he was also a believer in miracles. That's why none of us were overly shocked when he survived his heart attack in what could only be described as a miracle. You can read about it on my Web site at www.KarenKingsbury.com.

Clearly because of what we went through with my dad, the idea of miracles was on my heart like never before. I've heard from thousands of you who told me how glad you were that Ashley's baby didn't receive a miraculous healing at the end of the last book, *Summer.* It wasn't that you wished bad things for poor Ashley. But you wanted a real story, a way of seeing God's hand at work even when life doesn't go the way we want.

I'm glad you were happy with that ending. It was the only one I could've written, knowing the powerful God we serve and the very real certainty of heartache all around us. And so in this book, I had the chance to bring to light the fact that even in death, God can work miracles. We've seen that a number of times in people close to us and in our community. With the passing of my dad, we saw it personally.

God is at work, even in our storms.

The story of Ashley and Dayne and Luke all finding their someday by the end of this book was also one in which I felt compelled to talk about the battles of life. The deaths and illnesses, the broken relationships and ruined finances. God tells us in 2 Chronicles that we don't have to fight our battles alone. He'll go before us.

Isn't that the greatest news? For those who love Christ, wherever you go, you're protected. The battle is won, no matter how grim the situation seems.

At our house, we love when Donald takes out his guitar and everyone gathers around to sing songs of praise to God. We'll sit outside on the front porch or gather in one of the kids' bedrooms. Between songs, Donald often has one of the kids pray, and as the hour progresses, the heart of each of the kids becomes more tender. Sometimes a few of them will have quiet tears as the time wraps up. Why? Because victory comes in praising God.

Now, about the Baxters. I know. . . . I know. I hear from you, my faithful friends, many, many times each week. "Please," you write, "don't let the Baxters end! You can't stop writing about these people."

Believe me, I'm as upset about writing the final chapter of *Sunset* as you are. And so I've decided to keep the characters alive in a different way. With the conclusion of the Sunrise series, after the final book, *Sunset,* releases, I will start a blog on my Web site and in my monthly newsletters. One day you might hear from Ashley and another day from Dayne. John will weigh in on his new marriage, and Katy will share the joys of being a first-time mother. There won't be whole chapters or books, but you'll be kept aware of how the Baxters are doing and what's happening next.

And of course there will be more stories, more families and issues and emotionally driven characters and plots in the years to come, God willing. I have so many stories in my heart, so many times when we will meet again between the covers of a book. So stay posted.

Also, if you chose to start a relationship with Christ for the first time while reading this book, please get ahold of a Bible and read the book of John. Mark it and highlight it, underline it and memorize it. Scripture is the strongest weapon we have as we march into battle with God at our side. Then find a Bible-believing church where you can grow in the love and knowledge of our mighty King.

If you're unable to find a Bible or you can't afford one and if you've chosen now to start that life-saving relationship with Christ, then send me an e-mail. In the subject line simply write, "New Life." Include your address, and I will send you a Bible.

As always, you can find out more information and sign up for my newsletter on my Web site. I have contests in the works and journal entries about my life as a Christian wife and mother as well as my ministry of fiction. In addition, you can find photos of soldiers who need your prayers as they serve our country. My contact information is there as well. Don't forget: I love hearing from you!

On that note, find a song and sing it as often as you can. Oh, and if your parents are still alive, call them and tell them you love them. Today, while there's still time.

Until we meet again,
in His light and love,
Karen Kingsbury

ABOUT THE AUTHOR

Karen Kingsbury is America's favorite inspirational novelist. Her Life-Changing Fiction™ has produced multiple bestsellers including *Even Now, One Tuesday Morning, Beyond Tuesday Morning,* and the popular Redemption Series. Her novel *Oceans Apart* was chosen by the ECPA as the top fiction title of 2005, and her Christmas novel *Gideon's Gift* is under production as a major motion picture.

The employees of Thorndike Press hope you have enjoyed this Large Print book. All our Thorndike and Wheeler Large Print titles are designed for easy reading, and all our books are made to last. Other Thorndike Press Large Print books are available at your library, through selected bookstores, or directly from us.

For information about titles, please call:
  (800) 223-1244

or visit our Web site at:
  http://gale.cengage.com/thorndike

To share your comments, please write:
  Publisher
  Thorndike Press
  295 Kennedy Memorial Drive
  Waterville, ME 04901